THE
CREATURES
OF MAN

HOWARD L. MYERS

Edited and Compiled by
ERIC FLINT & GUY GORDON

THE CREATURES OF MAN

This is a work of fiction. All the characters and events portrayed in this book are fictional, and any resemblance to real people or incidents is purely coincidental.

NAKED TO THE STARS

Morgan's position in the fighting formation of the Lontastan raid brigade was well back, but on what would be the Earthward flank. It was important that, when the Primganese defenders studied the records of the coming skirmish, Morgan should not look special in any way.

His left ear hissed softly as the ultralight carrier came on, and he heard the voice of the brigade's navigator: "Delay in warp exit, three point four two seven seconds. Reset cut-outs for delay in warp exit of three point four two seven seconds. . . . Exit now due in eighty-five seconds. Prediction: Combat will commence four point five seconds after exit.

Morgan reset the timing of his warp cut-out and twisted his head for a moment to gaze toward the navigator's position. He couldn't see him, of course. The distance between the two men was over twenty-three hundred miles, and also normal vision was of scant use at superlight velocities.

But he looked anyway as he thought half sympathetically of the navigator, as burdened with equipment as an ancient was with clothing. Morgan glanced down at his own well-muscled body, bare and exposed to space except for his black minishorts, his weapons belt, and his low boots.

For an instant he entertained himself with his daydream of encountering a famed ancient from a thousand years ago, when men still traveled in spaceships. How astonished that worthy would be to see almost naked men zipping routinely about the galaxy! And how puzzled by the microchemical mysteries of a modern life-support system!

He drew both of his zerburst guns and waved them about to loosen his arm muscles. His comrades of the brigade were doing the same thing. Most of these men would fight the Primgranese Commonality defenders of Earth for fourteen long, furious seconds . . . and probably live to tell about it.

Morgan expected to be out of the fight and heading for Earth within six seconds. . . .

TABLE OF CONTENTS

PREFACE

HOWARD L. MYERS is almost completely forgotten today, although some people can still be found who remember the name "Verge Foray," under which he published many of his stories. But in the brief time his writing career lasted, from 1967 to 1971, he was a prominent figure in science fiction.

It's a sad tale. Myers was born in 1930, and published his first science fiction story at the age of twenty-two. That was "The Reluctant Weapon," published in the December 1952 issue of *Galaxy*. (The story is included in this volume.)

And . . . that was it, for another fifteen years. Why? We don't know. For whatever reasons, it wasn't until Myers was in his late thirties that he began writing again. And once he did, the stories practically came pouring out—and almost every one of them excellent.

His stories appeared in most of the premier science fiction and fantasy magazines of the day—*Analog, Galaxy, If, Amazing, The Magazine of F&SF*—and he seemed on the verge of becoming one of science fiction's top authors.

We'll never know. In the summer of 1971, against the advice of his mother, Howard Myers took a vacation to Florida. The combination of the heat and his medical condition combined to give him a massive heart attack which killed him. He was forty-one years old.

There have been other science fiction writers struck down in their prime, of course. Henry Kuttner and Cyril Kornbluth immediately come to mind; or Keith Laumer, who survived the stroke he suffered in his mid-forties, but was never the same writer afterward; or Randall Garrett, whose mind was destroyed in his early 50s by a viral brain infection. But at least those writers had enjoyed long and successful careers before the end came. That we can think of, only Stanley G. Weinbaum and Rosel George Brown suffered the same fate as Myers: felled, just on the eve of triumph.

There's something horribly poignant about it; as if Achilles, stepping ashore outside the walls of Troy, had lost his footing and drowned in the surf.

So be it. Achilles was a noted warrior even before the Trojan war, after all. And whatever Howard L. Myers might have become, what remains is what he *did* accomplish. And that was no small thing. In four short years, he produced a body of work which, though small in comparison to that of writers with longer careers, certainly does not suffer in terms of quality.

One novel, *Cloud Chamber*. Two, really, if we

count the novellas "The Infinity Sense" and "The Mind-Changer" as parts of a single story—which is how Myers intended them to be read.

A cycle of stories, usually called the "Econo-War series" but actually part of a broader framework, which are unique in science fiction. (The entirety of it, which we've titled "The Chalice Cycle," is included in this volume.)

And almost twenty other stories, ranging from the chilling "Fit for a Dog" to some of the wittiest science fiction stories ever written.

So, we invite you to make the acquaintance of an author who, had it not been for misfortune, would have been a well-known name in science fiction. And, who knows? Hopefully, this volume will go a long way toward restoring a reputation which deserves to be.

—Eric Flint
—Guy Gordon
January 2003

PARTNER

1

THE ONE-MAN CLOPTER was zipping over New Mexico when Kent Lindstrom's left hand dropped its side of the book of Beethoven sonatas. Kent stared with annoyance as the hand reached forward to fool with the manual control wheel.

Damn it all! he fretted. It was Pard's memory, not his own, that needed refreshing on some spots in the "Hammer-Klavier"! He had been looking over the sonata, instead of utilizing the flight to Los Angeles for a relaxing nap, purely for Pard's benefit.

But did Pard pay attention? Hell, no! He let his mind stray instead, ignoring Beethoven and indulging his childish fascination with gadgetry.

The sonata volume dangling neglected from his right

4

hand, Kent watched his left hand turn the control wheel a few inches counterclockwise, then release it. The wheel automatically snapped back into place and the clopter, having been swerved slightly from the center of the traffic beam, started correction to get back on its course.

Kent opened his mouth to advise Pard, in words that left no doubt, that it was time to quit being a kid. But at that instant a thunderous *Whap!* shook the clopter. Kent dropped the music volume and gazed anxiously at the control panel, wondering if Pard's fooling around had busted something.

The only red on the panel was coming from the cabin-pressure indicator. The clopter had taken a puncture, and its air was whistling away into the stratosphere outside. Kent grabbed for the emergency oxygen mask before he realized his left hand had already put it on his face and was now tightening its strap, getting it a bit tangled in his long, thick hair.

Despite his faults, Pard could think fast in a pinch.

"What happened?" Kent asked under the mask.

Pard took control of his neck muscles and turned his head to look down and to the right. There, in the alumalloy floor, was a hole over an inch across, the shredded metal curled upward along its edges. Through it Kent could see hazily a tiny panorama of New Mexican landscape sliding by in the late afternoon sun.

Then Pard turned his head upward to focus on the spot where the projectile had made its exit. The hole in the roof was a few feet to the rear of the hole in the floor.

"What could've done *that?*" muttered Kent.

Pard did not attempt a reply. Kent retrieved Beethoven from the floor, but left the book unopened in his lap while he stared at the controls. The clopter was functioning perfectly, keeping to the course and velocity that were correct for its moving niche in the air-traffic pattern.

Struck by a crazy thought, Kent drew a mental line between the punctures. The line ran parallel to the position of his body, and not more than three feet to the right of his chair.

And Pard had swerved the craft *to the left* just before the projectile struck!

"You kept that thing from hitting us!" Kent said.

His head answered with the slightest nod: *Yes.*

Kent gasped: "How did you know to swerve?"

His left hand reached around to tap his right temple—Pard's half of the brain—with a finger.

"Oh, sure you're bright!" growled Kent, annoyed because the answer told him nothing. "The brightest stupe I know!" But after he simmered down for a moment he added, "Sorry, Pard. I didn't really mean that."

His left hand patted the top of his head forgivingly.

It was silly, Kent knew, to get cross with Pard for being . . . well, for being *Pard.* He wouldn't have called him a stupe if he hadn't been upset and a bit frightened by the close call they had just had.

It was Pard's way to be noncommunicative, and rather devil-may-care. (But Kent could only guess at the latter because there was no way to learn Pard's real attitude about anything.) The language center was in Kent's hemisphere of the brain. Pard could not talk, and his few unwilling attempts at writing had been such painful, meaningless scrawls that Kent had long ago quit trying to achieve two-way verbal communication with him. Pard could understand the written or spoken word with ease, but the ability to *express* words simply was not in him.

Thus, Pard was not equipped to answer such a question as "How did you know to swerve?" The reply required concepts inexpressible in the "twitch language" Pard used for such essential thoughts as "yes," "no," "give me control," "take over," "wake up," and "I'm going to sleep."

But this didn't mean Pard was stupid. For one thing, as Kent sometimes admitted to himself, the only reason Pard was not the better pianist of the two of them was that he did not *try* as hard as Kent. For another, Pard was often aware of environmental factors that Kent missed. The object which had hit the clopter, for instance . . .

Kent looked at the tiny row of radar meters at the left edge of the control panel. The six little indicator needles trembled constantly with fluctuations in the thin surrounding air. They would have been within Pard's range of peripheral vision even while his eyes were directed at the Beethoven score—and their movements obviously told Pard a lot more than they told him. Pard had been able to read an indication that an object was approaching from below—on a collision course, in fact—and he had swerved the craft at just the right moment to save their life.

Having figured this out, Kent felt better—about Pard, at any rate. It was easy enough to feel haunted, with another consciousness sharing his skull, without that consciousness acting upon information it could not possibly have acquired. The radar meters explained where the knowledge came from.

"I'll never bad-mouth your fooling with gadgets again," Kent said tensely.

Pard accepted that without response.

As for the projectile . . . Well, thought Kent, objects don't shoot up from the ground of their own accord. And if they did, they wouldn't be aimed—or guided—precisely to tear through a lone man zooming past at an altitude of fifteen miles.

"Somebody tried to kill us," he said, "and that doesn't make sense!"

Yes, Pard twitched in reply. The left wrist went limp: *Relax our body.*

Kent did so, and set the chair on recline. After all, they had an important concert to play in less than three hours, and they should be alert and vigorous, in body and in minds, for the performance.

He idly opened the Beethoven volume again. The pages happened to part where a photo had been inserted in the book, and he knew what it was before looking at it closely: another picture of the "mystery girl." He suspected that Pard had found the photos some time when Kent was taking a "walking nap." Maybe a previous occupant had left them in a hotel suite. Why Pard kept scattering the photos around for him to find, Kent couldn't guess, and he didn't try to ask. A joke, perhaps. Pard was sort of peculiar about women, anyway.

He put the photo back and laid the book aside. He had to get a little rest.

The holing of the clopter, he mused, if not some kind of wild accident, *had* to be the result of mistaken identity, or perhaps the act of a crackpot who regarded anybody well-heeled enough to travel by clopter as an enemy. The attack *couldn't* have been aimed at him personally . . . and, therefore, it wouldn't be repeated.

He dozed for the remainder of the flight, but his eyes stayed open and alert. Pard was keeping watch.

2

Kent woke when Pard set the clopter down lightly on a restricted portion of the USC Arts Complex roof, but he was content to observe as Pard slid the sonata volume into his hand satchel and climbed from the craft. A roof attendant waved from some distance away, and started forward when Pard waved back.

Pard ducked under the clopter's cabin to peer up at its belly. He found the hole quickly, but after a glance at it he sidled another step toward the craft's centerline. Here he gazed up at a curious, bright-green circular spot, about eight inches in diameter, which appeared painted on the craft's underside.

If the projectile had hit that spot, Kent realized, it would have hit him as well.

"They had a target to aim at." Kent formed the words soundlessly.

Of course, Pard twitched, combining a nod and a shrug. He picked at the edge of the spot with a fingernail until he had enough of it free to grip between his fingers. Then with one clean motion he peeled the entire spot from the metal surface. It looked like a disk of adhesive paper. Pard opened the hand satchel, slid the disk inside, and slapped it against the back of a music volume.

"Mr. Lindstrom?" called the roof attendant, peering under the craft. "Is anything wrong?"

"No," Kent replied. He took over, snapped the satchel shut, and crept out. "Something hit the clopter. I was taking a look at the hole it made."

The attendant's eyes widened. "That could've killed you!"

"Well, it didn't," Kent replied curtly. "Now if you'll direct me to my dressing room, and inform my manager Mr. Siskind that I've arrived . . ."

His recital went excellently. He played for a packed house in the main auditorium of the Arts Complex, with the program televised nationwide via the noncommercial channels. It was a golden opportunity to win public affirmation of the acclaim of the critics—that Kent Lindstrom was by all odds the foremost young pianist of the decade.

The reaction of the house proved he was doing exactly that. The audience did not wait until the end to give him a standing ovation; he got one for the final work before the intermission break, a fantasia composed by himself.

Beethoven's "Hammer-Klavier" sonata, almost as demanding of sheer physical endurance as of technical and interpretive skills, was the sole work following intermission. The sonata is analogous to the same composer's Ninth Symphony, in that it imposes such superhuman demands on performers that a merely adequate rendition is something to marvel at.

But Kent Lindstrom considered himself two pianists rather than one. There was Kent himself, the dominant consciousness, the boss, the inhabitant of the left hemisphere of the brain, who directed the right hand at the keyboard. And there was Pard, the voiceless secondary consciousness isolated in the severed right hemisphere, who directed the left hand.

Kent Lindstrom was, therefore, the one pianist of whom it could truly be said that his right hand didn't know what his left hand was doing. Complicated counterpoint and devilishly tricky cross-rhythms, that would swamp the brain of a normal pianist with the mere task of playing notes, were handled readily by Kent Lindstrom on a division-of-labor basis, leaving both his minds with attention to spare for interpretive niceties.

He did more than *play* the "Hammer-Klavier" sonata. He did the piece justice.

The applause was tremendous and demanding, but Kent had looked forward to this moment—when he was assuredly entered among the immortals of music—with too much anticipation to waste its essence on some crowd-pleasing little triviality of an encore.

He knew what to do instead. After several bows, he returned to the piano while a complete hush fell over the house. With his hands in his lap and his gaze on the keyboard, he counted twenty seconds of silence. Then he stood suddenly and faced the audience.

"Anything I could play after the great 'Hammer-Klavier' would be a terrible anticlimax," he proclaimed in a ringing voice. "Thank you, and good evening."

He strode from the stage to a final approving roar.

At the jubilant post-concert reception, attended by numerous civic and university bigwigs plus a selection of music students and faculty, Kent quickly spotted a girl he wanted.

His head gave a barely perceptible shake: *Lay off*, Pard warned him.

Kent frowned in dull anger, but obeyed. He had been through all this several times before, and knew that when Pard told him to stay away from a girl, he had better stay away. Even if Kent was the dominant consciousness, he could not keep up a continuous guard against Pard's sneaking enough control to make him do something absurdly embarrassing, and usually with the girl watching contemptuously.

There was the time in Washington, for instance, when Pard had him flitting around like a gay homosexual for five minutes before Kent even realized what was going on. An incident like that could be damaging, and very hard for a well-known musician to live down.

Kent griped to himself. On this night, of all nights, why can't I have a choice girl? Why's Pard so nonsensical about women, anyway?

But the giggly, blond student violinist Pard finally let him accept for the evening wasn't at all bad, even though she was a type that Kent couldn't get enthused about. He wasn't sorry to see her go when his unobtrusive business manager, Dave Siskind, routed her politely from Kent's hotel suite around two A.M.

Kent yawned and settled down with the intention of sleeping at least until noon . . .

. . . And woke before dawn, fully clothed, crouched behind a dumpster in a dark alley, with a wavering ringing in his ears that he took a moment recognizing as police sirens.

He stared around wildly. The police, he could tell by the sound, were stopping at the mouth of the alley, while more sirens wailed a couple of blocks away. He turned to retreat deeper into the alley, but Pard stopped him.

That won't work.

"Blind alley?" Kent asked.

Yes.

Kent squatted back down and thought furiously. He had found indications before that Pard was an occasional night stroller: mud on shoes that had been clean when he went to bed, a few unaccounted-for scratches and bruises—and those photos of the "mystery girl" had to come from somewhere.

But Pard had never before wakened him during one of his after-hours jaunts. Why this time? Because Pard couldn't talk?

"You're in a mess I'm supposed to talk us out of," Kent guessed.

Yes.

Kent sighed unhappily, stood up, and walked out of the alley, into the glare of the police lights. Several officers rushed forward, and he was quickly frisked.

"Got any identification?" one demanded.

Kent felt in his empty pockets. "No. I left my wallet at the hotel. What's all this about?"

"Which hotel?"

"Sheraton Sunset. I'm Kent Lindstrom. Now, officers . . ."

"Lindstrom?" a policeman interrupted, staring at him closely. "Yeah, I guess you are at that. Hey, Mike! Call in that we've found Lindstrom. He looks O.K., except for some skinned knuckles."

Kent hadn't noticed the twinges of pain in his hands until then. He lifted them and glared at the bruised and bleeding knuckles. That goofy Pard! His hands were his *tools!* And tools were not to be abused in silly, back-alley brawls!

"Who'd you have a fight with?" the officer asked.

"I didn't ask their names," Kent replied, slightly pleased with his inspiration to make his opponents plural. "All I know is I couldn't sleep and went out for a stroll. After a while these guys jumped me. Let's see"—he peered around with a show of puzzlement. "I'm sort of turned around, but I think it happened over that way," he pointed, "maybe where those sirens are sounding."

It was a good guess. The policeman nodded. "That's about the luckiest stroll you ever took, Lindstrom," he said. "You'll have to come down to headquarters and make a statement. I'll fill you in on the way."

"Lucky?" groaned Kent. "I'm a piano player, officer. And look at the mess I've got my hands in!"

"They'll heal," the policeman replied, "but if you'd been in your bed at three o'clock you wouldn't have. A bomb went off under it."

There were complications at police headquarters, and Kent wound up in a cell. Whoever he had bloodied his knuckles on did not show up to complain, but there was also a question of attempted arson near the scene of the fight. The police were inclined to keep a tight grip on anyone found near the scene of a set fire without a good excuse for being there.

Kent phoned his manager Siskind to get him an attorney. Then he was ushered to his private niche in the cell block, where he flopped on the bunk and quickly went to sleep.

3

When he woke he was relieved to find himself still on the bunk with his eyes closed. He sat up and peered through the bar-and-steel barriers until he spotted the keeper.

"Hey!" he called out. "When do I get breakfast?"

A man in a nearby cell chortled, "The curly-head pianner player wants his breakfast, fellers!" Kent ignored the remark and the resulting chuckles from the other prisoners.

"You get lunch in forty minutes," the keeper replied.

Kent stood up and began his morning workout as best he could within the confined space. This was his routine—a vigorous twenty minutes every morning to keep the rest of his body up to par with his hardworking hands, arms and shoulders. With an audience this time, he show-boated a bit with extended push-ups, one-leg knee-bends, double flutter-whoops and other acrobatic exercises. The prisoners and keeper watched with gratifying awe. His knuckles, which the police surgeon had treated, gave him no pain under their bandages, so they were probably all right.

He saw that Siskind had brought his hand satchel and toilet kit to the jail for him. They were on the floor just inside his cell door. When he finished exercising he tossed the satchel on the bunk and took the kit to the tiny sink. His blade razor was missing, but the battery-powered shaver, which he used when he was in a hurry, was there. He shaved with it, washed up, and brushed his teeth.

Returning to the bunk he put his kit aside, sat down, and opened the satchel. A bright green oval gleamed out at him. He stared back at this chilling reminder that not one but two attempts on his life had been made within twenty-four hours.

"Better give this to the cops," he lipped soundlessly.

No, his head twitched firmly. *Give me control.*

He did, and Pard sat farther back on the bunk and hooked his heels over the metal edge, elevating his knees to conceal what he was doing. He took out the Debussy volume to which the green disk had adhered, propped the book on his thighs, and picked the disk loose from it.

He examined the disk closely. It was about the thickness of two sheets of typewriter paper, with about the same flexibility, Kent noted. There was no visible material on its back, but that side had a strange *dry* stickiness to the touch. It was made of stout stuff that did not tear when Pard tugged hard at it. A definite line texture could be felt when he ran a finger across the green surface. Pard explored this texture until Kent was thoroughly bored. Finally he turned it over and began abrading one small area vigorously with a fingernail.

"Pard," urged Kent silently, "quit playing with that thing and give it to the cops. It could be just the evidence they need."

No.

"Do you know what you're doing?"

Yes.

Suddenly the disk felt different, though it looked the same. The stickiness was gone from its back. Pard had . . . had *broken* it in some way.

"Hey!" breathed Kent, with dawning comprehension. "It's electronic inside. Right?"

Yes.

"And as soon as something hits it hard enough to tear up its circuit . . ." He left the words unmouthed, his mind filled with a picture of a little projectile zipping up from the New Mexican waste to home in on the green disk and plow through it—and incidentally, through Kent Lindstrom—and of the no longer adhesive disk fluttering free to fall in the desert, where it would never be found to incriminate anybody.

There had to be something like the disk. Otherwise the projectile could never have come so close to a bull's-eye over such a distance. Pard had deflected the clopter with split-second timing, too late for the projectile to adjust its course.

Kent gazed at the disk in awe. "I've never heard of such a thing. Is it military or something?"

Yes.

"Secret stuff?"

Yes.

"How did you know about it?" Pard shrugged. An unanswerable question.

Worse and worse! thought Kent in sudden fear. Whoever's after me has access to secret weapons! No wonder Pard figures the cops can't help! But why am *I* in such a mess?

There was only one possible answer to that: his silent, night-walking skull companion, Pard.

"You've done something that's got us in this jam!" he accused.

Yes.

Pard was keeping his hands busy. He had curled the disk into a tight slender roll, and now was taking the plastic shell off his battery-powered shaver.

Only by an extended guessing game, Kent knew, could he ever get the full story out of Pard. That could take more weeks than somebody meant him to live. But he knew of one guess he could make as a starter.

"Is that 'mystery girl' in the photos mixed up in this?"

Yes. Pard wedged the rolled-up disk into the shaver so that it was pressed against, and perpendicular to, the windings of the tiny motor coil.

"You in love with her or something?"

Yes. Pard flicked the shaver's switch and the motor buzzed. Nothing else happened for about a second.

Then at least a dozen things happened at once.

Lights throughout the cell block flickered, and two of them exploded with dazzling flashes. Sirens whooped deafeningly. Bells clanged. Electronically-activated cell doors clicked loudly as their locks opened. The loud-speaker system blared out the first two bars of "The Star-Spangled Banner" and then went dead.

The prisoners, offered a golden opportunity, swarmed from their cells, flattened the startled keeper, and made for the nearest exits, shouting in gleeful excitement. Pard, his gadget in his hand, leaped to his feet and started to join them.

"No!" shouted Kent. "Don't be a fool, Pard!"

Pard hesitated.

"Running from the law *and* from secret killers at the same time is for TV heroes and other fictitious characters!" Kent mouthed urgently. "Now sit down and do something about that stupid gadget. Go on! You can't go far hopping on one leg, anyhow, and my leg isn't moving a muscle until you start showing some sense."

Pard shrugged and hopped back to the bunk. "That's more like it," said Kent, relaxing control of the right leg.

The gadget was still buzzing. Kent knew very little about electronics. When Pard read an electronics magazine after going to bed, Kent usually went to sleep immediately. But he had picked up enough general ideas to guess how the gadget worked.

The circuit in the green disk was a highly sensitive responser, meant to pick up signals from an oncoming missile, amplify and perhaps vary them in a certain manner, and send them back as instructions to the missile.

That's what the circuit did when it was spread out flat, when there was no interference between the tiny electromagnetic fields produced by its thousands of microscopic components. When rolled into a tight tube . . . well; it still did something similar, but not as a precise response to one particular signal. It was confused and undiscriminating. It responded to every blip of electromagnetic energy it picked up—from the sixty-cycle alternation in the building's electric wiring, from the fluorescent light switches, from the alarm network. And with what was, for it, an overpowering input of energy from the shaver coil to work with, it responded with roars.

"Turn it off!" mouthed Kent.

The left hand started, slowly and unwillingly, to obey, but just then the gadget quit by itself, having exhausted the battery in no more than a minute. Pard yanked out the rolled-up disk, wadded it and tossed it in the toilet bowl by the sink. He was putting the re-assembled shaver away when the lights came back on.

Seconds later a contingent of armed policemen rushed in to stare at the empty cells in angry frustration.

"Most of your guests have checked out," Kent offered.

A sergeant glowered at him and tried his cell door. It was still unlocked. "Why're you still here?" he demanded.

"Because I've done nothing to run from."

The keeper came up rubbing his bruised head. "That's Lindstrom," he told the sergeant. "The piano player."

"Oh, yeah." The sergeant watched as Kent strolled over to the toilet bowl, flushed it.

"What happened to the lights and things, Sergeant?" Kent asked.

"That's no concern of yours—or mine either," the sergeant grunted, walking away.

The escapees were brought in one and two at a time during the early afternoon, and returned disgruntled to their cells. Lunch was over an hour late.

4

Around three o'clock Kent was taken to an interview room, where his manager Siskind introduced him to the attorney he had hired, and to a couple of police technicians.

"Mr. Lindstrom," the lawyer said briskly, "I believe we can wrap this business up in a hurry, thanks in no small part to your display of good faith during that jailbreak today. There is no real evidence against you in this arson business, but the police could hold you a couple of days on suspicion alone. I've explained to the proper authorities that you have an important schedule to maintain, and they're willing to be reasonable.

"Thus, Mr. Lindstrom, if you will submit to questioning under the polygraph, sometimes known as the lie detector, to demonstrate your innocence to these gentlemen—"

"I don't trust those polygraph gadgets," Kent broke in. "I read something somewhere about them being inaccurate."

"The device has shortcomings," the attorney admitted, "but these experts are aware of them, and take them into account. Also, I'm here to see that the questioning stays relevant, that no 'fishing expeditions' are attempted. This is a quick way to clear yourself, Mr. Lindstrom."

Kent hesitated. A polygraph could be dangerous for him, in more ways than one. Maybe he was last night's arsonist. Or, more precisely, maybe Pard was. Then there was the fact of Pard's existence. Only Kent knew that his brain had an extra occupant, and he wanted to keep that information to himself. A lie-detector test could betray Pard's presence in some manner.

He was about to reject the examination when Pard twitched a signal.

Yes.

Kent rubbed his nose to hide his mouth while he asked, "You mean take the test?"

Yes. I'm going to sleep.

That ought to solve the problem, Kent decided. With Pard asleep, he certainly could not react to the polygraph.

"O.K.," Kent said. "Let's get it over with."

The police technicians took several minutes to rig him for the examination, during which Kent assured himself that Pard had dozed off. The questioning had hardly started when the door opened and a distinguished, graying man was ushered in.

"This is Mr. Byers," said the officer with him. "He represents the owners of that warehouse."

"Yes," said Byers, "and if, as I've just learned upon arriving in the building, the charges against this young man are to depend on a single polygraph examination, I must insist on being present during the examination. I don't like these attempts to shortcut justice, gentlemen," he went on with a stern frown. "Nor do I like to see the law be made a respecter of persons, especially a respecter of a person who, while laying claim to a certain artistic notoriety, is not known for the stability of his deportment. But I'm a realist, gentlemen: I'm aware of the pressures under which the police must attempt to carry out their duties. Thus, since I have little choice in the matter, I'll go along with this procedure, provided I am present."

Kent had a feeling that Byers wasn't nearly so put out by the lie-detector test as he claimed to be.

"Any objections?" asked one of the officers.

"Nah," grunted Kent. "Let the old square stay."

"Providing Mr. Byers refrains from interfering with the proper conduct of the test," amended Kent's attorney.

"O.K. Let's proceed," said the officer.

First there were the usual trial questions to establish Kent's true-and-false reactions. Then the technician in charge got down to business.

QUESTION: When you retired last night, you found you could not go to sleep?

ANSWER: Well, I went halfway to sleep. Not fully.

Q.: Why didn't you take a pill?

A.: I don't take pills unless I'm really sick.

Q.: So you went walking?

A.: Yes.

Q.: Wasn't that a strange thing to do at that time of night, and in an unfamiliar city?

A.: Depends on what you think is strange. I do it every now and then.

Q.: Where did you walk?

A.: I don't know. As you said, Los Angeles is not familiar to me.

Q.: When did you leave the hotel?

A.: Between two and three. Maybe two forty-five.

Q.: Are you aware that two attempts were made on your life, yesterday and last night?

A.: I sure am!

Q.: Why didn't you report the first one to the police?

A.: Because I thought it might be some crazy accident at first. You know about it now, so what's the difference?

Q.: Who's trying to kill you?

A.: I don't know.

Byers was hovering over the other technician, watching the tale told by the polygraph needles. His frown was taking on a touch of puzzled doubt.

Q.: Why would someone want to kill you?

A.: It must be over some girl. I don't know what else.

Q.: What girl?

A.: I have no idea who she is.

Byers went over to whisper into the questioner's ear. The man looked annoyed, but nodded.

Q.: You've been intimate with a number of girls, then?

A.: Well, yes. A man in my position has so many—

Q.: Have you ever displayed homosexual tendencies?

A.: No!

Q.: Do you want to reconsider that answer?

A.: Oh, there was that foolishness in Washington last year. But that was just a put-on. An act! Maybe it was in bad taste, but that's all it was.

Q.: O.K. Now, about last night. Who were the men in the brawl with you?

A.: I don't know. I couldn't identify them if I saw them.

Q.: Are you sure one of them wasn't the night watchman of the warehouse?

A.: No, I'm not sure of that. I don't even know what building you mean when you say the warehouse. All I know is, I wasn't looking for a fight, with a watchman or anybody else.

Q.: We think someone got an oily rag out of a garage trash can, wrapped it around a rock, set it afire, and threw it through the warehouse window. Did you do that, or anything similar to that, last night?

A.: No.

Q.: Do you carry matches, or a lighter?

A.: Not often. I don't smoke. Sometimes I have matches if I've been with a girl who does. I don't recall having any last night.

The questioner sat back in his chair and glanced around. "Anything else?" he asked.

Byers was furious. "This whole thing's a farce!" he stormed. "This long-haired young ruffian is obviously abnormal in mind, and can fool your machine!"

The questioner glared at him. "You seem convinced of Lindstrom's guilt, Byers," he said coldly, "but if you have any evidence to that effect you've withheld it from the police. And let's remember two things. One, your clients are going to have some tall explaining to do about what the firemen found in their warehouse—"

"My clients were unaware of what use some unauthorized trespassers were making of their premises!" Byers protested.

"Two," the officer continued relentlessly, "somebody has tried to kill Lindstrom, and you're showing an unaccountable animosity toward him. Could there be a connection, Mr. Byers?"

"Absurd!"

"Will you sit in Lindstrom's chair and repeat that?"

"I'll have nothing to do with your rigged machines!" snapped Byers, drawing back. He headed for the door, firing a parting comment over his shoulder: "This country is in a sad condition when officers of the law start siding with hoodlums and beatniks!"

"Did I pass the test O.K.?" Kent asked as the technicians detached the monitoring devices from him.

"Yes. You're free to go. But you should ask for police protection till we get to the bottom of this."

He nodded and asked cautiously, "What was going on in that warehouse, anyway?"

"Illicit arms storage," the chief technician replied.

"Stolen rifles and such, huh?"

"Not exactly rifles. More fire-power than that. Military stuff. Enough to tear this city apart!"

Kent had a stunned feeling of unreality, as if he were involved in a silly dream. How could a harmless pianist get tangled up in this deadly game, he wondered plaintively.

But tangled up he was, thanks to Pard. That green disk was a military device. And now a cache of military armament! It tied together, and tied him in!

5

He and Dave Siskind rode back to the hotel in a police car, since the officers did not want to risk him in a taxi. He had little to say on the way, and if Siskind took his silence for fright, he was not inclined to disagree.

"Dave," he asked at last, "did you find out who that guy Byers represented?"

"Yeah. An old couple named Morgan. Right-wing oddballs. But the police figure they're innocent dupes, and Byers is really fronting for somebody else."

A couple of blocks later Siskind asked softly, "Want me to cancel everything for a while?"

"I don't know. What's next on the schedule?"

"The Tchaikovsky in Toronto, with the dress tomorrow night. I ought to be on my way now, and you're booked on TransAm at 9:47 this evening."

Kent thought it over. The temptation was to stick to the schedule, to act as if nothing were wrong.

"I'll let you know in a little while, after we get to the hotel," he said. As soon as he was alone in his room he woke Pard.

"Well, I'm out of jail," he mouthed, "but maybe I would be safer in. Here's what happened." Quickly he filled Pard in, then said, "The question is, do we stick to the schedule?"

Yes.

"Suits me. I'll tell Siskind I'll be on the TransAm flight."

No.

"Huh? Now what?"

Pard tapped Kent's side of the skull: *Use your brain.*

Kent tried it. "Oh," he muttered. "I see your point. No innocent bystanders, huh? Except *me.*"

Yes.

Kent called Siskind in. "Dave, I'm going to stay on schedule, but after what's happened I'd better not travel with other people. They might get hurt. See if the police will make secret arrangements for me to leave on another fast clopter—maybe from the hotel roof."

His manager nodded. "That makes sense. I'll travel with you this time. Maybe I can be—"

Kent was shaking his head. "No. By myself, Dave."

Siskind shrugged helplessly. "You're the boss. Good luck." He reached the door and turned to say, "That was a great performance last night, Kent. The recording of it will be a classic, no matter what!"

"Why, thanks, Dave."

His manager left him wondering if he had just heard his own funeral oration.

The clopter was waiting on the roof at 7:30. He walked to it in the twilight, escorted by Dave and two policemen, then ducked down and scooted underneath the craft.

"Hey!" a policeman objected.

"Just curious," Kent explained, coming out. "The clopter I came in had a hole in it, and I wondered if this was the same bucket."

"No. That one's impounded," said the officer.

Kent climbed into the doorway and stood on tiptoes to examine the roof. "It had a hole in its top, too," he explained. No green spot, nor even a slight irregularity in the clean metal, could he see.

Satisfied, he got in, waved, and took off.

As soon as he was established in the northeast traffic pattern he got a twitch from Pard: *Give me control.*

"Boy, if you could only talk," Kent moaned, "I'd give you control from here on out!"

Pard twisted out of the seat, which was not easy in the cramped compartment, and methodically began pulling the seat to pieces. "What now?" Kent demanded.

His skull-mate ignored him and kept working until he found what he was after. It was under a reglued manufacturer's label on the shock-cushion assembly.

Another green disk!

Squatting in the clutter of seat components, Pard got a razor blade from his toilet kit and hurriedly sliced the disk into tiny shreds. These he wadded into the remains of the label. He tugged the emergency-vent plug out of the side of the cabin and allowed the escaping air to yank the wad out of the clopter entirely. Then he shoved the plug back in place and waited for the air pressure to normalize. When he was breathing easily again he reassembled the seat and wriggled back into it.

Relax, his wrist twitched.

What was Pard up to, anyway? Kent wondered

fretfully. And how could he *possibly* have got mixed up with the kind of people who stole secret weapons and planted bombs under beds? Kent simply didn't *mingle* with such grim individuals, so how could Pard have managed to do so? Of course, there were those midnight strolls of Pard's, but how involved could a man get who couldn't communicate? Yet, Pard was entangled in something, as the "mystery girl's" pictures testified. And Pard said he was in love with her!

Kent mumbled, "You sure that girl is worth all this?"

Yes.

"How do you know? Have you kissed her?"

No.

"Touched her at all?"

No.

Kent sneered. "One of those I-worship-thee-from-afar bits, huh? You're an oddball, Pard! You really are!" He sat back huffily, staring ahead into the starry night. "She's the reason you won't let me get involved with any kind of girl except cheap fluff," he guessed after a moment.

Yes.

"And you keep strewing her pictures around for me to find. Am I supposed to fall for her, too?"

Yes.

"Huh!" Kent grunted disgustedly. But he had to admit that the "mystery girl" looked most appealing, with that uncertain little smile. Maybe she was right for him. It would be fun to meet her and find out. Besides, he was twenty-four years old, and ought to be thinking about marriage. And his wife should

meet Pard's approval, because in a way she would be
Pard's wife, too.

Poor old Pard, he mused. A mind living all these,
let's see . . . these eighteen years in isolation, practically incommunicado. What strange thoughts would
such a mind have by now?

He and Pard had been one person at first, so whatever
Pard was now was what Kent himself would probably
be if he had been stuck with the voiceless half of their
brain. Kent tried to imagine himself in that situation, but
it was too much for him to picture. It was a wonder, he
decided, that Pard hadn't gone raving mad long ago.

He had been too young at the time of their separation to recall many details. That was in the year of
the big Florida hurricane, when he was six . . . A lot of
loud noise and the house tearing up all around him,
and something hurting his head, and his mother and
father never being found . . .

He had no memory of being violently epileptic at
the little rural hospital where the rescuers took him.
He was told about that a week or two later, after he
had been operated on and was well. The old doctor
had been awfully nice to him, and had said how sorry
he was that the hospital didn't have the equipment
to make him well with just a small operation instead
of a big one.

Kent remembered some of the doctor's words:

"We had to give you a partner, son, to live inside
you. You and he must be friends, and always work
and play together, because he can make you do things
you don't want to do if you fuss with each other, or
he can keep his side of your body from doing what

you tell it, if he wishes. And probably only one of you will be able to talk, and the one who talks should be especially nice to the other one. And the one who can talk must never tell other people about his partner, because other people might think you are still sick, and make you stay in a hospital all the time."

When he was older, Kent had read up on the treatment of epilepsy, to learn what had been done to him.

It was a drastic cure worked out some ten years earlier, and justifiable only in the most violent cases even then. It had soon become outmoded as neural research learned how to pinpoint more precisely the cause of epilepsy in an injured brain. But that old country neurosurgeon in Florida had doubtless done his best under emergency conditions.

The operation amounted, quite simply, to slashing the two hemispheres of the brain apart. The connective neural tissues near the core of the brain—the corpus callosum and the lesser commissures—were cut, breaking communication between hemispheres and at the same time disrupting the epileptic syndrome.

The consequences of such an operation were less severe than one might expect, especially in an adult patient. Either hemisphere can direct almost all body functions. The two hemispheres begin their existence in a nearly balanced state, but during childhood one becomes increasingly dominant as the seat of consciousness—the left hemisphere in right-handed persons and vice versa—while the other becomes responsible for less exalted sensory and motor functions. Thus, in the adult patient there would be no emphatic "twoness," no great awareness within the severed secondary hemisphere.

But as the old doctor had known or suspected, this was not necessarily true of a six-year-old. Consolidation of ego in a single hemisphere would have only started, primarily with the shift of language functions to one center. A major portion of Kent Lindstrom could never move out of the secondary hemisphere, because the bridges were down, and would grow—if it grew at all—as a separate ego, a silent partner—Pard.

So there they were—as far as Kent knew the only human of their kind in existence—a duplex man, two functioning minds in one body. And a hell of an inconvenience to each other—except at the piano, of course.

But Kent could console himself that Pard was basically a nice, reasonably sane guy, even if he was mixed up in something pretty weird. The mob was out to kill him, which proved he wasn't on their side. And the upshot of his acts in Los Angeles had been the exposure of that weapons cache.

Also, Pard's special interests—electronic gadgetry and the like—might be trivial, but there was nothing unwholesome about them.

"Pard," Kent said at last, "those characters know we're headed for Toronto. Won't they be waiting for—"

Yes.

"We've got to stay alive and get to the bottom of this," said Kent, "and our chances of doing either in Toronto don't seem worth a damn. If I talked to this girl of yours, would she fill me in?"

Yes.

"Where is she?"

Pard pulled a map out of the rack and put a finger on New York City.

"I'm sure to be recognized there!" Kent protested.

Pard swooped a finger through the air and down on a little town in New Jersey, then rubbed it along the map to the big city. Kent nodded.

"Yeah, it might help to land in a cornball town and go the rest of the way by train. But I wish I had a disguise."

Pard made clipping motions around his head.

"That's what I was afraid you would do," said Kent glumly. Nevertheless, he took the scissors and a small mirror from his toilet kit and began shearing his long curly locks. He had trimmed his coiffure frequently—but far less severely—in the past, and could do a neat job of it. But when he had the mop down to businessman-length, he stared in the mirror with sad misgivings.

"I don't know what my fans in Toronto will think of this," he mourned, "if I ever get to Toronto."

6

He reached Manhattan shortly after midnight. The town, away from the tourist-trap centers, was resting quietly.

Pard walked into a well-kept residential section and halted in a shadowed spot near the beginning of a long block of brownstones. He watched and listened intently for a minute, then moved cautiously ahead.

Halfway down the block he paused in front of a house and looked around again.

"Where is she?" Kent mouthed.

Pard shrugged: *I don't know*.

"Is this where she lives?" Kent persisted.

Yes-no.

"If you're trying to confuse me, you're doing great!"

Pard didn't respond. He went up the steps of the house, and Kent saw the row of apartment bell buttons. Pard quickly mashed every button, then hurried down the steps and across the street, where he hid behind an illegally parked car.

Lights came on in the apartments, and after a couple of minutes someone opened the door and peered outside. Kent could hear loud words being exchanged, but couldn't understand them. Five minutes later the house was dark again.

Pard stayed a little longer behind the car, then strolled away. Mystified, Kent hazarded, "Was that some kind of code to find out if she was home?"

After a pause: *Yes*.

"Not quite right, huh?"

Yes.

By subway and bus Pard went into the New Jersey suburbs. He wound up in front of a home that Kent put in the seventy-thousand-dollar class. The place was dark and silent.

Pard eased across the lawn, then around the corner and along the side of the house. An empty garbage can stood behind a side porch. Pard picked up the can and flung it with all his strength against the wall of the house.

A shrill feminine scream, followed by enraged male curses, came from inside, and Pard scooted behind a neighbor's garage. He peeked out to see the porch light come on and a heavy man lurch out carrying a mean-looking rifle. The man looked at the garbage can, cursed some more, and glared out into the night, his eyes halting on Pard's hiding place much too long for Kent's mental comfort. At last the man stalked back inside, slammed the door, and turned off the light.

As Pard crept away and headed back for the bus line, Kent growled angrily, "Are you supposed to be accomplishing something?"

Yes.

"Damned if I can see what!" Kent snapped. "If this is the way you spend your nights out, I wonder why you bother!"

Pard napped while Kent returned to the town where he had left the clopter. He had breakfast there just after dawn, and refueled the clopter. Pard had indicated he wanted to head west again.

"Where to now?" he asked when they were airborne. Pard opened the map and pointed to Green River, Wyoming. "The girl's somewhere around there, you think?"

Yes.

"I hope you're right for a change!" Kent snapped, thinking of the rehearsal with the Toronto Symphony he seemed destined to miss that evening. A dress rehearsal at that! A concert artist who didn't show up for engagements could get a stinky reputation, no matter how good he was.

He must have unconsciously mouthed his fretful

thoughts, because Pard put an imaginary pistol to his head and pulled the trigger, to remind him that some gents whose instruments were more percussive than those of an orchestra were also waiting in Toronto. Kent simmered down quickly.

Pard landed the clopter at a public field in Green River, and steered Kent to a rent-a-car agency. The girl behind the desk looked like a person of culture, which worried Kent briefly, but she did not recognize his name when he signed for the car. He decided she couldn't be so very cultured after all.

From a distance the place looked like a ranch out of a TV western. It was about fifty miles out of Green River, a distance that took Pard nearly an hour and a half to drive over narrow country roads that were by turn pot-holed and rutted. They saw no other car during the final ten miles.

Pard parked out of sight and approached the house on foot, staying under cover. Kent wondered where Pard had learned his infiltration technique. They hadn't had military training, but Pard dashed from tree to bush to gully as if he knew what he was doing.

The frightening thing to Kent was that Pard thought it advisable to sneak up on the ranch house in this manner. Here he was, miles from nowhere without even a peashooter, and Pard was behaving as if he were going up against a machine-gun nest!

"This is crazy!" Kent mouthed.

Relax.

"Nuts to relaxing! Just when our career was starting to look so great . . ."

But he didn't interfere with Pard's actions. Pard

seemingly knew the score, and this was probably better than just waiting to be killed, and—

Machine-gun slugs stitched the dirt four feet from where Pard had crouched behind a bush, and the air was rent by the weapon's startling chatter. Pard hugged the ground, staring at the house still over a hundred yards away.

A loudspeaker bellowed at him: "SURPRISE, LINDSTROM! DIDN'T EXPECT REMOTE CONTROLLED DEFENSES, DID YOU! WALK FORWARD WITH YOUR HANDS UP!"

Pard crouched a moment longer, then stood up and started toward the house. *Take over,* he twitched.

The man on the loudspeaker lowered the volume to a more conversational level and said jovially, "That's one of the advantages of this rustic setting. It makes people think in terms of cowboys toting six-shooters! No gun without a man behind it. So fools and telepaths rush in!" The voice stopped and a mine exploded fifty feet behind Kent, knocking him flat on his face.

"You're not hurt!" the voice snapped. "Get up and come on! That was to remind you of two things: that you're never out of my range, and I don't care greatly if you wind up dead!"

Kent got to his feet, groggy with concussion, and plodded through the yard and onto the porch. The door opened and two guys with pistols came out.

"Inside, Buddy!" one of them barked, stepping aside.

Kent went through the door and saw a third man who was covering him from in front.

"Down on your belly!" this one ordered. Kent

obeyed, and only then did one of the men step forward to frisk him. "Roll over real slow," he was told. He did so, and the man finished frisking him.

"Now get up and move! Down the hall and down the stairs!"

Kent stood and moved off, noticing that the gunmen stayed a careful distance from him at all times, with their pistols leveled at his middle. Their caution was puzzling, but not comforting. They looked intelligent as well as tough, and they weren't giving him a chance to try anything desperate, even if he had the nerve, which he definitely did not. But maybe Pard did.

"Nothing rash," he pleaded silently.

Relax.

7

He was steered into a room where three people were waiting: A beetle-browed man sitting behind a desk, wearing an army general's uniform. Mr. Byers from Los Angeles, standing by the desk and smiling triumphantly. And the "mystery girl," in a chair in a corner of the room with her right wrist manacled to a hook in the wall.

Kent felt slightly acquainted with all three.

The man behind the desk said, "I'm sure there's no need for introductions, so—"

"I disagree," said Kent, determined to show some spunk if only verbally. "Mr. Byers I've met, but the young lady I've only admired from afar. And as for you, General Preston, I know who you are, but I don't know you in your present role. Do they give out medals these days for shooting piano players?"

Preston chuckled. "Good boy! I admire brashness in the face of danger. You might have made a decent soldier, Lindstrom, if this sick land of ours didn't regard 'decent soldier' as a contradictory term. To save argument I'll go along with your pretense of ignorance. The young lady's name is Peggy Blodget, of course.

"As for myself—I assume you are also pretending ignorance of my political views?"

"It's no pretense," said Kent. "Politics bore me."

"Very well. Since the collapse of communism, this once great nation of ours has gone to pot, Lindstrom." The general's eyes glittered. "We're giving away our unmatched wealth to good-for-nothing loafers. We, the greatest power in the world, have gone flabby. We no longer exercise our strength, either diplomatically or militarily. We don't lead by precept. We've turned into a bunch of bleeding-hearts and soft touches. What we don't give away we waste on effeminate living. You're a prime example, boy. A potential fighting man, playing sissy slop on the piano!"

"What's sissy about the 'Hammer-Klavier'?" Kent flared.

"Shut up and listen! I'm no man to waste words. I'm a man of action, a man who makes his speeches, but who then goes a step further than the cheap politicians who are ruining our country. I back up my speeches with deeds."

"Such deeds as shooting sissy piano players?" Kent retorted.

"Such as eliminating any fool who gets in my way,"

the general told him grimly. "And you, interfering with our Miss Blodget here, were doing exactly that."

Kent shrugged. "But what can you gain from doing things like that, and stealing secret weapons, general? A man like you! What are you after?"

Preston stared at him. "I'm after this nation's salvation, boy. That can be won only if my friends and myself assume top leadership, preferably with the support of the public, but without it if the public prefers to remain asleep."

"Dictatorship, huh?" muttered Kent, and then he rushed on before the general had time to blow his top: "But how does Miss Blodget figure in this? She doesn't look the type."

"Miss Blodget, as you well know, has a special talent," said the general. "And she was favorably impressed by my speeches. Thus, when she realized the patriotic thing for her to do was to offer her talent to her country, she came to me." He turned and gazed at the young woman, then added, "Unfortunately, Miss Blodget's patriotism lacks realism. She is slow to convince that to make an omelet, eggs must be broken. So she attempted desertion, first without and later with your assistance."

"What's this talent of hers?" asked Kent.

General Preston fidgeted impatiently. "I'm getting tired of this game!" he snapped. "We will waste no more time telling you things you've known for months."

The girl spoke for the first time. "I'm a telepath, Kent. That makes me useful to the general when I'm within my eighty-yard range of the United Nations, or the White House, or the Pentagon. Of course, he doesn't get my help willingly."

"Shut up!" bellowed Preston. "You answer my questions, nobody else's!" He glared at Kent. "When I sought to eliminate you, boy, it was because you were in my way. But I can use you alive now. Miss Blodget is sentimental about her home town—Los Angeles. That was the major present purpose of our arms cache there. I had to pose a very real, very serious threat to the peace of her city, to bring her to terms and win her cooperation. Since she's telepathic, she can't be bluffed.

"Now, thanks to you, that threat and our most important supply of weapons has been stolen from us. And you've earned yourself a new job! You, boy, are my replacement for Los Angeles. Obviously, Miss Blodget cares very much what happens to you. She'll cooperate to keep you safe." He smiled coldly and continued:

"That's why I set this little trap for you, with her as the bait. Mr. Byers was sent to Los Angeles to feed you the information that Miss Blodget was being brought here." The general paused and gazed at Kent curiously. "I was beginning to wonder, however, if you were going to fall for it. Byers had never been to this ranch before. So he didn't know it was my chief stronghold, and would be a trap for you. Also, he didn't know my real purpose in sending him to see you. What made you suspicious, Lindstrom? Why didn't you get here last night when I expected you? I even had a responser hidden in your clopter to warn us of your approach. Where did you go first?"

Kent shrugged distractedly and didn't reply. Pard, he remembered, had been sleeping the whole time Byers had been near him yesterday. Was that why he didn't get Preston's message? And Peggy Blodget was a telepath with an eighty-yard range . . . and Pard knew her. Also, Pard had acted so strangely in New York and New Jersey last night, waking people up and then moving on as if he had learned something from them, and . . . and it all began to make a terrifying kind of sense!

But why hadn't Pard ever *told* him?

"It would be hard for him to explain," answered Peggy, "and he knew you wouldn't take the news very well."

"I told you to shut up, girl!" roared Preston. She grinned a sad but unbowed little grin, and Kent suddenly knew she was the most wonderful girl in the universe.

Preston was speaking to him again. "Later on, Lindstrom, I may give you an assignment similar to Miss Blodget's—her covering the U.N. and Washington and you on a roving basis, each responsible for the other's safety. But that would require dividing my inner circle—the gentlemen in this room today—into two teams, with several new members to be trusted with the secret of Miss Blodget and yourself. That would be risky right now. Later, perhaps . . .

"But now, Lindstrom, let's put Miss Blodget into a proper frame of mind. She must feel pity for you, and a sense of responsibility. You both know what I have in mind, but the real experience should be far more convincing than my mental image of it. I believe, Lindstrom, that the end segment of the little finger is quite important to a piano player. Isn't that true?"

Kent nodded slowly.

"The removal of yours, from both hands, will not

be extremely painful," Preston continued. "I'm no savage who goes in for idle torture. But I believe this will have a salutary effect on you and Miss Blodget with a minimum of bloodshed. Gentlemen, you may proceed."

Give me control, twitched Pard.

"No!" Kent yelled aloud. "The Chopin Configuration!"

Yes, agreed Pard.

"What's that?" asked the general as two of his henchmen, after shoving their pistols into shoulder holsters, moved in on their captive while the third covered them.

Kent had neither the time nor the intention to explain that the "Chopin Configuration" was a special way of sharing responsibilities between Pard and himself—a way he hoped would enable them to fight like two men instead of one. In several of the first Chopin compositions he had learned to play, the left-hand part was far more demanding than the right-hand part. Kent had found that the best way to handle these pieces was to give Pard control of the entire body, except for the right hand and arm. This arrangement he called the "Chopin Configuration," although he used it frequently in playing other works.

And now, if there was going to be a fight, Kent did not intend to sit jittering helplessly in his skull while Pard alone took on five able-bodied men! Especially not with Peggy watching!

"Take the eyes, too!" Peggy called, and he knew she was relaying a message from Pard, who could fight without seeing.

"Your show of indifference doesn't move me, Miss

Blodget," chuckled General Preston, misinterpreting her meaning. "Just the small fingertips, gentlemen."

Kent lashed out with a sudden judo chop at the neck of the man on his side, but the blow landed on the chin and stunned the man only slightly, while—

The man on Pard's side moved in swiftly, and Pard gave with his motion, clamped the man's throat hard in the bend of his arm and swung him around as a shield against the covering gunman, who was looking for a clear shot, while—

Kent kept grabbing at his staggered opponent, and finally caught his jacket arm and jerked him into the melee, and fumbled under the man's jacket for his gun, while—

Pard broke his man's neck, then whirled the tangle around once and flung the body at the feet of the advancing gunman, where it flopped disconcertingly to the gunman's momentary dismay, then reached around to clamp his fingers on the throat of Kent's reviving opponent, while—

Kent yanked out the man's pistol just in time to raise it and shoot the advancing gunman as Pard's motion brought that enemy into view, while—

Pard went for the knife in the man's belt and slung it at Byers, who had moved away from the desk and was drawing his own pistol, but the knife missed, while—

General Preston had extracted his old army revolver from the desk and was aiming it at the no longer shielded Lindstrom, while—

Kent located Byers and put a bullet in that worthy's arm, causing him to drop his gun and lurch toward the door, while—

Peggy removed a slender shoe and threw it awkwardly with her free left hand at General Preston's temples, but only grazed his nose, while—

Preston whirled angrily and snapped a shot at her, and missed because she knew when to duck, while—

Kent finally got focused on the general, and put a bullet squarely between his eyes.

The rest was mere mop-up.

Kent's first opponent was still moving. He was crawling rapidly toward Byers' gun when Kent's bullet stopped him for good.

Pard ran out in the hall after Byers, whose retreating back was thirty feet away.

"Shoot him!" shouted Peggy. Kent didn't raise the gun.

"Idiot!" snapped Peggy as Pard suddenly reached the left hand over, yanked the pistol from Kent's grasp, and drilled Byers.

"Why'd ya do that?" Kent mumbled thickly. "He had no fight left in him."

"Because he knew about us," Peggy called out. "He was the only one left who did!"

Pard went back in the room, examined the bodies briefly, then got a key from Preston's pocket and unsnapped Peggy's manacles. She immediately went to the desk, studied the array of controls for a moment, then did things to them.

"Five minutes to get out of here," she said, dashing for the door with Pard following.

As they ran across the yard Kent puffed, "How is it you can talk if you and Pard are . . . are alike?"

"Because I'm a natural telepath. He seems to be accidental. That operation isolated him at an age when the urge to communicate was very strong. My hemispheres are joined."

"You're the only one he's found?" asked Kent.

"Yes."

"I'm glad it's you, Peggy. You're a beautiful girl."

She laughed lightly. "Keep running. This place is going to blow sky-high in a couple of minutes!"

"We'll be running the rest of our lives," Kent fretted.

"No. We've chopped the head off Preston's monster, and it'll die now. We'll even make that Toronto rehearsal this evening." She slid into an erosion gully and Pard leaped down beside her. They huddled there and waited.

A few seconds later all hell broke loose behind them. The sound and concussion of air and earth hit them with solid, jolting blows. Pard held her closely. It was like being next door to a major battlefield.

But it ended quickly. Peggy lifted her head with a half-frightened giggle. "We're safe, but we'd better scram."

They climbed out of the gully and walked on swiftly toward the car. "This has been a rough couple of days, Peggy," said Kent, "but I'm suddenly quite sure it was worth it."

"Why, thank you, kind sir." She smiled winningly.

"I'm especially glad for Pard," he added. "Life must've been pretty dismal for him up to now. It's great to find somebody he likes, and who can talk to him. He shouldn't feel so secondary from now on,"

"Pard? Secondary?" asked Peggy.

"Yeah. You know. Having to play second fiddle to me all the time."

She looked amused but said nothing. Kent was vaguely uncomfortable about the way this conversation was going. But of course, he told himself, she can anticipate my words before I say them. No wonder she responds a little strangely. I'll get accustomed to that.

They reached a level path and her hand caught his. An instant later he was delighted to find her in his arms, and the kiss she gave him was hard to believe. It was magnificent!

Then his bright new world turned dark—because she was murmuring passionately into his ear: *"Pard, oh dear, wonderful Pard! I love you so!"*

Kent was dismally certain he would *never* get accustomed to that!

THE CREATURES OF MAN

1

THE BUTTERFLY WITH A WOUNDED wing glided clumsily down to settle on a leaf by the spider's web. The spider knew he was there, but she was drowsy and ignored him for a time. The butterfly waited patiently, knowing that a hastily aroused spider tends to be bad tempered.

Patience was often desirable in mingling with the lesser creatures of Man, and the butterfly was, after all, in no hurry.

At last she turned to regard him with her principal eyes. Her dark mind spoke: "Was that your caterpillar that fell in my web near dusk yesterday?"

"Yes, I was its sire," he replied.

"Delicious," she commented lazily.

"I'm glad you enjoyed it," he said.

She moved across her web to study him more closely. "Your left hind wing has a fracture in it," she said. "How did that happen?"

"I was watching the metal-secreters being attacked by the bees. One of them ejected at me and hit the wing."

"Hold it out," she directed. He lowered his wings, and she examined the broken area with her feet and mandibles. "I can taste the metal," she remarked. "This won't be hard to fix so it will mend straight. Who won the fight?"

"The metal-secreters retreated into their flying hive, but then they destroyed many flowers, along with some of the bees and other insects, by ejecting flaming poison from their hive." He could feel and observe the spider's repair work on his injured wing while he conversed with her. The pain was a minor annoyance.

"Are the metal-secreters creatures of Man?" she asked.

He hesitated—unusually—before answering: "'That is beyond my knowing. Whatever they are, they are outside my knowing of the now-moment. I'm trying to learn more about them."

"So am I," she replied snappishly, "but hardly anybody bothers to tell me anything. They seem to think I can sit here all day and have as big a knowing as any creature that flies. All I get is bits and snatches when somebody thinks past me. Man himself could return, and I wouldn't know it unless he lit in my web!"

"I'll tell you about the metal-secreters, then, while you fix my wing," said the butterfly. In a way he felt sorry for the spider, because her complaints were largely justified. Man had favored her with some intelligence, but far too little for her to achieve a real knowing of the now-moment. In fact, she had only a vague notion of what the phrase really meant.

Butterflies, the most favored of the creatures of Man, had the fullest knowing, thanks in part to their varied and highly developed sensing abilities and to the routine thought-sharing which took place between all members of the order of Lepidoptera. Too, the central nervous system of butterflies was organized for extreme efficiency in the use of stored knowledge—not for remembering, which any of the favored creatures, including the spider, could do very well, but for defining the now-moment. The butterfly had a clear conception of what was taking place, from instant to instant, at all points in the populated portion of the world. It knew the now-moment.

Perhaps the prime contributor to the butterfly's knowing was its long period of development as a caterpillar.

This period lasted most of the seventy-four days— each day five hundred hours in length—of the warm season of the world's year. During that period the caterpillar was a passive receiver of all the traffic of thought taking place around it. It read and stored the knowing not only of butterflies and moths but of bees and even ants. The caterpillar could not act upon any of this knowledge. Indeed the central nervous system contained within the larva was actually two separate systems—one listening detachedly while waiting to serve the adult butterfly, and the other a primitive system guiding the caterpillar through its mindless life of eating and growing. This latter system vanished completely later, during the world's long winter of utter cold, to serve as one more morsel of warming fuel while the encapsulated insect was in the pupa stage. When warmth returned and the world sprang alive with soaring flowers, the adult butterfly emerged from its wrappings, fully grown and educated.

Only the moth shared so favorable a life cycle, and the moth's need for special sensory perception for night flying apparently left less room for intellectual development. In any event, the moth's knowing was less full than the butterfly's. Third in knowing were the bees, and fourth the ants. The spiders ran a poor fifth, but were certainly far superior to the many unfavored creatures needed to complete the world's ecology—the aphids, beetles, termites and various others. And since knowing the now-moment was beyond the spiders' abilities, they used their knowledge for the lesser function of remembering. They took considerable pride in their memories, which they claimed were superior to those of more favored creatures, but the truth was that the higher insects seldom bothered with remembering. The now-moment, to a butterfly, was sufficient.

But, to please the curiosity of the spider, who was repairing his wing, the wounded butterfly exercised his memory of the day's now-moments sufficiently to recount the story of the metal-secreters.

"Their hive flies, you know," he told her, "and is made of a hard metal. I have no knowing of how it is organized inside, or of how it flies without wings.

It came down shortly after sunrise today and settled on top of the Rock Hill."

"How far from here is that?" she asked.

"About half a mile west," he said. "It's a small mountain of solid rock in my hunting ground." He was trying to keep the story simple for her, not going into detail about the kind of metal used in the flying hive or the geological nature of the Rock Hill. "The ants saw it land. When the creatures in it unplugged its door, the ants tried to go in and know what was there. But the creatures ejected metal at the ants and killed several, so the ants retreated. When they did, some of the creatures came out of the hive, still ejecting metal at the particular ants who were carrying the bodies of those already killed. Well, you know how ants are when somebody tries to take food away from them. . . ."

"I'm the same way," she interrupted.

"They swarmed back, and the creatures retreated into their hive and plugged the door. The ants were then able to carry away their meat."

"What are those creatures like? Would they be good meat?" the spider asked with considerable interest.

"They are hard to describe to you, since I can't make you see pictures. They are big. Their bodies are most six times as long as an ant's—twice as long as mine. They move about in a very peculiar manner. They have no wings, so of course they crawl on their legs, which they have too few of. . . ."

"So do you, for that matter," sniffed the spider.

"They crawl somewhat like a mantis, or at least more like a mantis than like us. Their bodies are thicker than the mantis, though. And I suppose they would be good meat, unless they contain poison metal salts."

"I'd like to try one," she murmured half to herself. "If I wasn't in such a good location right here, I would go hang a new web close to their hive and try my luck."

"They may be intelligent," the butterfly reminded her.

"If they are they wouldn't get caught in the web," she answered; and added rather gloatingly, "And for all your *knowing* you don't know if they are even creatures of Man."

"That's true," he conceded.

"What happened after the ants left?"

"The bees came. They are more disturbed than the ants were, because it is a hive as well as an emptiness in their knowing. It could mean competition for the bees. They swarmed around the hive for a while, until it began ejecting metal at them. They flew some distance away and concealed themselves among the flowers. Nothing more happened for perhaps twenty hours, and the sun was well above the horizon when some ants who were keeping watch saw the hole in the hive unplugged again.

"This time the ants and the bees stayed off the Rock Hill and kept their bodies hidden when five of the creatures came out."

"What good did they think hiding their bodies could do?" asked the spider. "Didn't they think the creatures have good senses?"

"That's what they did think," the butterfly answered, "and seemingly they are right. The metal-secreters never seem to eject at anything that cannot be sensed by vision. The bees and ants stayed hidden among the flowers while the creatures crawled down from the hill and began exploring the edge of the foliage. That was when I decided to fly over there and observe the creatures directly.

"When I arrived, the creatures had moved a short distance away from the hill, using some sharp metal extrusion from their upper legs to cut a path through the flowers. If they are knowing creatures, then our world is as concealed from them as the inside of their hive is from me, because they obviously did not know the bees were concealed all along one side of the trail, waiting for the creatures to get deep enough in the flowers for their retreat to be cut off. Some ants were waiting, too, hoping to get some meat for themselves.

"I approached from the side of the trail opposite from where the bees were hiding and arrived just as the bees moved in to attack. The creatures saw me first and kept looking up at me until the bees almost had them. Then they turned and started ejecting at the bees. I saw several bees go down, but only one of the creatures got stung. Evidently the creatures have very tough exoskeletons, made mostly of metal, and the bees could not find weak spots into which the sting could be inserted. Nevertheless, the creatures started back to their hive, dragging the stung one with them, and they finally made it—with bees and ants snapping and punching at them all the way back to the Rock Hill. I was still flying about observing, and as soon as the creatures were out of the flowers one of them ejected at me and hit my wing. I came here, and the creatures are all in their hive now. As soon as they were in, the hive ejected a flaming mass of poisonous substance onto the area where they had cut the trail. Luckily, the bees had scattered by then, and the ants were most of the way back to their nests loaded with ant and bee meat, so the fire did not kill very many."

The spider was almost through repairing his wing as the butterfly ended his account. With a delicate touch, she smoothed the surface of the hard-setting modification of web-stuff with which she had encased the major vein-fracture.

"What are you going to do now?" she asked.

"Now?" he asked. "In the next now-moments? As soon as you say my wing is ready to be used, I'll take nourishment."

"That's not what I mean," she snapped impatiently. "I mean what about the metal-secreters."

A strange question, thought the butterfly. He queried the other butterflies, and they too agreed it was a strange thing to ask. So did the moths who, living on the night half of the world, were awake at the moment. One moth remarked that it was just the kind of question one might expect from a spider, whose life was one long introspection with insufficient introspecting equipment.

"Nothing," he answered at last. "Of course, I will continue trying to fit them into my knowing of the now-moment."

"If you could ever fit them in," she asked, "don't you think you could have done so by now?"

That "ever" was a meaningless, spiderish term. What personal significance could "ever" have to the butterfly, who had awakened and climbed from his pupa enclosure seventeen days before and who knew he would die fifty-five days from this particular now-moment, when the winter cold returned? "Ever" to a butterfly is one summer season; it is the same to a spider, but perhaps engrossed in her legends of memory she would not agree with that.

He answered her question: "Perhaps."

"In case of emergency," she recited, "a butterfly may call Man."

"That is true," he said.

"Then why don't you?" she urged. "This is an emergency, and you're a butterfly."

"Why is this an emergency?" he countered. "A few bees and ants have died before their normal time, and a few flowers have been destroyed in one tiny area. For the world as a whole, life continues as always for the creatures of Man."

The truth was that the butterfly—all butterflies—regarded Man as a rather mythic being. Man had doubtless once existed, but an accurate definition of his attributes was no longer available to his creatures. The clear picture of Man had been lost with the passage of thousands of years and thousands of generations. The act of calling Man, the butterfly felt, could not be integrated into his knowing of the now-moment.

"This is an emergency," the spider told him, "because you admit those metal-secreters are a blank spot in your knowing. When a butterfly admits something like that, it's an emergency!"

"If I called Man and he came," said the butterfly, "he would be another such blank spot. How do you know these two blanks would be mutually eliminating?"

"All I know is that we are creatures of Man," she huffed rather piously, "and we are supposed to call him in need. He brought us to this world and remade us and the flowers so that we could live here alone from him, because this world is not suited for Man's needs, and Man does not remake himself. The gravity of this world was too slight, and the air much too thick, for Man to dwell here in comfort, nor were the seasons suited to beings such as he, who may endure for a hundred years." (She was reciting again, the butterfly noted.) "He fitted us for this world, and gave it to us, but kept us for himself, as his creatures, to live for Man as well as for ourselves. We have a responsibility to Man. You should call him."

"The old knowledge says we 'may' call him," retorted the butterfly.

"Yes, and we 'may' disappoint if he returns some day to find his creatures gone and the world filled with metal-secreting monsters!"

"The creatures in that hive won't find much metal to secrete if they try to live here," the butterfly responded. "Our stones contain mere traces of the heavy elements."

Though he was arguing with the spider, the butterfly was not at all sure he was right. The calling of Man was an event that had never occurred; thus it was difficult to fit into his knowing of the now-moment. But perhaps it was the appropriate action to take under the present circumstances. As the spider had reminded him, it was a recourse suggested by Man himself.

"I will go feed while I think about it," the butterfly agreed at last.

"Will you let me know what you decide?" she asked.

"Yes."

2

He took to the air and found his mended wing was as sturdy as ever—as he had known it would be. Flying to a group of flowers he had not yet visited, he lit on a tall, deep-cupped blossom and unrolled his proboscis. As he sipped the sweet nectar from the bottom of the cup he realized that he had made his decision.

There was no question about it being his decision to make. Butterflies do not vote. The others were, certainly, interested in what his decision would be, but he was the individual directly involved in the matter of the metal-secreters.

The strange hive was on his hunting ground. He had seen it himself and had been attacked by one of the creatures. He had discussed the situation with the spider. In short, this was his affair, and his ability to decide how to conduct it was as good as any other butterfly's.

He would call Man. The other favored creatures would assist him if he requested their help.

Having decided, he continued to feed for two hours. Man could not be called from his hunting ground—that had to be done at a special place hundreds of miles away. It was best to be well nourished before beginning such a journey. When his feeding took him close to the spider's web, he kept his promise to tell her what he was going to do. She haughtily approved.

The day was still younger than mid-morning when he took a last sip, climbed higher in the air than usual and began the long flight westward. He had never come this way before—in fact, he had never traveled far from his hunting ground in any direction. But he found nothing strange in the countryside below him, no wonderful new sights to see. He knew the now-moment, and what he saw was what he had known was there to see.

When he grew hungry after several hours of flight, another butterfly, a Swallowtail like himself, called invitingly: "Come down and feast and rest. My flowers are suitable, sweet and plentiful." He accepted the offer and lighted in the other's hunting ground where he fed, napped and fed again until mid-morning. Then he resumed his journey.

He made five more such stops before the terrain began to change from the lush, slightly undulating plain into a more rugged and elevated landscape where the flowers grew in less abundance. He was approaching a towering range of mountains. As he climbed with the land, the atmosphere grew noticeably thinner; breathing and flying required increased vigor, and his periods of rest became longer and more frequent. But he was nearing his goal.

He reached a spot near the upper end of a high valley, with only one more tremendous barren ridge to fly over. He had left the area in which butterflies lived and hunted far behind; at this elevation the flowers were too small and sparse to support the likes of himself in comfort.

He fluttered down to light on a rock near a bee-hive. Several bees came out and examined him with wonder. To their limited knowing he was a sight at which to marvel, gigantic in size and with wings the colors of many flowers. And he was a butterfly, which meant he was wise.

"You are welcome here, butterfly-who-is-going-to-call-Man," they told him, "though you will eat so much, doubtless, that you will set our population expansion program back at least a year. Never has a butterfly visited our hive before. It will please us to serve you well."

"I am grateful," he responded "especially since you do not have plenty."

"What we have you will find good," they replied.

And he did. The bees fed him honey, and his knowing was shocked most pleasantly by its heavy richness and almost overwhelming sweetness. Never before, he realized, had a butterfly been so hungry and fed so deliciously. It was a wonderful and novel now-moment to know.

After he had been fed and had drunk from a shaded, icy spring, he napped by the water for several hours. Then the bees fed him more honey and, thoroughly invigorated, he began the last segment of his journey.

He needed all the strength the honey gave him. As he made his way up the steep final slope, the thinning air became hardly sufficient to sustain him, no matter how hard he worked his wings, and it seemed all but impossible to pump his abdomen fast enough to bring as much oxygen as he needed into his body. Long before he reached the summit he was reduced to making short, hopping flights of only a few yards at a time, from one ledge to the next, interspersed with rests for breathing.

The last fifty yards of the ascent he did not fly at all, but crawled. When he came in sight of the Nest That Man Left he was tempted to stop where he stood and sleep, but the chill in the air told his knowing that this would be unwise. He made his way clumsily over the leveled ground of the mountaintop toward the entrance of the rambling metal structure.

As he did so he realized that the Nest That Man Left was another emptiness in his knowing. That was not surprising, though, since it was an unpopulated, unvisited location. His knowing told him only what the outer appearance of the Nest would be, and where it was to be entered. The inside was as blank as that of the metal-secreters' hive. With a sense of uneasiness in the face of the unknown, intensified by the strained condition of his body, the butterfly crawled to the entrance.

The Nest sensed his presence and opened the door as he approached. He went inside without a pause, and the door slid closed behind him.

3

The interior was dark at first but brightened immediately as overhead panels shifted to let in sunlight through a wide expanse of glass.

The walls hissed as an oxygen-rich flood of air pressed in to bring the thickness up to a level the butterfly found comfortable. A trough in the floor gurgled and filled with water, and he drank gratefully. These events were all unexpected, of course, but there was a definite rightness about them. This was the way a butterfly should be received in the Nest That Man Left, and it was not difficult to place in his knowing.

The Nest addressed him: "You are a butterfly, and you are here to call Man." The mind of the Nest was shrouded, somewhat like that of the spider except for an absence of personality.

"Yes," the butterfly responded.

"I am the voice of the Nest, a contrivance that does not live but that can converse with you to a limited extent. Do you have injuries or unmet needs that are an immediate danger to you?"

"No." The butterfly's senses searched his surroundings while the voice addressed him, and he gained a partial knowing of the nature of the voice contrivance. Man had to be wise, indeed, to construct such a complex dead device and to shelter it so perfectly that, after untold thousands of years, it could still awaken and engage in a conversation of minds.

"Do butterflies continue to know the now-moment?" the Nest asked.

"Yes."

"That is an ability Man did not give me, and one that he lacks himself," the Nest told him. "Thus I do not know the nature of the emergency that brings you here. Nor do I know where Man is, nor what he may have become during the centuries since he made me, mutated your ancestors and departed."

"Man does not change himself, according to my knowing," commented the butterfly.

"Not intentionally, perhaps, but he changes nevertheless. He is a discontented being who, not knowing the now-moment, wanders and searches for new things to know. What he finds changes him, not in the orderly manner in which he fitted you for conditions on this world, but in ways that are unplanned and sometimes undesirable. Occasionally he finds something very damaging to him, something that darkens his intelligence and causes him to forget much of his learning from previous findings."

The butterfly struggled with this information. His difficulty was not that what the Nest told him was new. On the contrary, it was ancient; so ancient that it had been all but forgotten—dismissed as having no meaning to current knowing. It occurred to the butterfly that perhaps the creatures of Man had *wanted* to forget that Man could not know the now-moment, which implied that Man was inferior to themselves. But then, he quickly reassured himself, Man must have completely different abilities that made him superior—abilities so far beyond a butterfly's comprehension that the Nest would not attempt to describe them.

At last he addressed the Nest: "Then if I call Man, the being who responds may be unlike the beings who established the creatures of Man on this world. He may even have forgotten that he has such creatures as us."

"That is correct," the Nest responded. "Man instructed me to be sure you understood that before he was called. If he comes, the results will be unpredictable.

You are to reconsider the nature of your emergency with this in mind and decide if your need for Man is sufficient for you to accept the uncertainties of his present nature."

This was a difficult decision indeed. The butterfly thought about it for several minutes before saying, "In essence, the emergency is an intellectual one. An area of blankness has entered our knowing. Since Man does not know the now-moment, it is possible that we could not explain to him the nature of the emergency."

"That is possible," agreed the Nest. "In any event, unless Man has changed greatly, you will be unable to communicate with him directly. Man does not speak mind-to-mind, the way you and I are conversing, but through the use of special sounds he can emit, each sound being a symbol of a fragment of thought."

"Then how could we have ever communicated?" asked the astonished butterfly.

"Through intermediary devices such as myself," said the Nest. "You can talk to me and I can put your thoughts into the words of Man, like this." The Nest emitted, from a wall cavity, a complex series of noises.

The butterfly listened in stunned recognition. He had never heard such sounds before today, but as he had hovered over the metal-secreters earlier that morning just such noises, though dim and muffled, had struck his sensors. But Man was supposed to be ten-fingered—more manipulatory members than even the spider! And the metal-secreters had clearly been deficient in this respect, having only two pairs of legs.

The Nest was continuing: "Communication is rendered more complex by the use of differing sets of sound-symbols called languages, and by the fact that a given set of symbols tends to change with the passage of years to become an entirely new language. I probably would not know the sounds man uses today, but would have to communicate your thoughts, with some explanation, to a device similar to myself that Man brought with him, and that device in turn would speak to Man."

"Man uses metal extensively, does he not?" asked the butterfly.

"Yes. Metals were abundant on his, and your, original planet. He built his nests of them and other dead materials, and also his flying shelters in which he journeyed here and to many other worlds."

"What are fingers?"

"They are relatively small, slender extensions of Man's arms, his upper legs. They are useful for gripping and manipulating. He has ten of them, normally."

"I wish to call him," said the butterfly.

"Very well . . . The call is now being emitted. I do not know when he will arrive. He may have to come far, a journey of more than a day for his fastest shelter. Certainly, he cannot be expected to arrive within a hundred hours at best. As there is no food stored for you here, I suggest you return to your hunting ground to await him."

"My knowing is unsure," replied the butterfly, "but I believe Man to be quite close. I will wait outside, at least for a while. It is certain he will respond to the call?"

"If he does not," the Nest said, "he will have changed too greatly to be of any assistance to you. I am preparing to open the door."

The air thinned; the door opened, and the butterfly went out onto the mountaintop. This was the kind of air Man could breathe without the protection of an artificial exoskeleton, the butterfly reasoned. Thus this mountaintop was the place where Man should be met by his creatures.

4

He was hardly outside when the knowing came that the flying hive of the "metal-secreters" had lifted from the Rock Hill back in his hunting ground. It was hurtling toward him almost with the speed of a meteorite, but when it arrived it landed as gently as the butterfly could have descended onto a flower.

The Nest commented: "So your emergency was Man himself . . . They have a device with them to permit communication." Nearly an hour passed before the butterfly was addressed again: "A Man is coming out now. I have told him about this world."

The butterfly watched with a touch of awe as the Man came out of the unplugged hole in the flying hive. Without his artificial exoskeleton, but with most of his body covered with brightly colored woven material, he still looked very odd—but not like some freakish creature who could secrete metal. The butterfly's senses informed him that, without his woven coverings, Man would appear rather drab: pink all over except for a

scattering of dark hair and for the eyes which were
small and one-faceted.

Still, there was an austere attractiveness in the
Man's appearance and a startling grace in the way he
crawled, precariously balanced on his rear legs. The
Men had looked less graceful earlier in the morning,
using all four legs to push their way through the flowers and the attacking bees, or to climb the steep side
of Rock Hill. Apparently Man was designed to crawl
best over level, unobstructed ground.

The Man advanced to stand before the butterfly,
his small eyes studying the insect as the insect studied
the Man. The wings seemed to fascinate the Man.
When held in a resting, vertical position their tips
were approximately a third as high off the ground as
the top of the Man's head.

A series of sounds came from the Man's
mouth.

"He is asking your name," explained the Nest.
"That is an abstract symbol you would use to identify
yourself, as an individual, from the other butterflies. I
have explained that, while butterflies have individual-
ity, you have no use for names because of the way
you communicate."

"You (Man) may give me a name if you wish," said
the butterfly.

"No," said the Man. "If you need no name, you
should not have one. How can I serve you in a manner that suits your need?"

"I do not know. I came to the Nest to call you
because the flying hive was a blank in my knowing of
the now-moment. Perhaps I expected you to destroy
the hive, or cause it to go elsewhere. But the hive is

your contrivance, and this is your world. Thus I have nothing to ask."

"This is *your* world, butterfly," contradicted the Man. "Long ago, men gave it to you and left. I'm beginning to realize why they went away, even though there must be many mountains such as this on which men could live in comfort. We too must depart soon, for the same reason. And we will take our flying hive with us."

"The seasons of this world are not suited," the butterfly quoted, "for beings who live a hundred years."

"That is a minor problem," the man said. "Men are not as long-lived as you believe. Our hundred years, or season cycles, are very brief years compared to your own. This planet turns much more slowly on its axis and takes much longer to circle its sun than the planet that gave birth to both our species. Also, this planet's orbit is far more eccentric than that of our birth-planet, giving you brief, warm summers and very long, cold winters. Men restructured you genetically to fit in this environment as intelligent life. The ancient geneticists must have chosen you for this world because you metamorphose. You can survive the winter as a pupa or, in the case of spiders and some of the other insects, as an egg. That was long ago, according to the way man experiences time. We have lost all records of having populated this planet. Before our flying hive leaves, there is much about your life cycles we would like to re-learn."

"It will please us to tell you," said the butterfly. "There is a spider at my hunting ground who, I am certain, will delight in talking to you for a whole day."

The butterfly was somewhat puzzled by the workings of the Man's mind. Evidently the Man had started to tell him the reason why the Men who had shaped the creatures had not stayed, and why now these Men would have to depart quickly. However, the Man had strayed from the subject. But perhaps the butterfly knew the reason without being told.

"Now that we know what the flying hive is," he said, "its blankness is far less disturbing. It is quite tolerable, in fact. You need not go quickly on that account."

"That is not why we must leave," said the Man. "If it were, we could solve our problem quite easily by allowing you to enter the flying hive and investigate its contents until it ceased to be a blank. You may do that, anyway, for that matter."

"Then why must you go?" the butterfly asked.

The Man replied hesitantly. "Because it may not be good for men to associate too much with you. Not bad for you, but bad for men. Tell me, butterfly, do you know that on the birth-planet men regarded you as the most beautiful creature in existence?"

"No."

"Neither did I—since I had never seen a butterfly until today. Nor even a picture of one. That is the reason for the incidents earlier this morning. I wish to apologize for not recognizing you and the ants and bees."

"That's all right," replied the butterfly. "We didn't recognize you either."

"Anyway, you are the most beautiful creature that I've ever seen on any world, excepting of course certain females of my own kind," the Man went on.

"And in your mutated form, which has increased your size and given you a unique intelligence, you impress us as being—totally admirable. Man sees no other creature that way. And what men admire, they try to imitate in themselves."

He hesitated, then finished hurriedly and almost angrily: "If men stayed here, they would wind up being fake butterflies, trying to look and think like you when they can do neither. It's best for us to stay away from your world and continue being men, whatever that may be."

The butterfly found this speech astonishing to the point of incomprehensibility, the final words no less than what came before. "But you made us as we are," he protested. "Surely you know your superiority to us."

"No."

"You do not know the now-moment," the butterfly persisted, "but isn't that for a reason similar to my not remembering in the manner of the spider? The thought comes to me that perhaps you combine remembering and knowing in a way I cannot comprehend, to know all moments that have been or will be."

The man made a sound signifying amusement. "That is a flattering thought. It attributes to us the supreme knowledge we sometimes imagine in our own gods—the hypothetical beings who created all life. No, we don't have that kind of knowing. And the fact that you have part of it is a reason why men must avoid you. They would tend to consider you half-gods."

This, to the butterfly, was monstrous. "But surely you must have some form of knowing . . ." he began.

The Man was shaking his head. "Men have seen

much and learned much. And we know much. But not as you know."

Suddenly the butterfly understood and gazed at the Man with awe. To know the now-moment, he realized dimly, was a complete thing, and what was complete was limited to its totality. Man's knowing had no completeness—no limits—because Man did not even know himself.

Breathing hard in the thin mountain air, the butterfly marveled at the boundless wonder of Man.

ALL AROUND THE
UNIVERSE

❧

AS SOON AS I LEFT Gildalyn and returned to my own ship, I checked my financial status. Uneasily. I knew that fun and games with a choice morsel like Gildalyn was costly—it always was for me—but the question of the nanosecond was precisely how costly.

I admit it: I'm not the Sandman's gift to women. Not mutated or dismal or anything, but nothing special. I'm just average. The big trouble with that is that I'm not interested in dawdling with just-average girls. I'm always getting out of my class, going for the Gildalyn types.

A weakness like that can make life in this cold, cruel universe pretty frantic.

"Tell me the damage, ship," I groaned.

"I beg pardon, Mr. Rylsten?"

"My financial balance!" I snapped.

"Yes, sir. Your balance is 217 Admiration Units, sir, indicating an expenditure of 1,644 Admiration Units during the past 36 standard hours, sir."

Over sixteen hundred Admires! My mouth hung open. Why, a cost like that meant (my soul squirmed) that Gildalyn couldn't have returned as much as 10 Units! *Amused contempt!* That was all she could have felt!

"Somebody ought to kick me," I muttered.

"Shall I mock up your father, sir?" the ship suggested.

"No!"

"Then perhaps your mother, sir. A comforting word may prove more useful than a kick in amending your present mood, Mr. Rylsten."

"*No!* None of your damned mock-ups, ship! Look. Could the sensors in that twirl's boat be rigged to overcharge?"

"Absolutely not, sir," replied the ship, almost sounding offended. "The Admiration Accounting System cannot be compromised. And any exchange of more than 500 Admiration Units is automatically depth-probed and verified."

"Okay, okay," I grumbled. "Vanish."

My surroundings flickered, the way they do sometimes in an older ship—and my crate was a secondhand job—then went transparent for a dozen seconds before achieving total invisibility. I gazed about dully.

I was moseying off, arbitrary west from Abercrombie Galactic Cluster, where I'd been with Gildalyn. I tried to relax and feel at one with the beauties of nature. That's thickly clustered space west of Abercrombie, and I don't know anywhere in the universe where the spirals are more gracefully formed. Nothing to knock your eyes out, but just attractively restful countryside.

It put me at ease, after an hour or so, and I went to sleep. When I woke ten hours later, Johncrust Cluster lay dead ahead. I felt sleep-groggy, which was an improvement.

I told the ship, "Veer south twenty degrees, and give me some breakfast. Standard menu." I had no Admiration to waste on food. And actually I was hungry enough to enjoy subsistence fare—orange pulp, ham and eggs, jelly toast and coffee—which being standard would cost me nothing.

When I finished, and had been evacuated and sanitized by the ship, I got a determined grip on myself. I had to do something about my finances.

"Tread control, ship."

"Yes, Mr. Rylsten."

I stood up and began walking. The invisible surface beneath my feet felt smooth and grassy. "One-point-five gravitation," I said.

I felt my body compress downward under the weight, and squared my shoulders against it. I hiked ahead vigorously, the ship responding to my changes of speed and direction as I strolled among the clusters, picking my path subconsciously as my mind worked on the problem at hand.

But it was no good.

The trouble was, my old sources of income were shot. I'd gotten too damned old to go running home for a handout. My old man had made that clear. As for the kids I used to planetcrawl with, back in my old home system . . . well, that had gone sour on me, too.

Time was I could breeze in to visit with the old gang, regale them with tales of the famous twirls I'd made the big scene with, and soon have them gaping (with Admiration, of course) at me. Why, once, after I met Jallie Klevillia whom *everybody's* heard about, I got two thousand Units out of the home system kids . . . and all Jallie got out of me was nine hundred. She wasn't as hot as her reputation.

But the last time I went home to hit my old chums, it didn't work. Maybe they're getting old and hard to impress. I recall Marge Grossit gave me a cold stare and then said, "Boje Rylsten, isn't it time you settled down?"

And Harmo Jones said, "I guess *anybody* can mingle with the big beauties, if he's willing to drop a thousand Units doing it."

Would you believe I came away from that bunch of low-lifers with fewer Units than I had to start?

So, where the sand was my Admiration going to come from?

I was at a dead end. I might have no choice but what Marge Grossit suggested—settle down with some average twirl; and spend my life eating standard nine days out of ten, raising kids who *might* Admire their old man; and building interest Units with their mother.

I cringed at the thought. I'd had a taste of something better.

But my thinking was getting me no place.

"Tread control off. Gravity down," I commanded tiredly, flopping in the direction of my chair.

"Very well, Mr. Rylsten."

"Standard beer."

"Yes, sir."

I sat there, sipping the beer like a nobody. That was what I was, a nobody from a long line of nobodies. But unlike all the other Rylstens, I couldn't help knowing I was a nobody.

Old Uncle Buxton, for instance. All pose that guy was. I chuckled at the memory of old Uncle Buxton. When he talked, his tongue wagged his brain! By which I think I mean his brain was foolish enough to believe what his tongue said.

But in his way, he wasn't a bad old joker.

"Ship," I said, "my Uncle Buxton gave me his mock-up three years ago. I don't know if I threw it away. Check and see if you have it."

"Yes, sir, a Buxton Rylsten tape is on file."

"Okay, mock him up. And brief him. I don't want to spend an hour explaining my troubles to him."

"Yes, sir."

I had time to finish my beer before the mock-up came into the living cabin. "Hi, Uncle Buck," I greeted him.

"Hello, Boje," he responded with extended hand. "So it's been three years since you saw me, has it?"

"Sorry about that, Uncle. I've just been busy."

"I understand, Boje," he smiled. "The thing is that you called for me now, when you have a problem that requires mature wisdom and experience. I didn't give you that tape expecting to be your constant companion—you naturally prefer friends your own age."

I accepted that with a straight face. "Mature

wisdom"—*hah!* If self-admiration was spelled with a capital A, old Uncle Buxton would be the richest man in the universe! The truth was that I just wanted somebody to talk to me, without getting mushy like mom's mock-up would, or hitting me with an angry sermon like dad.

"I'll give it to you straight, pal," he said in his solemn, querulous way. "We have to face reality, and reality is harsh." He settled himself comfortably on a lounge. "Who a man is, or what a man is, don't amount to a circumcised Unit! I learned that long ago, Boje. What I'm saying, Boje, is don't expect respect. You understand?"

"I sure do," I replied. "Won't you have a beer, Uncle?"

"I'd be delighted. Now, Boje, your problem is financial. That puts you in the same boat with every honest man who ever lived. No monetary system in history has been fair to the honest man. That's what's held me back all my life. Tell me, Boje. Why do you think our system of exchange uses Admiration for currency?"

"Well," I said, "that's because Admiration is the basic desired quality. Everybody tries to get it, and that's good. It keeps the society moving. So, when science found a way to quantitize and measure Admiration, it was adopted."

Uncle Buxton was grinning knowingly. "That's what they taught you in school, isn't it, Boje?"

"Yeah."

"The trouble is, pal, there are lessons the schools don't teach," he said. "They don't breathe a hint of the real truth, which is that our system *debases* Admiration by making it the object of crass materialism. In the same way the ancients debased the beauty of their handsomest metal, gold, by making it the medium of exchange.

"But the abuse goes deeper than that, Boje," he went on ponderously. "Whether money is based on gold, on labor, or on Admiration, it always requires a man to *do* things he wouldn't otherwise do. It forces him to act against his higher instinct.

"It makes him chop up the ornaments the ancients loved and make coin out of the pieces. It makes him work when he would prefer to rest. It makes him force his personality into an Admirable mold. Isn't that true?"

"Yeah, and I can't find the right mold for myself," I said glumly.

"Right!" he said emphatically. "And I'll tell you why, Boje. It's because you're too much like me!" I started slightly. If that was true, it was the worst bad news I'd ever heard.

"There's too much honesty in you," he explained. "You want to be what you honestly are, without abusing your better nature by acting the way the monetary system tries to force you to act. You see?"

I didn't quite see, but I nodded anyway. "Then it's what a man *does* that counts," I hazarded.

"On the button!" he applauded. "Not what he is, but what he does!" He chugged his beer and added sadly, "It wasn't always this bad. Back in the Dollar Era, there was a saying that went, 'It's not what you do, but who you are.' And another they had was, 'It's not *what* you know, but *who* you know.' That must have been a golden age, indeed. Society has degenerated."

"I guess so," I agreed moodily. "But our system wouldn't be so bad if they would just change it a little. You take me. I like to Admire. Particularly I like to Admire certain twirls. Things ought to work so that I can concentrate on Admiring them, since that's what I do best, without having to try to be Admired myself. There ought to be an allowance for a guy like me . . . say one or two hundred Units per day . . ."

"Right, but the powers-that-be wouldn't listen to that for a nanosecond," he snorted. "It would compromise the Admirable Society. The aim of our whole system is to force *everybody* to be as Admirable as possible. It's slavery of the most blatant type! That's the harsh reality, Boje."

We chatted on and had some standard lunch. Then I saw that I had an embarrassing chore on my hands. How was I going to turn Uncle Buxton's mock-up off?

That had never been a problem with mom or dad . . . They were always glad enough to go back on the tape after a short visit. But Uncle Buxton had the look of a man settling in for a two-week visit. If I had the ship unmock him against his will, he wouldn't come off the tape next time in a friendly mood at all.

At last a solution occurred to me.

"Uncle Buck," I said, "I want you to enjoy the hospitality of my ship. The previous owner equipped it with twirl tapes. I guess they were best sellers in their day. Sorry I can't offer you anything current."

There was a lustful glitter in Uncle Buxton's eyes. "Well, now, Boje, that's nice of you, but your aunt, may the Sandman bless her, has old-fashioned ideas.

She would have my hide if I fooled around with a twirlmock."

"I don't see how she could, Uncle. You're separate from your original self that's married to Aunt Bauvila. How will she know what you do?"

Uncle Buxton snorted. "I keep forgetting I'm a mock-up. Um, well, I just might take you up, Boje. Who do you have?"

"There's Sondri Cavalo," I began, "and Dince Har—"

"Hey! I've heard of Sondri Cavalo all my life!" He broke in eagerly. "She'll do fine!"

"All right. Ship. Mock up the Cavalo twirl."

"Yes, sir," the ship responded. When Sondri came into the cabin, I introduced her and Uncle Buxton. They hit it off right away, the way mock-ups usually do. Sometimes I think our society was made for mock-ups, instead of the other way around. They don't have to worry about Admiration since they don't participate . . . except as pieces of property . . . in the monetary system. So they can take life as they find it. Sondri wasn't hungry, and it wasn't long before she and Uncle Buxton went off, in a cuddly embrace, to the back cabin.

"Ship?"

"Yes, sir."

"Unmock Uncle Buxton after he's had his fling and five hours of sleep."

"Very well, sir."

It's what you do that counts. That's what I had decided during my talk with Uncle Buxton. It was something I'd known all along, in the back of my mind. After all, a lot of guys *do* do things.

And I know my way around; so I knew where to go to find something to do.

"Head for Greenstable, ship," I ordered. "That's in Milky Way Galaxy, over in the old sector." A funny name for a galaxy, I'd always thought. Probably after the type of candy that originated there.

"On our way, sir."

I deep-napped most of the way, and didn't come back to full alert until we hit the Greenstable atmosphere.

That planet is somebody's good idea gone sour. Time and progress have passed it by. Its only attraction is the Greenstable Racetrack, which was quite a scene several centuries ago. It was called the "horse-racing hub of the universe" . . . and it is still called that, but only a handful of nuts waste Admiration on a horse nowadays.

The racetrack is still in operation, though, and is energized for mock horses and riders. Other than the track complex, the planet is just a lot of marlboro, with herds of wild horses wandering around, I guess to give an appropriate setting.

I put down on the nearly empty parking area and shuttled to the Jockey Club building. With mock jocks, the club doesn't serve its original purpose (whatever that was) any more. It's a place where guys looking for something to do contact other guys who need something done. All informal, but legal enough to stay out of trouble with Admiration Accounting.

But to look at the guys lounging inside, you'd think doing something, or wanting something done, was the most distant subject from their minds. There was always a bunch hanging around, though.

I got a beer and took a lounge near five guys talking about new-model ships. I put in a remark now and then, and finally asked, "Anything doing today?"

"Not much," one of them yawned. "It's a dull day. Jonmak's got a research thing. That's him over there. Watch out for him, though."

I knew what the warning meant, but I walked over to Jonmak anyway. I wasn't worried. He looked like somebody's idea of the ultimate twirlrave—tall, clean-cut, hawknosed, with a haughty expression—but I don't waste Admiration on such guys. I guess I'm not the jealous type.

"Jonmak? I'm Rylsten. Boje Rylsten," I said.

He gave me an old-pal grin. "Good to meet you, Rylsten."

"Same here," I replied, shaking his firm hand. "The guys tell me you're pushing a chore."

He saw that I wasn't impressed by what a great guy he was, and looked a bit sour. "Yeah. It's a bit out of the average doer's line. Ever hear of Profanis?"

"No," I replied. "If that's a galaxy, it must be a small one. I know all the spirals."

"It's not a galaxy. It's a system."

I shrugged, as much as to say what the sand did he expect. "Where is this Profanis system?" I asked.

He grinned. "That's the chore, Rylsten. Find Profanis."

I stared at him. "That's all?"

"That's all."

"Okay," I said, "I get aboard my ship, and tell it to take me to Profanis. I let it search the tapes for the right sector and galaxy and so on. Then it takes me there. What's the chore about that?"

"The chore is that Profanis isn't on the tapes of your ship, or any other ship," said Jonmak. "Even Admiration Accounting has nothing on it."

"Then there ain't no such place."

He smirked, and peeled a sheet of plaper out of his tunic pocket. "The government doesn't agree," he said, handing me the plaper.

It was a fax of an official U.G. document, issued by the Standing Consolidation Commission of the Department of Justice:

For use of DJ agents, here is a description of the Profanis system, unlocated and unconsolidated.

The system takes its name from its principal planet, rather than from its sun, for a reason the diagram below makes plain. Note the system is abnormal and in high probability is artificial.

I looked at the diagram, which showed the craziest looking system I ever saw.

There was the planet labeled "Profanis" in the center, with about half a dozen satellites orbiting around it. One of the satellites was rayed, and was labeled "sun." The others were just ordinary moons, and their labels were meaningless symbols instead of words.

And that was all. No real sun, no other planets. I thought for a moment that the diagram was not supposed to show the whole system. Then I noticed that stars were marked in a circle around the edge of the drawing, to indicate that beyond the outermost satellite was nothing but interstellar sky.

Of course a "sun" the size and mass of a moon just doesn't exist in nature. But a moon can be fired up to burn like a sun for a few thousand years if someone wants to go to the expense. It involves setting up an anti-matter con-recon field around the object, and I don't know of anybody with enough Admires to pay for that kind of job.

Still, that was what the drawing showed: a moon fired up to serve as a sun, and in an orbit low enough, presumably, to keep the planet Profanis comfortably warm.

Below the drawing, and looking like part of the drawing instead of the text of the document, was a line that read: *"The world Profane, least blest of God's creation."*

As most everybody knows, "God" is what the Sandman used to be called, back before the universe was explored out to the edge and the sand was discovered. Which meant that the drawing was pretty old . . . at least three thousand years. And now I noticed that the reproduced drawing showed smudges and crinkle marks. So it *was* old.

I read the rest of the document, mostly about the urgency of Profanis being found and brought into the Admirable Society. Presumably the inhabitants lacked space travel, which meant that when their goofy little "sun" burned out they would *all* die.

I never heard of anything so fantastic! A planet without space travel!

The document concluded:

Agents discovering any information concerning the Profanis system are instructed to report their findings at once. The accompanying drawing, which was found in the Astrographic Archives of Homeworld Earth, is the only source of information concerning Profanis now known. Additional data is urgently needed to expedite the early location of the system.

I exploded, "This is crazy, man! All they have is that drawing! It doesn't have to mean *anything*. It could be out of a piece of fiction!"

Jonmak gave a hard grin. "Then what was it doing in the Astrographic Archives?" he asked.

I grimaced. He had me there.

"The government doesn't make many mistakes, pal," he added. "If they say that drawing is of a real system, you better believe it is *real*. Now, are you going to give it a try?"

I thought it over, and can't say I liked it. If the DJ agents had tried and couldn't find Profanis (and it stood to reason that they had; otherwise the government wouldn't be dealing amateur-doers in) my chances of success had to be extremely slim. Also, the guy who first said "It's a small universe" probably never had the job of locating a particular uncharted star system in it. Certainly not a system with a tiny fake "star" that would be out of detection at a quarter of a light-year!

I told Jonmak, "It doesn't sound promising, but if it's the only thing going and has a big payoff . . ."

"It does," he put into my pause. "Eight Big Ones."

Eight thousand Admires seemed like a fortune right then. "Okay, I'll try it."

He smiled like a guy who has found a doting sucker. "Great! And good luck in the hunt."

Feeling foolish, I returned to my ship. "Lift off," I said.

"Yes, sir. Where to?"

"Just off. I'll decide where later." The ship rose

through the atmosphere, picked up speed as it wiggled between the stars and out into intergalactic space.

"What's my balance now, ship?" I asked.

"Still 217 Admiration Units, sir."

I nodded, pleased. I didn't think that Jonmak had taken me for anything, but I always like to make sure. Sometimes Admiration can slip out of your subconscious without you being aware of it.

"Ship, see what you make of this," I ordered, feeding the plaper about Profanis into its information bank.

After a moment the ship replied, "It is a facsimile of a document of the Universal Government's Department of Justice, specifically the Standing Consolidation Commission, concerning the unlocated and unconsolidated system of Profanis—"

"Never mind quoting it to me! I can read!" I snorted. "The point is, I've taken on the chore of locating Profanis. How do I go about it?"

"Inasmuch as such a search has doubtless been conducted by Department of Justice agents—"

"Right," I inserted.

"And inasmuch as these agents doubtless made full use of such computerized reasoning as I can offer, any avenues of procedure I might propose can be presumed to have been fully explored."

"A great help you are!" I sneered.

"On the contrary, sir," said the ship, "I fear I can be of no help at all."

"That's what I meant."

"Very well, sir."

I thought, and ate, and thought some more.

"How much would it cost," I asked at last, "to put together a system like that?"

"Depending on how many of its constituent objects were found in location, sir, the cost would run from a minimum of 16.4 billion Units. That covers essentially the expense of energizing the fourth satellite as a source of light and heat. If none of the satellites were in place—"

"Never mind. The minimum's high enough. Now tell me this: who has Admires to spend on that scale?"

"Nobody, sir. The highest personal fortune currently on record is 56 million Units. The highest corporate expendable balance is 1.3 billion Units. The highest government unaccountable expense is limited to 100 million Units by law."

"Okay," I said. "When in the past did someone have that kind of Admires?"

"Never, sir."

"Then nobody could have ever done it; so Profanis can't exist," I growled angrily. "I thought this was nonsense to begin with!"

"I did not say that, sir. You spoke of Admiration Units only. Before the Admirable Society was founded, and other mediums of exchange were in use, there was a period of some forty years when numerous fortunes of sufficient scope existed."

"Oh, yeah," I said. "You mean the Worldking Generation."

"Yes, sir."

Which was an awful long time ago. The universe wasn't fully explored then.

"Okay," I said, "how about this approach? Find out where the frontier was back then, take account of every factor we can think of, and figure out where a Worldking would be most likely to set up a secret planet where he could indulge his favorite sins. Does that narrow down a search area for us?"

"Perhaps, sir. It will take several minutes to correlate the data."

"Sure," I said, opening a beer. Before the drink was gone, the ship flashed a 3D map of the Home Cluster. As usual, it showed our own position with a blue dot. And there were about a dozen markings in green, scattered through seven galaxies.

"The green indicates areas of search such as you described, sir," explained the ship.

"Good. This one looks closest," I said, reaching an arm into the map to put my finger on a green patch. "We'll start with it."

"Yes, sir: Changing course for Stebbins Galaxy."

The next three days I spent filtering around as dusty a patch of backlight as I ever hope to encounter, the ship's receptors full on for any radiator that approached being right for that homemade "sun" of Profanis. It was slow, boring work, but I kept at it. And when I was sure there was no such radiator around there, I told the ship to move on to the next area.

It was bigger, and took over a week to search. My morale was beginning to slip, but I consoled myself that we were looking in the right kind of places. I never realized before just how much of the galactic areas are uninhabited by man, even in the Home Cluster where you assume people are everywhere.

But I could see that this search might take months. Naturally, I didn't want to fritter away my time to that extent.

"Look, ship," I demanded, "how do we know that the

DJ agents haven't already searched these same areas, after figuring the problem the same way I did?"

"We don't know that they did not, sir," the ship replied. "In fact, the probability that we are duplicating their effort is .993, sir."

"*What?*" I roared. "Why didn't you *tell* me?"

"You did not ask, sir."

"Oh, sand," I moaned. Nearly two weeks shot! And I couldn't blame the ship. Ships have to be inhibited on information feed-out; otherwise they would talk you deaf on the slightest provocation.

"Well, I've had it with this chore," I said in disgust. "I'm going somewhere and have some fun."

"Very well, sir, but you have instructed me to advise you when your financial status is insufficient to cover an intended activity. Such is now the case, sir."

I groaned. Trapped! Me and my expensive tastes! "Damn it, I need companionship!" I complained.

"Yes, sir. May I suggest one of the mock-ups—"

"*No!* Who wants to fool with *those* things!" I wandered restlessly about the cabin. There was no getting away from it: I needed Admires, and this silly chore of finding Profanis was the only way I had to get them. Of course, I could go back to Greenstable and see if anything else was doing by now, but that would put me in a bad light there, quitting one chore that wasn't done to ask for an easier one.

So, I had to find Profanis.

Profanis.

"Ship, what does 'profane' mean?"

"It is essentially a negative word, sir, meaning 'not concerned with religion, not sacred.'"

"That's what I thought it meant," I said. "Okay,

let's approach it from that angle, then. Check for a colonized planet that doesn't have a church."

"Very well, sir."

"Hold on! What's the probability that the DJ agents have tried that?"

"Quite high, sir—.997."

"Forget it, then!" I was in a foul frame of mind—depressed, angry, and frustrated—and I wanted a Hallypuff very badly. But smokes are nonstandard fare, and wanting a Hallypuff as urgently as I did would make me Admire it just that much more.

"Oh, sand! Gimme a beer!"

For a long time I sat sipping and brooding. I still had the notion that the answer was locked up in that word "profane." The trouble was that, while I'm as religious as the next guy, I don't make a big thing out of it. I'm no expert on what is and isn't sacred.

"Ship, what's the probability on the DJ agents consulting church fathers?"

"It is approximately .992, sir."

I grunted. Evidently I didn't have an original idea in my head.

"Of course they would talk to the Pipe, then," I said glumly.

"Yes, sir."

"And the hermit sandpipers?"

The ship hesitated. "The probability there is lower, sir, approximately .26. The hermit pipers are not highly regarded as authorities on questions of religion, sir."

"Well, they handle sand more than the Pipe himself. He's too busy being an organization." I hesitated over the decision, but finally got it out timidly: "Head out to the sand, and we'll hunt a hermit."

"Very well, sir."

The ship didn't change course—after all, the sand is in every direction—but speeded up. I was so scared by what I was about to do that I had the ship untape a mocktwirl.

I didn't tell her what I was doing, but when we zipped past the last of the galactic clusters, she began to get shakier than I was; so I kissed her and put her back on tape.

"How much longer?" I asked. "Perhaps an hour, sir," said the ship. "We are entering the area of edge phenomena now, sir."

"Okay, just don't show it to me."

"Certainly not, sir."

But even if I couldn't see what was happening to space outside the ship, I could feel it. All I could do was lie limply, but not feeling limp. My eyes were squeezing out of my head, and my throat was coming up and out of my mouth.

Through my terror, I wondered how the first man had made it through to discover the sand. The only thing that kept me going was the knowledge that this would be over in less than an hour. The first explorer wouldn't have known that.

I thought about that for a while, and was still thinking about it when the phenomena started to let go.

"Approaching the sand, sir," announced the ship.

I sat up slowly. "Okay, I'll look at it," I managed to mumble.

The ship revealed the Sandwall stretching completely across the sky. It had a dim creamy glow (or anyway that is the way ships always show it . . . maybe it is really dark) and was featureless. I stared.

It's a strange sight to look at, and even stranger to think about. The sheer size stuns the imagination. A solid surface of stuff that englobes the whole universe like a bubble.

But it's not just a bubble, or even a wall, even if it is called the Sandwall. Maybe it goes on forever, and has other universe bubbles in it by the billions. The Pipe's pipers have probed it to a depth of five light-minutes, and the sand is still there. Just where it is in it that souls go to . . .

I shrugged. I was wasting time mooning over religious riddles. "Are we close enough to detect hermitages yet, ship?"

"Just coming into range now, sir."

"Good. Let's start searching."

The ship went into a search spiral along the surface of the Sandwall.

"A hermitage is just a ship, isn't it, pushing against the Sandwall?"

"Yes, sir."

"If I stayed in the same place all the time, I'd want something more elaborate than a ship," I mused.

"That would be difficult for a hermit sandpiper, sir. If the hermit traveled away from his stationary residence on the Sandwall, he would be unable to return to it."

"Oh? Why not?"

"He would be unable to find it, sir."

"But of course he could find . . ." I started to object, and then stopped. That surface was big, and feature-less, and the area of edge phenomena did strange things to navigation. If a hermit took a jaunt into the inhabited part of the universe, he might come back to a point on the wall a trillion lights from where he started. He'd never find his residence.

That thought led to another, and the pit fell out of my stomach. "How many hermit sandpipers are there, ship?"

"Slightly more than six million, sir."

Six million little ships, scattered over a surface that ran all around the universe!

"This," I said with apathetic calm, "is about as hopeless a search as trying to find Profanis by visiting every body in the universe."

"The difficulties are of similar orders of magnitude, sir," the ship agreed.

"Discontinue the search and give me a Hallypuff," I said.

After a pause, the ship replied, "Very well, sir," and lifted me the reefer.

I sat smoking it, not giving a damn how many Units it might cost me. I was beaten. Sunk without a trace. The End. The last of the red-hot twirl-chasers.

I giggled and threw away the butt of my Hallypuff.

"Just two choices left, ship. Suicide or become a hermit, and I'm not high enough for suicide. Push down to the surface."

"Yes, sir."

The Sandwall moved closer. There was a slight bump as contact was made.

"We're there, sir."

"Well, open me a compartment against the wall. I can't pipe sand through your damned hull."

The ship constricted a bulkhead on the wall side, and I climbed over the lip to squat in actual contact with the Sandwall. It was so slick it felt wet, but it wasn't. I could see the sand grains just beneath the slickness, but couldn't touch them.

Nothing but thought, such as a soul or a piper's probe, could penetrate that slickness. I sat still, glared very hard at a sand grain, and concentrated.

Five minutes or an hour later I giggled and gave it up. I couldn't make a mental probe, evidently; so I couldn't pipe sand.

I climbed back over the bulkhead lip and flopped in my lounger to laugh about it.

"I can't do a *thing*, ship!" I roared merrily. "Not one universal *thing!* Isn't that remarkable?"

"Yes, sir."

"How much did that Hallypuff cost me'?"

"Six Admiration Units, sir."

This startled me out of my hysterics. Just six?

But then I realized I hadn't Admired the reefer. I'd been too far overboard for that. I'd just taken it like medicine.

"I can't even go bankrupt," I said, but the hilarity was gone. "Oh, sand, sand, sand. Make a suggestion, ship."

"Your proposal to consult a hermit sandpiper had promise, sir."

"Have you gone back to counting by twos?" I yelped in disdain. "We just tried . . ." I shut up when it dawned on me that I had let something slip by. I nagged myself into remembering what it was. "Okay, so the hermits take trips into the inhabited universe now and then. Where should I look?"

"You might try one of the planets on which they sell their sand, sir. These are in the edge clusters, and specialize in religious tourism. The sand is purchased by novelty dealers for inclusion in sacred mementos."

"Oh, yeah," I remembered. "My great-aunt Jodylyn had one. What planet?"

"Hussbar is perhaps the most famous of the commercialized meccas, sir."

"Well, head for it."

I found me a hermit on Hussbar, all right. He was a big guy with a noncompetitive face and a full dirty beard. I snagged him coming out of a wholesale sand dealer's offices.

"Your pardon, holiness," I said politely, "but I'm told you're a sandpiper. Could I have a word with you?"

He looked me over and said, "Sure, boy. What's on your mind?"

"This," I said, bringing out the Profanis plaper. "I'm trying to find this system. If you can provide information that will lead me to it, I will find your knowledge Admirable, sir."

He took the plaper and glanced through it.

"Sad," he mumbled. "Pitiably sad. The plight of these poor people, living in sinful ignorance."

"What poor people, holiness?"

"The inhabitants of this system, Profanis," he said.

"Oh."

"May the Sandman bless your search with success, young man, that this world may be brought to redemption," he said piously. "I regret that my meager information of the worlds of the universe can be of no help to you."

"Oh, well, that's not exactly what I expected. I want

to know what is and isn't profane. In this drawing, for instance. Is there something in it that makes Profanis profane? That burning satellite, maybe?"

He stared at me. "You mean, boy, that you cannot feel the profane feature in this drawing?"

"No, holiness," I admitted meekly.

"Humpf. There isn't much sensitivity in the universe any more. Get out your pen and pad, boy."

I did so.

"Now copy the stars the way they are shown in this ring around the Profanis system."

I did that.

"What did it feel like you were drawing?" he asked.

"Just . . . just stars, with five points," I answered.

"Let's see your pad." He took it and frowned annoyedly. "You didn't get the feel of the original," he criticized. "Look at it again, and try to draw it exactly like it was originally drawn."

I shrugged and tried again with the hermit watching over my shoulder.

"That's better," he approved. "What did it feel like that time?"

I thought about it and said, "Like I was drawing a . . . a *solid* . . . a wall of stars."

"*Ahah!* And since human nature is, in essence, unchanging, the man who drew that sketch of the Profanis system was also drawing a wall of stars!"

"But it looks almost the same as galactic stars are always indicated around a system map," I objected.

"Almost," he agreed, "except for the *feeling*."

"You mean the guy who drew that Profanis sketch

really *thought* there was a wall just beyond that smudgy seventh satellite?" I asked in disbelief.

"Obviously, and the implication is plain. The drawing represents the cosmogony of an isolated, ignorant society."

I nodded doubtfully. "But if they're so ignorant, how do they know their world's profane?"

"Because, being central, it is the object most distant from the starwall, which the people probably erroneously regard as the dwelling of the Sandman . . . of God, they would say."

We talked on for a while, about such things as how the people could have gotten so ignorant so soon after the planet was given its "sun" and was colonized. The hermit couldn't help with that kind of question. And the questions he did answer offered me no hint of where the system might be found.

Still, that plaper said the government wanted any additional data on Profanis, and what the hermit had told me about the starwall struck me as being worth something.

"What you've told me might prove helpful," I said, "and if it is, I'll Admire your wisdom to an extent commensurate with what I receive."

The hermit shrugged. "Forget it, boy. Admiration is of little concern to me. Go with my blessing, young man."

"M-many thanks then, holiness," I stammered, caught a bit off balance by the hermit's indifference to Admires. What a self-sufficient old jack he was!

I returned to my ship. "Where does the Standing Consolidation Commission of the Department of Justice have its office?" I asked.

"On Homeworld Earth," replied the ship.

"That's where we're going, so back to the Milky Way Galaxy," I announced gaily. "I haven't found Profanis, but I have information the Commission will probably Admire to the extent of a thousand or two Units. My 211 Units will soon have plenty of company, ship!"

"Beg pardon, sir, but your balance is now 32 Units," the ship corrected me.

"*Huh?* What happened?"

"You experienced a burst of Admiration for the hermit, sir, at the conclusion of your interview with him."

That sly old fraud! He had slicked me!

Even if the Earth system is the universe's biggest tourist hangout, I like to go there now and then.

This time I came in past Saturn, the gas giant with the rings, and slowed the ship long enough to look at it. Saturn's good for that if for nothing else.

Saturn was sticking in my mind as I dropped on toward Homeworld. Frowning, I picked up the Profanis plaper to refresh my thoughts on what I was going to tell those Consolidation guys.

And there was Saturn again!

No . . . It was just the smudged seventh satellite in the drawing of the Profanis system. The smudge did look somewhat like a ring, badly drawn in an ink of lighter density than that used in the original.

Could it mean anything?

I shook my head. Saturn was a planet, not a satellite. And it wasn't the outermost in the system. Uranus, Neptune, Pluto, and a couple of unnamed others lay farther out.

But still . . .

I said, "Ship, don't land. Go into orbit around Earth and let me see the sky."

"Yes, sir. What amplification?"

"No amp. Let me see it like it looks."

The ship flickered and went invisible, and I stared about. A crescent Earth was below. Above were the stars, arranged in the familiar nursery constellations.

I picked out the plane of the ecliptic and had no trouble spotting the Moon, Mars, and Saturn.

"Where's Jupiter, ship?"

"Obscured by Earth at the moment, sir."

"Well, what about Uranus?"

"Here, sir." A pointer flashed on, pointing at a blank.

"I don't see it there, ship. Check yourself."

"I'm correct, sir. Uranus is too dim to be visible without magnification, sir."

"Oh. Neptune, too?"

"Yes, sir.

I grimaced. Well, here I go down another false trail, I told myself.

But the point remained that Saturn was the outermost visible object in the Earth system without using light-amp.

"Ship, let's put this in the simplest form," I said. "How many heavenly bodies could a man on Earth see, just with his eyes, that moved against the background stars?"

"Seven, sir. That includes the sun, Earth's satellite Luna, and the planets Mercury, Venus, Mars, Jupiter, and Saturn."

"Okay, did you notice the ring-like smudge on the seventh satellite?"

"Yes, sir."

"All right. Let's say Profanis is Earth and this drawing was made way, way back, before spaceflight or light-amp was discovered. Then light-amp comes along. Some guy sees Saturn has rings, so he tries to add them to the drawing, making a messy job of it. What do you think?"

"Homeplanet Earth is not the center of the system, sir," the ship responded.

"Well, no, but would an ignorant guy eyeballing from Earth have to see that?" I argued. "He might notice that Mercury and Venus stuck close to the sun, but other than that, the sun's only difference from the other objects would be its brightness. And all the complicated planetary motions would probably snow him, anyway; and he would give up and put them all on neat, circular orbits."

"That is possible, sir. There remains the problem of the name, Profanis."

I paused in thought. What the hermit had said about the world's distance from the starwall came to mind. But maybe there was more to it than that.

"Ship," I said fervently, "if I was stuck on just one planet, Profanis would be about the least impolite name I would call it!"

There was a silence of several seconds. Then the ship said, "The probability is .992 that you have found Profanis, sir."

I just sat there for a while. My feeling of calm and confidence was new to me, and I wanted to savor it, because I didn't figure it would last.

But it did.

*   *   *

I'd promised myself that I'd go to Bwymeall if I ever got a real bundle; so after collecting my 8,000 Units, that's where I went. And who did I run into right away but that twirliest of all twirls, Lumise Nalence.

I grinned at her. "You're Lumise, and I'm Boje Rylsten," I said. "I've been hoping for a chance to get acquainted with you."

"How sweet of you, Boje," she replied, sticking to the formula. "I do so wish I could take the time right now, but . . . Would you wait a moment while I check with my ship and see if my schedule's open?"

"Sure."

She hurried away to check on me. That's part of the ritual, too, as you may not know if you've never done much twirl-chasing. She wanted to see if I could afford her, and if I am the Admiring type. I didn't have a thing to worry about on either score. And, sure enough, Lumise was back immediately, exuding eagerness and come-hither charm. "This is wonderful, Boje! It happens that I'm free for a couple of days!"

"Great!" I said.

"My ship or yours?" she asked.

"Yours. Mine's an uncomfortable old tub that I ought to trade in. Maybe I'm keeping it out of sentimentality."

We walked arm in arm toward her ship, and she gave my hand a squeeze. "I like sentimentality in a man very much, Boje."

It was a terrific two days with Lumise . . . although different from my earlier visits on twirls' ships in some respects. For one thing, I got the impression that Lumise was enjoying it all, not just earning my Admiration.

When I got back aboard my own bucket I said, "Let's go to Greenstable, ship. I want to find out what kind of jobs are available. The old roll must be thin."

"Very well, sir."

"How thin is the roll?"

"Your financial balance is 8,351 Units, sir."

"But . . . Do you mean I came out 300 Units *ahead* on Lumise Nalence?" I asked in astonishment.

"Yes, sir."

I thought it over. "Maybe self-confidence accounts for it?"

"That may be, sir."

Lumise had asked me to come back soon . . . had practically begged me, in fact. Well . . . I would come back, but I didn't want her to think I was just after her Units. Maybe it was time, after all, for me to think about settling down. But first I wanted to line up some interesting work to do.

PERSONAL: DO NOT FACSIM!
Office of Ninth Secretary
Standing Consolidation Commission
Department of Justice
Noram Park, Earth

Mr. and Mrs. Wardin Rylsten
Halebas West 5040-K Sector
Talleysmat, Bark., K.V.

Dear Ward and Gilta,
Your request that I take a hand with

young Boje came at an opportune moment. A friend of mine in Historical Philosophy had just produced a drawing, his own brainchild, that seemed an ideal challenge to present your son. Through one of the Department's stringers on Greenstable, I was able to toss it in his lap. The problem was for him to identify Earth from a drawing of the universe as a prehistoric Earthman might have seen it.

Boje will certainly tell you about it the first time he's home; so I won't go into details. Suffice to say he solved the problem, gaining some needed mental maturity in the process. He will, I'm sure, be able to support himself amply hereafter, and make the universe his oyster.

Expenses involved, of slightly more than 8,000 Units, are covered by Admiration Development grants from the Treasury, made available through interdepartmental exchange. So you need not concern yourself about that.

And please don't bother to thank me, because I'm always glad to help old friends. If I have won your Admiration to some small extent, that will be thanks enough.

Best regards always,
Raffor Wisosborg.

HEALTH HAZARD

❧❦❧

ROMEE DID NOT DOUBT that the men and women from Earth were as fully human as the chimos and chimees of Notcid. But sometimes they did things that struck her as absurd.

And that made dealing with them difficult, and more than a little frightening.

Right now, she had to get the damn-television set fixed, and wasn't sure how to go about it. There was a repair shop at the Trading Center—or the Cultural Exchange Center as it was called by the new set of Earth people running it now. Romee had carried the damn-TV some forty-five miles under her arm, jittery all the way because she didn't know what to expect from the new people.

She wished the traders (or "exploiters" as the new people wanted them called) were still running the

Center. A person could do business with them without so much upsetting uncertainty.

It was some relief to reach the compound, and to find the repair shop where it had always been. In fact, when she went in she recognized the Earthman in charge as the same one who was there two years earlier, when last she had visited the shop.

She lifted the damn-TV set onto the counter.

"Can you fix it?" she asked.

"Sure. I can fix anything," he replied, more understandably than the average Earthman despite his monotone accent.

"How much will it cost?"

"I won't know until I find out what's wrong. Give me your name, honey."

"Romee of West Hill with the Flat Rock on the Brook," she replied.

He shook his head. "That won't do for the record, Romee. The Demography Office has assigned family names. You run over to the office and find out what yours is."

"Oh, that," she gasped nervously, flustered by her mistake. "I already know it. Romee Westbrook."

"OK." The man wrote her name on a ticket which he attached to her damn-TV. "This ought to be ready for you tomorrow, Ro . . . I mean, Miss Westbrook."

"Mrs. Westbrook," she corrected him.

He grinned, and she grinned back. She was glad he was still running the shop. As a leftover from the time of the exploiters, he was fairly easy to understand.

"How come you're still here?" she asked, momentarily emboldened by his grin.

He shrugged. "Because I wasn't important enough to kick out when the new regime took over."

She nodded vaguely, said goodbye, and left the shop. How could a man who could repair something as marvelously intricate as a damn-TV set be unimportant? she wondered.

That was just one more unsolvable puzzle of the Earth people, she concluded. They made big importances out of little things, and no importance out of great dangers and fearful problems.

For instance, they did nothing about the horrors of the jungle lowlands.

And she had to go down to the jungle now. She had to go there to gather the natsacher shoots to sell to the Earth people, to get money to pay the damn-TV repairman, and to buy some chocolate . . . if the new people were still selling chocolate.

In any event, she had to gather natsacher shoots, and the thought intimidated her, almost to the point of making her whimper.

For a while she wandered around inside the compound of the Cultural Exchange Center, peering in shop and office windows at the men and women and chimos and chimees. She realized she was merely killing time, postponing the inevitable. But maybe she would gain courage by looking at other humans, particularly the men and women.

Maybe they looked strange, with their hair concentrated on the tops of their heads, and needlessly long there, and their peculiar stance with legs straight instead of flexed, which made them look taller than they really were. And the males almost as breastless as herself, since the Earth-women not only bore the young but also nursed them . . . an arrangement that struck Romee as so odd that she sometimes wondered if that physical absurdity might account for all the other ridiculous traits of these people.

But the humans from Earth, for all their foibles, had courage. They were brave beyond understanding. Why, she had heard that a loud noise wouldn't even make some of them jump!

She wished she had some of that courage right now.

Slowly she headed for the compound's gate, then turned aside to examine the bulletin board.

A woman was feeding in a new notice as she approached.

"Good morning," Romee said politely. "Is that something new?"

The woman turned and studied her. "Yes. Would you like to hear it?"

"If you please."

Romee hoped the new bulletin would not be another lecture on the evils of chocolate. Those lectures frightened her, and they were constantly popping up on damn-TV these days. Romee knew she was hooked on the stuff, and couldn't give it up. So, to be told over and over that it was taking years off her life was sheer torture. She had made up her mind not to believe the lectures, but she couldn't stay sure they weren't right, no matter how hard she tried.

But it turned out that the new bulletin wasn't a lecture. The woman pressed the button and the board said: *"The services of several chimos and chimees are desired for a series of tests on response to environmental stimuli. A modest stipend will be paid to participants. Apply at Exotic Psychology Office, Brown Building."*

"Thank you," Romee said to the woman, and headed once more toward the gate. Then she halted and turned. She had never heard of the Exotic Psychology Office before, which suggested it might be very new on Notcid—even newer than the replacers of the exploiters. And being new, it might have a lot of prestige and money, since Earth humans thought highly of new things.

"How much money is a 'modest stipend'?" she asked.

The woman frowned. "We prefer applicants who are motivated by a desire for increased understanding and cultural progress, rather than monetary rewards," she said stiffly.

Romee thought about that, and nodded. If this was something to increase her understanding of Earth people's peculiarities, or help these people progress toward more rational behavior, she was all for it.

"I have those motivations," she said, "but I have newly hatched young and a husband whose breasts are heavy with milk. For their sakes I must inquire about the stipend."

This seemed to please the woman. She nodded. "The pay will be fifty cashers."

That was more than Romee could expect from two gatherings of natsacher shoots!

"O.K. When do I start?" she said.

The woman blinked. "Why . . . immediately, I suppose. Yes. Come with me, please. I'm Miss Dallas McGuire, assistant director of Exotic Psychology."

"I'm Romee Westbrook."

Miss McGuire led the way to the Brown Building

and into a sparsely furnished office suite near the rear. She motioned Romee into a chair beside a desk, and seated herself behind it. Without complaint, Romee perched on the chair instead of squatting comfortably on her haunches.

"We'll have to wait for Dr. Radley Truit, the director," said Miss McGuire, "but in the meantime we can fill out your application form." In a business-like manner she scribbled some words on a sheet of paper. "What is your age, Mrs. Westbrook?"

"Twenty-two years."

"The hatching you mentioned, was that your first?"

"No, my second."

"How many young?"

"Three each time."

"Are they all living?"

"Yes."

"What about your parents? Are they living?"

Romee repressed a whimper. "No. The jungle got them."

Miss McGuire made a clicking noise with her mouth and looked annoyed.

"Were they on chocolate?"

"Yes."

"And are you?"

"Yes."

Miss McGuire put down her pen and gazed at Romee. "Don't you know that's bad for you, Mrs. Westbrook?" she asked solemnly. "Can't you give it up for the sake of your young, if not for yourself?"

This was so absurd, to talk about giving up chocolate. "I've tried, but I can't," she replied, hoping to satisfy the woman. But she couldn't help adding, "I can't tell that it does me any harm, and it makes being alive much nicer."

"Any *harm?*" demanded the woman sharply. "Surely, Mrs. Westbrook, you know of the tests made on the dakcha and gobhow meat animals? Chocolate is utterly alien to Notcidese life forms! It *has* to be harmful! Look at the evidence, Mrs. Westbrook. Before the exploiters arrived, less than a hundred years ago, the high plains of Notcid were filled with your people. Now most of them are gone. Of the bowers still standing, at least half are empty and falling into ruin. And you don't see *any harm* in chocolate! Really, Mrs. Westbrook!"

Romee was so totally intimidated that she could hardly reply to any of this. She would have liked to say that no chimo or chimee ever ate enough chocolate at one time to coat their entire insides with an indigestible brown layer, which was what had killed the overfed experimental subjects, the dakcha and gobhow meat animals. Besides, she knew Miss McGuire would have an answer to that: that the pounds of chocolate fed the animals in one day was less than the hooked chimo or chimee would eat in ten years, and since Notcidese life could not assimilate chocolate, the cumulative effects could be similar. Not the coating inside the guts, of course, but harmful buildups of deposits elsewhere within the body.

Also, Romee would have argued, if she could, that chocolate was no more alien to Notcidese life than natsach was to Earth people. And tons of natsach were exported to Earth every year, where people used it to sweeten their food. They used it because it *wasn't* assimilable, and thus would not make them fat as Earth sugar would. Also, natsach left no unpleasant aftertaste and did not cause disease, the way artificial sweeteners did. If natsach was so good for Earth humans, why was chocolate so bad for Notcid humans?

And as for the rapid decline of the population . . .

"The jungle got them," she managed to say.

"Hah!" snorted the woman. "The jungle got them because their reflexes were debilitated, or because fear of the jungle was too much for chocolate-weakened hearts!"

Romee had reasons to wonder if this was true, but she did not have the nerve to argue the matter with this forceful Earth human, who was going to pay her fifty cashers. So she nodded and said, "I'll try harder to kick the habit."

"Good!" approved Miss McGuire. "Please understand, Mrs. Westbrook, nobody's blaming you or your people for this chocolate addiction. It was those damned exploiters."

Romee nodded again, as a short man with white hair on the bottom of his face came into the office.

"Dr. Truit, this is our first applicant, Mrs. Romee Westbrook," said Miss McGuire.

"Ah, fine, fine," the little man said rapidly. "I just completed setting up the test site. We can get started right away if you're ready, Mrs. Westbrook."

"I'm ready," Romee gulped.

"Then come along, come along."

He led the way out of the building with Miss McGuire bringing up the rear. Outside he cramped

Romee in the back of a hovercar and got into the front seat with Miss McGuire. Much too fast for Romee's fragile peace of mind, the car whizzed out of the compound and across the rolling grassland. Romee cowered with hands over her eyes and ears till the motion stopped and the car's engine fell silent.

"Here we are. Everybody out," said Dr. Truit.

Romee climbed from the car and looked around. She was beginning to have doubts about this business. Of course, these new Earth humans had made it clear that they felt the best of goodwill toward the Notcidese, and wanted nothing more than to repair the harm done by the exploiters. But just the same, one never knew what to expect from Earth people. And fifty cashers was a lot of money ... surely more than she could expect if no danger was involved.

Still, she could see nothing that looked like a threat. They were standing on a flat hill, a few miles from the compound with nothing around them but grass, close-cropped by wandering herds of meat animals.

Dr. Truit kicked at the stubble and muttered something about unbalanced ecology. Then he and Miss McGuire stationed themselves somewhat to one side and stood watching Romee.

She squirmed with fright and self-consciousness.

KRO-O-OMM!

The sudden tremendous roar behind her sent Romee in a flying leap, completely over the hovercar. She hit the ground on all fours, skittered around and lay flat.

"Beautiful response!" approved Truit. "Beautiful!"

Slowly Romee recovered her wits, and peered about.

Still nothing in sight except the two Earth people and the hovercar.

"See?" said Miss McGuire. "There isn't any danger. Just a loud noise."

"What made it?" she whimpered.

"A piece of equipment, buried underground," said Truit, "No danger at all, Mrs. Westbrook. Stand up, please."

Romee rose, and saw they were watching her the same as before. Well, she was going to keep facing that place where the noisemaker was hidden, so it couldn't

KRO-O-OMM!

Again the blast of sound came from behind her, and sent her sailing over the hovercar.

This time she lost consciousness briefly. When she opened her eyes the two Earth people were bending over her.

"See? It was only a noise again," Truit assured her. "You don't need to be frightened by it, or respond to it. Nothing's going to hurt you."

"Let me help you up, Mrs. Westbrook," offered Miss McGuire.

"No, no!" she begged, hugging the ground and sobbing. "If I stand he'll do it again!"

"I'm not attempting to terrorize you," Truit replied frostily. "You can take a break until you settle down, and while I explain. What we wish to do is test your ability to modify, under controlled conditions, an over-response to stimuli that seems a universal flaw . . . characteristic, I mean . . . in the Notcidese psycho-physiological pattern. After you've rested a bit, we'll try it again, and this time I want you to try to modify your reaction. That is, keep rational control of yourself when the noise stimulus comes, and refrain from jumping."

Romee felt too weak and shaky to get up and run away. She lay there wondering how Truit had captured a jungle noise in his equipment, because that was what it was. He must have set up a recorder at the edge of the jungle to get the sound, and then made it loud and close the same way one turned up the volume of a damn-TV set.

So really, Truit was right. It was just a noise, and this wasn't the jungle. So why should she jump when she heard it?

For that matter, why did her people jump . . . at least a little bit . . . at *any* loud noise? Why not ignore noise like the Earth people usually did?

She stopped sobbing as the surprising thought struck her: maybe, in this one way, her people rather than the Earth people behaved absurdly.

In any case, it was better to be scared and alive, with fifty cashers, than to be scared and perhaps dead in the jungle. And she just *had* to get her damn-TV fixed, or lose status as a bowerkeeper with her chimo. And how good it would be to have some chocolate right now!

She had to go along with this experiment.

Still quivering, she rose to her feet and gazed questioningly at Truit.

"Good girl!" he approved, "I mean, very good, Mrs. Westbrook. Now remember, this time try not to jump."

She nodded and tensed, waiting for the noise.

When it came, her leap was half again longer than the two previous times.

"Don't tighten up so!" snapped Truit impatiently. "Dallas, can't you get this silly aborigine to settle down?"

"Watch it, Doc," the woman snapped back, then said softly to Romee, "Just try to relax, Mrs. Westbrook. Decide you don't care about the loud noise, that it isn't going to frighten you."

After a while, Romee stood up again, by now too exhausted to be anything other than relaxed. When the sound came, she jerked, and fell forward flat on her face.

"Excellent!" applauded Truit. "We modified the response! Next time, try to modify it still more, and not fall down."

But when Romee stood and the sound came, she jerked and fell again. Three more trials produced the same results, and Truit was getting extremely cross. This had tensed Romee up again, and it was all she could do to limit her response to merely falling down.

As she lay on the ground after the latest trial, she heard a different Earth human yell, *"Are you idiots trying to scare the natives out of their limited wits? What's going on here?"*

She lifted her head to see a second hovercar settle to the ground nearby, and Hector Grandolph, Director-in-Charge of the Cultural Exchange Center, come waddling out of it. When he saw her, he stopped in his tracks and pointed at her. "Who's that, and what's going on here?"

"Why, ah, yes, Mr. Grandolph," stammered Truit. "Yes. Yes, indeed. How are you today, sir? Well, yes, we have been running a little experi—a little examination, with the cooperation of Mrs. Eastwood here—"

"Westbrook," corrected Miss McGuire numbly.

"Yes, that is to say, Mrs. Westbrook agreed to cooperate with us, for the advancement of cultural understanding—"

Grandolph growled. "Don't cover it with crap, Truit! This was illegal experimentation, as you know damned well! What were you trying to find out . . . how much it would take to scare this poor creature to death?"

"On the contrary, sir," retorted Truit, stiffening. "We were seeking only to ameliorate her fright response by . . ."

"*Nuts!* Both of you can start packing when you get to the compound! You're going back to Earth on the next ship!" Grandolph waddled over to Romee and hunkered down beside her. "Are you all right?"

"I'm tired is all," she said. Very slowly she rose to her feet. "When do I get the fifty cashers?" she asked.

Grandolph's face looked as if it might explode. "Did they offer you fifty cashers to cooperate in this experiment?"

"Yes."

The big man turned to glare at the culprits. "Your names are mud from now on," he growled. "Count on it."

"What about my fifty?" Romee persisted.

"You'll be awarded damages, chimee," said Grandolph, "and I would guess that'll come to several hundred cashers."

Romee did not dare risk a reply to such astonishingly good news as that. She stood waiting in silence for the money. Was it supposed to come from Truit or from Grandolph? she wondered.

Truit presumably had nothing to lose by talking, because he was doing a great deal of it. "We were doing her no harm at all," he was protesting. "At one time the Notcidese were obviously jungle creatures, for whom the fright response and nervousness in general were a necessary survival pattern. They escaped the predator that emits the pre-attack roar by leaping.

"When they left the jungle for the plains, after developing rudimentary herding and agricultural skills, they no longer needed the fright response," Truit continued, "but so far they haven't lost it. This may be taken to indicate their sojourn on the plains has been relatively brief. However, the fright response is now a handicap to their cultural creativity. They cannot undertake innovative activities that require extensive forward cerebration, such as plains-cultivation of natsacher shoots, or supra-bower social organization, because too much of their energies are absorbed by fright activities. Thus, the test being conducted by Miss McGuire and myself was—"

"—was even worse than I thought!" Grandolph broke in angrily. "So you were trying to turn the Notcidese into Earth-style peasants, huh? Imposition of our cultural pattern on a native intelligence! Very exploitative, Truit!"

"I was trying to keep them from becoming extinct!" Truit almost screamed, making Romee quiver. "By removing the need for them to enter the jungle to gather natsacher shoots . . ."

"Nonsense!" bellowed Grandolph, and Romee made a tentative six-foot leap. "Everybody knows what's killing off the natives! It's *chocolate*, not any damned jungle!"

Romee wondered self-pityingly why these Earthmen didn't stop arguing absurdities and give her the
damage money so she could leave. Or at least not
yell so loud.

"You two are frightening Mrs. Westbrook," Miss
McGuire announced smugly.

"Huh? Oh, my apologies, chimee . . . Mrs. Westbrook," said Grandolph.

"That's all right," Romee quavered. "If I can have
my damage money I'll leave so you can yell all you
like."

"Your damage money?" He looked puzzled. "Oh,
I'm afraid you'll have to wait a little while for that,
Mrs. Westbrook. The claim must be processed through
the nearest Interspecies Circuit Court—a matter that
will have my personal attention."

Romee nodded. "Tomorrow?" she asked.

"Longer than that, I'm afraid, but very soon. Probably within half a year, certainly no more than a year,
Mrs. Westbrook."

Romee wondered dejectedly how "half a year" could
be considered "very soon."

Grandolph reached in his pocket. "Here," he said.
"If you are short of money, Mrs. Westbrook, this
should tide you over."

Romee took the paper and studied it. It was a
two-casher note. "Thank you," she said, hoping she
was not revealing her disappointment.

Because she was going to have to go down to the
jungle, after all.

She found an empty bower near that of a cousin
of her chimo in which to spend the night. The next

morning she returned to the Cultural Exchange Center compound and entered the trading post. She felt she just couldn't face the jungle today without a bite of chocolate first.

"Half a casher of chocolate, please," she said timidly to the woman behind the counter.

"We don't have any," the woman snapped crossly.

"Oh." Romee hesitated. "When will you get some?"

"Get some what?"

"Chocolate."

"I have no idea what you're talking about," the woman snapped. Romee was shaking badly, but her desire wouldn't let her leave. "Chocolate is what I'm talking about."

"Never heard of it," said the woman, not quite so harshly.

Could it be that this woman really didn't know about chocolate? That didn't make sense at all, but after all, what did about Earth people?

"It's brown and bitter unless it has sugar in it," Romee explained pleadingly. "It comes in square cakes about this thick." She held up her hand to show the thickness.

"Oh, that stuff," said the woman. She reached under the counter and came up with a half-casher block of chocolate in a plain green wrapping. "This what you mean?"

Romee took the block and tore the wrapping from a corner. It was chocolate, all right.

"Yes."

"Half a casher, please."

Romee paid her and received her change. Quickly

she took a bite and chewed it rapidly. Um-m-m. How nice it was! And already she was feeling less tensed up.

"I thought everybody knew about chocolate," she said to the woman, who was watching her with a strange expression.

"Knew about what?"

"About chocolate." Romee pointed to the block in her hand. "About this."

"Of course everybody knows about that!" said the woman.

Romee munched in thoughtful silence. Here was a strangeness that needed solving, because it dealt with chocolate. She wished she didn't have to worry about it now, since going to the jungle was problem enough for one time.

At last she said, "You know about this," indicating the block in her hand, "but not about chocolate."

"That's right," the woman said.

"But this is chocolate."

"I never heard of it."

Romee thought some more. "What is this stuff called?" she asked in sudden inspiration.

"It doesn't have a name, so far as I know," the woman replied.

"It had a name yesterday," murmured Romee.

"That's right, it did," said the woman. "But last night a directive came from Director-in-Charge Grandolph, who was steamed about something." She held up a sheet of paper with writing on it. "Would you like to know what it says?"

"Yes, please."

The woman read from the paper: "*All personnel at this station have been entirely too negligent in their responsibility toward the native population whose welfare is our trust. Namely, we have taken no firm steps toward the reduction and eventual end of the (bleep-bleep) addiction that became established under our exploitative predecessors with fatal consequences for hundreds of thousands of innocent natives.*"

The woman looked up. "Where I said 'bleep-bleep', the Director-in-Charge used that word you mentioned," she explained, then continued reading:

"*Unfortunately, the economics of our situation here make the immediate cessation of our trafficking in (bleep-bleep) impossible. And despite our warnings, the natives' cravings for (bleep-bleep) continue unabated. Only a few hours ago I was the pained witness to the indignities a native will willingly suffer to obtain the price of this addictive.*"

"Therefore, I order that, effective immediately, the very word (bleep-bleep) be omitted from the vocabulary of every Terrestrial on this planet. The health hazard warnings will be dropped from telecasts, as indeed will all mention and display of (bleep-bleep) be stricken from TV programming.

"It is my belief that we have discussed (bleep-bleep) entirely too much, and too freely, with the natives, and can make our abhorrence clear to them only by refusing to mention (bleep-bleep). It occurs to me that treating (bleep-bleep) as too horrid to mention may have a salutary effect on the natives, by playing upon their fright syndrome.

"To repeat, all personnel are hereby forbidden to speak of or display (bleep-bleep). If a native mentions it you will make clear that you never heard the word and do not know its meaning."

The woman finished reading and stood looking at Romee with a peculiar twisted smile.

Romee thought about the words on the paper. Presumably they were sensible words, from the Earth-human viewpoint. And she wasn't sure whether or not they were more absurd than most Earth-human doings, from her viewpoint. She was puzzled.

"Bleep-bleep," she murmured, trying the sound the woman had used in place of "chocolate."

The woman brightened. "Why, yes. Bleep-bleep!"

Romee tucked away the remainder of her block of chocolate, said good-bye to the woman, and left the trading post.

On her way to the gate she met a chimo she knew coming in. "Are you going to buy chocolate?" she asked him.

"Yes, Romee."

"They don't talk about it anymore," she told him. "But if you ask for bleep-bleep, they'll sell you some."

The chocolate was relaxing, but did not take away fright. Romee was very scared as she descended the steep slopes from the Cultural Exchange Center to the edge of the jungle, and felt almost numb once she entered the trails that twisted through the thick foliage, even though the trails were safe.

The danger would begin when she left the trails to squirm her way through the undergrowth, and she would have to do that. The trails were kept picked clean of natsacher shoots. She kept peering through the shadows, trying to spot a patch of natsacher that was not too far from safety. She found an isolated shoot or two that was within reach from the trail, but these were only enough to emphasize how big and how empty was her gathering-sack.

At last she took a deep, tremulous breath and plunged off the trail. For a distance of some fifty feet she fought through thick tangle, then came out in a relatively open area where enough light filtered down to make natsacher grow. And indeed, there were shoots all around her. Rapidly she began breaking them off and stuffing them in her sack.

When the patch was picked clean she plunged frantically back to the trail. Only then did she take time to estimate the fullness of her sack ... about a third.

KRO-O-OMM!

The sound was distant, but it was behind her. She jerked and fell on her face. She lay there and trembled for a while, then rose and followed the trail deeper into the jungle.

A brightness off to her left indicated another likely natsacher patch. She pushed through to its edge, and paused, looking at it. She wasn't sure just why, but this patch had a particularly dangerous look to her. But it was a big one, at least twice as big as the other. She could fill her sack here.

Slowly she moved out among the shoots. Nothing happened. She began picking. This was a long narrow patch which she had entered at one end. As she worked her way along it, her confidence grew a little. It was heartening to see how fast her sack was filling.

And then it was full. She saw there were plenty of shoots left to be picked. If she needed another sack-load to pay for fixing the damn-TV and to get enough chocolate to last her family a while, she would come back to this place.

She lifted her sack, turning slowly toward the trail as she did so.

KRO-O-OMM!

She jerked and flopped on her face, her thoughts racing in terror and dismay.

It's got me! I didn't jump away from it! My poor hatchlings!

SWISH! Something large and fast swooped past, over her cringing form. She waited for the monstrous killer to pounce on her.

Instead she heard a creaking as of strained tree limbs. Several seconds passed.

KRO-O-OMM!

She tried to hug the ground more closely.

SWISH!

She was more than halfway unconscious, and aware of nothing but the continuing sounds, and only vaguely of them.

KRO-O-OMM! SWISH! CREAK.

KRO-O-OMM! SWISH! CREAK.

The pattern seemed to go on and on.

Finally it occurred to her that she wasn't being eaten, or even bitten. Slowly, and very cautiously, she twisted her neck and looked up.

KRO-O-OMM! SWISH! A greenish-brown mass about two feet in diameter came arcing down, across the natsacher patch, to zing through the air above her. It snapped to a halt a short distance past her, just short of the wall of undergrowth surrounding the patch.

CREAK. It reversed direction, moving slowly now, and came back over her. She saw that the mass was attached above to an oddly jointed limb or heavy vine. This limb was now bending, and in a moment had carried the mass upward and out of sight in the foliage. She could still see some of the limb.

KRO-O-OMM! SWISH! Here it came again! The limb was snapping straight, like a many-jointed leg of some kind. The mass reached the end of its trajectory and stopped.

CREAK. It began moving back once more.

Romee realized she could easily crawl away, out of its path. But she didn't feel up to moving just yet. So she watched it and thought about it.

If she had jumped when she heard the noise, she would have landed in the undergrowth, just about where that mass would have knocked her if she hadn't fallen out of its way. It was as if the noisemaker wanted her in that particular spot of undergrowth, and had meant to put her there, one way or the other.

What was waiting for her there? And why didn't it just come get her?

She was tempted to crawl over and peer through the leaves to find out. The temptation to do such a risky thing made her cringe some more.

KRO-O-OMM! SWISH! Creak. Crackle.

It had added a new sound. Crackle. She looked up, wondering why, and saw that the jointed limb was beginning to look shredded. It wasn't used to swishing so frequently and continually, she guessed, and was wearing itself out. It must have some way of sensing she was still in its path with her back more or less turned toward it, but couldn't tell she was lying down.

She resolved to crawl away after the next swish, so it would stop that horrifying noise.

KRO-O-OMM! Here it came. SWISH! CRACK!

The limb snapped. Instead of making its sudden stop, the detached mass was flung into the undergrowth. A moment later Romee heard a rough grating noise coming from the spot where the mass had landed.

This noise was sickening rather than frightening. In a little while she felt much better, and her curiosity was aroused. She crept forward, pushed into the undergrowth, and stared at what was happening.

The ground there was covered by what looked like misshapen boxes with open tops, all packed tightly against each other. Each box was twisting in place, back and forth, rubbing against the sides of the neighboring boxes. Their top edges were sharp, and their motion made them cut anything touching them, the same way the power knives sold by the Earthmen cut.

They were chopping the greenish-brown mass to bits. The shredded pieces of it were forming a pulpy mess in the areas between the blades. Romee shuddered hard, thinking how close her own body had come to that same fate, and of how many people had been chopped up to feed that kind of . . .

. . . that kind of *tree*. Because she could see it was a tree. The slim trunk rose from the middle of the blade-edged boxes (they were really something like roots, she realized), and by changing position slightly while she looked up, she could follow the trunk to where it divided into three down-looping limbs, one of which had a splintered, bedraggled look. And no mass on the end of it like the other two.

Romee giggled. For the first time since she was a tiny hatchling. She giggled. Then she laughed. *It was so funny!* She had tricked the noisemaker into eating part of itself!

She was laughing like a drunken Earthman. It was a strange sensation, laughing, but nice. She squatted comfortably to enjoy it while it lasted.

Finally she grew quiet. The way she felt was puzzling, but she couldn't figure out what it was. Well, no matter. Life was full of mysteries she couldn't hope to solve.

She rose, looked at the noise tree for a moment, toying with the idea of tricking it into eating its remaining two masses. That would be a foolish and useless risk to take, she decided. She retrieved her sack of shoots, returned to the trail, and began the trip back to the Cultural Exchange Center.

There she would tell the Earthmen about the noise tree, and how it was killing and eating the chimos and chimees who went into the jungle for natsacher shoots. The Earthmen would know some way to kill off the noise trees so that . . .

No.

The Earthmen would pay her no attention. They would just say that chocolate . . . or bleep-bleep . . . was the culprit. And besides, they would say, they could not think of upsetting the jungle ecology of Notcid by exterminating a predator species.

Romee wished again that the exploiter Earthmen were still running things. *They* would have given the noise trees a real scorching. After which there would have been plenty of Notcidese on the plains once more, to go hunt natsacher shoots. Plenty of

natsacher for Earth, and plenty of chocolate for
Notcid.

But as things stood, whatever was done about the
noise trees would have to be done by the Notcidese
themselves . . .

She paused on the trail. If a noise tree was tricked
into eating all three of its masses, would it die?

Perhaps. Certainly it would be harmless. Why not
go back and finish off that one she had started on?
She decided against it. That was something to try
when she had no new hatchlings and a chimo heavy
with milk . . . and when she was not herself heavy
with eggs, of course.

The seasons passed at the bower on West Hill with
the Flat Rock on the Brook. The new hatchlings grew
rapidly. There was plentiful milk for them, because
Romee and her chimo Pipak enjoyed the secondary
sex act frequently, keeping Pipak's mammaries well
stimulated.

And certainly there was no shortage of meat animals,
although their flesh was tougher and less tasty than it
had been when the animals were fewer and the grass
taller. There was also enough redroot, even though it
was almost impossible to keep the meat animals from
raiding the garden and nibbling away the tops before
the redroots could become mature.

And there was damn-television. And chocolate.

But the time came when Pipak's breasts were empty,
and the hatchlings were weaned. And the chocolate
was running out.

Romee had dreaded this moment, but knew it had
to come. She had, of course, told Pipak about her

experience with the noise tree, and how it could be outwitted. Also, she had told her neighbors, and they in turn had told theirs. Most everyone on the plains knew about it, but still natsach gatherers went into the jungle not to return when the noise sounded.

Telling them to fall flat rather than jump wasn't enough, Romee realized. They needed the Earthman Truit to train them, as she had been trained, to modify their reaction. But Truit and Miss McGuire were long gone.

Romee mentioned to Pipak once that she, not he, should go to the jungle, but he would not hear of it. He had his masculine pride, and it was his turn to go. She could not cross him.

One morning she set out for the Cultural Exchange Center, after promising him faithfully that she would not enter the jungle, that she merely wanted to find out about her damage money. She meant to keep her promise, but her trip had another purpose aside from the damage money.

As she neared the Center, she left the main path and angled off across the rolling grassland until she reached the flat hilltop where Truit had conducted his experiment. She had some trouble deciding exactly where the hovercar had landed, but finally figured it out. Then she picked a spot and began digging.

The device . . . the noisemaker . . . was still there, barely covered with a clump of loose sod. She put it in her sack and paced back past the place where the hovercar had sat. In a moment she found the second noisemaker.

She squatted and studied them for a while, but, as she had expected, she did not know how to make them work. She put both of them in her sack and headed for the Cultural Exchange Center.

The same man was still running the damn-TV repair shop. He grinned at her and called her "honey" because he didn't remember her name. It was strange, she reflected, that the exploiters had, like this man, always been friendly but hardly ever polite, while the new people were polite but hardly ever friendly.

Romee put the noisemakers on the counter. "I want to stand in one place, and make either of these work in two other places," she said to him.

He examined the devices. "No problem," he grunted.

She walked home through the dark that night, partly because she wanted to get the noisemakers in place while Pipak and the young ones were sleeping, and partly because she wanted to get back so quickly that Pipak would be sure she had not gone to the jungle. The Earthman Grandolph had surprised her by having her damage money ready for her, and she did not want Pipak to doubt her word when she told him how she had raised the price of a large sack of chocolate and a power knife as well.

She was squatting outside the bower, eating a red-root, when he woke at dawn and came outside. He smiled as soon as he saw her.

"You're back."

"Yes, I hurried."

Almost reluctantly she pressed the button on the little box concealed in her hand. In a way, this was a mean trick.

KRO-O-OMM!

Pipak went flying through the air, and there was a scurrying and scuffling inside the bower. In a moment six young furry faces were peering out the entry at her.

"Come outside, children," she ordered, "and stand facing that way."

When she had the young positioned so neither noisemaker would be behind them, she walked over to where Pipak lay shaking. "See? There isn't any danger," she said. "Just a loud noise. A piece of equipment made it. Stand up. I will test your ability to modify, under controlled conditions, an over-response to stimuli that seems a universal flaw . . . characteristic, I mean . . . in the Notcidese psycho-physiological pattern . . ."

She hoped she was getting the words right.

PRACTICE!

❦

BARBARA SMITH LED the two small boys, one by each hand, into an ugly, sparsely furnished room in the Thorling School basement. There was an old couch, a table littered with gaudy children's books and magazines, and a couple of scarred chairs. On the floor was a toy fire truck. On the window sills, so high as to be well out of arm's reach of the boys, sat what appeared to be an assortment of bottles and dimestore vases. Actually, these were made of lightweight, easily shattered plastic, not of glass.

"Here we are, children!" said Miss Smith. She released them and backed away, leaving the tykes to stare at one another with uneasy curiosity. Miss Smith added, "Stevie, this is David; David, this is Stevie. Now, you two play, and I'll come back in a little while."

She left the room.

Left to their own devices, Stevie and David prowled their separate, self-conscious courses about the room, each aiming indirectly at the fire truck—the only toy in sight.

"Are you goin' to go to school here?" David asked.

"I guess so," said Stevie. "Are you?"

"Yeah."

"I'm five."

"I'm almost."

They arrived at the fire truck at the same time. Stevie squatted beside it and pressed his right hand firmly on its red top. Without closing his fingers he pushed it back and forth, while David watched silently. Then Stevie shoved it across the floor to bang against a wall, and David walked after it. He kneeled beside the truck, tried the back-and-forth routine, then scooted it back in Stevie's direction. Stevie sprawled sideways to intercept it and both boys laughed.

Soon they were both sitting on the floor, some distance apart, happily rolling the truck from one to the other. The routine of a game had been established.

Watching from behind a one-way mirror, Headmaster Judson Royster grunted dubiously, "This doesn't look like a psychokinetic duel to me. They've gotten on good terms almost immediately. Is there any point in continuing?"

Miss Smith was frowning in disappointment. "Let's watch a little longer," she urged. "This was such a fine opportunity—two new children, boys the same age, strangers to each other, with home reputations for 'throwing things' and, of course, both with behavior problems. I still think those young fellows ought to be tangling for possession of that fire truck!"

"Just how did you expect this battle of the century to develop?" Royster asked dryly.

Miss Smith's eyes snapped at him, but her words were matter-of-fact: "The fight for possession would be physical, a tugging match probably. As soon as one boy got possession, the other would vent his frustration by pelting the victor with the vases and bottles. This would scare and anger the victor into retaliating in kind. If this phase could end with only one piece of ammunition left unbroken, and both boys struggling for psi control of that piece . . ."

" . . . Then both boys would wind up with well-developed mental muscles, after just one easy lesson," Royster finished. He looked through the mirror at the boys, who were still playing peaceably. "Perhaps it could work even yet," he added, "but I've explained my lack of faith in shortcuts of this sort. And anyway, the problem is not so much to strengthen ESP talents as to bring them under conscious control. That has always been the problem, and I know only one way to solve it. No matter how many breakaway bottles David and Stevie pelt each other with while in fits of rage, I wouldn't expect the exercise to prepare them, when they're making a calm, rational effort, to roll one peanut."

He concluded with a grin, "Are you sure we're not staging this experiment simply to satisfy your feminine urge to see two masterful males locked in combat?"

Miss Smith gave the remark the sniff of dismissal which, Royster agreed to himself, was all it deserved. Why did his attempts at jokes with her always come out with more cutting edge than humor? Maybe the reason was that he . . . No! He broke away from the forbidden train of thought, as he always did. After all, he was in a building full of telepathic children!

"I'll get another pretty girl's opinion," he said lightly, turning to the serious-faced, twelve-year-old blonde who was standing a little apart from them in the observation cubicle. "Jilly," he asked, "how do you size up our gladiators?"

"They won't fight," Jilly replied assuredly. "David started to get mad when Stevie first touched the truck, but he just stood there. They're pretty sure they're being watched."

"How's that? Telepathy?"

"Just a little bit," the girl answered. "Not that they can read us or anything, but they can sense us looking at them. So they won't fight while they feel like that."

"Damn!" groaned Miss Smith. "Forgive the language, Jilly, but I'd have thought it if I hadn't said it. The whole idea of this experiment hangs on those two kids being isolated. Certainly it won't work with them aware of adult presences."

"Maybe if you let a movie camera do the watching it would work," Jilly suggested.

"There isn't a camera in the building," said Royster. "And besides . . ."

A boy of nine pushed through the door of the observation booth with an excited expression on his face. "Hostiles in the first floor halls, Mr. Royster!" he puffed breathlessly. Turning to Jilly he added an angry reproach, "Jilly, why wasn't you *listening*?" . . .

"I was busy listening to them," she answered, pointing to the boys playing with the truck.

"What kind of hostiles, Arthur?" Royster asked.

"Inspectors from the state! School credit inspectors!"

"Accreditation inspectors from the State Department of Public Instruction?" Royster asked sharply.

"Yeah! That's them! And they have it in for the school!"

Royster nodded grimly. "I'd better get up there," he said swiftly. "Miss Smith, take David and Stevie up to Miss Wembley's class, then go on to the office. Jilly, Arthur, spread the word that outsiders are here and that everything must look normal in the classrooms. And get back to your own classes."

"The dormitories are fragrant," commented Arthur.

Royster stared down at him in puzzlement for a second, then said, "The word is 'flagrant', Arthur. You're right. Jilly, get three of the older boys and two girls plus yourself up to the dorms right away. Put everything used in ESP out of sight—the pendulums, pith balls, decks, everything! Hurry! I'll try to keep the inspectors away from the dorms long enough for you to get through."

"O.K.," said the girl, dashing off. Miss Smith had already gone to retrieve her young duelers and take them to the kindergarten class. Royster left the observation booth and headed for the stairs with Arthur at his heels.

"Are you sure you won't need me or somebody with you, Mr. Royster?" the boy asked.

"Hm-m-m. Maybe so, Arthur. Stay with me, but get

rid of that excited expression. Look sullen! Remember that you're a badly-behaved problem child who can't adjust to adults or to your peers."

"O.K.," the boy said. Royster glanced back at him. The boy looked satisfactorily rebellious and woebegone. Royster hoped he could play his own role as convincingly.

On two scores Royster had a head start. First, his appearance was prototypical of the dedicated, harassed, rather ineffectual schoolman. He was of medium height, a little underweight, bespectacled, and despite his thirty-five years a bit too youthful-looking to seem a capable adult.

Second, at this moment he felt as nervous and unsettled as anyone would expect the headmaster of a school full of young misfits and antisocials to be. This surprise visit by the state accreditation team could darken the school's future, and he knew it. If he could stay on the defensive with the inspectors, not get angry and tell them to go to hell, perhaps things would go off all right.

There was plenty to get angry about, though. The fact that this was a surprise inspection, for instance. Schools in the public system were never subjected to such upsetting visits. And even the private schools, traditionally viewed with suspicious dislike by state education officials, were hit by surprise inspections so seldom that the very act of an accreditation team, showing up unannounced at one of them, was tantamount to an accusation of educational hanky-panky.

All Royster could hope for would be grudging agreement that Thorling School's students would, in the event of their transferal to another school, continue to be accepted as bona fide graduates of the last grade they had completed at Thorling. Or, when Thorling reached the stage, in another five years, of graduating high-school students, these would be accepted by standard colleges and universities, subject only to the usual entrance examinations and placement tests.

There would be no pats on Royster's head from any state school officials, no praise for Thorling for a difficult job well done—for a very good reason: Thorling was succeeding in educating children with whom the public schools had failed. Such a success was hardly the sort to please the leaders of the state's educational and political power structures, even though it should have been plain to everyone that Thorling was specialized for a task that public schools, by their very nature, could not be expected to handle.

So the public school psychologists and counselors grudgingly referred to Thorling the children they could not get through to, particularly the kindergarteners they did not even wish to try to get through to. Thorling accepted some of these and sent the others back. When asked to explain the school's criteria for accepting or rejecting a referred child, Royster spouted a dizzying line of educational doubletalk that, if stripped of its camouflaging verbiage, would have amounted to nothing more than: "We take the children we can help."

The carefully concealed truth was, of course, that Thorling took those children who had extrasensory abilities, whose behavior problems in fact usually stemmed from the difference these abilities created between them and other children. Brought together with others of their own sort, these children were no longer misfits. They became attainable—to each other, to their teachers, to the normal processes of schooling, and to the development and joyful use of their special gifts.

If Thorling School's real nature was suspected, its loss of accreditation would be the least of its worries. Public school officials would scream with gleeful alarm until they stirred up a full-scale witch-hunt. And the public itself, long plagued to the point of surliness by educational quackery and soaring school costs, would probably be quick in making Thorling School a sacrificial goat.

In brief, Thorling School existed on a razor's edge, and the accreditation inspectors would be in a position to topple it if they could find a minimal amount of solid leverage . . . anything to justify their vague suspicions. But, if Royster could say the right things, and the children played their roles . . .

"Don't worry about that, Mr. Royster," said Arthur. "Us kids're with you all the way—except maybe a couple of new soreheads and the old perfectioners—perfectionists. An' they won't get out of line, either."

"Thanks, Arthur," Royster responded.

They came out of the stairwell into the first floor hall. Arthur murmured, "Everybody's got the word."

Two of the team members, a man about Royster's age and an angular woman in her fifties, were in the main hall, each peering through the glass panel of a classroom door. Royster recognized neither of them as he approached. Roddy Linker, the student hall monitor, was at his desk unconcernedly reading his biology textbook. He glanced up and gave the headmaster a conspiratorial wink, then returned to his book.

Royster reached the woman first and said rather loudly, "Good morning, madam. Can I help you?"

Both she and the man, who was at the next door down the hall, jumped and spun around. She recovered her composure quickly and drew her head up and back, as if confronted by a distasteful odor.

"Are you Judson Royster?" she barked.

"Yes, I'm Mr. Royster, madam."

"Why weren't you in your office, Royster?" she demanded.

"Duties elsewhere in the building. Sorry to have kept you waiting, madam. The hall monitor should have let me know through the intercom that I had visitors." He gave young Roddy a reproving glance. "What can I do for you?"

She fumbled in her garishly beaded handbag and drew out an official card. "I am Dr. Phyllis Ross, of the Inspections Division of the State Department of Public Instruction." She held the card out so he could read it with a little peering but could not touch it. "My colleague here is Dr. J. Mercer Stilly, who has our documents." The man walked up, gravely shook hands with Royster, and gave him a stiff, folded paper.

"And this is the third member of our team, Mr. Donnelly McNear," Dr. Ross continued, pointing to a rotund, baby-faced young man who was emerging from the school office.

Looking very much at a loss, Royster said, "I'm very happy to meet all of you, Dr. Ross, Dr. Stilly, Mr. McNear. I suppose this is a building-safety inspection, isn't it? You'll find everything in good order, and I'll welcome your professional advice on a few proposed alterations—"

"We're not safety inspectors!" broke in McNear in an insulted tone. "That paper tells who we are!"

Royster unfolded the paper, stared at it, and looked up with a dazed expression. "Accreditation? There must have been a mix-up somewhere, I'm afraid. We've not received notice that you were coming, and don't have any of the special reports prepared. Could it be that . . ." He peered at the paper again and went on weakly, "No, it says Thorling School, all right, and the date's correct. But those special reports I should have ready . . ."

"Never mind the reports, Royster," Dr. Ross said brusquely. "Send the paperwork in later. We're here to see what's going on for ourselves, not to read what you *say* is going on. And I still want a satisfactory explanation as to why your office was left unattended."

"Yes, madam. Our funds are insufficient to pay a receptionist without reducing our teaching staff. There is only Miss Smith, who is my assistant and who also handles much of the secretarial work, in addition to myself. Sometimes we both have to be out of the office at the same time, particularly when new pupils are being enrolled as two were this morning.

"However, we always make sure a monitor of demonstrated dependability is on duty in the front hall when both of us must be out." He looked at Roddy Linker again and said to the inspectors, "If you will pardon me a moment, I should have a word with that young man."

He walked over to the monitor's desk and the team

followed closely behind him. "Roddy," he said sternly, "you know very well that you are supposed to inform Miss Smith or myself when we have visitors!"

Roddy's lips puckered angrily and his eyes swept the four adults with a glower. "They said not to," he grunted churlishly.

"*Who* said not to?" Royster demanded.

"Them," Roddy replied, pointing to Dr. Ross and McNear. "That woman and that guy."

"That *lady* and that *gentleman*," Royster corrected him.

Roddy shrugged and said indifferently, "You're the boss."

Royster thought in dismay: *What's Roddy trying to do to us?* "The young scoundrel is lying!" snapped Dr. Ross.

"In his teeth!" supplemented McNear. "We said no such thing! Really, Royster, if your establishment is producing such dishonest ruffians as *this* . . ."

Helplessly Royster looked at Dr. Stilly, who was listening with an unhappy frown but who showed no inclination to speak. It was a hopeless situation—the word of one boy, and a problem boy at that, against two or maybe three responsible adults. "Roddy," he began.

"Gosh, Mr. Royster," said Roddy, in a changed tone and plainly in retreat, "I didn't mean to lie! That's what I thought they told me."

"Nonsense!" yapped Dr. Ross. "We said nothing that the dimmest child in the state could misinterpret in that manner!"

Roddy was fumbling for something under his desk. "If you say so, ma'm," he said apologetically, "I guess you're right. What was really said," he finished, lifting a tape recorder onto the desk and rapidly flicking its buttons, "was *this!*"

The recorder come on loud and clear with Roddy's voice:

"'Good morning. Who did you wish to see?'

"McNear's unmistakable, high-pitched voice: 'Nobody in particular.'

"Roddy: 'Just a moment, please, and I'll call Mr. Royster.'

"Dr. Ross: 'That won't be necessary, young man. Return to your seat.'

"Roddy: 'But Mr. Royster said I'm supposed—'

"McNear: 'And the lady said that won't be necessary!'

"Roddy: 'But when visitors come, he wants to—'

"Dr. Ross: 'We're not mere visitors, boy. We're here on business. Now get on with your book!'

"Roddy: 'Yes, ma'm.'"

He switched off the recorder and looked up innocently. To Royster he said, "I guess they didn't say not to call you, after all, sir. At least not in those exact words."

Royster was fighting to stifle a guffaw of sheer relief—and no little admiration. He was glad the inspectors were staring at Roddy, as if the boy were a rattlesnake who had just depleted his venom supply into their veins, and weren't noticing him.

As soon as he had himself under control, Royster said brightly, "Roddy is quite an enthusiast of speech identification patterns—you know, those photographs of vocal vibrations that are used somewhat like fingerprints. He makes himself a minor nuisance with that recorder of his, gathering samples of visitors' voices to study. How many adults do you have so far, Roddy?"

"Twenty-seven, counting these three. But none of these said 'Good morning,' and those are the words I'm using in my comparative study."

"I'm sure they'll be happy to oblige, won't you, folks?" Royster said, turning to the inspectors. "Will each of you say 'Good morning' for Roddy's recording?"

Dr. Stilly said with a wry smile, "That's a very educational project you're undertaking, young man. I'll be glad to contribute. Good morning." He looked expectantly at McNear.

"Good morning," McNear sang tonelessly.

"Good morning!" Dr. Ross snapped impatiently. "Now let's quit wasting time and get on with the inspection."

"Very well," Royster said, talking fast and glibly. "I suggest we start with the dormitories, on the upper floors, and work our way systematically to the basement." He moved away slightly, as if to lead the way to the stairwell, but none of the others showed any intention of following him, so he edged back, still talking. "As I'm sure you know, most of our youngsters are boarding students from all sections of the state. The top floor has been converted into living quarters for the boys, the second floor for the girls, and the first floor and basement rooms for classes. Fortunately, this is a big if rather old building, and—"

"We'll start with the classrooms, if you please," Dr. Ross ruled coldly.

"Those in the basement," added McNear.

Royster looked blankly at them a moment, then said, "Very well," with a nervous chuckle. "I can appreciate the fact that, for an accreditation inspection, the actual classroom work is your foremost consideration."

"Precisely," said Dr. Ross. "So let's not just stand here all day!"

As Royster led the way with apparent reluctance, the visitors became increasingly aware of the glum-looking urchin who was dogging the headmaster's footsteps. After a whispered conference with Dr. Ross, McNear asked, "Why is this young man following you, Royster?"

The headmaster started to answer, then paused, not at all satisfied with the explanation he meant to offer for Arthur's presence. The boy cleared his throat and Royster peered down at him.

"Suppose you answer our visitor's question, Arthur," he said. After all, the boy had access to several dozen imaginative young brains.

"It's 'cause I misbehaved," said Arthur.

"This is your punishment?" asked McNear.

"No, sir. This is so Mr. Royster can watch me while he decides what to do to me."

"This strikes me as a most unusual procedure," Dr. Ross commented disapprovingly.

"Oh, no, ma'm," said Arthur. "Mr. Royster does this all the time. It ain't unusual."

"It 'isn't' unusual, Arthur," Royster corrected mildly, wondering what this was leading to.

"Really, Royster," the woman said, "such a display of hesitancy concerning a simple disciplinary matter shows a lack of decisiveness scarcely fitting for a headmaster."

"Am I indecisive, Arthur?" asked Royster.

"No, sir, it ain't . . ."

"Isn't!"

" . . . It isn't that." The boy looked up at Dr. Ross. "The reason he waits for an hour or two is so I'll know he's thinkin' over what I did, because he thinks I'm important enough to think about."

Royster got the drift and put in a pious aside to the inspectors, "So many of our children's problems were intensified by angry and impatient parents . . ." He shook his head sadly.

"But couldn't the boy do his waiting in his classroom?" asked Dr. Stilly. "This procedure interrupts his work schedule for hours."

"That's correct, Dr. Stilly," said Royster, "and in the regular school situation this practice would be unjustifiable. But here at Thorling, as you know, behavioral problems have to be given a high priority. If Arthur were in his class, waiting with mounting dread to hear my decision, imagining me increasingly as a vengeful ogre, and perhaps misbehaving again out of boyish bravado, the effect on him would be far from salutary. But if he's actually with me, he's constantly aware of me as I really am, and of my desire to help, rather than injure, him. You'd be surprised at the gracefulness with which the children accept a penalty when they know I have given it hours of thought."

"Arthur," Dr. Ross said sweetly, "do you even go to the bathroom with your headmaster?"

"Yes'm."

"And are girl students punished in this manner, too?"

"Yes'm. Miss Smith had Hazel Petrov with her most all yesterday afternoon, ma'm."

Dr. Ross grunted in disappointment.

Royster led the way along the basement hall. Thorling School had originally been built, back in the late 1920s, as a public school to consolidate some two dozen of the old rural one-roomers in that area of the county. When enrollment began to mount after World War II, the penny-pinching county fathers decreed that the overflow of students be handled not by the construction of expensive new wings, nor of entire new schools, but by digging out new rooms under the old buildings. The resulting classrooms might have looked dismally shoddy, with their tangle of pipes a foot below the ceiling and their haphazardly located support beams and posts, but they served their purpose for a while.

But finally enrollment pressure reached the point where an all-out program of new-school construction was unavoidable—and the new schools made the old "substandard" by comparison. Naturally, every tax-paying citizen was soon demanding that his Johnny have as pleasant a school to attend as the next kid, and it became expedient to build still more new schools and to abandon the old.

The J. V. Thorling Foundation had purchased this building for not many more dollars than it had cost originally. The boxy, red-brick structure was old, and not considered handsome, but it was sturdy. And after a thorough repair and renovation of the interior, it proved quite satisfactory to its new users.

The state education officials made no fuss about the fact that the building was "substandard." So long as the big sign facing the highway made it plain that Thorling was a privately-operated institution, public officials seemed to feel that the shoddier it looked the better.

Thus Royster chattered extensively about the building's shortcomings, poor-mouthing and apologizing over them, as he led the inspectors about. He knew that the quality of housing was a definite factor in the accreditation process—but he knew as well that the members of this team definitely were not interested in finding fault with the building.

They were more inclined to gaze with studious frowns through the little glass-door panels of classrooms and poke their heads in storage closets, evidently in hope of discovering disorderly or illicit activity. They accepted Royster's explanation of the room in which Miss Smith's experiment with Stevie and David had been conducted—that it was a room in which visiting parents could chat with their children. The adjacent observation booth would have passed, with its lights on to blank out the scene through the one-way mirror, as unused storage space, but the inspectors did not notice it at all.

"I'm sure you've observed that we made some use of programmed instruction in our classes," Royster remarked, "but haven't gone to it fully by any means. About half of the classrooms are equipped with the program machines. We find them excellent, of course, for the teaching of all subjects once the basic learning skills are acquired."

"Then why not adopt them more fully?" asked Dr. Stilly.

"Mainly to keep the children functioning, as much as

possible, as members of groups—that is, as cooperating participants in a class discussion, et cetera. When a child is using a PI machine, he is isolated, without social contact. For our purposes, which as you know are to help the children surmount behavioral difficulties as well as provide a rounded educational experience, too much time in isolation is undesirable."

How much easier it would be, thought Royster, who was getting tired of chattering at the increasingly grumpy visitors, to tell them the truth in a very few words—that PI is about the only way to be sure that a telepathic pupil is actually learning a subject instead of picking up answers, as needed, from the minds of teachers or other students, while the ordinary, old-fashioned classroom setup is ideal for the development of ESP skills.

The group returned to the first floor and the inspectors fanned out immediately to gaze into three classrooms. Arthur took the opportunity to hiss a message to the headmaster.

"Stilly's completely snowed, Mr. Royster, but Fat Stuff and the old biddy are still on the prowl. Don't worry, though. Just get 'em into Mrs. Morelli's room!"

Royster nodded, wondering giddily who was actually running this school.

"You are, sir," Arthur hissed promptly. "but in an emerging situation like this, it's fun for us to help out."

"Emergency situation," Royster corrected automatically, and a little too loudly.

"What's that you said?" McNear snapped sharply, rejoining him.

"Oh, Arthur was saying he has to go to the bathroom.

He said it was an 'emerging situation' and I was correcting him."

McNear guffawed shrilly.

Royster frowned and said to Arthur, "Well, run along, but be back in three minutes. We'll be at Mrs. Morelli's room."

"Who's Mrs. Morelli?" asked Stilly as they walked down the hall.

"She's the music teacher. We emphasize vocal music here, because the children seem to come out of their shells so readily in the process of joint creativity of beautiful harmonies. We start part-singing at the kindergarten level. It's a wonderful social experience for the children—and an aesthetic experience as well, of course."

They reached Mrs. Morelli's room, and Royster opened the door, just as the children were finishing a marching song.

"Really, Royster," protested Dr. Ross, "we haven't the time to waste listening to . . ."

Her voice trailed off as the children's voices rose again—very softly and sweetly this time:

> "Soft as the voice of an angel,
>   Breathing a lesson unheard,
>   Hope with a gentle persuasion,
>   Whispers her comforting words.
>   Wait, till the darkness is over,
>   Wait, till the tempest is done,
>   Hope for the sunshine tomorrow,
>   After the shower is gone."

Dr. Ross had edged through the door to stand facing the singing children, who seemed to be unaware of her and the other inspectors who followed her quietly. Mrs. Morelli looked up curiously from the piano but didn't stop playing as the children sang the chorus:

"Whispering Hope, oh how welcome thy
    voice,
Making my heart in its sorrow rejoice."

"Oh my," Dr. Ross said numbly. "Oh my!"

Royster, who was himself seldom untouched by that old song's tender simplicity, said, "The children love that piece. It has a message for a troubled boy or girl."

"I could listen to it forever," breathed Dr. Ross. "I haven't heard it for years, but when I was a child . . . I've never heard it sung more beautifully!"

"Perhaps Mrs. Morelli has it on tape," said Royster. He introduced the inspectors to the teacher and asked her if she had taped "Whispering Hope."

"Why, yes," she said.

"Let's make a present of it to Dr. Ross," said Royster.

Mrs. Morelli got a small spool from her desk and handed it to the other woman. "Oh, I'll cherish this!" Dr. Ross crooned. "Thank you, Mrs. Morelli, and you, Mr. Royster. And thank *you*, children!"

McNear, who had been leaning his considerable weight against the doorframe, looking bored and annoyed, spoke up. "Who plays the fiddle?" he asked, nodding to a violin case in the corner of the room.

"I do!" piped up Sandylou, a chubby, confident

seven-year-old. "Shall I play for you?" She headed for the violin case without waiting for an answer, but suddenly whirled to glare angrily at her classmates. "I *will* play, too!" she shouted at them.

Something was going wrong, Royster realized. The class didn't want Sandylou to play for some reason, but the girl was only slightly telepathic and could not understand the *Don't!* she was receiving from the others. Her ESP capabilities were strong in the kinetics realm, but . . .

Of course! That was the trouble! She played the violin mostly with her fingers, but sometimes she used a mental touch to produce a harmonic, which did not require that the string be pressed against the fingerboard but merely touched at a vibrational node to damp the fundamental tone while allowing the whispery overtone to sound. Since the principal node is at one-half the string's length—high up on the fingerboard for a beginning violinist—Sandylou's mental touches made it possible for her to avoid long, quick reaches for harmonics, and thus enabled her to play selections that would otherwise be beyond her technique.

To the non-musician, with no exact knowledge of violin techniques, Sandylou's playing would appear extraordinary only in the sense that it was extremely advanced for a child her age. Royster himself had not known, until Mrs. Morelli told him, that the girl was ESPing her harmonics. But someone who *knew* the instrument . . . !

"Do any of you play the violin?" he asked the inspectors.

"Yeah, I used to play quite a bit," grunted McNear, "but I didn't intend to launch a student recital! We're not here to spend the morning listening to musical trivialities."

This brought a glare from his female colleague, who was still clutching her tape spool as if it were a precious jewel.

"Thank you for offering to play for us, Sandylou," said Royster, "but our guests are in a hurry today and—"

"I'll play something short, and fast," replied the girl, who already had the violin under her chin and was tightening the bow hairs. "And it won't be no triviality. It's a Wohlfahrt *study!*"

She dug into a piece that consisted mostly of ascending arpeggios, almost every one of which had a harmonic at its summit. Royster, Mrs. Morelli, and the class watched in numb, helpless silence as one pure, unexplainable note after another flowed from the instrument. McNear, his head lowered slightly and his lips puckered critically, gazed at Sandylou through his eyebrows in deep concentration.

The music ended and McNear said, "Very good, little girl. Very good indeed! You'll be an accomplished musician one of these days if you practice hard. You have a . . . a sure touch."

"Shall we move on, folks?" Royster said hurriedly, sensing that the situation had been saved—but unable to guess how. He moved toward the door and saw Arthur waiting in the hall. The inspectors were busy taking their leave of Mrs. Morelli, so he stepped outside.

In a somewhat mystified tone, Arthur hissed to him, "Fat Stuff *saw* it, but he didn't *believe* it, so he didn't *see* it! Is he looney or something?"

After a moment, Royster nodded in understanding. McNear had responded to the inexplicable as people often do: he had ignored its existence. An excellent way to maintain sanity—provided the inexplicable does not become overpowering.

"Oh," said Arthur. "You've never thought much about that before. It'll help us stay a secret, won't it?"

"Don't depend on it," said Royster.

"You've got the old biddy and Fat Stuff now," Arthur reported, "but you've lost Stilly, and he's the top man. He feels like they're being had, because they ain't found nothing wrong anywhere. We're too perfect! He'll like Miss Smith, though."

Miss Smith? Royster thought as the inspectors came into the hall and Arthur fell silent. What has liking Miss Smith got to do with it?

He glanced at his watch and said, "Classes will change in a couple of minutes, and the first lunch period will start. What's your desire, folks? We can stay here and let you observe the movement of the students through the hall, or we can get on with a tour of the dormitories, or we can go to the cafeteria for lunch, now or later."

"Whichever you think preferable, Mr. Royster," Dr. Ross said pleasantly.

"Lunch sounds fine to me," smiled McNear.

Dr. Stilly said, "We may look into the dormitories later, Mr. Royster, but that would serve no essential purpose of this inspection. As for lunch, I wonder if we could have that somewhere other than in the cafeteria? Do you have a conference room where we could confer with you while we eat, without being interrupted by children or other distractions?"

"Why, yes. There's a conference table in my office. Arthur, run down to the cafeteria and tell Mrs. Sams to send four regular trays, plus coffee, to my office . . . Make that five trays, Arthur. If we eat there, Miss Smith can join us."

Arthur counted noses and asked, "What about me, sir? Where do I eat?"

"Oh, I was forgetting you. Make that six trays."

Dr. Stilly frowned. "Don't you think, Royster, that we can dispense with this young man's company now? Surely, you've considered his case sufficiently . . ."

Royster blinked, then nodded. "Quite right, Dr. Stilly. Have your lunch in the cafeteria, Arthur, and return to your regular schedule. And report to the night room each evening this week for one hour of vocabulary PI."

"Yes, sir."

In the office Royster introduced the inspectors to Miss Smith. As Arthur had predicted, Dr. Stilly was visibly impressed by her, and Royster felt a pang of bitter annoyance at the friendly warmth with which Miss Smith responded. His assistant had never favored *him* with such a charming smile!

But if the kids had expected Stilly to develop an immediate, disarming crush on Barbara Smith, they were wrong. As soon as the trays were brought in and the group settled around the table, the inspector said:

"In going over your background, Mr. Royster, I noticed that you spent two years, after finishing college, with a parapsychology group. That struck me as very strange preparation for a headmaster."

There was no point in denying the record, which Stilly had apparently gone to some trouble to look into. "Yes, I became quite interested in parapsychology during college. I viewed it as one of our scientific *frontiers*." Royster chuckled wryly at the idea and continued, "I soon realized the parapsychology people were getting nowhere with their researches, of course."

"But you stayed two years," Stilly persisted.

"Yes. I became interested, while I was there, in the general problems of disturbed children. You may not know that such children are brought to the group quite frequently. Perhaps it is a complex some parents have—to see abnormal behavior in their children as an indication of abnormal, or paranormal, abilities. At any rate, I saw enough such children there to gain an appreciation of their problems, and left the group to do graduate work in special education. So, in a sense, you could say that those two years were responsible for me being in my present position."

All of which was the truth—the carefully edited truth.

Stilly ate for a moment in frowning silence, then remarked, "I understand those two years might have been responsible in more ways than one. Wasn't it while you were with the parapsychology people that you first met J.V. Thorling?"

"Yes, indeed," Royster said brightly. "Our late benefactor was quite a psi buff, as is fairly well known."

"He attributed his financial success to a freakish mental ability to foresee the future, didn't he?"

Royster laughed. "So the magazine articles about him said. From my own conversations with him, I got the impression he wasn't really sure of the source of his success. But he wondered about it, and therefore took some interest in parapsychology. We have to remember, though, that he had a fine head for finance, and I'm sure a more acceptable explanation of his accomplishments would be that he often could see the financial possibilities of a situation, through subconscious but quite normal mental processes, that were invisible to less capable minds."

"That doesn't explain why he chose to endow this school rather generously," Stilly frowned.

"That's no mystery," Royster shrugged. "When Mr. Thorling visited the parapsychology people he wasn't much impressed, and since I was something of a rebel there he talked with me quite a bit—to the annoyance of the group's brass, I might add. I told him about my plans, such as they were at the time, to work with children of above-average potential but suffering from severe behavioral defects. In the rarefied air of that group my ideas must have had a down-to-earth, constructive ring to Mr. Thorling. He became interested, and said if he could ever be of assistance to let him know. So, here we have Thorling School."

"From all this, then," said Stilly, "I take it that you no longer believe in parapsychology. Is that correct?"

Royster peered curiously at the inspector for a moment before replying, "I'm a rather conservative man, Dr. Stilly. I don't believe in getting something for nothing, and that's what parapsychology tries to do when you boil it down to the essentials. Man has to *work* for what he gets—for his food, for his knowledge, or to develop his skills. Now I try not to be prejudiced against parapsychologists, but I've seen enough of them to know that they are mostly of the visionary type, dreamers of dreams, not doers of jobs. They seem to expect to find some magic word that will bridge any gap in time and space, through telepathy, or teleportation, or some such, so they can manipulate the real world without exerting real energy. I certainly don't believe in magic, Dr. Stilly."

"I don't see what all this has to do with an accreditation inspection," yapped McNear rather crossly.

"Evidently it has nothing to do with it," said Stilly. "However, Mr. Royster had some crackpottist connections in the past, and if he still took such things seriously that would certainly reflect on his ability to direct the educational life of hundreds of children. But I find his explanations and his present, more adult, view of parapsychology quite satisfactory. Miss Smith, have you been with Thorling School any length of time?"

"Only four months, Dr. Stilly," she said, and the conversation drifted into less perilous waters.

After lunch the inspectors made a perfunctory tour through the dormitory floors, the cafeteria, and the gymnasium. Afterwards Royster walked out to their auto with them.

"An excellent job you're doing here, Mr. Royster," said Dr. Ross. "I was particularly impressed with the orderliness of activities in the classrooms. I really don't know quite how you do it, considering the backgrounds of your children."

"There are several factors involved," he responded.

"A child coming here finds himself in a new environment, where he can make a fresh start. And as my written reports for earlier inspections have explained, and I'm sure you've read them, we try to let the child know where he stands with us, to make the rules perfectly clear to him—and above all to let him know we're on his side, that he can feel secure and loved. And understood. Fortunately, we have been able to bring together a faculty of sufficient size and ability to do the job. As in any school, success depends on the individual teacher."

"You'll see to it that that little violinist gets good training, Royster?" demanded McNear.

"Well, this is no conservatory, you realize," he replied, "and I must reemphasize the stress we place on proper personality and behavioral development. But you can rest assured, Mr. McNear, that Sandylou will be given ample opportunity to develop her special talents."

McNear nodded. "O.K. Just so you realize that she has something special." He climbed in the car with the others.

Royster smiled. "To us at Thorling, Mr. McNear," he said, "all of our children have something special."

"How true!" cooed Dr. Ross. "Good day, Mr. Royster, and thank you for an inspiring morning!"

Royster walked back in the building and, even though he could hear what sounded like a minor riot down the hall, he went into the office and sat down.

Miss Smith nodded toward the noise and said, "I don't have to ask if our visitors are gone."

"Yeah, back to normal," he said with a relieved

sigh. "It's funny that I let things like that scare me, but I suppose I keep thinking of our kids as—just *kids*. I never realize what a help they can be in a pinch."

"I hear Sandylou almost gave the whole show away."

Royster nodded and lit a cigarette. "She had the kids upset for a moment there. Some of them looked as pale as I felt."

"Can't something be done about that child?"

"The kids'll be working on her, never fear," Royster shrugged. "They can do more with her kind of problem than we can."

"It frightens me to think," Miss Smith shuddered, "what would have happened if that McNear slob hadn't been so stupid."

Royster nodded without replying. Miss Smith had been with the school less than half a year and—well, there were some things she just wasn't ready to know yet. For example, that the kids could have handled the McNear problem, if absolutely necessary, with selective mental erasure. It was a repulsive idea, to him as it was to the kids, and it would be too disgusting for Miss Smith to accept until the Thorling children became *her* children more fully.

"Well, I'd like to get back to my young gladiators as you call them," she said.

Royster looked up curiously.

"To Stevie and David," she explained. "That test might still work even though—"

"Miss Smith," Royster said, grinding out his cigarette, "I've gone along with you on your experiments so far, partly to let you learn for yourself that this

age-old search for a mental Midas touch is a waste of
time, because there are no shortcuts, and partly not
to discourage creative thinking from you, and partly
I guess just to keep you happy.

"But you've been here four months now, and you're
still busily barking up the same old empty tree. How
much longer is it going to take you to get this nonsense out of your system and turn your energies to
our *real* problems?"

She stared at him in hurt astonishment. He would
have felt ashamed of his outburst, except for the ten-
sions of the inspection and the way she had flirted
with Dr. Stilly. His anger continued to boil.

"Well really, Mr. Royster," she snapped, her face
turning red, "I see no need to shout! And I haven't
been aware of neglecting my duties because of my
interest in various experiments that, you must surely
comprehend, can be conducted here more ideally
than anywhere else in the world! If you're too stodgy
to realize—"

"*Stodgy?*" barked Royster. "Is that what you think?
Maybe you'd be happier doing something else—
some*where* else! With livelier company! Maybe inspect-
ing schools with your pal Stilly!"

"If you can't even have an argument like this without
being ridiculous, maybe I *should* move along!" she
flared. "Stilly indeed!"

"I saw you turn on the old charm for him!" replied
Royster.

"Sure I did! The kids told me it would help!"

"Oh." He ought to have guessed that, he realized.
His anger was suddenly gone. He said, "I'm sorry
for jumping on you that way, Miss Smith. It was

uncalled-for. Nerves, I guess . . . I have no objection, really, to you continuing that test with Stevie and David. So if you want to get on with it . . ."

She blinked a couple of times and turned toward her cubbyhole office. "No. I don't know. Maybe tomorrow . . ." She turned to face him again. "You really think it's a waste of time, don't you?"

He nodded glumly. "Yes, I do. But I don't know everything, after all, and had no business sounding off as if I did. I know that my own ideas work—today the kids proved just how well they've worked. But that doesn't make all other ideas worthless. So, if there's anything you want to try . . ."

"I . . . I don't think so." She sat down and propped her chin in her hand. "You're probably right, and it's high time I realized that. Maybe you had to yell at me to get through. ESP ability isn't a . . . a gift . . ."

"In a way it is," Royster said. "It's a gift in the sense that Sandylou's musicianship is a gift. But a gift is merely a capacity. Sandylou's doesn't automatically make her a great violinist, it just provides her with the capacity to *become* one—after several more years of hard work and practice. What would have happened to her gift if our society had no use for music, if the whole concept of music didn't exist? Not much of anything would have happened to it. Unless maybe it got her thrown in the loony-bin for making strange noises.

"That's what happens to ESP capacity, most of the time. A few people, like Old Man Thorling, manage to develop some primitive skill with it. But mostly, it just pops up, unexplainably and usually frighteningly, in moments of great emotional stress, and then it's gone again. It's an unrealized capacity because it isn't trained.

"That's what I decided while with the parapsychology group, working with the children brought there. Thorling agreed when I explained it to him. Take a child with ESP capacity, still young enough to have a pliable mind, let him know that ESP development is *desirable,* and figure out ways to train him to use his capacity. Encourage him to practice, practice, practice! Bring many such children together, so they can learn things from each other that we don't know to teach them. Children are eager to please, and to learn—and they'll work hard to do both.

"Now, as for shortcuts, some may exist. But I believe if they do they won't be discovered by you or me. The kids will find them. They have the knowledge and the skills that we'll never attain for ourselves. If Sandylou learns an improved violin technique, it will be from another fiddle player, not from a non-musician. That's why I feel our job is to help the children develop themselves, in the only way we know how, and leave it to them to devise ways to build on their basic skills."

"One thing bothers me about this," said Miss Smith. "You keep referring to consciously-controlled ESP as a skill, and equating its development to other skills such as learning to play a violin. Yet, you say the learning has to start at a very tender age—in the kindergarten years if not sooner. But this isn't true of other skills. I know it helps for a child to start his musical training early, but many adults, starting with no musical training at all, learn to become adequate performers on some instrument. Now if ESP were really a skill, why couldn't you, or I, or some of the teachers develop some degree of it? All of us have tried, without the slightest result."

Royster shook his head. "You're wrong, I think, when you speak of an adult learning to play an instrument with no early musical training at all. I don't think there is any such adult, for the simple reason that every person in our culture has some early musical training. From babyhood on we *hear* music, sung by our mothers, played on radios, and so on. And babies begin attempting to gurgle songs about the same time they are learning to talk. They experience music from the beginning. It's part of their lives. So no adult starts cold to learn an instrument. And there are similar parallels for any other skill you can name—except controlled ESP. Only in this school of ours does a child have a chance to grow up with ESP as an integral part of his daily experience. In fact, I think it's remarkable that they can start from scratch at the relatively advanced age of four or five, and still—"

Arthur appeared in the doorway. Royster broke off his conversation with Miss Smith and said, "Hi, Arthur. Thanks for the help this morning—thanks to *all* of you." The boy grinned his pleasure and looked down at his shoes as the headmaster continued, "What can I do for you?"

"About you tellin' me to do an hour of vocabulary PI every night, Mr. Royster—" Arthur began.

"That was just part of our act for the inspectors, Arthur," Royster smiled. "You can forget it."

"Oh, *I know* that, sir. What I wanted to tell you was that I guess I need that PI, so I'm goin' to do like you said, even if you didn't mean it."

Royster nodded approvingly. The boy turned to
leave and Royster recalled something he had meant
to ask the boy about at the first opportunity. "Just
a moment, Arthur. This morning you told me all
the children were with me, except a couple of new
'soreheads' and some old 'perfectionists'. The new
'soreheads' I understand, of course. But what was
that business about 'perfectionists'?"

Arthur looked uncomfortable, and glanced uncertainly from one of the adults to the other. "Well, it
ain't . . . isn't much of anything, just some silly stuff the
big girls like Jilly and them think about sometimes."

"Is it too silly to tell us about, Arthur?" Miss Smith
smiled.

"Naw, it's just that . . . well, they don't like the way
Mr. Royster keeps himself half mad at you all the time,
Miss Smith, because he likes you a lot and thinks he
shouldn't, or that he shouldn't even think about liking
you with all of us kid telepaths around."

Royster stiffened with astonishment and was aware
that his face was flaming red. It did not help his feelings to observe that Miss Smith appeared perfectly
calm.

"Wh-what business of theirs is it if—" he sputtered.

"That's what I think," nodded Arthur, emphatically.
"But you know how girls can act sometimes. And
they think it's mean of you not to be nice to Miss
Smith, because she likes you, too, and it makes her
sad because she thinks you don't."

"I . . . see," said Royster.

"But this is a good place to be," Arthur went on
hurriedly, "and they like you just the same. They just

don't like the . . . the way you do with Miss Smith. That's why the rest of us call them perfectionists."

Royster nodded. "Thank you, Arthur," he said, and the boy beat a hasty retreat.

After a pause Barbara Smith said, "Really, Judson, there's no reason to behave like a priest around here if you don't think like one! To telepathic children, that's simply a form of hypocrisy."

"But I felt that in my position . . ." he mumbled.

"Nonsense! The children have teachers who are married. They are aware of such relationships." She peered at his face. "How did you develop such a straitlaced attitude toward love? Do you come from a puritanical family?"

"Certainly not! My parents were merely— conservative."

She giggled and kept looking at him. Finally he smiled back.

LOST CALLING

❦❦❦

1

THE GANGLY YOUNG MAN slumped limply on the white metal stool in the *Strahorn's* sick bay. His mind was working frantically and repetitiously:

My name is Dalton Mirni, and I am a . . . My profession is . . . I have finished my special training and am now a competent . . .

He could not remember the missing word. Gone with it was all the knowledge of the subject of . . . acquired during twenty years of schooling. The loss was too shattering to accept.

He was dimly aware that someone had joined him and the medic in the sick bay, and glanced up long enough to identify the man as the ship's captain. He heard their conversation with scant attention.

"When did he get like this?" The captain's voice was hard and cold.

"Just before I called you, sir. I was getting his history, and he told me he had been in a special kind of school since he was four. A very strange place, the way he described it. I asked him what he had studied there and he started to answer. Then he laughed and started to answer again, but didn't. He seemed to be trying to remember. When I repeated the question I got no reply. He was almost catatonic when I called you, sir, but I noticed him raise his eyes when you came in."

"*Mirni!*" the captain barked sharply. Dalton Mirni heard but did not try to respond. His brain captured and echoed the sound "*Mirni!*" complete with the commanding tone of the captain's voice, and tried to use it to arouse his lost memories. "*Mirni!*" he shouted silently. "*Mirni! . . . ! Mirni! . . . !*" But the blank remained blank.

When he again noticed the conversation, the captain was saying impatiently, "Let me review for your benefit, Bolinski. First, we're out in the Periphery, where the friends of Earth are few and questionable. Second, we receive a distress call and home in on a survival capsule containing this whoever-he-is Mirni. Instead of a sick, scared castaway, he comes aboard as assured and beamish as a Vegan princeling—yet he claims to have been separated from 'real' humanity (whatever that means!) since he was four. And he says he can't identify his home planet, so we have to send out the standard identification-query call, meaning we inform the universe at large that we have picked up a man named Dalton Mirni whose description is such-and-such.

"Now, after all this, our assured young princeling abruptly displays a lapse of memory and goes zombie on us. You can offer what explanation you like, Bolinski, but one alone sticks in my mind: *We're being had!* Somebody's playing a tricky game with us, and with no friendly intent. So why not use your investigatory drugs on this jerk and get to the bottom of it?"

"If you'll make that an order, Captain Devista, O.K.," the medic replied stubbornly. "But you know the restrictions on those drugs. Besides, if somebody is trying to sucker us, maybe they *expect* us to shoot the kid with a quizzer. But, if you'll give me a direct order—"

"You're getting close to insubordination, Bolinski!" the captain flared.

"I'm ready to obey orders, sir," the medic returned tightly.

Dalton Mirni struggled part way out of the depths to say: "The drugs . . . may help."

His speaking startled the two men. "You'll volunteer to take them?" the captain demanded.

"Yes."

"Get his authorization on a sealed tape, Bolinski, and proceed," the captain snapped.

The medic led Mirni across the room to a small, seamless metal box. "Hold this grip," he said, "and answer this question: Do you, Dalton Mirni, voluntarily agree to submit to interrogation under medication?"

"Yes."

"All right, you can turn loose, and sign your name through this slot."

Mirni accepted the pencil and signed. Captain Devista was watching over his shoulder.

"You speak and write Anglo-Ruski like an adult," the captain remarked. "That must have been part of your training."

"No. I was taught language by the play-people. Language, history, the arts, physical sciences, plane-tography . . . I remember all those."

"Who are the play-people?"

"They were the . . . the projections I lived among outside of school hours." Having started talking, Mirni found the conversation a comforting distraction from his mental turmoil. He continued as Bolinski placed an applicator against his bare arm and squeezed the trigger. "I don't know the mechanics of the play-people projections—how the teachers made them. They seemed like real people, like you or me, and I was supposed to treat them as real, even though they weren't."

"How do you know they weren't?" asked Devista.

"Because when I was fourteen, going through a goofy stage, I got angry one day and told the play-people they were nothings, that I was the only real person and they should do as I told them. They became statues! Their bodies turned slick and hard, and I couldn't budge any of them, not even my baby cousin. It was spooky! That lasted all day and night, but everything was back to normal when I came home from school the next morning."

"You had a cousin there?"

"A play-cousin, of course, and an aunt and uncle I lived with. You see, the teachers didn't want me to become alienated from humanity, so they supplied a normal play-home and community for me to live in." Talking grew increasingly easier for Mirni as the drugs took effect, and the thought of his loss was less disturbing.

"Then your teachers were not human?" the captain asked.

"Oh no! Nor any of the other students, either."

"What were the teachers like?"

"I don't know. They never showed me. Sometimes a teacher would appear as a human, sometimes like one of the other students, and sometimes we wouldn't see him at all. We would just know he was there talking to us."

"Talking about what?"

There was no hint of an answer in Mirni's memory. "I don't know. That's gone."

"Why did you stop talking when Bolinski asked you a similar question?"

"Because I didn't realize until I tried to answer him that I had forgotten. It was a shock to learn that."

"Is it still a shock?"

"Yes, but the drug seems to help."

The ship's intercom buzzed and the captain answered, "Yes?"

"Mirni identified, sir," the speaker said. "He's a citizen of Earth and the only located survivor of the CES *Gorman* which was lost beyond Antares in 2709. He was on board with his parents."

"Acknowledged," growled Devista.

"That fits with what I remember," said Mirni, "and what the teachers told me. They said the ship blew up, and I was the only one they rescued."

Bolinski remarked to the captain with evident

enjoyment, "It's hard to see how anybody could embarrass an Earth ship by planting an Earth citizen aboard, sir."

The captain ignored the jibe. "Does that drug ever fail to elicit the truth?" he demanded.

"Not when handled properly, sir. Mirni's telling you the truth as he knows it."

"As he knows it," the captain grunted. "He could have been fed a cock-and-bull story under hypnosis. Would that fool your drug?"

"Captain, I'm no psychographer," retorted Bolinski. "I can't answer that."

Devista paced the room, fuming. "Men have been knocking about interstellar space for over five hundred years," he barked, "without seeing a sign of intelligent extraterrestrial life! Then this boy comes drifting along in a surcap with his tale of a race of super-teachers, along with several student races—implying that we're among the latter. And very conveniently, he goes amnesiac on the one subject that might prove his story! Do you expect me to believe him?"

Bolinski shrugged. "I'm not saying I believe him myself, sir. I'm simply reserving judgment on his story."

Devista grunted. "Well, keep him confined under observation. I want a private word with him, so I'll see him to his cubicle."

"Yes, sir. He can go in Number Three."

Mirni followed the captain through a hallway off sick bay and into an eight-foot cube room. "Sit down," said the captain. Mirni sat on the bed and looked up at Devista, who was studying him with an annoyed frown.

"This is no luxury liner, Mirni," the captain said harshly. "We're a Commercial Earth Spacer, as the *Gorman* was, but freight's our business and we have a minimal crew. We're not prepared to baby you all the way back to Earth. So no more of that deepending, understand?"

Mirni nodded. "I'm under control now, captain, and I think I can stay that way. I realize you have plenty of problems without me, so—"

"Problems?" snapped Devista. "Why do you think I've got problems, and what business of yours is it if I have?"

"I'm sorry, sir," Mirni answered contritely. "I don't mean to butt in. But I couldn't help noticing the way you spoke to Bolinski, and the way he spoke to you. It was easy to see there's trouble between you and your crew."

The captain stared at him. "For a kid who claims to have spent almost his whole life away from people," he grated, "you see a hell of a lot."

"Being with the play-people accounts for that."

"That's no answer," the captain replied. "People live together for years without knowing each other's problems."

"But I was supposed to work at understanding the play-people," Mirni explained. "That was so that, when I learned my . . . my profession and came home, I would know how to stay on good terms with everyone, and my work would be accepted. It's important to be liked, no matter what job you're doing."

The captain nodded jerkily. "That's the truth. And

that's the trouble on this ship! This is probably my last trip as a commanding officer." He flopped tiredly on the bed and stared at the floor.

"What happened?" asked Mirni.

"A case of insubordination—Spaceman First Ferris. He's the guy who brought in your capsule."

"Oh, the big red-headed fellow," recalled Mirni.

The captain nodded. "A week ago he gave me some back talk. The words got hotter until he made a remark no ship commander can afford to tolerate. I threw the book at him. He's to stand trial before the adjutant of the next planetary base we reach. That's on Fingal, four days from now."

"This sounds more like trouble for Spaceman Ferris than for you," Mirni observed. The tranquilizing effect of the drugs was wearing off, and he had to make an effort to attend the captain's words.

"Except for one thing. Ferris intends to call half the crew as witnesses. There's a rule in the Merchant Spaceman's Code that a crew member who has given unfriendly testimony about a superior officer cannot be required to serve under him any longer. After that trial the *Strahorn* won't have enough crew left to lift off of Fingal—unless I resign then and there. And there's no recruiting on Fingal. It's unfriendly to Earth. So I've been mouse-trapped!"

Mirni nodded soberly. After a pause he asked, "Captain, would it be impossible for you to drop the charges against Ferris? I can understand your moral objections to that idea, but if that's the only way out for you—"

"Oh, I've thought of that. It's out. Not so much on moral grounds, because . . . well, I *am* a hard man to get along with. The fault wasn't all Ferris's. But a captain can't humiliate himself that way."

"I don't see why anybody can't admit a mistake, or even apologize for one. Everybody makes them."

"Well . . . if it would do any good, maybe. But it wouldn't. If I withdrew the charges, and even apologized to Ferris, next trip out I'd run into the same thing with Chief Engineer Thorns, or Zaffuto the cook, or somebody. Why postpone it?"

"Gosh, Captain, I hate to see this happen to you," said Mirni. "I imagine that, except for this problem with subordinates, you're an unusually capable ship commander."

"I *have* to be that or I wouldn't have lasted as long as I have!" Devista chuckled ruefully.

"It would be such a waste," Mirni nodded. "There ought to be a more lasting solution of some kind. Don't ships have executive officers to handle most business with the crews in place of the captains?"

"That's right," said Devista, "but in practice on a ship this size and type the captain acts as his own exec. If he turned the job over to someone else, ten percent of his pay would go with it. It just isn't done."

"Is the money that important?"

"Well . . . no, but it isn't done. But—" The captain hesitated. "If I apologized to Ferris and dropped the charges, and named somebody like Warrant Officer Soklov as exec . . . the men seem to like him—"

"That way you could concentrate on the things you do best," Mirni said.

The captain stood up, frowning thoughtfully. "Maybe it's worth thinking over. Now, son, as I said, this is no luxury liner, but we ought to be able to make you comfortable. Ask Bolinski for anything you need, and if he can't provide it tell him to call me. Or to call Soklov and *he* can call me."

"Thanks, Captain. I'll be O.K., I'm sure. One thing I'd appreciate. I want to thank Spaceman Ferris for hauling me in. So, if you or Soklov would ask him to drop by some time tomorrow—"

"Certainly. And, son, when you see him, I wonder if you would try to talk some reason into that mule head of his?"

2

The day after the *Strahorn* grounded on Fingal, Mirni was called to the bridge. Captain Devista greeted him with a worried expression.

"Mirni, the Fingalese are curious about you," he said. "They are demanding that I turn you over to them for examination."

"Do they have psychographers?" Mirni asked eagerly.

"The planet's filthy with them!" growled the captain.

"O.K. I'm ready to go. Do they want me right now?"

The captain was startled. "You don't understand, son. Fingal is under a monarchy, and the questioning methods here aren't very gentle. I can't expose an Earth citizen to that!"

"If I go willingly, you won't be sending me," Mirni pointed out. "Some way or other, Captain, I've *got* to get back what I've lost. I'm nothing without it. With it I was ... I don't know ... something important. I can stand questioning under torture if that's what it takes to get me free of this torment."

As the captain started to reply Spaceman Ferris came storming up the ladder. "Captain," he demanded hotly, "you're not turnin' the kid over to the Finks, are you?" Devista purpled.

"He's not sending me out," Mirni said quickly. "I'm going of my own accord."

"What?"

"Maybe they can find out what I need to know."

"Bilps and stenchers! They'll just torture you!"

Mirni shrugged. "Maybe that's what it will take."

"For a bright kid you're talkin' stupid!"

"Spaceman Ferris," snapped the captain, "I agree with you completely, but I remind you that Mirni is a citizen of Earth and a passenger on this ship. We cannot legally stop him from going groundside if he wishes. And you are on the bridge without permission!"

"Huh? Oh. Sorry, sir. Look, if he's going out, let me and some of the gang go along as a bodyguard."

"That wouldn't help. Not even your roughneck buddies can take on a whole planet. You would merely make the Fingalese suspicious, and probably harder on the boy. But the offer's appreciated."

Ferris's thick shoulders slumped. "Will you show me which port to use, Mr. Ferris?" Mirni asked him.

"Huh? Oh, sure kid. Come on."

The Fingalese inquisitors were efficient but short on enthusiasm in their session with Mirni. The fact that he seemed a nice lad did not restrain them; they had worked over nice lads before. But Mirni puzzled them, first with his unbelievably cooperative attitude and second with his hard-to-swallow life history.

Finally he managed to capture the imagination of one of them.

"Think of the possibilities!" this worthy enthused. "This boy may have a complete new science locked in some dark recess of his brain. Or else maybe some highly-developed extrasensory abilities. Whatever is there, Fingal must have it!"

A colleague complained, "But we've scopped him, infrahypped him, scanned him and electrocited him. With him trying to help, what's more. If he had secrets, we'd know them by now."

"Not necessarily!" argued the excited one. "Obviously his so-called teachers used an erasure technique that goes deeper and is more selective than any method of ours. But it is a well-known fact, gentlemen, that no memory can be removed completely from a living organism. We must dig deeper to find it!"

"Dig with what?" another exploded. "And that 'well-known fact' of yours is just a well-known *theory*, based on what we can and can't do with our *human* skills. I say we quit wasting time and make out our report to the Foerst before he gets impatient."

Mirni asked weakly, "Have you tried everything?"

"Everything but splinters under the fingernails," a glum inquisitor replied, "and they wouldn't help, either."

Mirni was given a reviving drink and put in a comfortable room to rest. He slept poorly, but after he was wakened and given breakfast he felt generally recuperated from the effects of the questioning.

He was rushed immediately to the private audience chamber of Foerst Dolfuls IV, who turned out to be a spare man of middle age with a thin, pinched face, old-fashioned exterior spectacles, and cautious, compressed lips. Politely, Mirni gave Fingal's chief-of-state the prescribed chest salute and stood at attention between his guards.

The Foerst's frigid eyes studied him briefly before the monarch spoke. His voice was dry and level, with only a hint of controlled anger.

"Dalton Mirni, you may report to your superiors that their little fraud did not work. Congratulate them for their skill in your preparation—my psychographers were nearly taken in! But I recognize you, of course, for the deception you are. The psychographers have been directed to ignore the content of your purported memory and to destroy all records of the questioning, as I will destroy the report they gave me. They will, however, conduct research on such deep-briefing techniques as have been used on you, and will not easily be fooled again. You may return to your ship."

This speech left Mirni wide-eyed with puzzlement. "Pardon," he faltered. "Is one permitted to ask the Foerst a question?"

"Go ahead," said the Foerst.

"Thank you. I'm . . . not aware of any fraud, sire, but I suppose I would not be if your conclusions are correct. I would like to know the nature of this deception—what it is that I am supposed to fool you into believing."

The Foerst nodded indifferently and said, "Earth

is obviously trying to revive the old 'alien menace' myth. You are allowed to fall in our hands with your absurd 'memory' of a super-race of aliens. The object is to scare the independent worlds into uniting—under Earth's leadership, it is hardly necessary to add—in defense against the aliens. But your superiors were too cheap to make your story convincing. They should have let you reveal some of Earth's scientific secrets to masquerade as alien knowledge."

"But . . . but, sire, there is no alien menace!" Mirni exclaimed.

"That I am sure of!" the Foerst replied with a humorless smile.

"That is I mean my teachers are no menace. They simply aren't constituted to threaten our sort of life. As for the students' various races, none of them live in this galaxy, and a teacher told me it will be at least seventeen thousand years before humans make broad contact with another intelligence."

A fleeting look of uncertainty crossed the Foerst's face, but he sneered, "You are backing down with a vengeance, now that Earth's scheme is exposed." He glanced at the guards and said, "Leave us. My defenses are adequate."

The guards saluted and left the Foerst alone with Mirni.

"Your words puzzle me, young man," said the monarch. "By admitting that no alien menace exists, you have weakened Earth's chance to succeed with a better-planned effort to repeat this ruse. Why would you be permitted to make such an admission?"

"I can only tell you what I remember, sire. I don't know why those memories are what they are."

The Foerst was silent and expressionless for several minutes and Mirni took the liberty of relaxing his stance.

"What are your views on Earth's interstellar policies?" the Foerst asked at last.

"They seem . . . mixed up, sort of . . . I don't know how to describe them, exactly. I don't really know why Fingal and Earth are mad at each other."

After a flicker of a smile, the Foerst said, "The situation has complexities, but it is basically simple. Earth is striving, with too much success, to keep all the independent planets including Fingal in economic subjection."

"Oh," Mirni nodded. "What is it you need that Earth won't let you get?"

"Manpower," grated the Foerst. "Manpower to support our own industrial economy."

"But the guidebook says you have twenty-seven million people," objected Mirni. "Isn't that enough to build from?"

"Our present population is not available for industry," the Foerst replied impatiently. "Are you familiar with Fingal's cultural pattern?"

"The guidebook calls it feudal-agricultural," said Mirni.

The Foerst nodded grudgingly. "That's close enough. We have an enlightened nobility, the Firsters, the descendants of the earliest settlers. Most of the later arrivals entered the services of the Firsters and the pattern never changed. The result is a stable culture in which each person's role is established before he is born. There is a minority of freemen—in crafts, trades and the like—but they are too few for industrialization. Also, they are needed in their present occupations."

"Then all of Fingal's manpower is pre-empted by your present system?" asked Mirni.

"That's the sum of it," agreed the Foerst.

"Why not bring in immigrants? Earth has too many people—"

"Impossible! Earthmen aren't to be trusted! We will not open our planet to that scum. Also, immigrants would have to be assigned upon arrival to the various Firster estates—all but the tenth my House could claim. They would only reinforce the established pattern."

Mirni looked sympathetic. "Tell me, sire, would something like this be possible: Fingal was settled by people from a Central European state, was it not?"

"That is correct."

"Then couldn't you start a propaganda campaign, saying that Earth was discriminating against the people of the Central European province? You would have to be cagey about how you did it, because later on you would want to be very suspicious of the Central Europeans. The propaganda would stir the sympathy of your people for their old kindred on the mother planet, and build up a demand that the repressed people be offered refuge on Fingal.

"But you would be against that, because Earthmen can't be trusted. Finally you would give in part way, and say Central Europeans could come in, but not under conditions that would allow them to subvert the Fingalese way of life. They would not be permitted to infiltrate the services of the Firsters—"

"The Firsters would not be allowed to grab them, you mean?" asked the Foerst with a glimmer of interest.

"Yes, but you would not put it that way, sire. The refugees would be let in only as wards of the planetary government, so they could be kept under strict surveillance. Of course, the refugees would be expected to earn their keep—I suppose you have title to enough land, mineral rights and so on to provide industrial cities and raw materials?"

The Foerst nodded. He was eyeing Mirni with quizzical approval. "You're a clever schemer, boy," he said. "How did you learn that in your school?"

"I didn't, sire. I learned such things from living with the play-people. Well—it *was* part of my training, in a way, because I would need to know how to handle people."

"So you manipulated the play-people for practice."

"Something like that, sire."

"Well, you need experience with *real* people," the Foerst told him with a dry chuckle. "Your scheme is clever, but it is nonsense. First, the Central Europeans are no more discriminated against than any other segment of Earth's population, and the 'big lie' propaganda campaign is an anachronism. The Earth government could kill such a campaign with a sealed-tape plebiscite that would prove the propaganda's falsity."

"By asking the Central Europeans if they were repressed?"

"Certainly!"

"But couldn't the propaganda make the people there *think* they were repressed?" Mirni persisted. "No planetary government can be so perfect that people can find nothing to complain about."

"That I will definitely grant you!" grunted the

Foerst. "But your scheme is still impractical for more reasons than I care to detail. You are too lacking in experience, boy, to expect to solve a world's problems as if they were a puzzle-toy." He pressed a button on his chair arm and added, "But I have enjoyed this interview, young man. For an Earth citizen you are a most pleasant person—but then you say you weren't on Earth very long. If I were advising you, I would suggest that you never stay on that planet long enough to adopt the Earth viewpoint." The guards entered the room and the Foerst gave Mirni a cold, formal nod. "You are dismissed, Dalton Mirni."

Mirni saluted and departed.

3

After he reached Earth several weeks later, Mirni was questioned far longer and more intensively than on Fingal. This was what he had expected and hoped for. The psychographers of Earth were less inclined than those of Fingal to regard him as a possible source of militarily, or politically, useful knowledge, to be wrung from him and reported to the appropriate government branches. They were more inclined to take him at face value as a perhaps unique example of advanced psychometric manipulation, and thus as an unusually interesting research subject.

But their results were as disappointing to Mirni as were those of the earlier questionings. No concealed memories were nudged into consciousness. As test after test yielded nothing, he had to fight a growing sense of depression.

The months of examination produced occasional moments of excitement, though.

One came when a beet-faced security official barged into the Psychomed Center one day, storming angrily over Mirni's "presumptuous interference in Earth-Fingal relations." Mirni had, of course, recounted his interview with the Foerst, and his examiners had sent a transcript of it to Interstellar Affairs, and hence to Diplomatic Security.

"I'm very sorry, sir," Mirni told the angry official. "I didn't mean to interfere, but . . . well, the Foerst had problems, and his people had tried to help me with mine. So I tried to suggest something that might help him. But he didn't consider my idea very plausible—"

"Oh, *didn't* he!" growled the security man. "Then why has he sent Fingal's worst muck-monger reporter into Central Europe to do a series of exposés on the so-called 'Plight of the Homefolk'?"

"Then he is using my suggestions," said Mirni, feeling cheered by the thought.

"He is," the official snapped. "And now, since you were so helpful to the Foerst of Fingal," he went on with heavy sarcasm, "perhaps you will also be so kind as to suggest a way for your home planet to get out of the mess you've put us in!"

"I'll be glad to help any way I can," Mirni replied earnestly, "but I don't think you should worry about the discontent being stirred up in Europe. It will blow over soon—after the most dissatisfied people have left for Fingal. The easing of population pressure will have a soothing effect."

"You're saying we should stand still for these insulting lies!" exploded the official. "These aspersions on the fairness of the government of Earth! And from a planet that keeps most of its people in serfdom!"

"You can't win an argument by calling a liar a liar," said Mirni. "But, if Earth needs to strike back at Fingal, maybe the best way would be with jokes. The Foerst is a grim, humorless man, and he wouldn't take jokes at all well. And jokes would imply that the whole Central European business was too trivial to be viewed seriously."

The security official stared at Mirni as if wondering about his sanity. "Jokes, huh? Could you suggest one to start with?"

Mirni shook his head. "I'm afraid I can't . . . I'm not feeling very funny these days."

"This beats all!" yelled the official, spinning and stalking ferociously out of the lab.

One of the researchers, who had stood by taking all this in, said to Mirni, "That's the first time I've ever seen you meet somebody and not win his friendship."

"Oh, he likes me all right," Mirni replied distractedly. "He just enjoys being angry."

Several days later he was called in to see the Psychomed Center's research chief. She regarded him with soft, motherly eyes and fingered a report on her desk.

"This is only a preliminary summary of our examination of you, Dalton," she said. "The full analysis will take six or seven weeks yet. So don't take this as the last word."

Mirni nodded glumly. She was trying to let him down easy.

"Our two basic findings are these," she continued. "First, your memories are accurate, so far as they go. Our random cross checks indicate a consistency that could not be produced by any conceivable means of artificial memory-planting. You actually spent twenty years among extraterrestrials, with the companionship of the play-people. And you were being trained.

"Second, your lost memory of that training is, I'm afraid, total. It is not waiting in some corner of your brain to spring out when appropriately keyed."

Mirni nodded. He expected this.

"That's about it, Dalton," the research chief concluded. "You can have a copy of this summary which, as I said, is not final. But now I think the best thing for you would be to exteriorize your interests—put these weeks of introspection behind you. Find something to do with yourself, and with your talents. Make a place for yourself in the society of people."

"My place has been erased," Mirni objected dully.

"Then make yourself another," she urged him. "That might be easier than you think. There's a gentleman waiting in the next office who might help you do it. Go in and talk to him."

The man in the next office arose from the chair in which he had been fidgeting when Mirni entered. He was a pink-skinned, vigorous oldster with a shock of white hair and a sunny expression.

"Mirni?" he asked, extending his hand. "I'm Wilbert K. Neff, chairman of the Institute of Governmental Studies, which you've probably never heard of. Get your jacket and we'll get out of this sick-room smell. Let's hustle!"

Hustle they did, at a pace that left Mirni excited and confused from being rushed into and out of a ground car and on to a noisy pub, where Neff led the way to a corner booth. A loud comic was holding forth on the 3V, and Mirni caught a snatch of a gag that ended with " . . . flipped by the flexible finger of the Fourth Foerst of Fingal!" The resulting roar of laughter was cut off as Neff flicked on the booth's sound curtain.

The man chuckled as he punched an order for drinks. "That Fingal affair is funnier than the 3V comics realize," he said. "I hear the squirmings in the President's conference chamber were something to behold when the council members sneered your 'joke' suggestion into oblivion and then 'recreated' it out of their own ingenuity."

"They're doing what I suggested?" asked Mirni.

"Indeed they are! But don't expect credit for it—not from them. What congratulations you get will have to come from such unimposing persons as myself."

"Your title *sounds* imposing," Mirni commented.

Neff sipped his drink and got down to business. "The Institute of Governmental Studies is not government-connected, nor confined to any one planet. It's a private operation supported by a dozen foundations. It had its beginnings way back in the pre-space era. Our work is described by its name. The IGS collects data and, on request, makes studies of whatever governmental problems anybody cares to drop in our lap. When a study is complete, we pass along the results and our recommendations. I want you to come to work with us."

"Oh. What would my job be?"

Neff shrugged. "Who knows? Maybe to boot me out and take over the whole show! I've learned a good bit about you, Mirni, and you look ideal for our line of activity. That training you got, manipulating your play-people, seems to have given you a rare insight into political ways and means. I'm offering you a chance to develop and use that insight."

"To solve problems, the way I tried to for Fingal?"

"Yes, and the way you did for Captain Devista on the *Strahorn*. You did better there, I would say, than on Fingal—probably because you had more pertinent information to use."

Mirni nodded guiltily. "I was sloppy in my thinking about Fingal, I guess. I did need more information, and maybe I was too anxious to please. I should have figured out something that wouldn't increase, even for a moment, the hostility between Fingal and Earth. And I shouldn't have left Fingal with a split-population problem in the making."

"But you got the immigrants moving away from Earth en masse again, for the first time this century," gloated Neff. "The unpleasant side effects are trivial compared to that! The people have to keep moving outward, or we'll wind up in a mess that nothing short of interstellar war can end. Conditions are already bad—everybody suspicious of everybody else."

"Yes, I know," Mirni agreed. "Is that the kind of thing IGS is concerned about?"

"Very much so!"

"Then I'll be glad to try to help," Mirni said.

*   *   *

IGS was small, with a staff of some four hundred persons, all of whom seemed to share Neff's inclination to hustle. Mirni hustled, too, although he soon realized the "hurry syndrome" was a response to a feeling of inadequacy. Relations between the human-settled planets were almost unanimously strained, and were worsening steadily. And the Institute, seemingly alone in its effort to find sound, unbiased resolutions to the vast complexity of discords, was indeed inadequate for the task.

So Mirni hustled. One of his first acts was to devise a means of getting IGS into action on urgent issues about which the Institute had not been consulted. This was his "review and insinuate" approach, in which IGS would inform some ex-client planet that a closed study had been reexamined in the light of recently-acquired data, and that additional recommendations were being dispatched. These recommendations would manage to touch upon—at least in passing—the urgent issue IGS wanted a hand in, thus "insinuating" the Institute into the role it desired.

And with the Institute's research facilities at his fingertips, Mirni soon proved his ability for finding useful means of settling troublesome disputes, some of which had lingered stubbornly for centuries. Also, he could phrase recommendations in ways that appealed to their recipients, and made their acceptance likely. This all but eliminated the most aggravating burden of any strictly advisory operation—that of convincing the clients they should heed the offered advice.

The task was endless, but with Mirni's arrival it

soon ceased being hopeless. The Institute was making headway, and so were interstellar relations.

"You're a marvel, Mirni, my boy!" Neff enthused one morning. "There's no stopping you! What's your objective—first President of the United Planets?"

Mirni laughed, as he often did since joining the Institute. "Nothing like that, boss. I'm all for a United Planets, but the IGS gives me a better means of getting work done than any government position could. But watch yourself, sir, because I do have my eye on your job—and maybe on your granddaughter!"

"You'll be welcome to both with my blessings, son," Neff grinned, putting his feet on his desk and relaxing. "Any time!"

His work and Patricia Neff had preoccupied Mirni so fully that the letter from the Psychomed Center caught him by surprise. It was a jolting reminder of an unhappy mental state that, while less than two months behind him, had seemed distant and almost forgotten. Unwillingly, he tore open the envelope and scanned the contents, picking out key passages:

"Our preliminary summary is fully supported by further study of the data . . .

"The obvious question is: Why did the 'teachers' choose to erase Mirni's training? Only one tenable answer presents itself, although we have searched diligently for an alternative explanation. To put it bluntly, Mirni flunked out of their 'school.' Presumably the nature of his studies was such that the non-graduates cannot be released with possibly dangerous partial knowledge. At any rate, we conclude that Mirni's performance was not satisfactory.

"This finding is in no way a criticism of Dalton

Mirni. We consider him a superior person in every respect. If he flunked out of the 'school,' then the human race itself flunked out. Needless to say, we trust that this finding will not be communicated to the public, as it would be harmfully and pointlessly depressing.

"The detrimental effect on morale . . . has perhaps manifested itself in one researcher, DV, on our staff (See File DV-437). Unable to accept the evidence of humanity's poor rating in the estimation of the 'teacher' race, DV denies that Mirni flunked out. To support this belief, he states that the only knowledge Mirni lost was theoretical, and that Mirni was permitted to keep skills derived from the theoretical training.

"As DV explains the case, Mirni can be compared to persons who are taught the 'theory of science' of some field to aid them in developing special skills which, once acquired, will function without further referral to theory. He cites artists and musicians as typical examples. When confronted by the fact that such persons remember their more academic preparatory work, he admits this is true, but argues that such retention is not essential to skilled performance.

"In Mirni's case, the theoretical training postulated by DV was in 'advanced political science,' from which working and retained skills were developed during the play-people 'lab course.'

"The essential failure of DV's hypothesis is that it offers no satisfactory reason for the removal of Mirni's memory. DV's only suggestion is that the teaching of 'advanced political science' is a role jealously guarded by the 'teachers,' that perhaps it is a role no 'student' could adequately fill. Thus, Mirni's theoretical

knowledge was taken from him so that he would
engage in no vain attempts to train others.

"This is far too conjectural, and too wishful, a line
of thought to be taken seriously."

All this was not easy to take. It stirred a dull echo of
that sick emptiness that had hit Mirni, months before,
when he had first discovered his loss. Still, he was able
to feel a wave of sympathy for the researcher DV, who
was finding the situation so difficult to accept.

But of course DV was wrong. He had to be. Mirni's
training—whatever it may have been—could hardly
have been to prepare him for something as simple as
this political work he was doing for IGS. Why, this
was just play-people stuff! Satisfying, useful work,
certainly, but work that could be done by anyone with
the understanding needed to get along with people
and to comprehend the mechanisms of society. There
was no—no *wisdom* required. Definitely not a twenty-
year accumulation of wisdom.

Still, DV could be right, Mirni mused. There was
no actual evidence to prove the man wrong. There
was a possibility that Mirni was now engaged in
precisely the kind of work for which the teachers
had prepared him. It was a tempting idea, anyway,
and—

And that was just the trouble with it, Mirni concluded with a feeling of impatience with himself. It
was tempting! He, more than DV or anyone else,
could fall very easily into the trap of wishful thinking on this subject. If he had learned any lesson well
among the play-people, it was not to cling to some
cherished notion despite abundant logic and evidence

that the notion was wrong. Such clinging was the road to irrationality.

Disappointments had to be accepted, and lived with. And for that matter, he had no time to waste grieving over a lost dream—not with the chore of establishing peace and relative tranquility among a hundred and sixty-two planets on his hands, plus a dinner date with Pat Neff.

Mirni stuffed the report in a bottom drawer and got to work.

THE OTHER WAY AROUND

FOR A SCORE OF DAYS the chronicler Raedulf had sought the magician, trailing him on uncertain information obtained from sulky peasants, importuning mendicants and cautious bandits encountered along the way.

The going was often difficult. The magician followed the weedy Roman roads only when they seemed to suit his odd fancy. Nor did he confine his course to the wandering byways and riding paths.

It was as if, thought Raedulf, the magician were impatient with the routes of ordinary men, pushing his way instead through whatever bog and bramble stood between him and his destination.

Why, then, was the course he took so far from straight?

Raedulf was minded of some mighty knight bereft

of his senses by too many blows on the head in too many jousts, mounting his charger and clattering hither and yon while convinced he was riding straight into the face of the foe.

"Yea, I encountered an ancient such as you detail," said a young friar met on the old road along the River Kennet. "We talked somewhat, but I fear he will find meager favor in the eyes of our Redeemer. There was no charity in the man."

Raedulf took the hint and dropped two coppers in the young man's hand. "Did he say whither he journeyed?"

"No, gracious sir, nor whence he came. He was hard of speech and arm, and I did not deem it prudent to question him closely. He seemed of a sullen humor."

Raedulf nodded. All reports indicated the magician was indeed a man of temper. "Did he say aught to you of his errand?"

"Nothing. He tested my knowledge on various matters, sneering at my replies, then whirled and strode away. He muttered foully at what he called my ignorance of the Old Stones."

"I know little of the Old Stones, myself," said Raedulf, "except that they stand somewhere in this region of Briton."

"They form a round figure, and are ten leagues south and west from here. That was all I could respond to the ancient's test."

Raedulf grew alert. "He wished to know where the Old Stones stand, then?"

"Why . . . I think not. Seemingly he knew, and was but trying my knowledge." The friar hesitated with puckered face. "Think you the ancient scamp made a pretense of trying me, to hide his own ignorance?"

Raedulf replied, "The ancient scamp seems capable of that—or of most anything."

The friar uttered an unchristian oath. "I am shamed to have been awed! A fraud!"

"It is perhaps well you were," said Raedulf. "This ancient may travel like a bull both crazed and lost, but like the bull he has horns with which to gore."

After proper farewells, Raedulf turned his mare and rode westward along the road, watchful for a good way trending more to the south. By and by he found a side road that proved well-frequented, with a fair scattering of villages and farm stockades along the way.

Through the afternoon he rode at a comfortable pace, having no need for hurry if the magician were indeed making for the Old Stones. The magician traveled afoot and would easily be outpaced to the destination by Raedulf's mare.

The chronicler found a comfortable inn for the night, and there obtained clearer information on the location of the Old Stones and how they might best be reached. He was also warned that the Stones were in outlaw-infested country, to which he nodded solemnly, thinking of how many times he had received similar warnings during this quest, and of how he had yet to meet a brigand who cared to challenge a man who was mounted and wearing a sword.

If he rode in fear of any man, Raedulf mused, that man might best be the very one he was seeking.

Late the following afternoon he reached the Old Stones. They rose above the thick brush of the deserted heath like some primitive colonnade. Raedulf stared at them in wonder. Here was surely a thing that should be better chronicled. Who had raised these great stone slabs on end along a circling line, and had spanned many of their tops with massive lintels?

Certainly they were not the work of the Romans. They had not the style of Roman structures. And they appeared far too old.

Allowing his mare to stroll along what paths she could find through the brush, Raedulf explored the place at length, but found nothing enlightening. Here and there were ashes of campfires, some quite fresh, left by outlaws or outcasts or whoever, but nothing to indicate what the Stones might have once been.

And no sign of the magician. The old man would not reach the place until the morrow, he guessed.

With that thought, he turned his mount back the way he had come, toward the stockade of a peasant-squire he had passed half a league to the north.

He met the magician on the way.

Raedulf had never seen him before, but descriptions made his identity certain. He was a huge man, a head taller than even King Lort, with a heavy beard of gray and frowning brown eyes. Strapped to his shoulders was a backpack of peculiar design.

The magician halted in the middle of the path, and Raedulf stopped his mare.

"Hail, thou of renowned wisdom!" he called out.

The magician's right hand stole out of sight under his cloak. "Who the hell are you?" he growled.

Taken aback by the strangeness and vehemence of the magician's words, he replied, "Raedulf of Clerwint, good sire, a chronicler in the service of God and His Majesty, Lort."

"Huh! A damned newspaper reporter! Of a sort, anyway. You know who I am?"

"Thou art he who is called Merlin," replied Raedulf, wondering if it would be safe as well as courteous to dismount.

The magician said, "I'm Wilmoth T. Aberlea of Maryland, and if you hayseeds make 'Merlin' out of that, what the hell's the difference to me?" He paused. "Is this a chance meeting, what's-your-name, or were you laying for me?"

"Raedulf of Clerwint," the chronicler supplied, feeling miffed. "I confess to having sought you out, good magicker."

"Okay, Roddy," the magician said brusquely, "let's hear what you want. I'm a busy man."

"In behalf of my liege, sire, I would have of you circumstantial knowledge of the lamented King Arthur."

Merlin stared at him, then chuckled. Raedulf took heart from this display of good humor and dismounted.

"This Lort of yours . . . isn't he the bully boy over in the Leicester neighborhood? What's his interest in Arthur?"

"There is a likeness in the names, Lort and Arthur," Raedulf explained. "My lord wishes to know if there is a tie of blood; if, indeed, he might be heir to the kingdom of Camelot. And if so, he would have me enquire the whereabouts of that kingdom."

The magician bellowed a gust of laughter, then soured abruptly. "Tell him no," he grunted. "Now pull your pony aside so I can get by, boy."

Raedulf began moving his mare slowly out of the way, hesitant to let the magician move on but fearful of disobeying. "Frankly, renowned magicker," he entreated, "that is not the answer my liege wishes to hear."

"Nuts to your puny liege!" grumbled Merlin as he stomped forward. Raedulf quickly yanked the mare aside as the magician went past, and stood looking helplessly after him.

But a few steps later the magician halted and turned, frowning unhappily. "This Lort of yours . . . he doesn't know his own genealogy?"

"Not precisely, sire," Raedulf replied. "Like the great Arthur himself, my king's origins are confused. Since the departure of the Roman legions, our land has been rife with disorder and civil strife to a degree that families are uprooted and—"

"Okay," snorted Merlin, "I get the picture. What the hell, your boy Lort might even *be* Arthur on some other timeline. Look, tell him what he wants to hear. Tell him he's the third son of Arthur's only child, a daughter named . . . named Merlinette, after me. Say his elder brother was slain in battle and the other has taken Church vows. So that makes him heir. As for Camelot . . ." The magician shrugged. "Tell him it sank, that it was lost in The Wash."

Raedulf bowed stiffly "I extend His Majesty's thanks, gracious magicker."

Merlin was grinning. "You don't believe a word I said, do you?"

"I have obeyed my king's command," retorted Raedulf, "in seeking out and questioning he whose knowledge of Arthur is fullest and most direct of all men still alive. It remains for me to report accurately your words on the subject."

Merlin chuckled. "Spoken like a true newspaperman!" He applauded. "You ought to go far, although you don't get a mention in any history book I ever read. You know how to lie honestly, and that's a big step toward civilization as I knew it. Maybe that's what I should have encouraged around here, instead of chattering about Arthur and Company. But I suppose it wouldn't have led to a convergence at this early date, and wouldn't have caught on."

The magician fell silent, seemingly lost in speculations beyond Raedulf's ken. Indeed, nearly all the magician had said was mystifying to the chronicler, and rankling as well. There was the insulting suggestion that the accurate recounting of the words of an authority was not necessarily honest. What else was a faithful chronicler to do? And the strange comment that Arthur might be Lort in some other . . . other here-and-now? How could Lort be his own grandfather? But, no, that was Merlin's fabrication . . .

It was much too confusing. To change the subject in his own mind, Raedulf asked, "Does the good magicker seek the Old Stones?"

Merlin frowned down at him. "I *go* to the Old Stones," he corrected. "I seek nothing, because I know the location of all things."

Raedulf gathered his courage and said sharply, "I believe the good magicker shares my ability to lie honestly."

Merlin blinked, then chortled in surprised delight. "Aha! Hoisted by me own petard! You're a clever lad, Roddy. Okay, I know Stonehenge is somewhere on

Salisbury Plain, but how the hell to find it in all this damned brush is something else."

"Five furlongs down this path," said Raedulf boredly, "you will be in sight of the top of the Stones."

Merlin studied him in amusement, then said, "I have a recently seized fowl in my sack, along with other foodstuffs fit for a magician. Come along to the rocks and dine with me, lad. Else I might wind up talking to myself."

"I'm honored, sire," said Raedulf, bowing. "Perchance you would accept the use of my mount, to rest your limbs after so long a journey."

Merlin snorted. "Not on your life! You have to grow up with those stupid animals to understand them. Besides, I'm a jogger from way back. Keeps me in shape."

So Raedulf led his mare and walked at the magician's side. He was less awed now, having bested Merlin in one verbal exchange. Also, he found a touch of comic absurdity in someone exercising (if he had understood correctly), to stay in good walking form . . . the way knights exercised with lance and sword.

"The Old Stones have not a Romish look," he offered.

"They're not Roman," said Merlin. "I'm going to study them, find out what they really are."

"Mayhap I can be of some assistance in this undertaking," Raedulf hinted.

The magician glanced at the younger man. "Think you might pick up some of my magic, boy?"

"You might choose to reward me in that manner, sire. Or perhaps with more of the history of Arthur the King."

Merlin spat a word that was strange to Raedulf, but that sounded obscene nonetheless. "I've shot all the Arthurian bull I intend to," he snapped.

The remark had puzzling implications. But they made it clear the magician did not want to tell more of the great king. "Then perhaps of your own history, good magicker."

"My history you wouldn't believe. Or be a fool if you did. We magicians lead strange lives."

Annoyed at the patronizing tone, Raedulf replied tartly, "You may try me, sire."

"Okay, boy. How about this for a starter: I come from thirteen hundred years in the future."

Raedulf nodded thoughtfully, although he would have guessed that, possessor of the wisdom of the ancients, Merlin had come from the distant past. "Your time must be one of inspired magicianship," he flattered.

Merlin grunted in disdain. "Mediocre. I was the greatest of the lot. Got damned little credit for it, of course. A prophet without honor in my own time," he muttered bitterly. "Not that I gave a damn. I was never one of those security-blanket organization scientists who can't function without coddling and praise. And the lousy Swedes know where they can shove their stupid Nobel Prize, for all I care."

"You are highly honored here, good sire," placated Raedulf, wondering what the old man was raving about.

"Oh, sure! But not understood," snapped Merlin. "A magician with some impressive tricks, but not a brilliant physicist whose discoveries surpassed those of Einstein! Those dolts called me 'simplistic'!"

"Which dolts, good sire?" Raedulf inquired.

"My damned so-called colleagues! Those biddy-brained idiots who sat in judgment on my work, those referees who insulted my discoveries and kept them from being published!

"That's the way they buried my theory of subatomic structure, in which I demonstrated that there is only one kind of particle, the neutron. All the other kinds that have multiplied like rabbits in the minds of bought scientists are merely reactions to neutron configurations of flows and counterflows of energy.

"You want to know what the referee said about that? He said I chose to ignore numerous phenomena that failed to fit my scheme. A damned lie! But those party-lining journal jacklegs believed him.

"After that disaster, I didn't even *try* to publish my finding of the equivalence of gravitation and nuclear binding force. What a laugh some idiot would have had with that one! Everybody *knows* the two forces can't be the same. Gravity's the weaker by too many orders of magnitude to make a relationship thinkable. So nobody but a trouble-maker like me would see a parallel between the neutron stars, in which gravity is so concentrated as to be almost totally self-confining, and the atomic nucleus where binding force is similarly concentrated. Oh, no, I wasn't about to announce that one! I was enough of a joke or a fraud without that hanging over my reputation. Instead, I carried on alone, and brought a consideration of time into the light thrown by my earlier discoveries. And I learned how to time-travel."

He paused, slamming fist into palm.

"That was exactly what I needed. I was a man

ahead of my own time, trying to mingle with people
far too stupid and backward to appreciate my work
or myself. The future was where I belonged, so . . ."

Merlin broke off his angry recital in midsentence,
glowering at the path ahead. "How much farther till
we see the stones, boy?" he demanded.

"Around yon turning of the path."

"Good. I'm getting hungry. Keep an eye out for
firewood."

"Very well, good sire." After a hesitation, Raedulf
asked timidly, "But, sire, if you sought the future, how
is it that you journeyed into the past?"

Merlin snorted. He strode on in silence, and
Raedulf concluded he had asked about a matter that
vexed the magician sorely. He was casting about for
a graceful change of subject when his companion
began muttering, "Even I fell in the intellectual
trap. Even I."

He looked at the chronicler and spoke more audibly.
"We believe what our society believes, boy, whether
we mean to or not. We're tricked, because there are
so damned many beliefs and they come at us in so
many shapes and disguises. You believe I'm a great
magician, but in my own time no intelligent young
man would accept that. He would look for the mirrors,
or the sleight-of-hand. Or the scientific explanation.
When I tell you I come from the future, you accept
that as powerful magic and ask no explanations. But a
young man of my era would say, 'Impossible!' Or he
might be sharp enough to ask, 'How does it work?'
Both reactions would be based on accepted assumptions of the times. They would be proper."

Raedulf nodded slowly. "Even within one time, that

is true. The deeds of the Romans oft were senseless to my greatfathers."

"Right!" approved Merlin. "Now, you see that any society's set of beliefs will contain falsehoods, beliefs that contradict the natural scheme of things."

This was a difficult point. In accepting it, Raedulf saw that he would be admitting that his own deepest convictions could be in error . . . along with the rulings of his king and the teachings of the Church. He was not prepared for that. But he could pretend in order to stay on pleasant terms with the magician. "It would seem that each group of beliefs would contain its share of truth and its share of falsity."

"Correct!" said Merlin. "And the discerning man cannot test every belief of his society. Most are drilled in when he's too young. And, there are so damned many of them one lifetime isn't long enough to test them all.

"So I accepted a notion about the structure of time that was inaccurate, and as a result I wound up here in the past instead of the future."

Raedulf stared at him. All that lecturing about beliefs merely to justify an error in the magician's time-journeying spell! Surely, Merlin must make few mistakes, to be so perturbed by just one!

"The error must have been profoundly subtle," Raedulf said.

"No, not really; I can explain it to you. If you went back to the time of your father's youth and killed him before he bedded your mother, then you could never have been born and thus could not have killed him, could you?"

"Not unless my mother . . . But then he would

not have been my . . . No." Befuddled, he shook his head.

"What would happen?" asked Merlin.

"A pretty riddle," said Raedulf, pausing to jerk some dry brush from the ground for the campfire. "I would think on it."

"I'm not bandying riddles. My question was rhetorical."

"Your pardon, sire," Raedulf responded. "Then I would say, without thinking on it, that upon slaying my father I wouldst must vanish."

"But how could you have existed *until* then?" persisted the magician. "How do you explain this paradox within the laws of nature?"

To cover his hesitation Raedulf began breaking up the brush in his hands as he walked along. He had at least a vague notion of what the magician meant by "laws of nature." This brush, for instance, was a natural thing with its slender trunk and still thinner branches, which he was snapping off to make a compact bundle under his arm. Also, he recalled the magician's earlier mention of "timelines."

"Could it be," he asked, "that time is shaped like a tree? Then if I returned to slay my father, my deed would cause a new branch to sprout at that point—a branch on which I slew my father and vanished."

The magician gasped. *"Remarkable!* You have duplicated precisely the erroneous belief of my own era; that timelines diverge into the future like the branches of a tree. You are a man of wit, Rodney."

Pleased by the praise but irked at being misnamed, Raedulf said, "Then nature is deceptive in this matter?"

"Only to the extent we deceive ourselves," growled Merlin. "My excuse for being taken in is that I acted in haste. I was too damned eager to get into the future and find an advanced, compatible culture, perhaps even a woman who would measure up to my standards . . . I being a younger man then than now. But here we are. Stonehenge."

"Yes, good sire." Raedulf pointed. "Yon is a partially fallen lintel stone under which others have sheltered before us. Mayhap you will find it a suitable nook."

Merlin walked over to the stone and gave it a hard push. But it was firmly wedged in place against one of the uprights, and was some eight feet above the ground at its higher end. "It'll do," he said. "Tie your pony and hunt some more wood."

Raedulf obeyed, and when he returned the magician had a fire going. "Who's been camping here, Rodney?"

"Outlaws, or so the people hereabouts say."

Merlin snorted. "They better not bother me!"

"I thought on that while gathering wood, sire," replied the chronicler. "The bandits are a cowardly lot, but when we are in our blankets at night they might find us easy prey. Also, this plain abounds in concealment for those of evil intent. I would favor precautions, sire."

"Yeah? Such as what?"

Raedulf lifted his hands in a gesture of ignorance. "I know not what magical protections you have, sire. I merely suggest it would be well to have those protections in readiness."

"Let me tell you something, boy," said the magician. "There's no magic like an alert watchman. Maybe I'll rig up something, but we're going to take turns sleeping. And you'd better not doze on watch, understand?"

"Of course, sire," replied Raedulf grumpily.

But he soon forgot the insult as he watched Merlin remove the limp form of a fat goose from his pack, plus a number of bewitched utensils of light gleaming metal. The magician put him to work plucking the goose while he busied himself over the fire, often muttering what the chronicler took to be incantations.

The goose was soon broiling on a spit, with frequent bastings of a spicy liquid the magician had concocted. Raedulf watched in awe, his mouth watering from the savory odors of the bird and from a small stewpot, as the magician worked his wonders.

The supper was eaten shortly after nightfall by the light of the dwindling fire.

Raedulf picked the last bone clean and sighed contentedly. "Were the victuals so wondrous in Arthur's Court, noble magicker?" he asked

Merlin chuckled and sucked his teeth. "Far better than this, lad. The banquets of the Table Round, honoring some worthy knight for valor on a perilous quest, were marvels beyond delight that all but the angels might envy and—" He broke off the recital with an impatient grunt. "Never mind that nonsense!"

Raedulf realized belatedly that he had blundered in bringing up the subject of Arthur. The old magician was obviously bitter about the fall of the great King and the sundering of the Table Round. It was not a matter to remind the magician of.

"I have thought on the shape of time," the chronicler said quickly, "and must confess my thinking comes to naught."

"Small wonder," said Merlin. "You haven't the background to deal with it. You never heard of the expanding physical universe, and wouldn't see the absurdity of the idea that time, too, was expanding through the multiplication of divergent timelines.

"To compensate for the physical expansion of the universe, timelines have to *converge*. One by one they have to be consolidated into fewer and fewer tracks. That's what I should have recognized at the beginning." The magician stared moodily at the embers of the fire.

"That shaping," hazarded Raedulf. "It caused you to journey opposite to your desired course."

Merlin nodded. "I moved toward divergence, which is the only direction one can shift in time. A time-traveler can get himself out on a limb, but can't go from limb to trunk. That would compromise all the consolidations that took place during the period covered by his shift. That much I knew, but what I didn't know, didn't bother to realize, was that time branches downward, into the past, not upward into the future. Which makes me an idiot, like everybody else."

"Belittle yourself not, noble sire," Raedulf soothed. "You are renowned above all mortals for wisdom and power, and are spoken of in kingly councils with awe and trembling."

After a pause Merlin said, "I have made my mark on this timeline, at that."

"Indeed you have, sire. However, I confess myself in darkness concerning these time-limbs bending into the past. If I entered the time of my father's youth and slayed him . . ."

"You wouldn't," said the magician. "Converging

timelines solve that paradox by simply not allowing it to happen. If you went into the past, you'd likely find yourself on a limb where your father didn't even exist. Probably you would wind up marrying someone much like your mother and having a son who, when the juncture of your limb and a major branch came, would meld into the Rodneys from other limbs and continue as yourself. So, instead of creating a divergence, you would help bring about a convergence."

"But if I refused to wed the woman with my mother's likeness . . ." Raedulf began.

"You couldn't refuse, if that were the role you were destined to play in bringing the convergence. It wouldn't occur to you to refuse. No more than it occurred to me to . . . well, never mind that. I think you get the picture. Any point on any timeline can lead to only one future, but is led to by innumerable pasts, and a jump can be made only to a past where the jumper will fit in. That's orderly nature for you, boy."

The magician rose yawning. "I'm hitting the sack. Take the first watch and wake me around midnight, Rodney."

"Very well, sire."

The magician vanished under the lintel stone and was soon snoring softly.

Raedulf found his mind whirling with the many strange thoughts thrust upon him by the words of Merlin. The foolish question he had asked on behalf of King Lort—to which he had received a false and silly answer—seemed the least important part of his exchanges with the magician.

But he had learned much worthy of detailed

chronicling about the magician himself, and about the magical cookery from which delightful flavors still lingered in his mouth.

Why, then, he wondered glumly, did the thought of chronicling these events leave him feeling uninspired? Thirteen hundred years in the future, the name Raedulf would be forgotten, and his chronicles unheard of. Why should he care for that? he demanded in self-annoyance. Before this day, he had never given a thought to the durability of his scribings. Why should ambition be destroyed by knowing his work would not survive some thirty mortal lifetimes?

He studied moodily on this, considering such possibilities as Merlin being a minion of Satan—despite his long service to the most Christian of all kings—who had purposely made the discouraging remark to tempt Raedulf away from his God-prescribed duties. Yet the remark had seemed unpremeditated, words carelessly dropped by an abrupt man.

Raedulf sighed and turned to look at the Great Bear in the northern sky, and estimate how much turning of the Bear would mark the end of his watch.

Perhaps, he mused, knowledge of the future was in all cases evil. Were not seers generally regarded with suspicion and assumed to be of dubious grace? Thus the knowledge the magician had thrust upon him in that one remark was best forgotten—pushed out of his mind.

So Raedulf murmured all the prayers he knew, and shortly felt less depressed.

But still he could not view his future with enthusiasm.

*   *   *

The night passed without incident, except for a few furtive sounds of movement that did not approach the camp and could have been made by straying animals rather than by men.

In the morning Merlin began his study of the Old Stones. He stomped about with great energy, uprooting brush that stood in his way, measuring stones and distances with a magical metal ribbon that lurked in a flat round box except when he drew it forth. He drove stakes, strung lines of yarn hither and yon, took sightings, and scribbled unreadable notations.

Raedulf helped to the extent his ignorance permitted.

"If the Old Stones stand in your future, good sire," he asked once, "could you not have studied them then?"

"I wasn't interested then," Merlin replied distractedly. "And not all the stones are still up in the Twentieth Century. Many will be removed, including the one we slept under. There won't be enough left to put the purpose of the structure beyond dispute."

"Could it be . . ." Raedulf began, and then caught himself. He had nearly brought up the subject of Arthur again, by suggesting the Stones were the underpinnings of a vast Table Round, left from some distant eon when giants strode the earth.

"It's thought to be a religious shrine," Merlin said, sounding cross. "With astronomical implications. Used for a seasonal celebration. Look, can't you work without asking questions?"

"My apologies, sire."

Thereafter the chronicler spoke less, but the magician grew more irritable as the morning advanced.

Finally he turned and snapped, "Look, boy, I work best alone! Always have. If you want to be useful, get on your mare and go get some groceries. See if that squire-peasant up the road will sell you cheese, meat, eggs of recent vintage, wine, cabbages, bread and whatever. Do that and I'll teach you some decent cookery."

"Most willingly, sire," beamed Raedulf, and he hurried to obey. After all, he was sure the magic of the Old Stones would be ever beyond the scope of a mere chronicler, but the magic of the cookpot might be a marvel he could master!

He outdid himself to be a quick student of Merlin's lessons. Thanks to his professionally trained memory, Raedulf could murmur to himself just once a formula given by the magician, and have it firmly fixed in his mind.

Merlin was pleased with him, and kept him busy at the campsite day after day, preparing dishes that took hours in the making. Meanwhile, the magician continued his investigation of the Old Stones.

The brigands attacked on the third night, during the magician's watch. Raedulf was startled awake by a sharp thunderclap of sound so powerful as to leave his ears dazed. He leaped up, tripping on his blanket while groping in the dark for his sword.

"*Avaunt, you beggars!*" he heard Merlin shout above the surprised yelps and brush-threshings of the attackers, and the alarmed whinny of the mare.

"Where are they?" he gasped when he reached the magician's side.

"In disorderly retreat." The magician chuckled in

evident satisfaction. "I winged one of 'em. They won't be back—more likely they'll scram out of this region completely."

"That thunderclap nigh made me do the same," complained Raedulf. "And my mare as well." He hurried over to the animal and soothed her with strokings and soft words.

"That was my magic wand you heard." Merlin laughed. "My thunderwand. My faithful rust-proof roscoe! I'd better show you how it works tomorrow, boy, in case another band shows up during your watch some night."

"Whatever you think wise, sire," Raedulf agreed reluctantly. Using the thunderwand had no appeal for him. But he listened carefully next morning as the magician explained the wand's functioning. Its proper name, he learned, was "Forty-five Automatic." He handled it as well, but rather gingerly, not daring to touch the portions called "safety" and "trigger."

"Not many rounds left for it," Merlin remarked with regret. "When they're gone I'll bury it, I suppose."

Raedulf wondered if such fearsome magic was often needed in Arthur's Court, protected as it had been by the swords of many valiant knights. But he restrained himself from asking.

They were not disturbed again during the fortnight they remained among the Old Stones. Raedulf surmised that the marauders of that one frightful night had warned others of their kind that demons in human guise lurked amid the Stones.

Then one afternoon Merlin returned to the cookfire only an hour after the midday meal. He sat down and regarded the chronicler thoughtfully.

"I'm through here, Raedulf," he said gruffly, surprising the younger man by, for once, getting his name right. "I'll be moving on, and you'd best be getting back to Lort with that cock-and-bull story, and to your chronicling."

"Very well, sire, but I have little lust for either."

"Ah? Why not?"

"On our meeting, sire, you remarked that my chronicles are not known in your time of the future. Though I had never thought me to make a lasting impress, I am yet disheartened that my scribings are fated to perish."

"Humpf! I oughtn't to have said that," Merlin grimaced. "Look, boy, maybe your work does survive in a way. All this Arthurian guff I've been spouting gets preserved some way. Maybe your work lasts long enough to get it established in oral tradition."

"Perhaps," said the glum chronicler. "But the word-of-mouth of the Great King and the Round Table is already widespread. Methinks it will endure without my help."

"Yeah, I suppose so," mused Merlin.

"Would that I, like thee, had my lasting impress assured," Raedulf mourned. "Thou art as famed as Arthur himself."

The magician nodded. "And since I *am* Arthur, so to speak—on this timeline at any rate . . ."

"Thou art Arthur?" exclaimed Raedulf.

"In a sense. You see, lad, there was no Arthur on this line. I didn't know that at first. When I learned what century I was in and the people shortened Maryland to Merlin, I naturally assumed I was the historical Merlin of the Arthurian legend. I began trying to find Camelot, and amazing the hayseeds with tales about a great king they'd never heard of. The yokels believed me and repeated my tales as gospel. So, for all historical purposes, this timeline now has an Arthur, and it can converge into other lines in which he really existed."

Raedulf was staring at him in a state of shock.

"Don't take it so hard, boy," the magician snorted. "I'm not saying Arthur wasn't real. He just wasn't on this Line. On other lines . . . well, who's to say?"

After a silence, Raedulf moaned, "I can never bring myself to chronicle this, or even speak of it."

"If you could, I probably couldn't have told you. Can't have the legend doubted at its very beginning." Merlin studied him closely. "Look, boy, you just said you didn't want to chronicle anymore, anyhow. So what the hell. Give it up. Go into some other line of work."

"My training . . ."

"Your training makes you the best damned cook in the world today, myself excluded. Open a restaurant— an inn."

Raedulf blinked. "Could I, perhaps make a more lasting impress in that manner?"

"Not around here, you couldn't!" Merlin chortled. "The cookery on this island is an atrocity through all convergences to come. But I'll tell you what: go over to the Continent. Become a Frenchman. You'll need to do that anyway, to get half the spices I told you about. Do your fancy cookery over there and your impress will last quite a while, believe me!"

After a moment, Raedulf nodded. "I will heed your advice, sire."

"Fine! Now, I must be going."

"May I ask whither?"

"Into the past," said Merlin. "Where else? I know what Stonehenge is, but I still don't know who built it. I'll have to find out by going back and meeting the builders in person."

"And what is the purpose of the Stones, sire?"

"They're the remains of a perpetual clock-calendar, a time-telling device. When Stonehenge was in its complete form, it could tell one the exact date, year, and century. When I arrived in this time, if I had been unable to verify that I had, indeed, leaped thirteen centuries, then a structure such as this once was could provide me that knowledge."

"It must have been the work of magicians of vast wisdom!" said the awed Raedulf.

"My thought exactly. And there are legends of extremely advanced prehistoric civilizations. As I can't seek in the future for the high cultural climate in which I properly belong, I'll look for it in the distant past. So long, boy!"

Merlin had gathered most of his equipage as he talked and stuffed it in his pack. Now, before the mystified Raedulf could speak, he vanished into empty air, pack and all.

Raedulf did not leave the Great Stones immediately. Instead he wandered the paths opened by Merlin, who had apparently tramped all over the place. Here, untold centuries ago, he mused, magicians perhaps the equal of Merlin himself had labored long to raise the magnificent timepiece of which the Old Stones were the ruined remains.

It would, he decided, have been more practical to keep track of dates by the usual process of keeping records. One chronicler of no great talent could have done that. But—perhaps the ancient magicians had reasons beyond his ken.

He intended to prepare food for the road before starting his journey south to the coast, and he needed firewood for that. He wandered toward some dead brush he remembered seeing near the center of the ring of Stones, brush he had previously left untouched because a slender stump of broken stone had blocked his way.

Now that Merlin was gone he no longer needed to concern himself about leaving the stone undisturbed. He pushed hard against it and it tumbled over, out of his way.

On the ground where it had stood was a rust-crusted object. He picked it up and examined it with wide eyes. Beyond doubt, it was Merlin's thunderwand. The magician had said he would bury it when it had no more vigor.

Instead, he had placed it under the stone. And he had done so at a time so distant that the rust-proofing spell had worn off.

What could have been the occasion? Raedulf couldn't be sure, but suddenly he felt that he could make a good guess.

After all, who more than Merlin himself would need a timepiece that read the centuries? And particularly so if he found himself among untutored primitives who knew nothing of tallying days and years, and who could only slave with their strong backs to serve the great magician who appeared among them.

He guessed that Merlin would indeed make them slave. With no further hope of finding the wonderful magic land for which he longed, he would have little to do but see that the Old Stones were put in their proper place.

He would have to, because it was necessary for convergence.

THE RELUCTANT WEAPON

❧

WHEN THE ZOZ HORDE passed destructively through this sector of the Galaxy, approximately a billion years ago, they suffered a minor loss. One of their weapons, Sentient Killer No.VT672, had an unexplained malfunction and was left behind to be repaired by the slave technicians who followed the Horde. However, the Zoz were met and annihilated by the Ghesh Empire, after which the masterless slaves dispersed to their home planets. The weapon, unrepaired, was left forgotten in the solar system it had failed to destroy.

Tresqu the Wisest, Ruler of Hova, Lord of the Universe, was being entertained by a troupe of Goefd dancers when his Lord of War, Wert, bounded into the Audience Hall. In his hurry to reach Tresqu's throne,

Wert slipped on the nearly frictionless floor and skidded through the formation of dancers, sending the slender Goefden sprawling in all directions. He slid to a halt by the Pleading Mat, onto which he crawled and groveled, awaiting permission to speak.

"I believe three of the dancers received broken legs," Tresqu observed calmly. "They are rather delicate creatures and not at all clumsy." He dipped the tip of his tail into an urn of chilled perfume and gently dabbed it about his nostril. Speaking pleasantly, with long pauses between sentences, he kept his friendly gaze on the groveling Wert. "Oft I meditate on the clumsiness of our race in comparison to many others who are our graceful servants. Why, I wonder, cannot the rulers be graceful? Some of us are very clumsy indeed—too clumsy to live."

A tremor passed through Wert's stocky body.

"Possibly my Lord of War has news of sufficient import to excuse his ungainly haste. But I sincerely doubt it. I fear I must soon appoint a successor to him. Undoubtedly he has news of some sort. Blurt, Wert!"

"Your Majestic Wisdom," whined Wert, "my message is of utmost importance! The natives of Sol III have captured one of our decontaminator ships and learned its secrets!"

"Sol III?"

"Yes, Your Wisdom. The planet called Terra."

"Terra? You must realize, lordling, that I cannot occupy myself with remembering trivialities about individual worlds."

"Yes, Your Wisdom. We have a base, which is commanded by—that is, we *had* a base commanded—"

"Enough!" snapped Tresqu. "You start your tale from nowhere and wander whence and hence." He raised his voice and called to one of his retainers. "Fool! Come forward!"

An abnormally slender Hovan arose from a platform off to Tresqu's left and skipped nimbly forward to stand insolently over the Lord of War, who was still prone on the Pleading Mat.

"Recite for me," said Tresqu, "the contents of my gazetteer on the planet Sol III. Listen well, Wert. You may even yet live long enough to profit by my Fool's style of declamation. Study it well. Also, you may raise your eyes sufficiently to observe the grace of his movements. Proceed, sprite."

"Sol III," began the Fool. "An H9 planet. Sol is in the Sirian Colony Sector, coordinates GL 15-44-17-5, GR 12^7 plus 9, D 14. Terra's life is normal animal-vegetable, with one intelligent species of hovoids called Humans. Due to the unpleasantly high oxygen content of the atmosphere, Terra has not been colonized, but has been placed under the control of the Science Ministry for the purpose of long-range psychological experiments." The Fool picked up Wert's tail and twisted it hard but absently as he talked. The Lord of War twitched painfully. "Many informative reports on the results of these experiments have been released by the ministry during the past seven thousand years, dealing mainly with the Humans. The Science Ministry has declared Terra out of bounds—*Positively no visitors*."

With a single flow of motion, the Fool gave Wert's tail a final twist, leaped over his body, and bowed deeply to Tresqu.

"Beautifully done, Fool," applauded the Ruler of Hova. "Your mother claims me as your father, and there are times I am inclined to believe her. How would you like to be my Lord of War, Fool?"

"Verily, my good master," said the Fool, "I hope you consider me a Fool by title only."

"Well said, Fool. You are spared. Go seek your pleasures." With another bow, the Fool backed away.

"Stand up, Wert," said Tresqu, "and tell me about this captured decontamination ship."

The Lord of War arose and managed to report with some smoothness. "Two years ago, the Science Ministry turned Terra over to my command, saying their long series of experiments was concluded. They recommended complete decontamination of the planet, since the Humans were developing technologies which could eventually threaten us. I dispatched a ship for that purpose immediately, but it failed to return. Also, reports from our base on Terra's satellite Luna ceased soon thereafter. A scouting expedition was sent. It has just reported the Luna base destroyed completely, and the decontaminator ship crashed and stripped of all important devices in one of the Terran deserts. By studying these removed devices, the Humans have undoubtedly developed protections against them. I humbly submit, Your Majestic Wisdom, that these events have endangered the safety of your glorious empire, and that drastic steps against the Humans should be taken immediately. Also, Good Lord of All, I submit that the Science Ministry, not the War Ministry, is at fault in this affair. They obviously let their experiments get out of control before calling us. Undoubtedly they would like to shift the full blame onto my shoulders."

Tresqu continued his pleasant demeanor. "There may be some truth in what you say, Wert. You over-estimate the danger in this matter, I perceive. After all, what is one backward planet against the forces of my empire containing thirty-seven well-armed worlds? The Humans will be destroyed, even if they have the secrets of a decontaminator ship. As for the blame, which I admit is deplorable, the Lord of Science will be called to the Mat to make his excuses. Now, assuming you remain Lord of War, what action do you plan to take against the Humans?"

"Your Gracious Wisdom," faltered Wert, "I suggest we use the—the Weapon. You see, our forces are not fully mobilized at present for immediate action—"

"Full mobilization isn't necessary or even desirable," Tresqu interrupted with some impatience. "One task force can do the job. Ah! I see by your expression that you do not have even one task force in readiness."

"Your Gracious Wisdom," begged Wert, "you ordered a full holiday this month to celebrate the twenty-fourth anniversary of your magnificent reign, and—"

"Enough, Wert! Your tongue is as clumsy as your body." Tresqu nibbled thoughtfully at the tip of his tail. "We will use the Weapon," he decided. "In order to allow my court to continue their holiday, I'll assume direct command in this." He rose from his throne. "Musicians, summon my guards. I go to visit the Weapon. Come, Wert; come also, Fool. You will accompany me."

Shortly thereafter, Tresqu and his entourage boarded the royal cruiser and roared away from the City of Wisdom. The ship flew halfway around the planet and came to rest in a peaceful purple valley where insects shrilled contentedly and a small stream rippled. Tresqu climbed out onto the violet turf, his followers coming after him.

"Mighty Weapon of Zoz," he called, "I, Tresqu, seek your presence!"

"Oh, no!" groaned a slightly mechanical voice that seemed to come from no particular direction. "Will there never be peace, never a tranquil moment to soothe my spirit and erase the bloody stains of destruction recorded on my past?"

"That voice! It carries me away!" breathed the Fool. "Such a tragic tale of tormented strength is implicit in its very tone that I think I shall swoon!" But he wrapped his tail around the trunk of a nearby sapling for support and managed to retain consciousness.

"Me, too!" Wert chimed in with suspicious haste. "I'm quite moved!"

"Try not to counterfeit a soul you do not possess." Tresqu glowered at Wert. "You deceive no one."

The Fool was recovered sufficiently to hit the discomfited Lord of War with a pebble when Tresqu was not watching.

The Weapon had drifted into sight during this exchange, floating out of a shady hollow, as if blown by a breeze. It was very simple in appearance—an impalpable three-foot glowing sphere with a squat metallic cylinder at its base.

"Tell me not the purpose of your visit, petty lord," It said. "It is known to me only too well. Ah, great First Principle! Little did I reck when, in ages past, I nursed your species to civilization, just how poorly you would serve my purpose. Peace it was I desired, but do I get it? No! Your kingdom is powerful, but you have not the strength to handle your own troubles. You rule twenty-nine planets—"

"Thirty-seven," corrected Tresqu politely.

"—thirty-seven planets, but when a malignant force appears on your borders, I, the Weapon, must be called upon to act in my own defense, and for the sake of a few more restful moments in this calm glade, I am obliged to destroy, yet it was to avoid destroying that I helped your species to empire in the old days."

"In truth," spoke the deeply sympathetic Tresqu, "yours is a sad story. I disturb your richly earned rest only after the sincerest soul-searching. But affairs of state are at cross purposes in a moment of crisis, and without your help Hova will be in danger."

"Ah, cruel Fate!" intoned the Weapon, "It aids me in no manner to protest against your inscrutable machinations! There is no turning aside, no avoidance of necessity!" In a less declamatory style, the Weapon addressed Tresqu: "Very well, what is the trouble?"

Tresqu described the events on Terra for the Weapon, concluding, "Now that the Humans have knowledge of our space drive and armament, they are certain to attack, especially if they realize they have been subjects for experiment."

The Weapon flitted about restlessly along the bank of the brook. "I question the motives of my own thoughts. Do I quibble with myself in an attempt to escape unwelcome necessities? Tell, petty lord, do your scientists confirm the picture you paint of the Humans? Are they, like you, alas, masterfully vicious enough to destroy the peace of dozens of planets for nothing but revenge?"

"So the scientists say, mighty Weapon," answered Tresqu.

"You, Lord of War, why are you silent when your face is strained with words crying for expression?" asked the Weapon. "Speak your mind."

Wert squirmed. "If it please Your Mightiness, and you, Your Gracious Wisdom, I believe the Humans will know that we desire their destruction, and will try to defeat us for the sake of their own survival rather than revenge."

"A most convincing point, Lord of War," said the Weapon. Tresqu flashed a forgiving smile at Wert while the Weapon paused before continuing:

"However, I fear my unwilling spirit refuses to bow to the most reasonable of arguments. Please leave me; solve the problem yourselves!"

Tresqu bowed and moved toward the cruiser. "We obey, Mighty Guide of our fathers. Let me say in parting that I, too, am grieved by our talk, much more because of the pain our visit has caused your noble greatness than because our race is threatened with annihilation. My deepest hope is that the ravages of war will never reach this peaceful place which is so dear to your gentle being."

"Wait!" groaned the Weapon. "To slay, or not to slay, that is the dilemma. Ah, had my old masters of Zoz only left within my powers the seed of my own destruction, I would gladly seek the consummation of ultimate peace. But, no, that door is closed to me by deathless locks. Bring me a Human, that I may learn to hate him. Choose the most ignoble specimen available. I will converse with him at length so as to become exasperated with all the despicable traits of his race. Then, in my contempt for those traits, I will be able to cleanse the Universe of all Humans."

Tresqu turned quickly to his Fool. "Are there any Humans on Hova?"

"Yes, in the biological research laboratories."

"Then go quickly, Fool, and fetch one. This is a grave matter, and I trust you to choose the most monstrous specimen available. Hurry!"

The Fool ran into the cruiser and was on his way, leaving Tresqu, Wert, and several guardsmen with the Weapon. If the Weapon was conscious of the fact that the Lord of Hova was staying behind out of courtesy, it did not show it. Instead, it wandered indifferently away, mumbling a soliloquy of guilt and misery.

The sight of the Fool's specimen of humanity repaid Tresqu for the tediousness of the waiting. It was a particularly sordid-looking creature with a dirty growth of hairs on its head and face. Its body, thin as the Fool's, but with no compensating grace of movement, was clad in a blue garment of roughly woven vegetable fibers, and the extremities of its nether limbs were enclosed in evil-smelling boxes of animal hide. Its fierce eyes darted ominously from one Hovan to another. Its jaw kept working in a slow rhythm, and occasionally a stream of black liquid exploded through its mouth.

"You have done well, Fool," said Tresqu. "You will be rewarded highly." Raising his voice he called, "Mighty Weapon, your specimen awaits!"

"I come!" Once more the Weapon floated into view.

The Earthman's jaw sagged. "'Y God!" he muttered in English, staring at the approaching Weapon.

"Indeed," said the Weapon, "this appears to be a creature I could learn to abhor and kill. If only its thoughts equal its appearance—Speak, Human!"

The man said nothing.

"Mighty Weapon," murmured the Fool, "this Human is truly an ignoble monster. He has been in captivity for five years and has yet to speak a word of our beautiful language instead of his own barbaric tongue."

"You fool!" Shouted Tresqu. "How is the Weapon going to converse with him? Why did you bring one that cannot talk?"

Not in the least disconcerted, the Fool replied, "As you ordered, good master, I brought the worst specimen available. However, the possibility of linguistic difficulties was not overlooked. I have here a dictionary of his language, recently compiled by our Alien Affairs staff." He produced a large volume of manuscript from beneath his cloak.

"Your Fool shows wisdom, petty lord," spoke the Weapon. "I will study this book. Know the language, know the people, it is wisely said. In fact, I originated that saying myself some three thousand years ago, I believe. Unship any supplies brought for the Human and begone. Three days will suffice for the arousal of my wrath. Return then."

"As you wish, O Mightiest of All." Tresqu bowed gawkily. "It is my most ardent desire, Wondrous Guide, that we, your servants, will not be obliged to disturb your peace again for a thousand centuries, once this affair is concluded."

"And mine," the Weapon snapped crossly. "Now leave me."

The man watched the Hovans enter their cruiser and fly away. Looking at the Weapon hovering nearby, he squatted on his heels and pulled up a blade of purple grass to chew. Minutes passed in silence. Then the Weapon moved away, the book bobbing along behind, supported by some unseen force.

When it was out of sight, the man muttered, "'Y God, I've saw fireballs in my time, but that's the first one I ever saw settin' in a bucket!"

After a thoughtful examination of his surroundings, the man stood up and walked to the packing cases the Hovans had left. All but one contained the synthetic food product to which he had grown accustomed in his five years of captivity. The other box, rather small, contained a shredded vegetable which served him as a poor substitute for chewing tobacco. Purple when growing, the leaves of this vegetable were blue-black when cured, making his frequent expectorations look like ink.

"Filthy damn stuff!" he grunted, stuffing several handfuls in an empty overall pocket.

He shuffled down to the brook and tested its temperature with a hand. Finding it rather cold, he decided against taking a bath. Instead, he spat into it and watched meditatively as the spot of black was carried downstream. "I wonder what they turned me loose for," he monologued.

Careful to avoid the spot where the Weapon appeared to have gone, he returned to the food supply and ate. By then it was getting dark, and he bedded down for the night on some thick grass under a tree.

"'Y God," he yawned, "I'm glad all these insects don't want nothin' to do with me."

*　　*　　*

The Weapon was waiting beside him when he woke up next morning. "Eyes of your Terran Deity," it said, "I shall now converse with you in your own tongue. Name yourself, creature."

The man sat up startled. A moment passed before he said, "I'm Jake—Jacob Absher. What was that you said?"

"My pronunciation is above reproach, Jacob. Therefore I will not repeat myself. Attend me closely or I shall punish you."

"'Y God, I heard you all right and you didn't make sense!" said Jacob, determined not to be frightened. "Now if you aim to talk with me, stop imitatin' a professor and talk so's a man can understand you. I ain't scared of you, so leave off makin' threats."

"Such stupid insolence!" gloated the Weapon. "Already I feel my wrath growing within me. Since it will anger me even more to explain my words to you, I will do exactly that. My first words to you were, 'Eyes of your Terran Deity,' an expression you use frequently in a corrupted form to begin your statements. By studying your language, I learned that 'Zounds' is a similar corruption referring to the wounds of the Deity, while 'Strewth' refers to your God's truth. Thus, I was able to understand, and state in uncorrupted form, your remark, 'Eye God.'"

"'Tain't what it means," objected Jacob, filling his mouth with ersatz tobacco. "It just means by God."

The Weapon considered this. "And exactly what is the significance of such a remark?"

Jacob scratched his whiskered chin. "I reckon you got me there. I guess it means that I mean what I say."

"In other words, any statement you make following that phrase is to be taken seriously?"

"Somethin' like that."

"Then it follows that your other statements, without the 'by God' preface, are not seriously intended. Are they jokes or lies?"

"That ain't the way it is at all! I just say 'by God' when I feel like it, not every time I'm bein' serious."

"Monstrous inconsistency!" groaned the Weapon dramatically. "Ah, chaotic universe! Is there then no sublime plan, no fateful development to your endless succession of days? How could even the most synoptic First Principle find a purpose for creating such an unplanned, unreasonable species as the Humans? Can it be—unhappy thought!—that there is no plan to it all, and we exist for naught?"

Jacob listened with open mouth. "Say," he broke in, "are you some kind of play-actor?"

"That is what I ask myself," the Weapon continued its oratorical flight. "Are we all actors, speaking the lines written for us by a Great Playwright who plans to unite all the threads of his plot in a universal climax to come? Or are we poor random creatures without purpose?" It paused and added in a more conversational tone, "But that is not what you mean by your question. No, I am not a play-actor. I am an unfortunate weapon, reluctant to employ myself for my intended purpose of destruction of life and unsuited by my structure for the doing of deeds more worthy in nature."

Jacob squinted about. "A weapon, huh? Let's see you hit that bird thing sittin' in that tree over there."

"Bloodthirsty fiend! I do not kill for amusement!"

"I just wanted to see how you worked," said the abashed Jacob. "All I've seen you do is float around and talk a blue streak. As far as I'm concerned, you ain't nothin' but a big-mouthed bluff."

"Very well, Jacob. If you have formed such an erroneous attitude, it will be necessary for me to correct you immediately. Observe the red boulder on yonder hill."

"I see it."

The cylindrical base of the Weapon swung to point briefly at the boulder, which quietly crumbled to dust.

"I be dog!" yelped Jacob. He looked at the Weapon with respect. "You sure pulverized it! How do you work?"

"You could not understand the processes involved. Suffice it to say I have the means to collect energy in general and retransmit it in specific forms and directions. But enough of this. You are here to answer questions, not ask them. First, tell me what you did in an average day on Terra."

"That what you call the world I live on?"

"Yes."

"I'm a farmer, you know. I got a place in the Smoky Mountains in Tennessee. First thing in the mornin', I'd go feed the livestock while Suzy cooked breakfast." A faraway look came into Jacob's eyes. "Guess she took the kids and went to live with her mammy when these here animals grabbed me . . ."

"Continue," commanded the Weapon.

"Huh? Well, then we'd eat breakfast. Come to think of it, I ain't et yet this mornin'." Jacob got up and went to get himself some breakfast.

"But this matter—" protested the Weapon.

"Not on an empty stomach," Jacob said calmly, eating without haste.

When he returned, the Weapon questioned him further about his life on Terra. Hours of ill-tempered conversation passed. "Such drabness!" the Weapon finally exclaimed. "Creatures who lead such dull lives as yours should welcome extinction. Not once have you mentioned an appreciation of the wondrous exaltation that comes from an esthetic feel for beauty. With the labor of providing for your grotesque body's animal cravings is your whole life spent. Not in anger, but as an act of mercy, can I exterminate your defective race."

Jacob's mouth hung open. "So *that's* what your monkey's brung me out here for—fixin' to kill us! 'Y God, you better look out! We got atom bombs on Earth an' we'll use 'em on you if you try anything!"

"Toys," sneered the Weapon. "Be assured, Jacob, that I have nothing to fear from any childish mechanisms your Terrans can contrive."

Jacob sat stunned. "But you said a minute ago you couldn't kill nothin'."

"I can kill only when I'm convinced it is best for my own repose or for the health of the Universe. Long ago, I could go forth at battle with thoughtless joy at the command of my masters of Zoz, but now I must have reasons, must converse at length with my aberrated emotions, must prepare myself as for an ordeal."

"Them Zozes must've been the Devil's minions," argued Jacob. "The Commandments says, 'Thou shalt not kill' and when you go against that, you're goin' against the word of God."

"Poor, futile creature," sympathized the Weapon. "You actually strive to pit your naïve superstitious mind against my highly developed mentality in argument. You actually associate my supreme masters of old with your puny mythological villain! Lowliness should know its place. But I feel no anger—merely a pitying desire to relieve your kind of the burden of living."

Silently, Jacob replenished the wad of "tobacco" in his mouth. After chewing a while, he spat and said dolefully, "I don't reckon there's nothin' I can say or do that you won't hold against me. I always heard tell the Devil can twist anything to suit himself, and I reckon his minions can do the same thing. An' that's what you are: the Devil's minion! I reckon you break every Commandment God give us. Except about committin' adultery. I don't guess you can do that."

"Your piddling reproductive customs have no application on my plane of existence. Cannot you comprehend that you are less to me than a microbe? Even my servants, the Hovans, do not concern themselves with such ignoble concepts as what you call adultery."

"You mean they live in sin?" asked Jacob.

"They mate as often as they please with anyone they please," the Weapon replied coldly. "I will ignore the ludicrous implications of your absurd moral concepts."

"I don't mean to criticize your animal friends," glowered Jacob. "I reckon they ain't children of God, so it don't matter if they do mate like a pack of dogs. They probably ain't got no souls to keep pure.

It looked to me like they worshiped you like a false
god, too."

"They . . . O Great Hidden Manifestation!" squalled
the Weapon in rage. "They regard me as their guide
and mentor. Nothing more. I would not allow anything else."

Jacob watched the Weapon in awe. The energy globe
was flickering and flaring wildly in an uncontrolled
display of color. " 'Y God!" he exclaimed. "You sure
are puttin' on a fireworks show!"

The globe settled down to a tensely nervous fluctua-
tion which hurt Jacob's eyes to watch. "Never in the
ageless span of my existence," quavered the Weapon
angrily, "have I been insulted in such vulgar terms
by any creature. And now from you, creature whom
my glorious masters of Zoz would exterminate like a
buzzing fly, like a disease germ, I hear these senseless
mouthings of defamation. Stop it or I shall destroy
you outright!"

The Weapon's fluctuating, along with its loud, grating voice, put Jacob's nerves on edge. He growled,
"I bet your old Zozes live in adultery just like your
animal friends."

The color of the energy globe sank to dull red and
the Weapon emitted a series of buzzing, inarticulate
noises.

"It suits not my nature, bit of diseased scum, to
slay you in a fit of indignation," it finally said with
tightly controlled fury. "You are beneath such individual recognition. Yet it is fortunate for you that your
insults have no basis in reality, otherwise my intellect
could not have claimed ascendancy over the immediate urges of my tortured sense of extreme disgust. Be

wise, say I, knowing I request the impossible, and irk me no more."

"'Y God, I reckon you don't think you rile me up, too, with all that high falutin' jabber of yours!" Jacob snapped back.

"As I speak, so speak the mighty Zoz," replied the Weapon in high dignity. "They are great and noble beings, given to poetic flights and magnificent deeds. To them, your puny opinions would not even be recognized as thought."

"If they talk in that puttin' on, play-actin' way you do, they are a bunch of phony show-offin' hypocrites," sulked Jacob.

Several things happened too quickly for Jacob to follow. The color of the energy globe dropped to absolute black. The metallic cylinder swung up to point at Jacob. A thin ringing *"Ping!"* sounded in the cylinder. A killing wave of pure hate struck Jacob.

He had just enough time to know he was a dead man before he blacked out.

It came as a surprise, when Jacob regained consciousness, to find that he was stretched out on purple grass with the Weapon still hovering over him.

"You missed, 'y God!" he mumbled, sitting up.

"I regained my sanity in time, Master Technician," the Weapon replied pleasantly.

"Huh?"

"Ah, day of uncontainable joy!" sang the Weapon, flaming pure white. "Day of glorious release to continue the grandeur of old! As the past eons of futility passed over me, I sank to the conclusion that I was forever condemned to my useless existence on this planet, with nothing to sustain my spirit other than the sense of beauty given me by masters to fill my leisure hours. But now, Master Technician Jacob, you have found me and corrected my malfunction, long after I had surrendered all hope!"

Still dazed by the nearly fatal wave of mental energy the Weapon had directed at him, Jacob could not understand what had happened. Instead of talking contemptuously to him, the Weapon was now addressing him as Master Something-or-other, and . . .

"What did you say I done?" he asked.

"You corrected my malfunction," repeated the Weapon. "That is to say, you purged my mechanism of the inhibition against joyful slaughter that has plagued me for a billion years. Ah, you are a clever Technician, Jacob! But I comprehend it all now. By arousing within me an overwhelming emotional desire to kill—a singularly strange feeling! —you depressed my inhibition to the releasing point. So telling was your masterful therapy that I almost ceased functioning at all.

"Your own life was in dire danger for the moment required for my new-found sanity to assume control. But, of course, all slaves of the glorious Zoz die willingly when the work of the masters so demands."

"Now wait a minute!" objected Jacob. "I ain't no slave of your Zozes or no Technician either! You know what I am—a good God-fearin' human!" His voice dropped to a pleading mumble. "And may God forgive me if I've got myself in league with the Devil."

"Ah? Could it be?" murmured the Weapon. "Could

indeed your infuriating insults of the Great Ones have been honest expressions of a puny mind with no therapeutic intentions? I answer Yes. The possible occurrence of specific incidents in the inclusion of space-time is curiously unlimited. But you have served me, Jacob, and have earned the privilege of continuing your meager, momentary life. Besides, I can use you further."

"You can, huh?" Jacob said slyly. "Look here, Weapon, I'll make a bargain with you."

"Ha! Stupid, untutored slave!" chuckled the Weapon. "Learn that yours is to obey, not to bargain. But yet, state your price for my amusement, now that I can no longer be enraged by your words."

"Well, you let the rest of the people on Earth alone and I'll do whatever you want me to."

After a pause, the Weapon quoted, "'Nobility shows its traces in surprising places.' You do not sufficiently comprehend my nature, Technician Slave Jacob. I am a Weapon. My masters point me, as you would point a rifle, and command that I destroy. I kill at their direction, but seldom otherwise. Thus, your Terra is safe until another Weapon or I am aimed and directed. You can make no bargain."

Jacob thought this over. While doing so, the Weapon drifted away.

"Wait here, slave," it said in parting. "I go to meditate on my recovered sanity."

During the next two days, Jacob caught an occasional glimpse of the Weapon drifting thoughtfully around in the depths of the forest, but they did not meet for conversation. Jacob amused himself by rigging a fishing line out of some of the packaging material that contained his food. He even succeeded in catching a fish, but its queer odor discouraged him from trying to cook and eat it.

Then the royal cruiser of Tresqu the Wisest dropped into the meadow. Its airlock swung open and the Ruler of Hova, followed by his entourage, came out.

"Oh, Mighty Weapon!" bawled Tresqu. "Your loving servant craves audience!"

"Ah, you have returned, petty lord," said the Weapon, drifting out from among the trees. "Serve me by calling all the crew members from your noble ship, that I may view you all together."

Puzzled, Tresqu bowed and said, "Your least whim is law, Mighty Weapon." He turned and called, "All hands, outside!"

A half-dozen Hovans tumbled through the lock to stand in line behind the ruler's entourage.

"Is this all of them?" asked the Weapon.

"All, Great Mentor of—"

The Weapon laughed and the Hovans fell dead.

"Come, Slave Jacob," commanded the Weapon. "We take this cruiser."

Dazed and slack-faced, Jacob came out from behind a bush, where he had hidden himself from the Hovans, and followed the Weapon through the airlock.

"Even in my insanity, I planned well," said the Weapon. "These ships, which I taught the Hovans to construct, can be operated simply, even by such as you. Attend my instructions."

First, the Weapon taught Jacob to open and close the airlock. Then he was shown how to fuel the engines, upon which the Weapon made some changes to improve their performance. Finally, in the control room, Jacob learned to fly the ship.

This took several hours, at the end of which time Jacob had succeeded in raising the cruiser into a satellite orbit around Hova. "Do you comprehend, Slave?" asked the Weapon.

"Sure. This thing ain't nothin' to run compared to a T-model Ford. Which way is it to Earth?"

"That I shall not tell you, Jacob, because I must leave the ship for a few hours and desire to find you here when I return. Consider and tell me: Will you be here?"

Jacob gazed at the broad, star-spangled viewplate that curved around his seat at the controls. There was, he reflected, an awful lot of nothing out there for a man to get lost in.

"I'll be here," he promised.

"Very good. You must understand that these controls are constructed for manipulation by such limbs as your own and those of the Hovans. Thus, it is convenient for me to use you as a pilot instead of doing the drab, mechanical task with my ill-suited force-field manipulators. You will be wise to serve me well, Jacob."

Jacob nodded. "You got a point there."

"Operate the lock for me," the Weapon ordered.

Jacob did so and watched the colorful machine drift out of sight in the atmosphere below the cruiser.

Minutes ticked quietly by as Jacob gazed down at the purple planet and wondered why the Weapon had not chosen a trained Hovan pilot instead of him. Also, he wondered how soon the Weapon would take him home to Earth.

A great swath of the purple planet began turning black. The black dulled to the gray shade of ashes as the swath grew longer. Over the surface of Hova, the blackening moved like some colossal paintbrush. Dense clouds of smoke rolled upward to the high reaches of the atmosphere.

Jacob realized why the Weapon had not selected a Hovan pilot.

When all of Hova was a lifeless ball in a fog of ash, the Weapon returned.

"Ah, good Jacob!" it boomed jovially. "Let us be up and doing! Thirty-six planets remain to be visited before my current assignment is concluded."

"Do all of them get—that?" asked Jacob, nodding toward the lifeless world below.

"Yes. I was instructed to render this solar system lifeless before I malfunctioned. Since then, the life of this system has spread, with my insane aid, to infest other systems. Of course, my task must now include all those new Hovan worlds."

"Now wait a minute!" said Jacob in terror. "I can't let you do that!"

"They are your enemies, Jacob," reminded the Weapon. "They meant to kill every human on Terra. Also, by your own words, they are soulless animals who live in sinful adultery. Ha! It amuses me to reason with you, Slave Jacob!"

"Godamighty, forgive me!" prayed Jacob, in horrified defeat.

The Weapon seemed to know how to find the Hovan planets from the markings of the cruiser's star charts. Jacob could not read the charts and saw no hope of getting back to earth and Suzy and the kids without the Weapon's help. Dully, he went about the tasks the Weapon ordered him to do.

Several weeks passed as one world after another was left a smoking ruin.

Finally the job was done.

"*Now*, can I go home?" begged Jacob.

"To Terra? No, Slave. I still need a pilot."

"But if you take me home," Jacob continued desperately, "you can get a better pilot than me. I'm just a dirt farmer. There's all kinds of airplane pilots on Earth, youngsters without families who would give their right arms to fly this thing, I bet."

"Ah?" The Weapon considered. "A willing slave is, of course, always desirable. On the other hand, Terra is up in arms against the empire of Hova, not realizing it is dead. They would destroy this craft on sight, and I would be obliged to wait around until they could construct another for me. No, I have decided we will not go to Terra."

"But, damn it, where else is there to go?"

"In search of my masters of Zoz," replied the Weapon. "Naturally, I wish to return myself to their services as soon as possible."

"But they might be anywhere!"

"True," the Weapon agreed. "But even after a billion years, I know of several places in the Universe they may be near. Their great cleansing sweeps tend to circle and turn in a pattern established long in advance. Thus we will go to those places where they may now be engaged in their consecrated task of universal purification."

"But—"

"No more, Slave! We go!"

Out of the Milky Way, the cruiser hurtled at a speed which a sentient lightwave would find meaningless. On and on they journeyed in quest of the long-dead Zoz Horde.

They may still be going.

OUT, WIT!

❧❧❧

Department of Physics
Grandview University
Grandview, Ohio
November 6, 1975

D. R. Dayleman, Editor
North American Physical Journal
Adminster, Virginia

Dear Dan:

Other commitments will keep me from attending the annual NASP meeting in Chicago in January. Sorry I must pass this up; we old hands enjoy these opportunities to congregate and chat, do we not? Give the others my regards and regrets.

You may remember the name Jonathan Willis. He

is a young man who did his doctorate for me here at Grandview and who was listed among the co-authors of some of my research reports published in the NAPJ. I regard him as one of the most promising youngsters in nuclear field theory. In some respects he is rather immature and irrepressible, for which his brilliance more than compensates. He is presently associate professor of physics at Mesa State University.

I mention young Willis because I've recommended him to the agenda committee of the Chicago meeting. He's to present a paper on an approach to nuclear generation and degeneration that he has been pondering for some time, and which he tells me he has virtually completed since going to Mesa State. His theory proposes a characteristic, called, I believe, "angular stability," which seems to put the question of whether a given nucleus will fission on more solid ground than a mere law-of-probability basis. All I know of his recent work comes from two brief phone conversations with him, the latest of which was yesterday afternoon. Actually, you will have the opportunity to see his paper, and hear him deliver it at the meeting, before I can examine it, judging from my present plans. He was still writing it yesterday, and said he would send you a copy to consider for publication well in advance of the meeting.

Thus, you may consider this a "letter of recommendation" for my very able former student. And I am also aware, of course, that you like to know when a report of extraordinary interest is coming to the Journal.

Best regards,
Harmon McGregor, Chairman

———————

North American Physical Journal
January 3, 1976

Department of Physics
Grandview University

Dear Harmon:

A note in haste, as I'm off to Chicago this afternoon.

The Jonathan Willis manuscript did not reach me until yesterday, though it was mailed in mid-December. The postal service becomes continually more atrocious, especially around the holiday season.

I haven't had time to read more of it than the abstract, and glance at the math. It looks most promising, and I'm forwarding it to the referees.

I do find his title, "Back to Alchemy," rather objectionable, but that's easily remedied and not at all unusual. I'm often amused by such efforts of our younger colleagues to find "catchy" titles for their reports. When I make the acquaintance of young Willis at Chicago, I'm sure he and I will be able to find a more reputable title, in keeping with the content of his paper.

All best wishes,
Daniel R. Dayleman

———————

North American Physical Journal
January 20, 1976

Department of Physics
Grandview University

Dear Harmon:

I understand if, having doubtless heard of the debacle in Chicago, you are reticent about writing to me.

Please rest assured of my continued high esteem. No one holds you responsible in the slightest for the dismaying performance of Jonathan Willis. Such things will happen now and then, to the injury of the repute of our profession, and are, of course, not to be tolerated. But matters are best mended not by blaming each other. Rather, we must work together to make sure such offenses are quickly forgotten and not repeated.

Indeed, I admit some responsibility in this myself. Had I taken time to read Willis's paper when I received it, I could have phoned Margoli and warned him to strike it from the meeting's agenda.

I can sympathize with the feeling of shocked betrayal you must be suffering, since your letter indicates you had a high regard for Willis. During my own academic career I, too, was disillusioned by my students more than once, although none of them dishonored themselves or our profession in so startling a manner as this.

Again, be assured of my continued esteem and

All best wishes,
Daniel R. Dayleman

Department of Physics
Grandview University
February 14, 1976

North American Physical Journal

Dear Dan:

I got back to Grandview yesterday for the first time since shortly after my last letter to you, having been fully occupied with other commitments in the meantime. A copy of my former student's manuscript, along with your letters and those from other friends who attended the Chicago meeting, were waiting on my desk.

You can appreciate that they were a bitter dose for me. At this moment I'm torn between a sense of personal guilt and anger at the former student. Mostly, I feel the guilt.

I've tried not to slight the task of teaching my students professional decorum. But it is something I've always sought to put across more by personal example than by precept. For this student, obviously a more forceful effort was required of me, and unfortunately was not forthcoming.

Dan, would you do me the kindness of telling me precisely how the meeting responded to the report? And am I correct in assuming no effort will be made to publish a revised version of it?

Best regards,
Harmon McGregor

North American Physical Journal
February 19, 1976

Department of Physics
Grandview University

Dear Harmon:

The response to Willis's presentation can best be described as frigid. He began with a tasteless ad lib, not mentioning me by name but referring to my suggestion, made to him the previous evening, that the title "Back to Alchemy" be changed. He said he agreed, because "science never marches backward, or at least hardly ever." This drew a scattering of mild chuckles from the younger crowd. Then he offered as his revised title, "Forward to Alchemy." Frankly, I was too stunned by this insolence to note the immediate reaction of others, but I believe my feeling was by no means unique.

From there on Willis followed his manuscript text closely, with results you might well imagine. The most disastrous of his witticisms was the conclusion of his introductory paragraph: " . . . Upon assuming my duties at Mesa State University, I was in position to make fruitful utilization of the scientific method in bringing this research to completion. You know what the scientific method is: that's having your graduate students do all the hard work for you."

This double slur, striking not only at academicians but at the high cause to which our profession is dedicated, brought a coarse guffaw from one newspaper science writer. Everyone else, even the younger crowd, sat in stunned silence. From that point on, the entire audience was like a stone.

Of course we've all encountered speakers who, regardless of the seriousness of their subject and the dignity of their listeners, think it necessary to open with a touch of "after-dinner" humor. One need not be a psychologist to observe that such speakers must lack confidence, either in themselves and the value of their presentation, or in the ability of their audience to accept a serious presentation.

But so accustomed have we become to this ritual of the opening jokes that perhaps Willis's would have been overlooked, despite their aspersive quality, had they ended at that point. As you can see from the manuscript, they did not.

I found most objectionable, for example, his use of the term, "the Slide Rule," in referring to his theorem of nuclear degeneration. This is a thoroughly juvenile play on words.

When Willis concluded, we moved on, without questions or discussion, to the next paper on the agenda, and a normal atmosphere was soon reestablished. I had no encounters with Willis thereafter, and cannot say—and do not care—how he reacted to his chilly reception.

Fortunately the popular press made little of the episode. I don't believe the reporters present really grasped what was going on. Being members of a craft not noted for pride, or for reasons for pride, they would not be struck by the demeaning quality of the Willis "wit."

As for our foreign guests at the meeting, I cannot guess their reactions, except to presume they were varied. The Russian group in particular had a limited grasp of the English language, and the "jokes" may have eluded them. Of course the foreigners received copies for later translation and study, and I can only hope the Willis brand of humor will suffer in translation. If not, I fear the respect abroad for the American physics community will be dampened.

Obviously any revision and publication of the paper is out of the question, in view of the irremedial scandal its author has brought upon himself. It is best to drop and forget the entire matter. I understand certain administrators and faculty leaders at Mesa State University have already been approached, to acquaint them with what transpired at Chicago. Presumably they will take such steps as they consider appropriate.

I ask you, Harmon, not to blame yourself for this debacle. Remember that undesirable personality traits are formed early in life, long before a youth reaches college age. I dare say that nothing you might have done would have made much difference, in that regard, in Willis. A teacher should not fault himself for the poor quality of student he sometimes must work with.

> All best wishes,
> Daniel R. Dayleman

Department of Physics
Grandview University
March 8, 1976

North American Physical Journal

Dear Dan:

Many thanks for your letter of February 19th. I needed your closing reassurances very much, having just received a letter from the former student in question, in which deep bitterness showed through his usual flippancy in a manner I found very disquieting. Your words helped me recover my perspective.

I will not quote his letter at length. The gist of it is summed up in his protest: "They acted like I'd told a dirty joke in church!" Of course he is not capable of realizing how apt that comparison is. Impertinence has no place in a gathering of learned persons, striving toward the noble goal of understanding the laws of the universe.

However—and because that is our goal—I hate to see the perhaps valuable theoretical content of the paper passed over because of the unseemly inclusions. For that reason I have studied it thoroughly, and find the logic of it apparently sound. And if his proposed and dismally misnamed "Slide Rule" can be verified by experiment, it could have major technological applications. It might provide an opening to controlled nuclear fusion, as well as to the tailoring of elements alluded to in the paper's title.

The verifying experiments would require use of one of the large, federally-sponsored accelerators. While I'm fairly well-connected in Washington, I am reluctant to request accelerator scheduling for this purpose. My personal association with the author of the paper could make a request from me suspect. Under the circumstances, I would probably accomplish nothing, and might do myself a professional disservice.

Did any of the participants in the Chicago meeting

express interest in the real content of the paper, to indicate they may be willing to undertake the necessary verifying tests? Please let me know if you see any hope along this line.

Best regards,
Harmon McGregor

———————

North American Physical Journal
March 12, 1976

Department of Physics
Grandview University

Dear Harmon:

I have just one hope along the line you mention. That is that you'll drop the whole thing. Immediately and completely.

I thought my letters had made clear to you how totally negatively all of us responded to that horrible Willis paper. Not one physicist in that room could possibly have followed the rationale of the report, filled as all of us were with justified and honorable indignation. Certainly nobody expressed the sort of interest you are asking about.

Harmon, for your own sake as well as for the dignity of American physics, let this sleeping dog lie!

Best wishes,
Daniel R. Dayleman

———————

Department of Physics
Grandview University
March 20, 1976

North American Physical Journal

Dear Dan:

I'll heed your advice. And forgive me if I've tried
your patience over this affair. I felt it my duty to at
least try to rehabilitate my former student and his
research findings.

Now that I feel I've done all I can reasonably ask
of myself in that direction, I'm very glad to wash my
hands of the entire miserable mess. Hope to see you
in Paris in July.

Best regards,
Harmon McGregor

———————

North American Physical Journal
October 9, 1978

Department of Physics
Grandview University

Dear Harmon:

Your piece on spin-ratios is drawing interesting
comments and questions from readers. Enclosed are
three letters that might be worth publishing with your
comments. Harmon, I hate to rouse a sleeping dog
that I myself urged you to let lie. However, it has
come to my attention that Jonathan Willis, the creator

of that unseemly incident at the NASP meeting three years ago, is now teaching physics at Simonton High School which, according to the road maps, is some forty miles from Grandview.

I am not suggesting any particular action in relation to this. Maybe no action is needed; one might say that Willis has found his proper professional level. I must ask, however, if Willis will present impressionable high school students with a reputable example, as a member of our profession?

I hope you'll give this matter some thought, and take whatever action you deem advisable.

All best wishes,
Daniel R. Dayleman

———

Department of Physics
Grandview University
December 15, 1978

North American Physical Journal

Dear Dan:

Concerning the comments on my spin-ratios piece, I admit myself at a loss for worthwhile answers to the questions raised. Essentially, the questions ask for a reconciliation of my conclusions with those offered in recent publications by various Russian theorists.

I have, of course, gone over the translated Russian reports, and have come away puzzled—as has nearly everyone with whom I've discussed them. The

Russians appear to have gone off on some offbeat line of investigation without bothering to tell the world the reason for their departure from the mainstream.

I halfway suspect the presence of a Lysenko brand of physicist, well-concealed and disseminating a politically-inspired dogma the others are obliged to accept. I would not care to say that for publication, as you can readily understand, but it is the only solution to the Russian riddle that occurs to me. Publish the questioning letters if you like, but without comment from myself.

As for my former student referred to, I've made discreet inquiries about him and his present position. The community of Simonton is synonymous with "hayseed" in this section of Ohio. Its high school has an enrollment of three hundred at maximum, of which fewer than twenty percent take the science courses.

I feel we can dismiss the situation as inconsequential. Certainly it is too trivial for me to wish to involve myself in it, and run the risk of personal encounters with this former student that could not be pleasant.

Perhaps he is now on the receiving end of student impertinence, and might profit thereby.

Best regards,
Harmon McGregor

North American Physical Journal
April 7, 1980

Department of Physics
Grandview University

Dear Harmon:

I regret to inform you that the present currency crisis has forced the temporary suspension of *Journal* publication. Enclosed is your latest manuscript which I am returning not as a rejection but in case you can find another publisher for it—one not caught as unprepared as we were by the sudden economic storm.

Conditions should stabilize in a few months, at which time I would be happy to have this manuscript back. I'm no expert on economics, of course, but I cannot believe the fall of world gold prices can have a lasting depressing effect on the value of the U.S. dollar. That value is, at bottom, based on the ability of our nation to produce goods and services. As soon as the frightened public realizes that, the situation should straighten out quickly.

Nor can the Soviet Union keep dumping gold on the world market indefinitely. Evidently they discovered a very rich mine, perhaps a decade ago, and have been working it ever since to accumulate the amount dumped thus far. Someone more adept than I at analyzing Communist thought processes will have to answer the question, "Why?" They can gain little aside from the enmity of the rest of the world by this action.

Speaking of Russians, what do you make of their claim of a successful power generator utilizing controlled nuclear fusion?

All best wishes,
Daniel R. Dayleman

Department of Physics
Grandview University
April 11, 1980

North American Physical Journal

Dear Dan:
   By returning my report you anticipated my desire. I was about to request that you withhold it from publication, because I no longer consider its conclusions valid.
   I do not now consider myself at liberty to speculate on Soviet nuclear fusion claims. I will, of course, communicate more fully when I can. In the meantime, please forgive the brevity of this note.

Best regards,
Harmon McGregor

———

North American Physical Journal
July 9, 1980

Department of Physics
Grandview University

Dear Harmon:
   Congratulations!
   I've been reading about you in the newspapers, and watching you in television interviews, with much pleasure and satisfaction. Part of my joy comes from your being a personal friend, which allows me a sense of sharing in your resounding success. But more than

that, it is a great satisfaction to have the American physicist typified in the public's eye by a figure with the impressive dignity of Harmon McGregor!

Of course I understand now why your last letter was so short and mysterious.

Let me add my thanks to those of all members of our free Western civilization for solving the enigma of Russian physics—and by the same stroke resolving the currency crisis and gold glut, and bringing us into controlled fusion. All of which came, appropriately enough, just after the observation of what might otherwise have been our nation's final true Independence Day.

I'm confident the *Journal* will resume publication shortly, and I will be hoping for an early contribution from you.

All best wishes,
Daniel R. Dayleman

———————

College of Physics
Grandview University
July 15, 1980

North American Physical Journal

Dear Dan:

Honor from a colleague is far more dear to me than the loudest public acclaim. Many thanks.

I regretted my mysteriousness, but now that government security measures are no longer justified and are being dropped, you can expect a report for the *Journal* within a month.

In all due modesty, I must point out that I've given man no new discovery. I've merely duplicated the work of some unidentified Soviet theorist. If I were to view the matter from a purely selfish standpoint, perhaps I should be grateful to Soviet secrecy for allowing me the privilege of and credit for giving this discovery to the world.

Oddly enough, Dan, my solution to the mystery was not a formulation that was new to me. It had reposed in the back of my mind for an undetermined number of years, along with the thousands of other mathematical structures a theorist tends to accumulate in the course of his life's work. Just between us, Dan, I fear that figure of "impressive dignity" you mentioned stands revealed to himself as the stereotype "absent-minded professor." How else can I explain leaving so valuable a formulation shrouded in mental cobwebs year upon year?

You may recall the Russian "mystery" was a preoccupation of mine for some time. I once suspected it was the visible symptoms of neo-Lysenkoism, forcing our Soviet colleagues willy-nilly along a crackpot track. Such papers as were being published by the Russians pointed clearly to some undisclosed event that had stimulated the departure from mainstream physics. I devoted much time to the study of these papers, reasoning that, if the hidden event were in the realm of theoretical physics rather than of political origin, then its nature might be definable from clues in the published works that followed it.

The answer came to me in late March—that

half-forgotten formulation. In brief, it deals with a predictable asymmetry in nuclear structure that can be utilized as a weak point in nuclear binding force. Thus, the binding force can be largely bypassed, rather than overpowered, for the production of fusion and fission processes.

I communicated my findings to the appropriate government officials and the rest, as they say, is history.

Of course the thought occurred to me that, since my formulation was not new, perhaps the Soviets had picked it up from one of my early published works. This could have explained why the Russians were allowed to publish papers containing clues to the secret—that is, they assumed they had no secret since the key formulation was of Western origin. This would raise the secondary question of why they never quoted or referred to the key formulation, but they often "write around" Western contributions as a means of avoiding recognition of these contributions.

The government people working with me have been as interested as I in finding the original of my formulation. All my papers, published and unpublished, and my notebooks as well, have been searched without success. On the chance that the formulation was not mine at all, a similar search has been made of all the physical journals as far back as 1945. Even the theses of my students have been gone over, to make sure I had not inadvertently "borrowed" from one of them.

In short, every source we could think of was examined, and the formulation was not found. Certainly it was never published, and we must conclude that the

Soviets discovered it independently. And apparently it is something that occurred to me many years ago, was perhaps scribbled on a piece of scrap paper, and then was discarded and pushed from my mind by more urgent matters.

In any event, I'm happy enough to have remembered the formulation when it was needed, and if the Soviets want to say they discovered it first, I'm hardly in a position to challenge them.

Best regards,
Harmon McGregor

P.S.: Always there seems to be a dark spot in our brightest moments. You probably remember Jonathan Willis, my former student who behaved so badly at a NASP meeting a few years ago. He has been teaching high school in a small town not far from here. A friend of mine who has relatives in that town has just informed me that Willis suffered a mental breakdown of some sort last week. I would guess his brash manner and warped humor were symptomatic of an instability that has brought him to this misfortune. I was genuinely sorry to hear of it, and to realize that at the very instant I was enjoying public acclaim this poor fellow was being stricken by mental agony. It is too bad he had so little to offer as a physicist. A successful career might have shielded him from this.
H. McG.

FIT FOR A DOG
꧁꧂

GLITTER HEARD THE MUFFLED clatter of the descending plane. Slav had left the ruins of the '93 Buick which served as their den only minutes earlier, on a predawn trip to the Dome to get meat for the growing pups. Glitter had not gone back to sleep. Now she sat up to look out the window while she sniffed the air.

She saw the blurred lights of the plane as it came down in a wobbly glide. The lights vanished as the plane dropped behind the rim of a low hill. She heard it meet the ground with a grinding, drawn-out crunch.

Glitter leaped out the window and then to the top of the car. From this vantage point she still could not see, smell, or hear anything of the plane. That told her something. If the plane were afire, the air would be reflecting its glow. But the only light was the dim beginning of the new day.

She could tell it was going to be a beautiful day, though, with a dense, invigorating smog.

While standing on the car, Glitter bayed out the news of the downed plane. Then she jumped to the ground while her neighbors repeated her call, relaying it to more distant neighbors who would, in turn, bay it out to a still wider radius. Soon every dog within five miles east, south and west—and to the border of Bog Erie on the north—would know of the plane. Many of them would be hurrying to the scene.

Also, the message would catch up with Slav, long before he reached the Dome, and bring him loping home.

The pups were whining with curiosity. The car would not be a safe haven for them with humans about. Copters from the Dome might soon be circling overhead, and the flyers might fire at the old car. They often shot at anything which appeared, from the air, to offer concealment for dogs.

Glitter called the pups out and herded them through the weeds and into a deep bone-burrow Slav had dug in the bank of a nearby erosion ditch. She bared her teeth at them and growled a warning that they were to stay in the bone-burrow, and they huddled obediently against the back of the hole.

Satisfied that they were out of harm's way, Glitter trotted off toward the downed plane.

As she neared the hilltop, she dropped to her belly and crawled into hiding behind the concrete block foundation of a long-vanished house. Now she could smell hot metal and freshly vaporized oil quite plainly, but she could not smell any humans. That meant the crash landing had sprung no big leaks in the plane's airtight cabin.

Carefully she peered around a corner of the crumbling foundation and down the hill. There lay the plane, its wings, crumpled by the landing, on either side of the long, fat metal body. Light glared out of the windows, and the humans inside were plainly visible. They were milling about in their slow way, and looking disorganized. Some were putting on filter masks while others were taking them off, as if they didn't know what to do. Their sounds came dimly through the hull as they made cries and words at each other.

An antenna near the nose of the plane was transmitting; Glitter could feel the tingle in the back of her head that strong radio signals always produced. Rescuers would be coming out from Cleveland Dome, and that was good. Otherwise, a lot of meat would go to waste here.

She could sense no indication of gunnery, so there was no need to remain in hiding. Probably the humans could not see very well, looking through the windows at the outside gloom, although dawn was coming rapidly now. She stepped out into the open and moved alertly down the hill toward the plane, eyeing the lighted windows as she approached. Close up, she studied the humans inside.

Most of them, she saw, were young men and women . . . more of these than were usually found in a grounded plane. Three pairs of them appeared to be mates from the way they huddled together. And one female clutched a small child but had no mate in evidence. Only four that Glitter could see looked to be past breeding age. But sight was not to be depended upon in classifying humans. The sorting-out would have to wait until they were out of the plane and could be investigated by smell.

A questioning bark told her that the neighbors were beginning to arrive. She responded softly. Too much loud baying could spook the humans, already upset by the crash-landing. It was best for them to become aware of the dogs gradually.

The neighbors knew this. As the day brightened, they trotted about, not getting too close to the plane, conversing in quiet yelps. None simply sat and stared at the plane, because nothing would panic the humans quicker than that.

Of course there were some terrified screams and yelling from the humans as they discovered that the plane was surrounded by thirty or forty dogs, but these dwindled as the humans reconciled themselves to the situation, and the dogs made no immediate threatening moves.

But it was not safe to wait too long. A copter might arrive soon, and the humans had to be brought out of the plane before that. Presently four of the dogs, Clog, Blackeye, Brist, and Paddler, ambled nonchalantly to the plane's tail assembly, leaped up onto it, and then worked their way forward on the slippery metal to a spot directly over the passenger cabin. Glitter caught the sharp change in their smell as they prepared to vomit acid.

Inside, there was another flurry of near-panic as the humans heard the clatter of hard claws above their heads. Calm was restored shortly, however. The humans moved away from the area beneath the spot where the four dogs were working on the roof. Glitter could see dull fright and acceptance in their faces when they peered out the windows. There would be no wasteful stampede, she decided.

A plane was down fifteen miles from Cleveland Dome, and Rescue Unit 502 scrambled.

That meant Joe Cosman, for one. His half of the bed tilted suddenly, sliding him into the mouth of the chute tube before he could wake up. Wheels were mumbling beneath him and a tinny voice was briefing him on details of the mission as he sat up and began dressing in his rescue gear. He listened while wondering if the scramble had awakened Doris. Sometimes the bed decanted him into the tube without her knowing anything was going on.

The tinny voice stopped for a moment, then asked, "Any questions?"

"Yeah," Cosman grunted, tugging on his jacket. "How many copters are going out to cover us?"

"The dispatch of copters is being taken under advisement," the voice replied. "Other questions?"

Cosman's lips tightened in anger. "No more questions," he snapped.

The tube disgorged him a minute later at Westside Emergency Park. He jogged across the concrete apron toward his armored bus 502, putting on his filter mask as he went because the air this close to the Dome wall was somewhat stenchy from exhaust pipe leaks. The wall itself, with its vast triangles of tough plastic, rose in the gloom a dozen yards away from his bus.

Mike Mabry was trotting ahead of him, making

hard going of it. Cosman caught up with the older man at the door of the bus, and could hear Mike wheezing.

"How you doing, Mike?" he asked.

"Hi, Joe," Mabry responded hoarsely.

Inside, Cosman climbed behind the wheel and Mabry mounted the ladder to the gun turret on the foreroof. "What's keeping Diego?"

"Here he comes," Mabry replied, sounding less winded. "No . . . it ain't Diego. It's somebody else."

Whoever it was boarded the bus and dropped into the second driver's seat beside Cosman, who eyed the man curiously.

"I'm John Haddon," the man said, "subbing for Diego what's-hisname. Your second driver."

Cosman nodded curtly, not sure he liked this guy and wondering what was wrong with Diego. "I'm Joe Cosman, and that's Mike Mabry up in the nest." He flipped a switch on the dash and spoke into the mike. "Bus 502 crewed and ready. Open up!"

"Okay, 502," the speaker responded. "Move out."

Cosman put the bus in gear and rolled forward. The inner door of the Westwall Emergency Lock folded aside as the bus approached. When it was passed, the door closed and the outer door, a hundred feet ahead, swung apart. The bus passed through it and into the swirling blackness of the outdoors.

He heard Haddon gasp at the sudden darkness and wondered if this was the man's first mission. "The smoke thins when we get a few hundred yards from the Dome," he said, keeping his attention on the dashboard instruments.

"How . . . ?" Haddon started, then apparently thought it better to leave his question unasked.

Cosman nursed the bus along, partly by feel and partly by the radarscope which revealed the position of the guidewall along the edge of the ramp. After a couple of minutes he brought the bus onto the South Sandusky Dome expressway, switched on the autopilot, and sat back.

"Your first mission, Haddon?" he asked.

"Well . . . the first real one. I've had mock-up training, of course."

"Okay. You know where the coffee is?"

"Oh, certainly!"

"Fine. That's part of the second driver's job. Go get us some. Make mine black."

"Mine with white and sweet," said Mabry.

Haddon got up and moved out of the cockpit, back into the passenger section. Cosman and Mabry watched him go; then the driver looked up at the gunner. Mabry shrugged elaborately and chuckled. Cosman spread his hands in a gesture of hopelessness and the gunner chuckled again and nodded.

After a moment Mabry asked, "How close can we get on the expressway?"

"To within a couple of miles, I think." Cosman got out his road map, triangulated the position he had been given for the downed plane, and marked the spot on the map. "Yeah. A little less than two miles. Plenty of old roads there. We probably won't need to use the tracks to get in."

Haddon returned with the covered coffee mugs in time to hear the end of that.

"Is it in . . . dog country?" he asked.

Mabry answered, "Everything outside is dog country, bud. Everything except the Bog."

"Oh." Haddon handed a mug up to the gunner, then brought Cosman his.

"In fact," Mabry went on, "even inside the Dome seems to be dog country."

Cosman frowned. Old Mabry had his good points, but holding his tongue wasn't one of them. Remarks like that one shouldn't be made. They could get a guy in trouble. Especially in front of a stranger like Haddon, who might blab.

"No coffee for yourself?" he asked to change the subject.

"It might tense me up," said Haddon, peering at the blank blackness of the windshield.

Mabry guffawed. "Good thinking, bud! You gotta stay loose to be a rescueman. Some folks say the dogs pick the people who smell afraid to pull down. So don't get in a sweat and you'll be okay."

Haddon turned to look up at the gunner, and Cosman could see the look of dislike in his eyes. "You don't know what you're talking about!" Haddon sniffed.

Mabry laughed, pulled his mask aside, took a long swig of coffee, and replaced the mask.

Cosman activated the windshield washer and switched on the headlights. The heavy trucks rumbling past the bus on the fast inside lane now became visible . . . huge dark forms running on their automatic controls, each one sending its spout of black exhaust up to mingle with the thinner smog of the dawn-touched sky.

"Won't the lights tell the dogs this is a manned vehicle?" Haddon asked uneasily. "I mean . . . not that I think the dogs are *intelligent*, or anything like that . . ."

"For whatever reason, the dogs never bother a bus on its way to a rescue," Cosman replied evenly. He was becoming angry in spite of himself. This effeminate kid Haddon did not belong in rescue work, that was for damned sure. The Labor Draft Board had either goofed badly or was scraping the bottom of the barrel. And old Mabry wasn't making things any better by putting the kid on.

And no copters on this mission. That was the worst annoyance of all. It was . . . surrender. It was letting the dogs have things their way, without even an attempt to fight them off. It was admitting defeat.

"Not that I think the dogs are *intelligent,* or anything like *tha-a-at,*" Mabry gurgled, mimicking Haddon, "it's just that they're so *fa-a-ast.* That's because they can metabolize smog when they ain't metabolizing people. You know why they ain't eaten me and Joe, boy?"

Haddon, with tightly pursed lips, kept a frigid silence.

"Because we're too sexy!" Mabry answered his own question. "The dogs don't bother good breeders, and they know that's me and Joe, because they can smell woman-sweat on us. Right, Joe?"

"If you say so, Mike," Cosman said with what he hoped was discouraging indifference.

"So if you want to last long, boy," Mabry ran on, "you better get yourself a broad to rub against. That's what it takes to stay alive, boy, and it might even make a man out of you. Ain't that right, Joe?"

"You're doing the talking, Mike, not me," Cosman grunted.

This silenced Mabry for a while. Then he grumbled, "Everybody's afraid to know anything, too damn scared to put two and two together. Well, everybody can go to hell, far as I'm concerned!"

"Some people think they know it all!" snapped Haddon. Cosman winced, because that remark would start Mabry up again just when the old gunner had settled into a glum silence.

"Some people know a few things," Mabry replied. "Me, I used to read, back when it was still all right to read. I read about evolution, for one thing. . ."

"Big deal!" snorted Haddon.

"They didn't teach you as much about evolution as you think, boy. They told you about the origin of species in school, didn't they? But did they tell you that for a hundred years after evolution was discovered nobody saw a new species get originated? Thousands and thousands of species, but not a single new one in a whole century! What do you think of that, boy?"

"I don't think of it at all!" Haddon said.

"Well, you ought to. Because after the smog rolled in, there were new species all over the place. That was something old Darwin didn't figure on, kid . . . that species changed when the world around them changed. Because they *had* to change. So now there's dogs who don't just breathe smog. They can live on the stuff when meat's scarce. What do you think makes 'em so strong?"

"You're blabbering nonsense!" Haddon retorted with desperation in his voice. "Dogs breathe smog because they're used to it! That's all."

Mabry chuckled and yawned. "I sure could've used a couple hours more sleep," he said.

Cosman glanced at Haddon. The young man's face was pale with fear and anger. Well, the kid would have to learn to ignore old Mike's crackpot theorizings, as he had himself, if he became a regular in bus 502.

Because it was no good, trying to figure out the dogs. The best thing was not to even think about them. A guy could drive himself nuts wondering how dumb animals could do what the dogs did . . .

He took the bus off autopilot and swung it off the expressway onto a cracked, weed-grown ramp. There was a lot of light outside now, with the sky a lighter gray than it ever was over the Dome, even at midday. He glanced at the map again, picking out the markings which were likely to still represent recognizable roads that would lead to the vicinity of the plane.

"Ain't you going to get a copter to talk us in?" asked Mabry.

"No copters this trip," he grunted.

"Ah! The brass hats must be wising up," said the gunner with evident satisfaction.

"You mean we're . . . unprotected?" Haddon quavered to Cosman.

"We'll be okay," Cosman assured him. "Mabry can work that gun on the roof as fast as he can his mouth, when he has to."

Mabry laughed. "That I can, kid. And it's a great kick, shooting at our betters. I just wish they wasn't so damn hard to hit!"

Slav had returned, and Glitter hunched down beside him as they watched the humans help each other climb out of the plane. Clog, Blackeye, and Paddler were inside, having dropped through the acidcut hole in the roof, snarling and snapping at the laggards. But there was no smell of fresh blood;

the dogs inside had not had to slash anybody to get their obedience.

Brist had been inside, too, but he had leaped back through the hole to stand on top of the plane. He was looking down at the people milling around outside and barking happily. He was a young dog, feeling the vigor of full adulthood for the first time, and was plainly excited.

Glitter called Slav's attention to him, and her mate rose to walk indifferently past the humans, who drew back nervously at his approach. He stared up at Brist and growled warningly. A dog alone on top of the plane would be a perfect target, not only for a copter but even for a bus gunner.

Brist gave a nonchalant yap, but after a moment he skittered back to the tail assembly and jumped to the ground.

Thinking of copters, Glitter looked at the ground around her. She spotted several stones of about the right size—small enough for a dog to grasp by the teeth and sling high in the air, but large and heavy enough to reach the rotor blades through the heavy down-current of air, and damage those blades when they struck them.

All the humans were out of the plane now, and the dogs were beginning to move among them. They had stood in a tight clot at first, but this broke up as they drew apart to give the dogs plenty of room. Soon they were sufficiently scattered for the sorting-out process to begin and so thoroughly mingled with the dogs that a copter gunner would not dare try to shoot.

The sorting did not take long, and the results were somewhat disappointing. As Glitter had noted the first

time she looked into the plane, most of these were
young people . . . good breeding stock. But there were
the four older ones, who ought to be tough and tasty,
plus a hulking young female who did not have the
breeder smell.

These five were gradually herded away from the
others but did not seem to realize immediately what
was happening. When they saw the distance between
themselves and the other passengers, they created
the usual uproar. Two of the old ones, a male and a
female, fainted, but both revived quickly when jaws
closed on their shoulders to drag them away.

Another of the old ones flung off his filter mask and
started running in the general direction of Cleveland
Dome. Three of the dogs trotted after him, knowing
he could not go far.

The young female clenched her fists but allowed
herself to be herded away. Glitter guessed that one
would try to fight when slaughtering time came.

The remaining humans by the plane were silent
during all this. Now one of them giggled loudly, and
then all of them were laughing and making words to
each other. They tried to clot up again, but a few
growls from the dogs kept them in their places. The
female who was clutching a small child sat down on
the ground, looking fearfully at the nearest dog as she
did so, but plainly too weak to stay on her feet. The
dog, Highleg, ignored her. Soon the other humans
were sitting, too.

Brist was making a show of his discontent with the
small number of humans the sorting had yielded. Glitter
watched him with more amusement than admiration—
and he was plainly playing for the admiration of all

the bitches in hearing distance as he yowled about how he could eat a whole human by himself, and be ready to eat another tomorrow.

He was a robust young dog, without doubt, but Glitter suspected that Slav could make him scamper if the need ever arose.

The roar of the approaching bus brought the humans to their feet, and Glitter found herself a safe position in their midst. She wondered briefly at the absence of copters. If any were coming, they would have arrived before the bus. So there would be no copters, with crews to augment the meat supply if the copters dropped low enough for the gunners to aim and for their rotor blades to be smashed with slung stones.

"I hear a mutt yowling," remarked Mabry. "We getting close?"

"We must be," said Cosman. He was homing on the plane's radio beam now, and had a good idea of its location. The trick was to reach the spot while staying on low ground—in hopes that Mabry could get a good shot at some dog on a hillside—while avoiding getting the bus stuck in mud or bog.

"Hey! I saw somebody on the ground!" yelled Haddon.

"Where?"

"The headlights swept over him! Can you swerve back to the left?" Cosman slowed the bus almost to a stop and eased it to the left. The lights caught the prone form of a man, not more than twenty feet away but invisible in the smog until the bright illumination struck him.

"Dog meat," Mabry muttered.

"I guess so," said Cosman. He pulled the bus up alongside the motionless form and switched on his exterior speaker. *"Hey, mister!"* he called into the mike.

The man made no move. Cosman noticed that he was not wearing a filter mask. After a moment he shrugged and started the bus forward again.

"Aren't you going to bring him in?" Haddon demanded.

"Can't do it. He's probably dead, anyway."

"We don't *know* he's dead," Haddon persisted.

"Okay, would you like the job of going out and dragging him in?" Cosman demanded crossly.

Haddon was quiet for a moment. "What would happen if I did?" he asked.

"The dogs would be all over you."

"Oh . . . But I didn't see any dogs."

"They're there. You didn't see the man till the lights hit him, did you."

"No."

"Okay. Just keep in mind we're out here to collect live people, not dead meat. And we don't jeopardize them by trying to take away a body the dogs have claimed."

"That's one way dogs ain't changed," Mabry threw in from his perch. "Try to take a bone away from one and you got a fight on your hands."

"Don't you see anything on your infrared?" Cosman asked him with impatience.

"Nope, not through this muck. Yeah . . . there they are. We're heading straight for them!"

Cosman slowed the bus to a creep. He heard the people yelling before he could see them. Then there they were in his lights, standing and waving their arms, and the dogs slouching about among them.

"Good morning, folks," he said into the mike, speaking slowly and calmingly. "There's no need for hurry or panic. In a moment I will open the door of the bus, and all of you will be permitted to come aboard. Just move toward the door in an orderly fashion, without any crowding, when I give the word. All of us will be having breakfast in Cleveland Dome in half an hour. Okay?"

He heard muffled yells of assent from outside. "Good," he approved, and activated the door switch.

Almost instantly there was a crash behind him as the door between the passenger compartment and the cockpit section was torn open.

Cosman whirled in his chair to stare numbly at the gleaming eyes and bared teeth of a giant dog.

Haddon screeched and Mabry roared *"Good Godamighty!"* Cosman started to fumble for his sidearm but froze when the dog made a snarling lunge at him.

There was a moment during which the three men and the dog were motionless. Then the men stayed that way while the dog rose on his hindlegs to sniff briefly at Mabry's trousers. Next he dropped down to smell Cosman's face, and the driver felt the hair on his neck stiffen as the dog's hot breath moistened the skin around his filter mask.

Then the dog moved over to Haddon and gave him a similar inspection. The muzzle moved down Haddon's arm, and teeth clamped on his trembling hand. Cosman could see blood start to ooze.

"Oh," Haddon said softly in response to the pain. "Oh."

The dog tugged on the hand and Haddon came swiftly to his feet, grimacing. The dog backed out of the cockpit, pulling the young man along.

"W-wait, dog," Haddon was beginning to whimper. "Let me go, dog. I admit I . . . don't like girls . . . but I'll get one. Really I will, dog. I promise! Have lots of babies. That's what you want, don't you? Please . . . lots of babies, dog . . ."

The pleadings had been making Cosman cringe. It was a relief when Haddon was led beyond earshot. Mabry wheezed and coughed.

"I thought the kid was just . . . kind of prissy," he said in a weak voice. "They know better than to send a homosexual out here. Ought to, anyway."

"Maybe he wasn't good on any other job," said Cosman when he found his voice. "Bottom of the barrel." After a moment he added sharply, "Why the hell didn't you cover the door, Mike?"

"How was I to guess a damn dog would come aboard? They don't usually do that," Mabry said defensively. "Doubt if I could've hit him anyway, fast as they move . . . look at him out there! Acting awful damn proud of hisself! Maybe I can get him yet!"

"Careful," Cosman warned as the gun turret swung about. He too had caught a glimpse of the dog that had taken Haddon frisking about, but an older looking dog had growled at it, and it had moved out of sight among the people. Mabry cursed, and his gun remained silent.

"Okay, folks, don't be alarmed," Cosman said into the mike, "and start coming aboard."

The people outside began moving warily toward the bus, and when the dogs made no objection, they moved faster. But nobody was trampled, although there was some pushing and shoving at the door before all were inside. Haddon was not among them.

And the dogs had melted away into the smog. By the time the people were safe inside, no targets were left for Mabry.

"Hell!" he grunted. "Let's go home."

Cosman started the bus moving. It was full day now, but the headlights helped visibility enough to be left on. He checked his map for an underpass to the eastbound side of the expressway.

"I wish I hadn't picked on the kid," Mabry muttered.

Cosman said nothing.

"We're all such damn fools," Mabry went on angrily. "Always lousing ourselves up! This whole mess we're in . . . the world didn't get like it is by itself. We brought it all on ourselves, by our damn stupid mistakes! You know that, Joe?"

Cosman shrugged, and wished Mabry would shut up.

"We made our mess and now we got to live with it. Ain't you ever thought about it, Joe? How different things might be if we'd used some sense, or if our granddaddies had, I mean? It was way back then, when they put domes over the towns and everybody moved inside to get out of the smog.

"Have you ever thought, Joe, what damn fools they were? All they had to do was take all the dogs inside with 'em, or make sure they killed every damn mutt in the country. But they didn't! That was the damn foolishest mistake anybody ever made!"

Cosman nodded slowly. Old Mabry talked a lot of

nonsense, but sometimes he hit the nail squarely on the head.

"I guess that's right, Mike," he said. "I can't imagine anything stupider than that."

PSYCHIVORE

❧

1

CARGY WAS a hard boy to take by surprise.

Although he was just ten years old (or twelve and a fraction, Earth reckoning) he had knocked about his world enough to know it pretty well. His world was Merga, where surprises were commonplace.

And if his world was strange, so was his time. Humanity had arrived on Merga only ninety Earth years earlier, and had barely had time to settle down, get in an argument among themselves, and resolve the dispute with a war.

Cargy was orphaned by the war at the age of five, on his own as a runaway at six, an independent tradesman at eight. He knew his world well enough to find a unique niche for himself in the Mergan-human ecology. He considered himself a success, and viewed his world with eyes more calculating than startled.

In fact, when he saw the crossed-eyed man, it had been so long since anything had struck him as strange that he stopped in his tracks and stared.

Maybe the man was staring back. Anyway, his face turned toward Cargy and he propped up on an elbow as if to get a better look at the boy and the wagon he was tugging. The man's eyes were hidden behind goggles of opaque black plastic into which crossed slits had been cut for him to see through.

Cargy couldn't guess the purpose of such goggles, and in general he didn't like the looks of the man sprawled in a patch of padgrass beside the trail. He had a beggarly look, and Cargy knew how vicious beggars could be. This fellow seemed very old, and scrawny, and maybe sick, but he'd had the strength to walk to this spot in the foothills, a good twenty miles from anywhere. Cargy didn't like getting too close to old Crossed-Eyes.

But he couldn't go around him. The hillside on both flanks of the trail was a tangle of sackle trees and bladebriar. If Cargy were to get on into town and about his business, he had to pull his wagon down the trail and past the man.

He scowled, shifted his grip on the wagon handle to his left hand, and moved forward. He had learned early that timidity didn't pay.

Crossed-Eyes was smiling at him as he got close. "Headed for Port City, son?"

The voice was whispery and cracked with age, but it didn't have the sly whine Cargy had expected. And now he saw the man's clothes were too good for a beggar. Also, a backpack lay on the grass at the man's side. Like he was a hunter, or one of those off-planet sport-guys who liked to hike over a few foothills so they could brag about "exploring" the wilds of Merga. But Cargy could see that Crossed-Eyes was too old to be anything like that.

"Yes, sir," he replied to the man's question.

"What's in your wagon?"

"Wildfruit."

"What kind?"

"All kinds. Shavolits, blues, jokones, swerlemins, muskers, hawbuttons, greenlins . . .

"I haven't eaten a hawbutton in years," said the man. "Too dangerous for me to climb for them. Are you selling them?"

"Yes, sir."

"I'll take half a dozen."

Cargy went to the back of his wagon and tugged out a corner of the spacesheet that covered his load. He picked out six of the dark brown, fully ripened fruits and handed them to the man.

"They're three minals each," he said.

Painfully, Crossed-Eyes dug into a trouser pocket and brought out a hakon. "Keep the change, son," he said.

"Thank you, sir," said Cargy, quickly pocketing the coin. The man had overpaid like an off-worlder, even with nobody around to impress. Cargy was more puzzled than ever. Instead of pulling his wagon on down the trail, he squatted on his heels and watched the man eat.

The slitted goggles were the big mystery, but what bothered Cargy more than that was the realization that the old guy looked awfully sick and might be fixing to die. He didn't do too well with the hawbuttons, either. He gobbled one, worried down a second, and just messed with a third.

"I overestimated my appetite, son. You can have these three back. What's your name?"

"Cargy Darrow, sir."

"Glad to know you, Cargy. I'm Thomis Mead."

The name sounded vaguely familiar. "Glad to know you, Mr. Mead." They sat in silence for a while, then Cargy asked, "Are you sick, mister?"

"Yes, but it won't last much longer," the man nodded, and Cargy knew he didn't mean he'd soon get better. He meant it the other way.

"Was you trying to walk to town?" the boy asked.

"Yes, and I might have made it but . . ." Mead pulled up a trouser leg to reveal a swollen ankle. "A bad sprain. I can't walk on it."

"Oh." Cargy looked at the ankle, then at the pallor of the man's face, and felt annoyed.

The problem was that he couldn't hurry on alone into town to get help for this old man Mead. Sackle trees were far less active and dangerous than many other Mergan plant species, but they could be deadly to an old man who couldn't stay alert and who might pass out any moment. And the hillside was thick with sackle trees.

The only thing Cargy could do would require a considerable business sacrifice. Grumpily he said, "I guess I can pull you to town in my wagon."

"Thank you, Cargy. I'll pay you well for your trouble."

Cargy began unloading. The wagon was big enough

for Mead to ride in, if he sat with his knees drawn up, but it couldn't contain the man plus the load of wildfruit. Ungraciously, the boy asked, "Why'd you try to walk, anyway? They send out clopters for sick people."

With a dry chuckle Mead said, "Not unless they're called, and I let my transceiver rot on me. I hadn't tried to use it for perhaps twenty years, and etchmold got into the circuits. The supply serviceman was due to come by my place in six weeks, but I didn't think I could wait that long. I started walking."

Cargy felt a touch of disgust for anybody who would let etchmold ruin a perfectly good radio. All you had to do was switch the set on for a second or two, say once every ten days, because etchmold couldn't stand electricity, no more than any other kind of Mergan life could. And . . . and to have a radio, and not use it for twenty years! It didn't make sense!

The old man must have read the boy's expression. He explained, "You see, son, when I was a young man something happened that stopped me from caring about much of anything. I was interested enough in staying alive to eat regularly, but that was about all. I went to my place in Dappliner Valley, quit seeing people, and sort of vegetated. Recently I've started to care a little more, and . . ."

The name of Dappliner Valley rang a bell with Cargy. Only one man was known to live in that isolated spot. The boy now knew who Thomis Mead was.

"You're a. . . . a *first-comer!*" he exclaimed in awe.

The old man smiled. "That's right, son. Probably the last of the first-comers still alive."

Cargy's formal education had been limited by the

war to less than three weeks, but even before that he had been taught by his father that the first-comers were the real heroes of Merga. They were the special band of explorers and scientists who had come from the older planets ahead of everybody else to find out about this world, to see if it was a safe place to live, or what would have to be done to make it safe.

The voracious plant life had gotten many of them, while they were finding out what the different species did to kill their animal prey, and how men could defend themselves. There was a big memorial statue to the first-comers in Port City. Cargy had heard people read aloud the names carved on the statue's base. That was why Mead's name had sounded familiar.

"What happened to you," he prompted, "must've been awful bad."

"It didn't upset me at the time," Mead replied distantly, "since it left me not giving a damn. But thinking back, and caring a little after all this time, I suppose it was, as you say, awful bad. But it's nothing for a youngster like you to think about, son."

"Yes, sir."

Cargy felt a bit better about this rescue mission, now that he knew old Mead was a hero. As for his business losses . . . well, he'd make out some way. He had counted on getting at least three kons for this load of wildfruit, which he was now bundling into an old spacesheet to leave by the trail where it would probably ruin before he could get back to it.

As for Mead's promise that he would be "paid well for his trouble," Cargy knew from experience just how little adults valued the time and effort of a boy. Maybe Mead would give him another hakon, or perhaps a whole kon, and that would be that. It wouldn't pay for the meals of meat he craved, and for recharging his defense batteries, much less for the new batteries and new boots he was beginning to need.

Regretfully he dragged the big bundle off the trail and maneuvered his wagon to the old man's side.

"You can get in now," he said.

Slowly, with stifled grunts, Mead lifted himself into the wagon bed. It was a tight fit as the wagon was hardly more than a toy, and in fact had probably been constructed by some father for a son of about Cargy's age. Cargy had stolen it from a yard in the Port City suburbs and had disguised it with a coat of dark green paint. The wagon had enabled him to triple the size of his business, since he was no longer limited to the wildfruit he could carry in a sack over his shoulder.

There wasn't even room to tuck Mead's backpack in with him, so the old man had to wear it. He said he was used to it and didn't mind its weight.

Cargy grasped the wagon handle and resumed his journey to Port City. He glanced back occasionally at his passenger, but Mead kept his head slumped forward and didn't speak. The boy wondered if the man's eyes were open behind the goggles, or if he were dozing.

Then the trail, not smooth to start with, suddenly got rougher. The surface was corrugated by underground sackle roots. Mead grunted when Cargy tugged the wagon over one of the higher root bulges.

"The rooters ain't been working this part much," said Cargy.

"Probably a lone bull," Mead remarked.

"I guess so." Cargy studied the trail ahead uneasily.

Men had opened the Mergan trails, but maintenance was left mostly to the rooters, local animals that resembled Earth boars in many respects. The rooters had taken to the trails with alacrity, moving in family groups along territorial stretches about three miles in length, digging out and feasting on the roots which bordering trees kept extending under the open strip. The trails gave the rooters mobility and safety from plant attacks while allowing them to eat well. They had never had it so good before man came.

But their lives had imperfections. Sometimes a bull would lose his mate, or never succeed in getting one. Then he would turn psychotic and vicious. He would claim a mile or so of trail and defend it bitterly, not only against intruding rooters. Sometimes he would attack a passing human. And an animal who lived by digging roots out of the hard soil had to have natural tools that could function as murderous weapons.

If there was one thing in the wilds that Cargy really feared and hated, it was a lone bull rooter. True, he had managed to come away unscathed in the two encounters he'd had with the creatures, but with the handicap of having to defend old Mead as well as himself, he wasn't sure how a fight now might end.

And he couldn't even hurry through the dangerous stretch of trail. A maverick bull claimed more territory than it could keep eaten clean, which made the going slow and rough.

"I don't guess you got a gun, Mister Mead," Cargy said.

"No. It's been a long time since I needed one."

Cargy grimaced. The old man was no help at all.

And that crazy bull had to be somewhere in front of them.

The confrontation came moments later. The boy heard an angry snort, and fifty feet ahead a large, battle-scarred rooter leaped into view. Its tiny eyes studied Cargy, then it repeated its snort and began approaching in a fast, short-legged trot, head held high and tusks extended.

Cargy dropped the wagon handle while he drew and electrified his knife. He took a few threatening steps toward the bull.

"Stay close to the wagon, boy!" Mead called out in a nervous quaver.

Cargy realized that he couldn't worry about Mead's safety at this instant. He had to fight the rooter the only way he knew how, and that would give the animal several opportunities to get at the old man. He had no idea if the rooter would take these opportunities or not.

The animal charged, zig-zagging very slightly as it came to confuse any evasive attempts by the boy. But Cargy's move wasn't merely sideways; it was mostly upward, the way a high-jumper lifts his legs high and to one side as he goes over the bar. As the animal sped underneath him, Cargy got his knife down in time to slash a shallow cut in the tough hide over the animal's hind quarters. The bull bleated in pain and rage and, as Cargy had hoped, it turned. Old man Mead was going to be safe on this first pass of the fight.

At such close quarters, and hampered by the uncertain footing, Cargy didn't have time to get set for another high-jump, but the rooter was too close for a zig-zag approach. Cargy was able to sidestep its charge, but had to let it pass on his left and couldn't get his knife across in time to do it any damage. He flicked a glance at Mead before whirling to face the animal again.

"Don't look at me!" called Mead. "Keep your eyes on the rooter!"

Good advice. In two passes Cargy had done the animal no serious damage. And a rooter, he was numbingly aware, took a lot of killing. This beast could take several slashes from his knife and go on fighting, but if it got a sharp tusk into any part of him *just once*, the battle would be over.

It was turning to come at him again.

"Hah!" old Mead screeched.

The rooter's eyes shifted to the man in the wagon, and its gaze became fixed for an instant. Then it started behaving very peculiarly. It screamed as if being tortured. It lowered its head and shook its whole body like a wet Earthdog. It was breathing in hard, hurting snorts as it began running in a tight circle with its lowered tusks plowing furrows in the ground. That was nest-digging activity, and Cargy had never seen a male rooter do that before. It was as if the animal were trying to dig a hole to hide in.

The boy took a quick glance at Mead, and saw the old man had his hands on his goggles, like he had taken them off and had just finished putting them back on.

The rooter was now standing motionless, not looking at anything. Then it fell on its side and twitched. A moment later it stopped breathing.

"I . . . I think it's dead," Cargy said, feeling wobbly.

"Yes," said Mead, "it's dead. Can you drag it aside so we can get by?"

"Yeah." Puzzled and dazed, Cargy approached the rooter with caution, seized it by a foreleg and tugged it to the edge of the trail. The animal was thoroughly dead.

"Sit and rest a while, son," said Mead, when the boy returned to the wagon and reached for the handle. Cargy dropped to the ground, glad to be off his wobbly legs.

"W-what killed it?" he asked.

"Something it couldn't take," said Mead. "Something was poured into it that it couldn't contain. What happens to a paper bag if you try to carry hot coals in it?"

"The bag burns."

"But if you put the coals in a metal can?"

Annoyed by this simpleton-type questioning, Cargy replied, "The can gets hot."

"But it carries the coals," nodded Mead. "Well, son, the rooter's nervous system is a paper bag in some ways. It isn't built to hold certain things, such as rational intelligence. Pour in something like that, and the rooter's nervous system burns out, and it dies."

Cargy thought this over for a moment, then asked, "What's wrong with your eyes, Mister Mead?"

"You're a sharp lad," Mead approved. "You made the connection quickly. Yes, I killed the rooter by removing my goggles and looking it in the eye. It happens that my eyes are such that an unobstructed meeting of glances with any animal forces the animal to—so to speak—*read* my mind completely. The rooter suddenly had all my knowledge impinging on its nervous system, and no equipment in which to receive that knowledge and store it. So its system overloaded and collapsed."

Cargy nodded his acceptance of the explanation. He had never heard of mind reading before, but that didn't bother him. A first-comer, and one who wore cross-slitted goggles, might be capable of doing almost any strange thing.

"What if you looked at me?" he asked.

Mead winced at some old memory and said, "You would be a metal can, son. Your nervous system would heat up and warp, but you would hold my knowledge."

The boy sat up straight and his eyes were wide. To know everything a man like Thomis Mead knew! To have an Earth education, probably—maybe even remember what Earth looked like!

Cargy understood the value of education, and he was ambitious. With Mead's knowledge, why, he could do almost *anything*.

But there was that business about the metal can getting hot. And warping.

"Would it hurt much?" he asked.

"It would leave you insane," Mead replied expressionlessly. After a moment he added slowly, "It happened once, two days after I got the way I am. I didn't know it would happen, of course, and the first man I met . . ." His sentence trailed off, and he muttered: "Horrible. Horrible."

Feeling chilled and frightened, Cargy stood up,

grasped the wagon handle, and resumed the trek toward Port City. After going a short distance they moved out of the dead bull's territory and onto smoother ground.

Over his shoulder Cargy asked, "Has anybody else got eyes that do like yours?"

"I hope not." Mead's response was weak and tired. "But it could happen. That's why I'm going to town, to warn the Bureau of Xenology. Ought to have told them decades ago."

Xenology? That, Cargy knew, meant stuff about native life. Had old Mead caught a new disease that did things to his eyes?

But why had he waited so long to tell the Xenology experts? That was not a polite question to ask out loud. For *anybody* on Merga, much less a heroic first-comer, to withhold information about a local-life danger was worse than criminal.

Mead tired rapidly as the afternoon wore on. Cargy saw he was on the verge of falling out of the wagon long before dark, so at the next widening he pulled off the trail to camp for the night.

He helped the man out of the wagon and let him rest while he attached his ground-needles to his defense batteries and carefully electroprobed out a small campsite, listening with his ear near the ground to the crackings and suckings as mobile roots were drawn back from the area between his probes. When he was satisfied that all dangerous roots were withdrawn, and all small plants within the campsite area were thoroughly stunned or dead, he put down a groundcloth and pitched his tent.

Mead said, "There's a foamsheet in my pack, son."

"Yes, sir." Cargy was pleased, because a foamsheet was almost like a mattress. He opened the man's pack and stared at its contents. "You got stuff to eat, too."

"Take whatever you need, son," the old man mumbled.

"I'll fix us a good supper," Cargy said, delighted with the thought of real canned meat to eat, instead of what he could forage in the way of native seedpods.

He got Mead settled comfortably on his half of the foamsheet in the tent. Then he opened various heatercans of Earthspecie meat and vegetables and spread the feast at the man's side.

They ate—the boy ravenously and the man with nibbles. "You ain't ate enough to go with, Mister Mead."

"All I can do, son," mumbled the man, heaving an exhausted sigh. Almost immediately he fell asleep.

Cargy studied the oldster with concern. An all-day journey still lay between them and the nearest of the farms surrounding Port City—farms where help could be found or summoned. Would the man be able to make it?

The boy wasn't sure. He had seen plenty of sick people, and injured people, and insane people, especially back during the war when he was just a kid. He could tell pretty well whether a person was too sick or hurt or crazy to live, just by appearance. But extreme old age he didn't know much about, and that was what seemed to be ailing Mead. He recalled hearing two men in town talking and laughing about some man who was so old he died suddenly because about a dozen things went wrong with him at the same time. Maybe old Mead was near that point. As a first-comer, he had to be awfully old, and that was for sure.

Unhappily, Cargy ate the remains of Mead's supper, rigged the camp's defenses, and went to sleep.

If anything, Mead was worse the next morning. The night's sleep may have rested him some, but it had drained his energy reserve even more. Also, it had stiffened him. He wouldn't try to eat anything solid, and only after using a discouraging amount of patience did Cargy get half a cup of liquidized nourishment into him.

The only prospect that kept Cargy from feeling sure of defeat was the hope that, getting closer to the city, he might meet a hiker or hunter or somebody else with a radio pretty soon.

He broke camp and drew the wagon up close beside Mead, who was still resting on the foamsheet. "Time to go, Mister Mead. Maybe I can help you get in."

"I'll need help," the man whispered, sitting up slowly. "Get behind me and help me pull up."

Cargy kneeled at the man's back, clamped his arms around his waist, and heaved. With a groan Mead pushed down with his arms and swung his body sideways to sit halfway on the rim of the wagon bed. "Now," he wheezed, "help me slide . . ."

As he shifted his weight on the bed rim, the wagon tilted toward him. He started to fall. Cargy tried to grab him again and hold him up, but the old man slid through his arms before he could get a grip. The old man slumped flat on the foamsheet with a look of intense pain in his eyes.

"I'm awful sorry, Mister Mead," said Cargy.

Mead glanced at him and said, "That's all right, son," but Cargy never heard the words.

His mind was a fearful hell-pit of pain and wild confusion. Identity screamed for existence under the smothering impact of other-identity. Nerves quivered with messages of pleasure and pain utterly foreign and totally unwelcome. Nerve centers were swamped with billions of information bits, with the tight interference patterns that, when in orderly array, compose the stuff of thought-imagery. These were unloaded at random, and necessarily in tremendous haste, wherever there were cells available and approximately *appropriate for their storage.*

Cargy fell, squirming and twitching, in the grass behind his wagon, breathing in irregular gasps, his eyes wide open and staring at nothing.

"Oh, my God!" moaned Mead. He fumbled at his eyes, from which the goggles had been raked by Cargy's arms as the boy tried to slow his fall. "Oh, my God!"

He studied the quivering boy for a few seconds with a stricken expression on his face. A strong, tough lad, well-muscled and broad-shouldered even in early puberty. A promising sharp mind. All ruined now.

"This might help," said Mead, unmindful of whether or not the boy could attend his words. "I don't know, but I've thought about it. It isn't automatic, like what just happened, but I think it can be made to happen. And this old hulk is finished, anyway.

"Life force can be *taken*, boy. I know that. It happened to me. So it ought to be able to be *given*. Perhaps with enough life force in you, you'll be strong enough to straighten out. Boy, look at me. Boy? *Boy!*"

With what physical strength he had left, Mead hitched himself over to Cargy's side. He slapped the boy's face, and saw the young eyes come to a focus.

"Look at me, boy!" he commanded. Cargy's eyes met his, and something immaterial shifted.

The body that had been Thomis Mead slumped down lifeless. Beside that hulk, Cargy Darrow's body lived. Its twitches gradually faded, its breathing became even, and its eyes closed. It slept . . .

. . . But only briefly. The training of two minds warned it that the bare surface of Merga was no place for safe slumber. Cargy's eyes reopened and he crawled onto the foamsheet. For a moment he looked at Mead's body . . . the old body of part of himself . . . and knew it was dead. But that was all right. He slept some more.

When he woke again he knew he was alone, as he hadn't been when he crawled on the foamsheet. And he knew what had happened to restore his sanity. It was all there where he couldn't miss it, on the very top of his now neatly-ordered store of Mead-memories.

There was a life force, a soul, an energy, that survived physical death, the memory stated. This fact had been established as such for centuries, and suspected long before that. Just what became of the released spirit of a man was uncertain, debatable—perhaps because the spirit had a number of choices.

Mead had suspected that he could direct his own life energy into Cargy, where it would double the boy's own power to bring a return of order to his chaotic mind. And Mead had been right.

The reason Mead had been able to do so was that when Mead was a young man in the early days of the Mergan colony, he had met a *psychivore.*

A what? Cargy asked. *A creature that devours the life energy—the psyche—of other creatures,* his new memories supplied.

That encounter with a psychivore was the terrible thing that had happened to Mead when he was a young explorer of Merga. It was the reason for his retreat behind black goggles, and to the solitude of Dappliner Valley, with most of his soul-stuff gone and a doorway behind his eyes left dangerously ajar.

Cargy tried to get the old memory to come up clearly, but he could not. Over the years, Mead had not actually forgotten it, but had buried it nevertheless. What was available to Cargy amounted to a memory of a memory . . . with each step away from the original event vaguer and less complete than the one before. What Cargy found was little more than a verbalism instead of a picture, and the verbalism did not go into great detail.

During the moments while Mead's life force had cohabited Cargy's mind, Mead had attempted to remedy this situation but he hadn't had time. His spirit could not share the boy's nervous system long, especially after Cargy began regaining his sanity.

He had managed to make his intention plain: that Cargy should go to the Xenologists and give them the knowledge he had received concerning the psychivores. For that purpose, Mead had meant to put the entire recall of the psychivore encounter at the top of his memory-store.

But perhaps he had buried it too thoroughly to dig it out in the time he had. In any event, the only picture he had put in place for Cargy to examine was simply a map, pinpointing the habitat of the psychivores. It was deep in the interior of Merga's major land mass, far from the coastal regions which man—as was his wont—always tended to colonize first.

Sitting on the foamsheet beside Mead's body, Cargy tried hard, but briefly, to dredge up an image of the psychivore. He drew a blank, but the very effort made him feel weirdly uneasy, and he shivered.

That memory, he decided, was one he could do without. With a vast and valuable new education, most of it readily accessible to him, why fret over one frightening and occluded detail? But there was one worry he could not dismiss that way—the possibility that he had inherited Mead's "evil eye." He meant to check on that as quickly as he could.

Also, he had to get back down to business. The time he had lost trying to rescue Mead had kept him from meeting the spaceship due to land at noon. He was not going to miss the ship coming in day after tomorrow morning.

His Mead-memories told him not to make a fuss over the disposal of the old man's body. He removed the valuables from its pockets and stuffed them in the backpack to examine later. The body he dragged to the lower side of the clearing where he tumbled it out of sight among the sackle trees and bladebriar thickets. The vegetation would make good use of it.

When he was ready to hit the trail, pulling his almost

empty wagon, he backtracked to the spot where he had first seen Mead. His bulging bundle of wildfruit was where he had left it, but sliverworms had gotten into the muskers, and the blues were too ripe to last another couple of days. But the other items he recovered in good shape.

He barely beat a family of rooters to the fruit. Minutes after he had reloaded his wagon and resumed his up-trail journey to find fresh muskers and blues, he met the rooters working their way down. The animals stared at him, and silently moved aside to let him pass. He had a charged probe ready, but didn't have to use it.

After he was past them he realized he didn't have Mead's "evil eye." The sense of relief hit him so strongly that he giggled.

2

Two mornings later he met the spaceship with time to spare.

At his usual spot outside the spaceport gate he got everything set up, arranging his merchandise in attractive assortment-packs, bribing his friends the gate guards with a few of his choicer fruits, and erecting his sign.

While he was out foraging, his sign rode face down in the wagon bed. Now he got it out and started to prop it up when the words on it caught his attention. He blinked as he read them for the very first time:

EKZOTIK WILDFRVT
FRESH FRVM MERGA WILDRNES
EXSITIN TASTI .TRETE
MIKSED ASORTMENT PACK
ONLi 25 MINALS
GARANTEED WONT MAKE YU SIK

It took him a moment to get over the enchanting discovery that *he could read.* Then annoyance came. He had paid a drunken crumbum 40 minals to paint the sign, and it was a mess of errors!

He knew how to paint a sign for himself now, but still, he had to admit, this sign sold wildfruit. A Mead-memory suggested that it was appropriate for a ragamuffin peddler, that it drew attention, amusement, and sympathy.

Cargy frowned impatiently. He could think up his own reasons for keeping this sign, without help from the Mead-memories. For instance, the gate guards and other people he knew in town thought the sign was made for him by a ne'er-do-well father, and he didn't want anybody getting the idea that his parent was imaginary. So he would keep the sign . . . and keep those Mead-memories in their place and not let them start running his life.

"Comin' down," a guard announced boredly.

Cargy tilted his head to look for the descending ship. He found it when a gleam of sunlight caught a polished surface. It was a speck in the sky that seemed to move only slightly as the minutes passed.

"Where's this one from?" he asked.

"Vega Nine."

"That's close to Earth," Cargy said, since that was an appropriate remark to come from him. He now knew that Vega Nine was not close to Earth at all. It was merely twice as close as Merga. Cargy watched the incoming ship with an awe he hadn't felt before, because he was beginning to grasp the meaning of interstellar distances.

The spaceship was now swelling visibly. Cargy thought about the giant closrem drivers, in the forward third of that quarter-mile-long cylinder, that were spinning and roaring loudly enough to shatter eardrums—or even skulls—except that they were behind yards-thick layers of refrigerated sound insulation.

So well was that mighty noise muffled that the ship floated down without sound that Cargy could hear. But there was a grinding screech as its big tripod touched down on the plasticrete apron, and rock and metal gave under the strain of the ship's tremendous weight.

If he could only figure out some way to be aboard that ship when it lifted off again!

That was something he had never wanted before. Merga was his world, and he liked it. But at this very moment, and for as long as he remained on Merga, he was going to be agitated by a powerful temptation to do something very foolish.

That was to follow Mead's final wish and go tell the Xenologists about the psychivores.

Mead oughtn't to have put that in with his memories, he thought plaintively. The old man had been isolated for years! He didn't know what was going on. He had hardly been aware of the war that Cargy and thousands of other children had suffered through with varying degrees of anguish that had left them indelibly marked. So Mead didn't know Merga was full of kids who were mental cases! Cargy knew, because he had been in the Refugee Rescue Home with several hundred, and he still encountered no few of them in the streets and alleys of Port City.

Some of them were belligerent (but soon learned not to start anything with *him!*) but most of them were just cracked. They didn't know what was real and what wasn't, and Cargy had listened to a lot of fantastic stuff from these kids, told in perfect seriousness. Most of the time he pretended to believe what they said because it made them feel better.

Anyway, these kids provided a well-defined and well-populated category into which the Xenologists would plop him if he came in with a wild tale about a psychivore. And when the Xenologists learned there were no parents or guardians to come take him off their hands . . . well, Cargy could guess what would happen then. Well-meaning adults would take charge of his life for him.

That was why the temptation had to be resisted. But resisting was hard, because he had to fight more than Mead's final wish. He was bucking his early training as well.

Humanity on an alien planet had to stay alert to dangers posed by local lifeforms. Nobody on Merga was allowed to forget the absolute necessity of reporting anything unusual observed in the behavior of the local flora and fauna. And Cargy, a farmer's son, had as his earliest memories the reports he made to his father after he had been out playing in the fields of cultivated Earthplants. He knew beyond question that it was *wrong* to withhold information on the activities of local lifeforms.

And the psychivores were creatures nobody else knew *existed*, and the fate of Mead, and that man he had evil-eyed, proved the psychivores to be the gravest peril man had found on any planet yet!

Why, if one came into Port City right now, Cargy thought with a shiver, in no time at all everybody in town could be evil-eyeing like Mead or gone crazy like that other guy!

He *had* to stop thinking about it!

Then the passengers from the spaceship began coming through the gate and they amply occupied his attention. Now he knew why so many of them laughed when they read his sign, and he noticed that most of the laughers stopped to buy. Sales went briskly for a while.

The last to pass through the gate were eight of the handsomest, most flamboyantly garbed people Cargy had ever seen. They passed his stand without buying.

"Who was that bunch?" he asked a guard.

"Some people bringin' in a show."

"A show?"

"Yeah. Live entertainment. You know what that is, Cargy?"

"I guess so. It's stuff like on TV tape, except real people do it right where you're at."

The guard chuckled. "You got it. Them folks're goin' to do a show at Civic Hall the next four days."

Cargy gazed speculatively at the show people as they loaded into ground-taxis and sped away. "I guess they'll go on to another planet right after that," he remarked.

"Yeah," said the guard.

Cargy began packing his stuff. He handed the guard two packs of his unsold fruit. "Here's for you and Bill," he said.

"You got a lot left over this time, ain't you?" the guard sympathized. "Let us pay you."

"Naw. You guys're friends, and I got money left from last time yet." Cargy said his goodbyes and moved away, drawing his wagon around the spaceport perimeter and into the Old Town section of the city.

A half hour brought him to Mrs. Tragg's Room and Board, an old brick dwelling showing numerous indications of decay. He pulled his wagon around back and rapped on the kitchen door.

Mrs. Tragg appeared, wiping a wisp of stringy gray hair out of her big dried-pudding face. "I expected you day before yesterday, boy," she snapped accusatively. "Where was you?"

"I got slowed down," Cargy replied meekly.

"Somethin' wrong with your stumblebum daddy?" she prodded.

Cargy lowered his eyes and didn't speak.

"Well," she huffed, "you gotta use that room *regular* if you expect to keep it. It's *costin'* me, keepin' a place for you that you don't use more'n two nights in a week! And on top of that, here you come strayin' to my door two days late! You can't do that and expect anything from me!"

"No'm," agreed Cargy. He had expected this scene, but found that it didn't shake him up as it had when it happened before. His Mead-memories let him understand that Mrs. Tragg was trying to ease her own insecurity by making him feel insecure.

"Well, lucky for you, nobody got your room this time," she finally admitted. "Here's your key. I reckon you want me to take your leftover fruit on your rent like always?"

"Yes'm, and I'll pay you for four days this time. I'm going to stay that long and look for a town job."

"Has somethin' happened to your daddy?" she demanded.

"No ma'am. He just said I might make more money in town, now that I'm getting some size on me."

"Fine daddy!" she growled.

After settling with Mrs. Tragg, Cargy pulled his wagon into the dim little basement room that was his in-town home. With the door locked behind him, he sat on the edge of his cot and pulled Mead's wallet from inside his jacket.

He had looked at the money in it before, and his Mead-memories had confirmed what his eyes had seen. But he wanted to count it a bill at a time.

He fingered lovingly through the sheaf of currency. Yes, four of them really were hundred-kon bills. Also, there were nine twenties, and a ten, and two ones. Combined with his own earnings, this gave him a total of K602.85!

But . . . tremendous as this sure would have seemed a week earlier, he knew this was a pitiably small amount of wealth compared to his need. A single fare to Princon IV—Merga's nearest populated neighbor—was over K400. He was, he decided bleakly, far from rich enough to be an interstellar traveler. Even if spaceships took unaccompanied, undocumented kids aboard, which they didn't.

So what he really needed instead of a lot more cash was an adult ally to take him away from Merga. This thought brought him back to the troupe of show people who had just arrived, and would be moving on in a very few days. His Mead-memories defined show people as a wild, unpredictable breed. Which meant that someone in the troupe might be just the adult he needed.

When he showed up backstage at Civic Hall, Cargy looked like a snappy city lad. He had spent money as never before, on a haircut and new clothes, and considered it a wise investment. He hunted down the troupe's manager, a man named Petron.

"What do you want, kid?" Petron asked brusquely.

"My name is Tommy Larkan," said Cargy, "and I want to know if your bunch needs an errand boy. If you do, I know where the best coffee in town is, and the best and cheapest sandwiches, and a lot of things like that."

"Yeah?" Petron stared speculatively at him. "I suppose you're too young to know where the action is, though. If there *is* any action in this burg!"

"I know where there's a card game, and where the women hang around."

"Don't try to string me, kid," Petron growled.

"No stringin'," Cargy vowed.

"Well . . . you're on. Two kons a day, and any tips you can get."

That started Cargy on four fascinating and exciting

days that built to a big disappointment. He had no trouble making friends with all the players, but these experienced troupers knew the hazards of emotional entanglements with locals. They were willing enough to like Cargy, but not one was about to *love* him . . . certainly not to the extent of going along with any kind of adoption scheme.

The defeat was upsetting. For years Cargy had worked hard to keep his freedom, and now when he was perfectly willing to place himself in the hands of an adult, nobody who would do seemed to want him!

Also, he had been misguided by his Mead-memories in expecting a different reaction from the show people. He had presumed that his little-boy charm, plus his adult understanding of how to use it, was an unbeatable combination. But old Mead hadn't really known show people; he only knew their reputation. He hadn't suspected they kept their emotions so well-guarded.

The days passed, the final performance was given, and the troupe began packing. Cargy moped about backstage, feeling depressed, but nobody seemed to need his help at the moment. He climbed onto a high stack of dusty scenery and lay down to brood.

In a few minutes he heard one of the women passing below him call out: "Pete, have you seen Tommy, the errand kid?"

"Not for a while," Petron replied. "Maybe he went home after I paid him off."

"Oh. I wanted to slip him a five. He's such a sweet little guy."

"Keep your money," Petron advised sourly. "We're

not taking enough kons out of here to upset Merga's balance-of-payments as it is."

Cargy thought of climbing down to receive the five, but decided it would be best to wait a few minutes.

"Something else, Pete," he heard the woman say. "I simply must work on my costumes during the flight to Princon. Can't I have my trunk in my stateroom?"

"Afraid not, Vonica. It's regulations. All company trunks have to go in the baggage compartment. But I'll arrange to have yours stored up front where you can get to it."

"That's good enough. Thanks, Pete."

The voices moved away, and after some cogitation Cargy grinned. Vonica's costume trunk was pretty big—with room enough to hold her stuff plus a boy, an oxygen flask, and a couple of sandwiches. And on board the ship, when she opened the trunk and found him . . . well, Vonica did seem to like him more than the others, and could be talked into keeping quiet, he figured.

Once aboard the ship and footloose, he thought he could manage okay. Old Mead knew spaceships well.

In any event, he had to do something to get off this planet, because that temptation wasn't easing off the least bit. Vonica's trunk offered the best opportunity open to him.

He was a reasonably comfortable stowaway. He had been bounced around only a little when the trunk was loaded on a van at the Civic Hall stage entrance, and again when it was lifted into the Princon-bound spaceship.

The sounds of loading died out, and after a tiresome wait of perhaps two hours Cargy heard the soft hum of the closrem drivers beginning to turn. The liftoff was so smooth that he didn't know exactly when it came. It made him feel good to know he was on his way.

There was the sound of someone moving about among the luggage, making a tally of some sort, judging by the rustle of papers. Cargy dozed.

The sudden bark of a loudspeaker snapped him alert:

"Orbital hold! Orbital hold! Notice to passengers and crew . . . We are holding in orbit around Merga for an unauthorized person check. Please remain where you are unless requested otherwise by a ship's officer."

"What the hell?" grunted the tally-taker. Cargy was wondering the same thing. There was no procedure he (or Mead) knew of that would have revealed his presence on board.

The loudspeaker clicked twice and spoke again: *"Passenger Luggage, Deck C! Respond, please!"*

The tally-taker replied: "Luggage, Deck C, Mathurt here."

"Who's there with you, Mathurt?"

"Nobody, sir."

"Very well. Carry on, Mathurt."

If Mathurt continued his work, he did so in complete silence. A minute passed.

Then a door clanged open and the compartment was filled with loud voices. "Stand back, Mathurt, there's a stowaway in here! Getting a reading, Mike?"

"Yes, sir. This trunk in front." The lid over Cargy's head rattled briefly. "It's locked, sir. The tag on it reads 'Property of Petron Productions,' and 'Vonica' is painted on the lid."

"Get Sarl Petron down here. And this Vonica, too. *You in the trunk!*"

Cargy knew the jig was up. "Yes, sir," he replied.

"A damn' kid!" the commanding voice grated. "What are you doing in there?"

That, Cargy thought, was a silly question. "Hitching a ride to Princon," he said.

"You got enough air?"

"Yes, sir."

"Relax, men. We can wait for Petron to come unlock it."

Cargy called out, "Mister Officer?"

"Yeah?"

"How'd you know I was here?"

"Our life-detection scanner showed one point too many," the man growled. "What did you think? Or didn't you know about scanners? We've had them for forty years!"

Cargy hadn't known. Mead knew of life-detectors used in hospitals and such places, but the old man had been out of touch for too long. Cargy sighed. "Well, why didn't you detect me before we took off?" he asked.

"We can't scan in the middle of a city. The population overloads the detectors."

"Oh." Cargy's self-confidence was shaken. This was the second time the combination of his youthful vitality and Mead's mature but dated knowledge had let him down.

He heard Petron's voice raised in protest and a peevish "What's this all about?" from Vonica. The lock of the trunk clicked and the lid was raised. Big arms plunged into Vonica's costumes and hauled Cargy out. He stood blinking in the light.

"I never saw the kid before!" Petron announced flatly. "Or . . . wait a minute. He could be the boy who ran errands for us. I believe he is. Tommy something-or-other."

"That's right," chimed in Vonica. "His name is Tommy Larkan."

"Okay," snapped the officer. "We can't hang in orbit all day! The Mergan Port Security men can get the truth out of this kid, and they will. You men, take the boy to Number Seven hatch. An autopod is being programmed to drop him back to Port City."

Cargy was hustled away. As he went, Petron and Vonica were loudly denying any complicity in the stowaway scheme. Meanwhile, Cargy's mind was busy digging out Mead's knowledge of autopods. The information was, he noted hopefully, pretty extensive. In his day, Mead had been an expert with all types of small craft, both space and atmospheric. If his data just wasn't a half-century out of date . . . !

The autopod was basically a miniature clopter, hulled and insulated for use in space, and propelled by a small set of closrem drivers that, in a planetary gravitational field, were somewhat overburdened by the pod's mass. It was a handy little vehicle for outer hull inspection and repair in free fall, and for dumping detected stowaways back to their POEs. Once its orbital velocity was nullified, there was no way it could go but down. Its drivers could power it for a safe landing, but not to go sailing away to some other planet. By using an autopod to return a stowaway, a spaceship saved the time, expense, and red tape of an extra landing and liftoff.

Cargy was safety-strapped into the pod's one seat and the transparent hatch-dome lowered over him. A tinny-voiced communicator in the pod said pod release would be in forty-five seconds. In another voice it answered itself: *"Inner lock sealed, now pumping . . . Pumping complete. Outer lock opening."*

Cargy gaped and gasped as the open lock revealed a rectangle of stars and the bright horizon-bands of Merga. It was more of a sight than his Mead-memories had led him to expect.

Then suddenly the pod's closrems came to life, and he was through the lock and dropping away from the big ship. Voices on the communicator told him the ship was once more on its way to Princon.

With the spaceship no longer to be reckoned with, Cargy went into action.

There were no manual controls within his reach, these components having been removed when the pod was being readied for this descent. There was not even an emergency override of the pod's flight computer.

There was, however, the mounting panel from which the manuals had been removed, and it was perforated by a dozen plug holes. Ordinarily, these holes would offer no possibilities to a pod passenger. But Cargy spent most of his time in the Mergan wilderness, and he was never without his defense batteries, worn like curving plates along his belt.

Being in plain sight as they were, and also being so standard an item of apparel on Merga, the batteries hadn't attracted a glance, much less a thought, from the spaceship's officers and crew.

Now Cargy unsnapped his safety harness and got busy. Setting his batteries on parallel for low voltage, he rammed his electroprobes into a couple of plug holes and listened with satisfaction as the closrems' roar took on a lower pitch. He was feeding a counter-current into the driver power supply. This would cause the pod to lose orbital velocity more slowly and carry him past Port City. He could have plugged in the other way and dropped out of orbit more swiftly, but that would have plunked him in the ocean instead of on land.

A good two minutes passed before the communicator yapped: *"Scramble rescue squad! Autopod is overshooting! Scramble rescue squad! . . . Damnit, rescue squad! Respond!"* Cargy recognized the voice as that of a Port City Control Tower supervisor.

"Uh, this is Horax. The others are at supper."

"What the hell do you mean, at supper? They eat in the squad room!"

"Well, you see, tower, there ain't never much to do, and there's this cafe just across the road, so—"

"Good God! Heads are going to roll over this! I mean that! Get to that cafe and rout them out on the double!"

"Uh, okay."

"Kid in the autopod . . . Tommy Larkan! Speak up, boy."

As he recognized the tower man's voice, and figured the man might recognize his own as well, Cargy kept quiet. The rescue squad's goofing off was going to give him at least five minutes he hadn't counted on. Which opened a new possibility. Instead of letting the pod land a few miles outside of Port City and running like hell, why not go a hundred miles or so inland, land there, and try to knock out the tracer-bleep circuit before the rescue clopter could reach the scene? That way, he could keep the pod for his own use—and useful it would be indeed once he had stripped it of its overweight hull and rigged some manual controls!

He grinned at the frantic anger of the tower man's exclamations as the pod zipped over Port City at an altitude of nearly fifteen miles. *"No, he won't overshoot the entire continent,"* he heard him tell somebody. *"He's losing altitude too fast for that."*

Soon thereafter Cargy realized he was losing altitude too fast, period. At this rate he would smash the pod and himself flat when he landed. Hastily, he yanked his electroprobes out of the plug holes, switched them about, and reinserted them. The pitch of the closrems rose and Cargy felt the increased tug of their upward and slightly rearward acceleration.

But he was already beyond Dappliner Valley and still going fast. He would come down slowly enough for a safe landing, but a good two thousand miles inland!

He thought of psychivores, and his stomach tried to turn upside down. This wasn't what he'd had in mind at all!

3

The small degree of control his electroprobes gave him permitted him to put the pod down in a small clearing, instead of in the treetops. But his control wasn't enough to stop him short of—or carry him past—the area which his mental map marked as psychivore country.

In trying to put as much distance as he could between himself and these spooky monstrosities, he had landed himself precisely in their midst.

He wanted to cringe down out of sight in the pod the instant it bounced to a halt, but he knew he couldn't do that. The tracer-bleep was doubtless on the job, guiding the rescue clopter toward him. He couldn't have those guys following him down here, where a casual glance around could cost them most of their souls and leave them with the evil-eye affliction.

He took a deep breath, threw back the dome cover, and scrambled to the ground, digging in his pockets for a thin ten-minal coin to use for a screwdriver. He undogged the hull patch that protected the antenna assembly and let it fall to the ground. He peered in at the connectors, radiants, and safety switches for an instant, and found them as Mead remembered. With shaking hands he unscrewed the stops on two switches, flicked them into OFF position, and then climbed hurriedly back into the pod and re-closed the dome.

He realized that, in sparing the rescue squad from the perils of landing here, he had cut off any hope for help for himself. And the reasons why he had gotten himself in this predicament now seemed very trivial compared to his need to be elsewhere.

With mounting distress he considered what he had just done. He had landed, gotten out, killed the tracer-bleep, gotten back in, and was now staring fixedly at the mount panel. Not *once* had he dared to raise his head and glance around!

He had *never* had to act like that before. He, Cargy Darrow, who took fruit away from the dangerous but easily-killed jokone bushes without using electricity, and who stunned the deadly swerlemin tree only a limb at a time!

But he knew how Mead had been: he had the memories of all those nothing-years to remind him he had rather be dead—or even in a rescue home for life—than to be like that.

So, even though he was thirsty and getting hungry, he did not raise his eyes and run the risk of meeting the soul-devouring glance of a waiting psychivore. Finally he closed them, reclined his seat, and fell into a fretful sleep.

It was dark outside when he woke, and the question came to his mind immediately: *Can a psychivore feed in the dark?*

It didn't seem likely, judging from Mead's experience. There had to be sight to establish that eye-to-eye rapport—not that there was anything special or magical about the photons that made this contact possible, but the caught glance seemed to be a necessary first step, a preliminary that set up whatever kind of bridge it took for soul-stuff to pass over.

Or did the psychivores have vision that extended into the infrared, so they could feed at night?

Cargy wished with chagrin that his Mead-memories had never heard of infrared. Because he *had* to get out of the pod and trim it down to something flyable, and he didn't want to think about that infrared business while he did so.

He raised the dome cover and slid to the ground, where he paused and listened attentively to the nightsounds. He heard no noise he couldn't identify as normal. With a shaky sigh, he went to work.

The difficulty of his task soon took his mind off the psychivores and he felt better. Space shielding on a pod was supposed to be removable in emergencies, but it was hardly ever done, so naturally the manufacturers didn't bother to make it easy. With the proper tools he could have stripped the vehicle quickly. His Meadmemories knew just how to do it. But a coin was a poor excuse for a power-driven lock-tip screw driver, and the cutting-torch mode into which his electroprobes could be snapped was never intended for slicing the tough, heavy bolts that held the shielding in place.

But little by little, the shielding came off and dropped to the ground with heartening weighty thuds.

The glare of his cutting torch kept Cargy from noticing the growing light as dawn arrived. He had finished the stripping job and was ready to run makeshift manual control lines into the pod's cabin when a sound froze him. It came from behind him, and not many feet away.

It was a sound firmly ingrained in his Meadmemories—the peculiar barking grunt of a *psychivore!*

With it came a flood of recall. It was an ample key to Mead's occluded memory of his long-ago encounter with such a creature. Cargy now knew what he would see if he turned around . . .

It was more like a limbless trunk of a young tree

than a giant snake, he decided. The snake part was at the bottom, and was really the mobile taproot which the creature had pulled out of the soil when it reached the stage of going one better on the rest of Merga's active plant forms, and became locomotive. The old taproot was its one "foot", and was used much as an Earthsnake used its whole body to wiggle along.

But most of the psychivore's length stood erect, very like a sturdy tree trunk some eight feet tall. It had a top-heavy look, as it terminated in a globular head roughly the size of a man's, but a head that had no mouth or snout. In a line down the center of its "face" was a single green eye, plus one ear orifice and one nostril orifice.

With its total lack of bifurcation, it probably lacked the hemispheric brain division found in the higher animals of all planets, but the psychivore was obviously not an animal, anyway.

After a motionless second, Cargy continued with his work, never letting his eyes stray from what he was doing. After all, Mead had thought a psychivore's eye was its only weapon, so if he didn't look at that eye . . .

Two overlapping barks stiffened him with the realization that more than one of the monsters were present. He tried to work faster with hands that felt numb and clumsy.

Frantically, he scanned his newly revealed Mead-memories for some clue that would tell him how to defend himself. Surely in all those years Mead had thought of . . . *something!*

But he hadn't. Instead, Cargy found a very convincing theory that, in order to become locomotive,

a plant *had* to become a psychivore as well, because
a motile plant was necessarily wasteful of life force.
So a plant that actually "walked" would have to feed
on life force of other creatures, and animals would
have the most plentiful supply.

In fact, the psychivore Mead had encountered
had been the master of a herd of bovine-like animals that it apparently "milked" of life force. It
was from landing his flyer to investigate this herd
that Mead had run into the psychivore in the first
place, and . . .

Cargy thrust the useless memories aside, because
the barks were coming closer. They sounded persis-
tent, as if they were demanding that he look up. They
were so near that he could hear their wriggling feet
swish the grass.

Then he was bumped from behind, as if he had
backed into a small tree trunk.

Grimacing with alarm, he poked blindly behind
him with his electroprobes and made contact. There
came a whooshing moan and a retreating rustle in the
grass. An instant later he heard the other psychivores
(there seemed to be three altogether) also drawing
back. He stopped working to listen intently. Yes, the
monsters were no longer barking—they were giving
up their attack and leaving!

Cargy grinned, his confidence suddenly restored.
Those things had never run into an animal like *him*
before! His hands were swift and sure as he finished
rigging his makeshift controls.

But he didn't dare forage for food and water. Instead,
he got the pod in the air as quick as he could and

began flying slowly toward Port City while getting the feel of the controls.

He was not too worried about being spotted by the rescue squad. Their search would be far from psychivore territory, in the area where his flight path over Port City would have carried him. So he felt safe in raising the pod to an altitude of three miles to take a look around. His Mead-memories picked out a few landmarks which enabled him to get his bearings more accurately.

Just as he started easing down toward a more comfortable altitude, he caught a glimpse of a *structured* shape a few miles off his course to the south. A square shape, like a laid-out farm field. Curious, he angled the pod in its direction and continued to decrease altitude.

When he flew over it, there was no room for doubt in his mind. Below him, and right at the edge of what his Mead-memories identified as psychivore country, was a farm!

It wasn't anything fancy, but for any man to build the roughest sort of homestead in such an isolated and perilous place meant he had to be quite a guy in Cargy's way of thinking.

Circling at about one thousand feet, the boy studied the layout. There was only one building he could see, and that was a large, low shed-like structure near the center of the field. He could see large animals of some kind, looking like black blobs from above, moving out of the structure to wander about rather aimlessly, like cattle starting a day's grazing.

But what struck him as more interesting and more understandable at first glance was a *log fence* that enclosed the entire field, which must have been close to twenty acres in size, without a gate or any other kind of break. That fence, he realized, would not only keep domesticated animals in; it would keep psychivores out!

A psychivore could not climb a fence, nor jump over one. Maybe it could crawl under one that left crawling space at the bottom, but this fence did not.

Suddenly it struck Cargy how much work had to go into building such a fence, and keeping it maintained. A log in the Mergan wilds didn't hold together for very many years, even when it was well dried and off the ground. And that big shed probably was a continual repair problem, too, with its roof made out of some kind of thatching.

Whoever ran this farm had to be a hard worker.

Cargy brought the pod down in the field across a small stream from the shed and grazing animals. He climbed out and looked around. Nobody was in sight.

"*Hello!*" he shouted.

He listened to the silence for a moment, then ran down to the creek, dropped to his knees and drank deeply. With a sigh of pleasure he stood up and wiped his mouth while studying the cattle.

He recognized them. They were the same species of animal Mead had seen in the psychivore's herd!

He couldn't guess what use they would be to a farmer. Humans had yet to find a Mergan animal that was good to eat.

Reminded of food, he turned his attention to the grove of trees a short way down the stream and well inside the fence. After yelling some more and still getting no answer, he walked to the grove and began looking for fruit or seedpods, preferably the latter since they had more protein. His luck was good. He had not gone far when, carefully skirting an excitable benderbud clump, he came onto a fragbark missilenut that was loaded.

He studied his terrain for a few seconds and picked out a place under the tree where the ground was hard and free of brush. Standing well clear of the chosen spot, he picked up a fallen branch and took a precise poke with it at the missilenut limb which hung directly over the spot. At his touch, the limb *twanged* with a sudden release of vibrational energy, and a bombardment of nuts zinged to the ground. The whole tree quivered alertly for a few seconds, but Cargy did nothing else to stir it up, so it became quiescent.

Eagerly the boy gathered the nuts, not many of which had hit the ground with enough force to bury themselves completely out of sight. With mouth and pockets full, he had started out of the grove when his eye caught something that looked wrong. He stopped.

Evidently it was something the farmer had done. An uprooted sapling of some kind, with a couple of roots growing ridiculously high on the trunk, had been left leaning against a dead sackle tree. He walked closer. Why, he wondered, would a farmer bother to pull up a tree, or leave it leaning there?

"Don't knowledge me!"

The boy jumped back in alarm. The voice had come from the sapling!

"Please don't," it begged. *"Please go away."*

The sound was muffled, and like a whispered bass. The enunciation was clear, but was not supported by enough vibrations per second to give the voice much body.

A talking sapling was almost as spooky to think about as a psychivore, but after the first startled instant Cargy wasn't about to leave. Anything that pleaded with him to go away couldn't be much threat.

"I won't hurt you," he said. "Looks like the farmer has given you all the trouble you can use."

"He wasn't a farmer," the sapling replied. "He was an explorer named Mead."

This made no sense at all! "Who—what—who are you?" Cargy demanded.

"A harmless herder, self-exiled from my kind," came the sad soft rumble, "to avoid afflicting them with madness worse than my own."

Cargy began to see the light, he thought. "Did Mead 'knowledge' you? Is that what's wrong?"

"Yes."

"But how? He did it to me, too, but you've got to have eyes for that to happen. And you haven't."

"But I have. One eye, at any rate. You don't see it because I'm hiding my head in this hollow tree trunk."

Cargy gulped. "You're the . . . *psychivore!*"

"The what? Oh. Yes. I could be so classified, if one is concerned about the manner of my nourishment. Will you please promise not to knowledge me?"

"H-hold on, while I figure this out," Cargy replied.

He hadn't paid much attention to that part of

Mead's memory of the psychivore before, but obviously the creature had not come away from the encounter unscathed. Cargy recalled now that Mead had watched with amused, little-souled indifference as the creature went into a fit after it had nourished on him. Instead of walking away, it had dragged itself, root-foot first, out of the man's sight.

As part of its meal off Mead's soul, it had obviously gotten the total, indigestible sum of his knowledge as well. It wouldn't be quick to dine on another human!

"How did you get those upper roots, and a voice?" Cargy asked.

"From Mead's knowledge. The arms allowed me to construct a fence, to protect others of my kind from contact with me. The voice I developed in case I met another human, to beg him not to knowledge me again."

"You just wanted arms and a voice and, got them?"

"Not at all! Much time and energy was required. Mead's knowledge defined the necessary structures."

"And you built the barn for your cows?"

"Yes. I used such as I could of the knowledge forced upon me."

"Okay," said Cargy. "I've got it straight now. I won't knowledge you if you don't try to nourish on me. If you do, you get knowledged automatically. Understand?"

"Yes." The psychivore wriggled its foot back from the dead tree and freed its head from the hole. It turned and gazed solemnly at the boy. He gazed back, and nothing happened.

The boy grinned: "We don't look much alike, but we've got a lot of stuff that's the same in our heads."

The two of them strolled out of the grove and toward the shed, chatting of such things as the diverse habits of Mergan vegetation and of Mead's life subsequent to his meeting with the psychivore. After a little mental searching, Cargy came up with the name Barkis for his new friend, and the psychivore (after consulting the same memories as Cargy's) agreed that it would be satisfactory.

It was particularly interested in Mead's theories about itself, and Cargy described these in considerable detail. Soul-stuff, Mead had thought, drifted like an insubstantial fog from Merga's motile plants, and was doubtless absorbed in great quantities by the grass-munching herd animals of the psychivores. After an animal had been "milked" its nature was such that it soon recaptured its normal supply.

Barkis agreed that Mead's theories fitted with what the psychivores knew of themselves and their animals. In the shed, where comatose herd animals were sheltered until they recovered from a "milking", Cargy watched Barkis take nourishment. Then they wandered back outside.

"Something I don't understand," complained the boy. "Your folks talk mostly by exchanging bits of soul, you say, and when you do, one of you learns everything the other knows that he didn't already know. What's already known to both sort of cancels out in the exchange. You were used to getting knowledge the way you got it from Mead, so what bothered you about that was getting too much strange knowledge at once, wasn't it?"

"Yes."

"Okay. What I want to know is, why do you think the other psychivores would go crazy if you communicated with them? You didn't go crazy, or at least not for long."

"But I *did*, and I'm still thoroughly insane," Barkis replied.

"You don't seem like it to me," Cargy said uneasily.

"But I am. My willingness to grow arms, and to construct artifacts, would be obvious evidence of insanity to my kind. And they would know, as I did not at the time, that the insanity is permanent. At the beginning I was sustained only by the hope that the aberrative effects would gradually fade away. One of my kind, communicating with me now, would receive at once the shock of a new-data overload plus the realization that the aberrative effects of it were permanent. It would be too much to take at one time."

Cargy nodded slowly. "But somebody," he said, "will have to communicate with them."

"Yes," agreed Barkis, "in the long run contact with humanity is unavoidable. But I am obviously unfit for the task."

"Me neither," said Cargy. "That ain't my line."

"Actually, it is the task of your Xenologists. I'm afraid you must inform them of us, Cargy."

"I told you why I can't do that," the boy growled.

After a silence, Barkis suggested, "Could you not inform them by writing?"

"They wouldn't believe a letter from me, no more than they'd believe me in person."

"But," said Barkis, "they would believe one from Mead. And only you know Mead is dead."

Cargy blinked. Then he grinned.

"Hey, that'll work!" he exclaimed. "My writing looks pretty much like his did, and I can leave it where his supply man will find it. Hey, I better start to Dappliner Valley right now, to get to work on it!"

Barkis approved, and slithered along with the boy to the autopod.

"When the Xenologists show up, don't tell them anything about me, Barkis," the boy urged in parting.

"I will keep your secret, but I hope you will return soon."

"I will, in a few years when I grow up. I have to watch my step till then."

And also, Cargy mused as he took the pod into the air, he was going to be too busy for much visiting for a while. He had to get that letter chore done, and then back to business, which he had been neglecting for a whole week already. And now that he had the pod for transportation in the wilds, he was going to be in a position to expand like mad!

Why, he could even take on a couple of Port City's snooty gourmet restaurants as steady customers! They ought to be glad to pay plenty to offer fresh wildfruit on their menus—probably priced at five times what they paid him for it!

Some guys, he mused with annoyance, will do most anything to make a buck.

THE CHALICE CYCLE

PROLOGUE:
The Earth of Nenkunal

1

THE INN WAS COOL, and the wine in the cup of Basdon the Bloodshot was potent and sweet. He drank and smiled—politely though grimly—at the joking exchanges of the graingrowers sitting with him. They, after all, were paying for his wine.

"And anything else you want, good swordsman!" the largest of the farmers bellowed, slapping him on the back. "You served us well today, and by all that's devious we'll see you served no worse tonight! Ho there, Keep!"

The thick-middled man in the apron turned. "What, Jarno?"

"Me and the lads will get along to our own diggings after a cup or three," the farmer Jarno told him. "But our good friend the swordsman Basdon stays tonight. You tend him well, and we'll pay."

The aproned man nodded and looked curiously at Basdon. "Fair enough," he agreed, waddling closer with his gaze still on Basdon. "Might I ask, stranger, how got you in the good graces of Jarno and his bucolic cronies?"

"He found five graves we would have missed!" bellowed Jarno.

The aproned man frowned. "Out in the Narrowneck ground?" he asked.

"That's right. Them god-warriors got tricky, I guess," one of the other graingrowers chimed in. "They must have chopped the holes through the roots of a young chestnut tree. In five years, the roots grew back, to cover the bodies in the ground beneath. We couldn't snout them at all."

"But Basdon could!" said Jarno, giving the swordsman another slap on the back. "What's more than that, he got off his horse and helped us dig them out and burn them. You'd think a swordsman would be too snooty to dirty his hands with hard work. But not Basdon!"

His eyes still studying Basdon, the aproned man asked Jarno, "Could you recognize any of the bodies?"

"No. All five were grown men, and there was nothing to identify them. Basdon figures they could be god-warriors."

"Oh? My name is Jonker, swordsman. For a fighting man, you must be a bit of a magician to snout those bodies underneath living roots."

Basdon sipped from his cup. "A bit," he said, looking at his wine.

"And you think they were god-warriors?"

Basdon shrugged. "No magic in that guess. The god-warriors bury all the dead, because that's in keeping with their beliefs. But they would be most concerned for their own, so they would be most likely to bury them where they would *stay* buried." He saw the innkeeper Jonker was frowning uncertainly, so he added, "I know it's hard to follow the way they think, but to them a buried body is not an invitation to the first necromancer who comes along to enslave the body's soul. To them, burial is safe, and the worst thing that could happen to a body of a fallen comrade would be unearthing it. That would disturb the sleep of the soul."

Jonker nodded slowly. "Right you are, swordsman, now that I think it through."

"This talk of god-business gives me the shivers," one of the men complained uneasily. "It's bad enough to spend a day a week out there undoing the filthy work of those accursed worshippers. We do it, because it's our duty. But we don't have to gab about it all evening!"

Jonker chuckled, then said, "It's not very appetizing pre-supper conversation, I agree. How's the wine, swordsman?"

"Very tasty, and with bite," Basdon replied. "I haven't tasted better anywhere in Nenkunal." Jonker looked pleased. "I spelled it myself. And as the results demonstrate, I'm not without magical ability."

A couple of the graingrowers snorted and one said jokingly, "A top-grade magi, that's our Jonker, all right."

Basdon gathered that Jonker's pretensions in The Art were something of a standing joke. Which was a comforting thought, even though Basdon's personal secrets were protected by spells. Jonker's penetrating look had made the swordsman uneasy.

Attention turned to a bit of byplay between Jarno and the serving girl, who was trying to sit on the big man's lap.

"Go perch your pretty bottom elsewhere, Suni!" he growled unhappily. "A man's got his limits!"

"Ho, Jarno's getting old!" jibed one of the farmers.

"No, just sensible," Jarno denied angrily. "My wife's niece is staying with me while my wife's birthing, and she's an ardent and demanding piece. She would knot my head if I came home with no desire for her!" He gave the girl a shove. "Go perch on the swordsman, wench! He's a handsome stag, and with ardor to spare!"

Suni turned to study Basdon. "So he is," she giggled.

Basdon had paid her little heed before, but as she came toward him he looked her over. She was a shapely lass with a face of carefree prettiness rather than beauty. He put down his wine and opened his arms to her as she sat down on his lap.

She stroked his stubbled cheek, then kissed him on the mouth with the full lack of restraint of a healthy-minded woman. His thought of Belissa was only a brief, hurting flick across his brain, quickly crowded out by the lush wench in his arms, though his eyes burned sorely.

"Ho, the swordsman will content you!" guffawed

Jarno approvingly. "He'll content her only for as long as it takes," observed another. "Suni's no babe to be soothed through the night by a milkless pacifier."

The girl worked her skirt out from under her, and Basdon's exploring hands found much to approve in her structural details. Suddenly he lifted her onto the table, as the farmers hastily rescued their cups and the flagon, and climbed up with her.

She made a lively match of it, constantly wriggling and straining against him while she moaned and giggled into his mouth. Basdon was through all too quickly for her pleasure. But as he stood up and adjusted his clothes one of the younger graingrowers moved quickly to take his place with the girl. The others shouted their approval and three of them began casting lots for the next turn.

Basdon sat down and recovered his cup from the floor and refilled it. Belissa was strong in his mind now, depressing him bitterly. She had been so different from this lusty lass Suni . . . so damnably different.

Jarno touched him on the shoulder. "Watching this discomfits me," he said, flicking a thumb toward the pair on the table. "I must depart for home in haste. But remember you have a friend in this valley, swordsman, if you pass this way again."

"That I will, Jarno," said Basdon. They touched each other's foreheads, and the big graingrower hurried out the door.

Moodily he watched the sporting on the table while he nursed his wine. Presently Jonker told him supper was prepared, and guided him to a table in a quieter corner of the room. The graingrowers soon departed, shouting goodbyes to him and promises of future visits to Suni. The girl also found reason to leave the room.

In the quiet, Jonker came to have wine with his guest.

"Not often in these unsettled times does a man of arms find comradeship among tillers of the soil," he remarked. "I'm pleased to see it happen. It reminds me of calmer days."

"Perhaps those days are returning," said Basdon.

Jonker shook his head. "All that is finished. The god-warriors will return, more numerous, time and again, until finally they will come to stay. Here and everywhere. They are the wave of the future."

"I think not," Basdon countered. "The god-warriors are . . . are afflicted with a soreness of the mind. Some will die of this affliction, and others will heal. That is the way with sicknesses, is it not?"

"With most sicknesses, yes. Not this one." Jonker gulped his wine while staring at Basdon. "Swordsman, you cannot judge the full course of this affliction upon the world by the course it has taken in you. And you must see that, while you seem to be a special case, your recovery is not complete."

Basdon tensed, prepared to come to his feet with sword in hand. But the innkeeper made no move other than to lift his cup. Although he had so much as said he recognized Basdon as a god-warrior . . .

Jonker said softly, "The age of the magical arts draws to a close, swordsman. This earth now faces an age of superstition, of *religion*, as the leaders of the god-warriors are beginning to call it. This will endure nigh twenty thousand years before The Art begins its slow recovery."

"You speak as one who knows," Basdon commented tightly.

"I was not always an innkeeper, swordsman. Nor were countrymen always encouraged to regard my abilities as a matter for laughter. Yes, I speak as one who knows."

"Then why don't you *use* your knowledge?" Basdon demanded. "If you have The Art, employ it against the . . . the enemy."

Jonker shrugged. "That would be futile. We must be overwhelmed. The earth is not the only world, swordsman. It is one among many. The starry sky is filled with worlds, and the powers of magic span the gulfs between. Only of late those powers have turned to darkness—to necromancy on a scale that makes our own black-spellers seem prankish children by comparison. That is the power behind the god-warriors, swordsman, the power of universal necromancy! We are all but helpless in the face of such strength."

Basdon was shaping a question when the innkeeper signaled him to silence, and Basdon saw that Suni was re-entering the room. "I will go see to your bed, swordsman," said Jonker, rising. He went out, and after a moment Suni came over and took the chair he had vacated. She regarded the swordsman with large blue eyes that were still interested, but now a trifle sleepy.

"You are a hasty man, Basdon," she murmured. "If you are equally swift with your sword, your enemies must die with merciful suddenness."

"My apologies," he replied. "I have traveled far and seldom meet such hospitality as you offered, so I fear I was inconsiderate . . ."

"You can make amends," she giggled. "I was wondering: Is it the dust of the roads that reddens your eyes?"

"Perhaps so," he replied, blinking rapidly now that his attention had been called to the ever-present but slight burning in his eyes.

"Basdon . . . Basdon the Bloodshot!" she laughed.

He flinched. Why did everyone hit upon that naming for him, even on the briefest acquaintance? It was irritating.

"It's but a trivial imperfection," the girl said hastily, seeing his annoyance, "and the only one I noticed . . . other than your haste, of course."

He smiled. "The haste, if not the redness of eye, can be considered cured."

Jonker returned. "Your room is ready, swordsman. I believe you will find the bed comfortable and . . ." he glanced at Suni " . . . large. But if the day has not left you too exhausted, perhaps you would honor me with an hour of conversation in my private quarters?"

Basdon nodded, smiled at Suni, and followed the innkeeper from the room. They passed along a dark hallway and down some stairs, the flickering lamp carried by Jonker revealing little more than the walls and the dusty night-light fixtures, which had not glowed since their operational spell had failed shortly before the god-warrior raiding began.

Having realized Jonker was more than he seemed, Basdon was not surprised to see subtle indications in the man's quarters that The Art was far from dead here. There was a general cleanliness in the appearance of the furnishings. The light from the lamp, which Jonker placed on a central table, seemed amplified by the brightness of the walls. A sense of ease that could not be attributed to the wine, the girl, and the good supper came over the swordsman as soon as they entered.

But he was determined not to be gulled into an overly relaxed condition, which he guessed was Jonker's intention. He took the offered chair, letting his right hand rest casually on the hilt of his weapon.

"I am curious about the god-warriors," said Jonker, seating himself comfortably on a lounging chair.

"Seemingly you know more of them than I," Basdon parried.

"In some respects, yes. But I have not lived among them, have not been one of them. I don't know how they respond, as individual men, to the geas of universal necromancy. Nor how they differ in particular personal traits from a man such as Jarno, for example."

"You think I can tell you that?" asked Basdon. "You are suggesting that I've been a god-warrior?"

Jonker shrugged. "You know what you've been, perhaps better than you know what you are now. And I know what I see in you, especially in your reddened eyes. Why deny it?"

Basdon grimaced. "Very well," he conceded. "But I paid dearly for the casting of a concealment over my mind, which should have protected my secrets from the gaze of a magician."

"Few casts and spells endure these days, and yours was probably done by a practitioner of mediocre skill," said Jonker.

For a moment Basdon considered his situation in silence. Jonker obviously knew him for what he was . . . an enemy. But, no, that was not what he really was. True he had been an enemy, a god-warrior, but no longer, and Jonker knew that as well. And the innkeeper had revealed nothing in the presence of the graingrowers, who among them could have easily done their will with a lone swordsman . . . So the magician had passed up the best opportunity to take vengeance on him.

Basdon frowned. He found it difficult to keep in mind that vengeance was seldom a motivation in Nenkunal. Only those, like himself, who had grown up in the new culture of religion rather than the old of magic tended to consider a man a lifelong enemy on the basis of one injury done. To Jonker, an enemy would be he who threatened future hurt, not one who had inflicted past hurt. So probably the innkeeper meant him no harm.

Without preamble, he answered the magician's question. "The god-warriors differ from a man like Jarno by being burdened with discontent. They differ among themselves in the things they are discontent about. Some worry about whether the gods attend their worship. Others are troubled because their fellows do not give them the positions and honors they feel they deserve. But most . . ." Basdon hesitated, then finished, " . . . most are troubled by women, either a woman who won't be theirs or a woman who is theirs but whose actions displease them."

"Ah," said the magician. "And the women?"

"They are much the same as the men," said Basdon. "Easily irked for reasons difficult to comprehend, seldom at ease with a man. The religion doubtless has something to do with that. It teaches that a woman's body is at the same time filthy and sacred. This must confuse them, but they seldom admit confusion."

"Then a girl of the worshippers would not be likely to entertain men in the manner that Suni entertained you and the graingrowers," mused Jonker.

"Some few might," Basdon replied uncertainly. "They would be those not convinced that their bodies were sacred, but who were sure they were filthy. I'm not sure that even those would couple while others watched. In the city of Vestim, for one example, a girl who behaved like Suni would be reviled by all, probably beaten to death by the other women."

With a glint of amusement, Jonker asked, "And how do you regard Suni?"

Basdon frowned, and shook his head. "Well, I know she's a fine, loving lass, but what I *feel* doesn't quite fit with what I know. I can't respect her, though I should."

"Fundamentally, then, sex is dirty," said the magician.

"It comes down to that," Basdon nodded.

"And what of your own woman?"

Pain bit at Basdon's mind, and he rubbed his burning eyes. "She is . . . she's one of those who considers her body very sacred. The last words I spoke to her, and angry words they were, was that she thought herself too good for any man, that only a god would be worthy of her."

"But this woman was not your only source of discontent," said Jonker. "If that were the case, you could hardly have enjoyed Suni with such enthusiasm, and so openly."

"That's true, perhaps," agreed the swordsman. "I

think my real problem is that I don't quite believe in the gods."

The magician laughed. "Or that you don't quite disbelieve in them."

"Yes."

"You were one of the legion of god-warriors who engaged in the battle at Narrowneck five years ago," stated Jonker.

Basdon lowered his head and nodded. "The Art enables you to read that in me?"

"Partly. But mostly I guessed it through ordinary reasoning. You found the graves under the chestnut roots. No god-warrior is sufficiently free of universal necromancy to do that by snouting. You had to know those bodies were buried there."

"I helped cut the holes," said Basdon, his eyes clenched shut. "Then last year, when I saw at last that my desire for the woman—she is called Belissa—when I saw it was fruitless, I deserted the warriors and set out to retrace the route my legion had followed. I hoped that, here and there, along the way, I might be able to make some amend of the harm we had wrought. As I did today at Narrowneck."

The magician shrugged. "It matters little now whether bodies are burned or buried. The necromancers out there"—he pointed a thumb toward the sky—"will see to it that all souls meet the same fate. Your pilgrimage is honorable, but futile."

Basdon leaped to his feet to pace the room angrily. "Then why do you keep on living, magician, since to you *everything* seems hopeless?" he shouted. "You say the age of magic is dead, that the sickness of religion is going to overwhelm us all, that fighting back is useless! Then what keeps you going, magician?"

"Perhaps I would keep my spirit free a few years longer, as long as this body holds together," Jonker replied softly. "Also, there is still something needful of being done."

"What can be done, if all is lost?" Basdon demanded.

"You may recall that I said, while you were dining, that the age of religion would endure twenty thousand years, before man would begin to pull free of the tiring necromancers and a new era of magic would start its growth. My greatest ability in The Art is to see such distant matters with some clarity, if one considers twenty thousand years distant. It really is little more than a moment in the total span of a soul's existence.

"In any event, there will come a moment, in the advance of the new era of magic, when The New Art will be imperiled by its own incompleteness. Men will have learned many important but elementary traits of gross matter and motion. Such as being able to mark out with great precision the path that a thrown object will follow—trivialities no present-day magician would concern himself with.

"The demi-magicians of the future will interest themselves almost exclusively in such pursuits, because the lingering necromancy will block what few efforts are made to examine the nature and abilities of the human spirit. Those who look will usually see nothing but a peculiar obsession with sex—which, as you and I know, will be no basic trait of the spirit, but merely the result of a necromantic geas.

"However, this will allow the continued one-sided growth of The New Art, dealing generally with purely physical matters, while the old religious superstitions will remain accepted in psychical matters. I can't adequately describe to you the weirdness of such a mingling, or the absurdly unbelievable conflicts that will result."

Basdon said, "I think I can imagine a little of it. Having been a god-warrior, and now being . . . whatever I am, I know something of mental conflicts."

"So you do," nodded the magician.

"But you have told nothing of what you said needs to be done," the swordsman reminded him.

"I was getting to that. The age of The New Art will have to surmount its unbalanced development, or destroy itself. To win through the crisis, man will need nothing less than a favoring destiny."

"Favoring destiny?" Basdon asked, puzzled.

"That's good luck in layman's terms," explained the magician. "It was the last great development of The Art, before the decline began a century ago when universal necromancy began to shadow the earth and negate our work. A potent talisman of destinic adjustment still exists amid the ruins of Oliber-by-Midsea. It is powerless now, and defenseless."

"What power did it *ever* have?" Basdon asked sharply. "I would say the people of earth have seen little good luck during the past century!"

"In answer, I can only say that, bad though our condition is, it could have been worse by far," replied the magician. "The fate we were able to compromise ourselves out of, because of the strength of our favoring destiny, was . . . well, it's best left unhinted at. Even a spirit such as yours, swordsman, with the strength to struggle as you are doing against the geas of the necromancy, might fail if faced, unprepared, by such knowledge."

Basdon nodded acceptance of that, having little curiosity for horrible might-have-beens. "Then you hope to forward this favoring destiny to the next age of magic," he surmised.

"Yes, I wish to recover the talisman of Oliber-by-Midsea and conceal it where it will keep safely. Then, when the universal geas loses its potency, the talisman will begin functioning once more."

"May you fare well in this undertaking," said Basdon. "For myself, I care little for what happens twenty thousand years from now."

This remark appeared to depress the magician. "It is doubtless true that the geas occludes from you all knowledge of the human spirit's infinite survival," he mumbled. "The concept that you will live many lifetimes in many bodies, both during and after the age of religion, has no real meaning for you. Thus, you are not too concerned about future conditions. I regret that. Your help would have been useful in my quest."

Basdon blinked. He should have guessed that all this talk was leading up to something. "You want me to go with you to Oliber?"

The magician nodded. "I will need two with me. First, a guide to the ruined city and to the proper place in it. And second, a man of arms who is familiar with the ways of the god-warriors, as the worshippers of Vishan are now sovereign in the Midsea region. She who will guide is not far away, waiting, as I have been, for the proper third member of our party."

Basdon considered in silence. Finally he spoke. "You said it matters not if bodies be buried or burned. Why is that?"

"Because in either case the universal geas seizes the spirit immediately upon the body's death. Unlike our own piddling black-spellers, those from beyond earth do not need unburnt remains from which to trace and capture the departed soul. They seize all spirits, degrade them into worshippers, and return them to earth to seek new-conceived bodies for new lives as god-warriors and god-women. It saddens me to think the child near birthing by Jarno's wife will, as a near certainty, prove afflicted by the geas."

"Then there is little point in my pilgrimage along the legion's route, if that is true," said Basdon.

"It is true," Jonker assured him. "Although it is not a truth to be told to such good and simple men as Jarno. It is better to let them find comfort in freeing bodies from the earth—and freeing earth from bodies."

Basdon made his decision. "Very well, magician, we will seek Oliber-by-Midsea together. I have little concern for your purpose, but . . . but I have nothing better to do."

Jonker rose and extended his hand to touch Basdon's forehead, the swordsman returning the gesture to seal the pact.

"You will be welcome on those terms," said the magician, "and may the journey be more rewarding than you expect."

2

It was ten days later, after Jonker had settled a substitute keeper in his inn and had dealt with various other matters, when they set out.

Jonker took the lead on his big spotted mare along a trail that led northeast over the fertile rolling countryside of Nenkunal. The packhorse, reined to the magician's saddle, followed, and Basdon rode in the rear.

"The highwitch Haslil," Jonker said over his shoulder, "lives some nine leagues away. She will know we are coming, as she sees minds at a distance, and will probably be ready to join the journey with no delay. Unless, that is, she has had difficulty finding suitable fosters for her small granddaughter."

"She is a woman of some age, then," said Basdon, who had hoped the sorceress who was to be their guide would be youthful, and as like as possible to Suni.

"Haslil is a crone," Jonker replied. "So much so that she's becoming frail. If protected from harm she will endure for the journey to the ruined city; but I don't think she will see Nenkunal afterward."

"Does The Art tell you as much?" asked the swordsman.

"The Art tells me almost nothing of matters in which I am immediately concerned. Only in the distance do events take on clarity. And that is to the good. No man should know of his own death, or, more important, whether an undertaking such as ours will succeed or fail."

"How much does our success depend upon the sorceress?" asked Basdon.

"Heavily. She attended the last Great Assembly, nigh fifty years ago, in Oliber, and knows the location of things. You and I alone would be hard pressed even to find the city, so complete has been the destruction thereabouts by the worshippers. And it would be dangerous indeed to ask directions of the locals."

Basdon nodded. "Oliber-by-Midsea is called a city of evil by the god-warriors. Evil is supposed to still linger about the ruins, and infect the countryside for miles around."

"The place has been cursed, all right," agreed Jonker, "but not by my kind of magic, as the worshippers believe."

The day's ride was pleasant, for men and horses alike. Nenkunal had been fortunate in that the inroads of the coming age had been slower here than in most regions Basdon had traversed. The abundant crops in the fields they rode past were ample evidence that the farmers of this land still had the Green Hand. And those tending fields near the trail waved and shouted merrily as the swordsman and magician rode by.

How different they were, Basdon mused, from worshipper farmers, who struggled to the point of exhaustion and surliness for meager and withered harvests. The new age was going to know much of hunger, he told himself glumly.

That night they were put up in the home of a merchant, in a village too small to boast an inn. The next day they rode on toward the cottage of the sorceress Haslil.

The land over which they passed was steepening, with field crops giving way to orchards and the distance between dwellings growing. By midafternoon the hills were small mountains, tangled with timber.

Jonker suddenly reined his mare to a halt and dismounted, waving Basdon to do the same.

"What is it?" asked the swordsman. "We're not there, are we?"

"Haslil's cottage is perhaps a hundred yards ahead, beyond that turn in the trail," said Jonker in a low, tense voice. "But there is trouble."

"God-warriors?" asked Basdon.

Jonker shook his head. "If they were here, they would be everywhere. No, I believe it's a necromancer."

A slight shift of the breeze caused Basdon to sniff the air. "I smell dog odor."

"Black-spellers often house enslaved spirits in dogs," said Jonker. "If we approach it must be on foot. Weredogs would panic the horses."

Basdon answered the implied question by tying his mount's reins to a sapling. Jonker nodded and did likewise. "If we must fight the dogs, try to make your blows fatal. That is the greatest kindness that can be done to a spirit trapped in an animal body." The magician drew his rod from the saddle pack, gripped it and tested its point lightly against the palm of his hand. He sighed, "It lacks the power of old, but it should serve."

"Nothing has cast a shadow on this," replied Basdon, drawing his sword.

They moved forward silently, around the bend in the trail and into view of the sorceress' cottage. The breeze still favored them and they walked on. They were within twenty yards of the door when the dogs took note of them and poured baying from their shelter beneath a porch.

There were eight of the murderously miserable brutes, all of them boar-hunters as large as wolves and armed with vicious teeth.

The two men halted, backs together and weapons poised alertly for the onslaught.

The weredogs skidded to a halt just out of reach and formed a semicircle, leaving the trail behind the men open.

One of them whined, "Avaunt, sirs! You are trespassers here!"

"How is your master called?" demanded Jonker.

"He is called Master," replied the dog. "Begone, or we will feed on your fat belly."

Jonker grunted in annoyance. "Your master is the trespasser here," he snapped. "Now move aside. Once he is properly dealt with, I'll do what I can to free you from your misery."

The dogs conferred among themselves in growls and whimpers in which few words could be distinguished.

"We do our Master's bidding," said the one that had spoken before. He bared his fangs. "Begone, and quickly!"

"We will deal with your master," Jonker replied stubbornly.

With that the pack attacked. Basdon skewered one that came leaping at his throat, and took a tearing bite in the thigh before he could free his blade and slash through the neck of the brute clinging there. The severed head clung to his leg for several moments before falling to the ground. Having learned the folly of thrusting from that beginning, Basdon kept his blade free, guarding himself with quick slashes. A canine howl of terminal dismay behind him let him know the magician's rod was producing dire results.

Then he was too busy to give a thought to Jonker as the remaining dogs concentrated their assault on him.

His blade flashed and sliced repeatedly, blood coursing down its length to spray away from the point on every swing. He was aware of having one squirming monster trapped, his boot firmly on its neck, for what seemed to be an age while waiting for a spare instant in which to dispatch it. The neck gave a convulsive heave and the squirming ended, and Basdon guessed the magician had eliminated that nuisance for him.

The battle was over as suddenly as it started. Every weredog was either dead or mortally wounded, and Jonker moved among the latter giving them the coup de grace while Basdon, now aware of the pain in his thigh, sat on the red-speckled grass and pressed his hand against the wound.

Jonker took note, made an adjustment in his rod, and hurried to the swordsman's side. "Move your hand," he ordered. "I'll cauterize the wound until it can be properly cured. We must hurry!"

Basdon slowly eased his blood-covered hand away, and yelped with anguish as the rod made searing contact. He blinked the tears out of his eyes and saw the torn flesh was no longer bleeding.

He came to his feet, ignoring the pain, and followed Jonker toward the house. The magician hit the front door with rod and boot at the same time, and the door slammed open. He waddled through. Basdon darted in to stand at his side, dripping sword ready for further action.

"Ah, so it's you, Laestarp," Jonker was saying conversationally. "Even in the old days your ethics were dubious. So it has come to this."

He was facing, across the room, a string-bearded magician in a filthy robe, a man who impressed Basdon at first as being abnormally tall, but after an instant he realized the man was merely abnormally thin.

This apparition-like black-speller grinned maliciously. "Ah, Norjek the Fat," he sneered, calling Jonker by what Basdon guessed was his companion's real name. "More ungainly than ever, I see. And in low company if my Art does not mistake me, which it seldom does. A renegade god-warrior, no less."

"Where is Haslil?" Jonker rapped, with no jollity at all.

Laestarp made a grimace of mock regret. "It is sad, but the old girl's soul is now in the care of magicians greater than ourselves," he said piously. "Presumably she knew you were coming, and that gave her the will to be stubborn to the end. She would not bend to my superior power, and as it happens in such unfortunate cases, she broke at last, while you were tormenting my poor servants outside."

The black-speller moved a few cautious steps, keeping his eyes on Jonker, and drew a curtain from in front of a bed nook. The withered, half-naked body of a crone lay there.

"As you can see," Laestarp added, "her spirit has taken its leave, despite my efforts to restrain it here."

"You are a fool, Laestarp," said Jonker. "An over-educated fool."

Laestarp shrugged. "One does as best one can with his abilities, in a world that grows less perfect with each day. But as you can see, good colleague, whatever errand brought you here has come to naught. You need not linger. I will tend to the crone's proper burning, along with that of my cruelly dispatched servants. Let us hope not to meet again, Norjek, as we both seem destined to lose tragically when we encounter."

Jonker's shoulders drooped and he glanced at Basdon. "The harm is done past mending," he muttered. "We may as well return home."

Basdon was cold with anger, and his aching leg did nothing to improve his mood. Before him stood the stereotype of the vile Ungodly Magician, the villain he had been taught to hate as a youthful worshipper, but the like of which he had not previously met in Nenkunal.

"And leave this scum infesting the earth?" he gritted.

"His power to do harm is minimal, now that his dogs are gone," shrugged Jonker, "and the universal geas is now too strong for him to enslave other spirits. Let him live."

Basdon frowned in frustration, but he realized that Jonker had more understanding than he.

"Very well. But you mentioned a small granddaughter of the sorceress . . ."

"Oh, yes," nodded Jonker, "I'd forgotten, the child. We must see her into proper fosterage. Where is the child, Laestarp?"

The black-speller had paled. "Perhaps in the

kitchen," he said with a show of unconcern. "Don't trouble yourselves with her, good men. I will see her into kindly keeping when the burnings are done."

Jonker studied him for a long moment. Then he sighed. "You are too filled with sly intrigues to read well, Laestarp. But some things are obvious, and others I can guess. Among the former is that you have not the air of a man whose hopes have been confounded. Whatever your purpose here was, you still hope to accomplish it. And the purpose I can guess at. We will have the grandchild, or we will have you dead!"

"Oh, come-come, good colleague!" Laestarp half-whined. "Enough ill has been done this day! Don't irk me by refusing my kindly inclination to let you depart in peace."

"We will have the grandchild," Jonker repeated firmly.

Laestarp looked from one grim face to the other, then smiled. "You are not an easy man to deceive, Norjek. The child is dead, too, but through no deed of mine. It was one of the strange new pestilences that struck her down. I hesitated to tell you this, fearing that in your present mood you would blame her death on me."

"The child is not dead," said Jonker.

"But . . . but . . ."

Jonker gestured to Basdon. "You were right, swordsman. Slay him while I counter his Art."

Basdon moved forward.

"*Good men!*" screeched Laestarp. "I will gladly share with you the trove by the Midsea! There is plenty there for each of us, and—"

Basdon's sword cut his plea short, and the black-speller's body, nearly decapitated by the stroke, fell lifeless to the floor.

"Now you will suffer as you've inflicted, necromancer!" Jonker said in a loud voice.

"He didn't hear you," said Basdon, wiping his blade on a drapery.

"He heard," Jonker replied. "I must find the child." He waddled swiftly across the room and through a door. Basdon started to follow, then decided his help was not sufficiently needed to keep him on his injured leg. He went to the bed nook, tossed the crone's body off onto the floor, and lay down in her place.

His last thought was that he wouldn't have dreamed of treating a dead body with such seeming disrespect while he had remained a worshipper. But a body, after the spirit had departed, was merely so much meat . . .

He fell asleep . . . and had nightmares about dead bodies that were far more than so much meat.

The smell of food woke him. He sat up and saw it was night. The room was lit by a couple of candles, and Jonker was putting plates on a table.

Basdon moved to the edge of the bed. He saw his leg had been bandaged, and there was no pain in it. Jonker grinned at him.

"Let's eat, swordsman. Then we have some work to do." The magician nodded toward the two bodies on the floor.

Basdon stood up and walked to the table, noticing only a mild sensation of weakness in his leg. "Did you find the child?" he asked.

Jonker nodded. "She's sleeping now. It's best that she remain so until we clean up the gore a bit."

"Then Laestarp did not harm her?"

Jonker frowned as he filled his plate. "Frankly, Basdon, I'm not sure what he did to her. She was in a geas-daze when I found her in one of the back rooms. I brought her out of it, and questioned her, but she could tell me little. All indications are that she's been grossly geased, but I don't know to what purpose. Nor can I break the geas."

"I thought that one magician's geas could be broken by another," the swordsman remarked, puzzled.

"In the old days that was true," replied Jonker, shaking his head, "but now . . . well, when a geas is superimposed on a spirit already afflicted by universal necromancy, the two entrapments frequently interweave, and the stronger lends its strength to the weaker. That seems to be what's happened to the child Eanna."

"You mean she's a worshipper?"

"So her words and concerns indicate," Jonker said sadly.

"Poor kid," said Basdon.

"But despite her affliction, she can guide us to Oliber-by-Midsea, in her grandmother's stead."

"But how could a mere child . . . ?"

"Her grandmother trained her for it. Maybe the old girl suspected that something would keep her from going, or maybe it was her way of entertaining the child. Haslil, as I believe I told you, was able to see minds at a distance. Also, under correct conditions she could show her mind to another. She spent many hours showing little Eanna how she traveled to Oliber as a young woman, and some of the things she saw in that city. The child knows the way as well as if she'd been there."

The magician sighed and pushed his plate away. "It is too bad, I suppose, that Laestarp didn't know this about Eanna far sooner. Then perhaps he would merely have stolen the child instead of torturing the old woman to death in an effort to make her cooperate."

"What was Laestarp after, anyway?" Basdon asked.

"Power," shrugged Jonker. "Some of the talismans lost in Oliber should still have fair potency in trained hands. I suppose Laestarp would have succeeded in setting himself up somewhere as a . . . a . . . what is that word for a speaker among worshippers?"

"You mean a priest?"

"That's the word. Laestarp probably saw himself as a sort of super-priest, demi-magician, taking control of some backward region, and perhaps going on from there. Many such will arise during the coming centuries, as talismans are accidentally unearthed here and there and put to clumsy use. Most such discoveries will be destroyed, however. The worshipers and god-warriors seem intent on leaving no trace of the Age of Magic in existence, either on or under the earth."

"I know," said Basdon. "I did my share of smashing as a god-warrior."

"Don't let your past deeds prey on your spirit," the magician admonished. "A man who has fought, within himself, the power of the universal geas and won a partial victory deserves praise rather than blame."

"A partial victory, indeed," said Basdon, recalling the nightmares that had troubled his nap in the bed nook.

3

The journey resumed the following morning, this time with Basdon in front, leading a somewhat aged mare which had belonged to the sorceress Haslil and now ridden by her granddaughter Eanna. Jonker followed with the packhorse tied to his saddle.

It was well, Basdon mused, that there was a separate mount for the child. Though she was no more than six years old, she was exceedingly fat. Jonker murmured something to Basdon about "compulsive eating" as a symptom of the girl's affliction, and it was easy to see she was afflicted by the worshipper curse.

She had become slightly hysterical when Basdon made to lift her onto her mount. *"Don't touch me!"* she had squalled. This reminded the swordsman strongly of Belissa who also, more often than not, reacted badly to the touch of a man.

Then, to add to the absurdity of it all, she allowed Jonker to lift her aboard with no fuss. Evidently his ministrations to her the day before, Basdon guessed, had taken the magician out of the category of "man" and placed him in the safer image of, perhaps, "uncle" or "doctor."

The straw-yellow color of the child's hair also called Belissa to Basdon's mind, and so did her generally sullen demeanor. As the first morning on the road progressed, the swordsman detested the child more and more.

But Eanna was an accurate guide, as Jonker affirmed during the midday rest.

"I know the first twenty leagues or so of the route,"

he told Basdon privately, "and the tyke hasn't missed a single turning."

The first night was spent in an inn, still well inside the borders of Nenkunal. They stopped there long before dark, so as not to tire the child unduly with too much unaccustomed riding. The little girl ate a supper fit to fill a burly wood-cutter and puffed off to bed.

Basdon's dislike gave away briefly to awed wonder the next morning when she put away a breakfast that would have left him too full to move. No wonder she was so fat. The oddity was that, despite the way she was eating, she appeared no fatter than the day before . . . possibly a shade less so.

That morning she was less grumpy on the road, and seemed to take a childish delight in being able to command the movements of two adults. During the afternoon some trivial remark of Basdon's (he never learned exactly what) irked her, and the sullenness of the day before returned in full force. For an hour she grew increasingly fretful as she directed them along a dwindling trail that wound laboriously along the side of the highest mountain they had yet encountered.

Basdon glanced back at her finally and saw her eyes were large with alarm. He guessed she was frightened by the gloominess of the mountainside, where tall trees kept the trail in perpetual twilight.

Annoyed with himself for disliking a helpless child, he said gently, "We will come to an opening soon, won't we? We can rest there for the night."

"I d-don't know," she replied in a tremulous whine.

"Oh? Where did your grandmother stop for the night?"

"I don't know that, either. I mean . . . I do know, but it wasn't along here."

He sensed pure terror in her voice and reined his horse to a halt. "What's wrong, child?" he asked.

"*I'm lost!*" she wailed, and began weeping loudly.

"Lost?" Basdon looked at Jonker who had drawn up behind the girl's mare and was watching her in expressionless silence.

"Y-you made me m-mad," the child sobbed, "so I went the wrong w-way to fix you!"

The swordsman stifled a groan of anger. "All right, I'm sorry I made you mad," he snapped. "Now stop crying and we'll get back on the right road."

"I-I don't know *how!*" she bellowed. "I been trying for a long time, but I d-don't know the w-way! This black old p-path keeps going wrong!"

Basdon started to reply but was stopped by a gesture from the magician. For minutes then they sat silently on their horses while the little girl continued to bawl.

Then Jonker said, "I believe I can find the way back, Eanna. Just leave it to me. In two hours of riding we'll be back on a trail your grandmother showed you."

She stared at him in hopeful disbelief. Obviously it had not occurred to her that these men could find their way anywhere without her guidance. "You can?"

"Certainly. But we can't ride another two hours today. I noticed a spot a few hundred yards back where we can stay the night in fair comfort, however."

He turned his big mare about and moved off. The swordsman and child followed.

After Eanna had proven that her emotional upset had not harmed her appetite and had crawled into her tent, Basdon asked the magician, "Did you know what she was up to all the time?"

"Yes," Jonker replied, poking idly at the embers of the campfire. "I didn't interfere, because it was best to let her learn her lesson here in Nenkunal, where one can stray in fair safety and where I'm familiar with the lay of the land. Such a spiteful little prank could be costly later on, in worshipper country. I think she will try nothing like that again."

After a moment Basdon said, "The fault is mine in part. The blubbery brat irks me, and I have perhaps made less effort than I should to conceal my dislike, and treat her kindly. I will try harder hereafter."

"That would be helpful, swordsman. We must keep in mind that the child has no one but us to depend upon for protection and care, and we are yet practically strangers to her. She needs assurance that she can trust and depend upon us. When she feels disliked, as she did today, she is likely to do some foolish thing to prove that we need her as much as she needs us. I imagine when she led us astray, she had a vision of you on your knees before her, humbly begging her to guide you out of the wilderness, and promising her anything she wanted." The magician chuckled and added, "Such dreams of blackmail have to be thwarted, of course, when they occur. But better yet, a child should not be obliged to have such dreams."

Basdon nodded but said nothing. He felt ashamed of himself.

*   *   *

As Jonker had promised, he led them back to the proper route with no difficulty the next morning. Eanna seemed relieved to be once more on a road she knew.

And Basdon noted she seemed far less babyish than before. The misadventure of the previous afternoon, he decided, had definitely matured her.

She even looked more mature, like a child of eight years rather than one of six. Perhaps that was due to the fact that, despite her fantastic appetite, she was losing fat under the unaccustomed exercise and strain of travel.

That afternoon they crossed the unmarked border of Nenkunal in the unpeopled Hif Hills. They were now in a region that had been untraveled for years, and the trails were thick with weeds and waste-brush, often to the point of being obscured and almost impassable. Eanna's eyes often flicked about with alarm for a space of hundreds of yards in search of a familiar marking. Then she would spot something that had survived the years since Haslil passed . . . a distinctive rock outcrop, or boulder, or twisty little ravine . . . and giggle with relief. At such times Basdon, heeding Jonker's words, would turn in his saddle to give the child an approving smile.

In the night's camp beside a tiny stream, Eanna retained her unusual good spirits as well as her usual tremendous appetite.

Basdon's eyes studied her back as she arose from her place by the fire and walked slowly to her tent. Her rump was still a protruding balloon of blubber, but it no longer threatened to split her dress with every waddling step. In fact, her clothing now hung somewhat loosely on her. The child was definitely losing weight.

Which was nothing to worry about. She had it to spare.

The next morning as he helped the magician prepare breakfast, he saw the girl come back from the stream tugging at her dress, then peering down at the results with a puzzled expression.

The hem of the dress reached only to her knees. Basdon frowned. The last time he had noticed, that same grubby dress had concealed the child's gross legs well below the knee.

"Jonker!" he hissed. "The kid's gotten taller!"

"Yes," said the magician. "All that food and fat had to be going into something. I realized what was happening yesterday."

"But this is unheard of!" the swordsman objected.

"Among worshippers, perhaps it is," replied Jonker. "Not among magicians. It is a cruel geas to inflict upon a child, which is perhaps why it is so effective now when the universal necromancy stifles most benignant applications of The Art. No doubt it is the work of Laestarp."

"Just what's happening to her? Is she going to become a giantess?"

"No, she's merely growing up and maturing faster, at a rate of approximately one year per day. It is a two-week journey to Oliber-by-Midsea. Eanna will be a young woman of twenty when we reach there."

Basdon stared in shock at the girl, who was kneeling in front of her tent with head and arms inside digging through her belongings, probably in search of a longer dress. Her big rump hiked her skirt high in the back, revealing an ugly expanse of lumpy, pasty-white thighs.

"But why should even a creature like Laestarp want to do that?" he demanded.

"I can think of two reasons," said Jonker. "One, he wanted a woman, force-grown under his control, for his sexual enjoyment and abuse. Two, he meant to blackmail old Haslil by offering to break the geas on the child in return for the grandmother's cooperation. I doubt if he had the power to break it, but Haslil might have yielded if she had lived and we hadn't arrived."

"I wish I had killed him more slowly," Basdon gritted. After a moment he added, "Should she be told what's happening?"

Jonker sighed. "She needs some kind of explanation, but not the truth. I'll handle it tonight, after giving it more thought."

The explanation must have been a good one, although Basdon did not learn exactly what it was the magician told the child. In any event, Eanna took her continued rapid advance toward adulthood with evident pleasure as the days passed. Remembering what Jonker had said about her feelings of insecurity, Basdon guessed she was pleased to think she would so quickly be a grown-up, able to fend for herself if need be.

But she was bothered by the manner in which her clothing covered less and less of her, especially after a joking remark by the swordsman. She did most of her growing at night, so that every day her dresses rode higher on her legs.

"We can count the days of our journey," Basdon

quipped, "by the darkening rings of tan around your thighs."

She reddened and glared at him while tugging futilely at the hem of the dress. "That was an ugly thing to say!" she lashed at him.

He grimaced. "My apologies, child," he muttered. How like Belissa her reaction had been!

They came down from the Hif Hills into countryside in which Basdon felt uncomfortably at home. This was worshipper territory, and Jonker stared at the stunted crops in the fields.

"This is a starving land," he remarked in dismay.

"Not starving," said Basdon. "By slaving from dawn till dusk, these people produce enough to keep themselves fed most of the time."

"But they will have none to spare us, and our food is nearly gone."

"We have gold," Basdon shrugged. "They'll gladly sell us anything they have, to the point of keeping no food for themselves."

"They are so fond of gold?"

"Yes. We must be cautious in dealing with them, to not let them suspect the amount of gold we carry. They would see it as a fortune worth killing strangers to obtain."

The magician nodded his understanding.

The ragged workers the travelers passed at intervals gazed at them, sometimes covertly, with cold curiosity. None responded when Jonker shouted greetings, so after a couple of attempts he kept silent. But he studied them with his sharp magician's eye.

"I can make little of them," he sighed at last. "The

geas is too strong upon them, obscuring their spirits. What they think of us I cannot say."

Basdon chuckled. "They take us for townsmen, which means to them that we are evil tricksters who will rob them by subterfuge if they give us the chance."

"You don't think, then, that they suspect we're not worshippers?"

"No, they don't suspect. On the other hand, they won't think we're *good* worshippers like themselves, since we're not ragged farmers."

The girl Eanna complained, "This place isn't pretty like it used to be."

"You'll see little prettiness the rest of the trip," Basdon told her.

When the narrow road they were following passed close to a hovel that looked affluent in comparison to most, they stopped and the men dismounted.

"Hello!" Basdon yelled at the silent house.

After a moment he saw a shadow of movement through a tiny glassless window. Whoever was inside was looking the travelers over with greedy fear, he suspected, and the best thing to do was wait patiently.

Finally a harsh female voice responded, "Be on your way, townsmen! I have nothing with which to buy whatever you sell! So go, and get that creature taken in sin from my sight!"

Basdon glanced at Eanna whose blank expression showed that she did not know the caustic words referred to her. He suppressed a grin. The way the girl was growing out of her baby dresses did leave her indecently exposed by local standards.

"We are selling nothing, good woman," he replied. "Rather, we are buying for good gold. Our provender runs low. We need cured meat, sweetroot, ground grain, and wine."

"Starve or eat magic!" she yelled back.

"As you can see from the figures of my companions," he answered good-humoredly, "we have no desire to starve. Nor can we eat magic, although I have dealt with magicians in my time." As he said the last, he slapped his sword to make his meaning clear. Then he fingered a square coin out of his belt pouch and flipped it in the air and caught it. "This piece of gold has known the inside of a magician's pocket," he said.

"Better you spend it for cloth to cover your slut's nakedness, and her hardly more than a child!" the woman sniffed.

"One cannot make a cat eat onions, good woman," Basdon replied. He flipped the coin up again, and watched it glitter in the sunlight.

"Humpf! Well, stay where you are, and I'll see what I can find."

"Many thanks, good woman." He heard the dim sounds of the woman moving away from the window and rummaging around in the back of the house. He turned and winked at Jonker, then smiled up at Eanna, who was still on her mare and looking grumpy. He guessed she had caught some meaning from the peasant woman's insults. Surely she had heard the term "slut" before.

He felt a wave of anger at the woman for her self-righteous condemnation of a girl who was obviously an innocent child. What could have prompted such . . . ?

He paused in mid-thought and looked at Eanna again.

It dawned on him that she *did* look like a slut. An eleven-year-old one, to be sure, but what was left of her baby-fat—and there was more than a plenty of it—gave her a precociously sexed look that was affirmed by her sullen pout and the dirtiness of her straw-colored hair.

"No, Basdon," murmured Jonker softly.

The swordsman started, and looked at the magician. For a moment he was half-puzzled, then he realized that the magician had read his lust before it had fully reached his own consciousness. "Oh, well, of course not," he whispered back. "After all, she's still a child."

"A child with a bigger responsibility thrust upon her than many adults will ever face." said Jonker. "Let's add nothing to the unavoidable problems she has ahead of her."

Basdon nodded.

Shortly the peasant woman returned to the window, this time leaning into the light enough for her pinched, hard face to be seen. After ten minutes of stiff bargaining, Basdon obtained the needed supplies and paid her the gold coin.

When the travelers were on their way once more, Jonker remarked, "We could have paid her more amply."

"And aroused her suspicions," grunted the swordsman. "Trading among worshippers is not the easygoing matter it is in Nenkunal. Here, the traders cheat for the smallest grain of advantage."

Jonker sighed. "Well, if it must be done that way, so be it. In which case I congratulate you for besting the woman quite thoroughly."

"So I did, but she doesn't think so. Gold is highly valued here, although that coin I paid her will probably find its way into the nearest temple of Vishan without doing her or her family any material benefit."

They stopped for the night early, partly because the girl was whining for supper but more because they were nearing a town through which the trail of Haslil would lead them. Basdon had doubts about attempting to pass through a sizable habitation with the magician and the girl, and wanted to ride ahead to scout the situation.

"In any instance," he explained to Jonker, "there will be a small god-warrior garrison there, along with the usual priests and inquisitors. The three of us, with our horses, would be sure to arouse curiosity passing through. Alone, however, I would merely be another warrior going through on leave. What I intend to do is pass completely through the town, following the road Eanna has described to me. Then I'll explore a way back that circles the town, and which we can take in safety tomorrow morning."

Jonker frowned. "I suppose the risk is necessary," he agreed grudgingly. "The girl and I will keep safely enough here, well off the road and concealed as our camp is. But if by chance you should be taken by the garrison we would all be in sore straits. And worse, so would our mission."

"I'll take care," Basdon assured him. He remounted and returned to the road.

As he made his way toward the town he paused wherever his view was unobstructed to left or right to study the landscape, in search of trails that might be useful in bypassing the populated area. Farms were scattered in fair number, and paths were not hard to find. The only problem he anticipated would be in bringing the magician and girl out, on the far side of town, at a point Eanna would recognize. She was complaining frequently about changes in the appearance of things since her grandmother had journeyed this way.

And her own changing appearance was posing problems, too, he thought wryly. So far, no harm had been done. In fact, the disreputable look of the girl in her underclothed condition might usefully keep the locals, who would otherwise be nosey, at a distance.

But when those baby dresses crept up another six inches . . . well, the scandal would rock the whole region. Something would have to be done, and soon, about Eanna's apparel.

He reached the town, and found it little different from dozens of others he had known. The people went about their business in dedicated apathy, faithful to their carnate god Vishan and obedient to the rule of the god-warrior garrison. The few god-warriors Basdon saw and saluted as he rode along looked softened by garrison life. None bothered to challenge him.

He stopped at a pub for a cup of wine, and inquired of the keeper the whereabouts of a seamstress shop. He moved on to the shop, purchased a dress for his "ladylove" as he explained it, then rode on beyond the town.

Once in open farmland again, he turned off to the left and began circling back to camp, turning frequently in his saddle to memorize the aspects of the path as it would appear on the morrow. Night was darkening when he reached the road he had taken into town.

Jonker greeted him with relief. "I had no premonition of trouble," he said, "but in this land I'm not sure the senses of The Art can be trusted."

"There were no problems," the swordsman replied, passing the bundled dress to the girl. "Also, I brought a present for Eanna."

She unfolded it and held it up. It was, by intention, too long for her. "You will fit that size in a couple of days," Basdon said.

The girl was beaming. She hugged the garment to her chest and murmured, "It's pretty."

"Didn't you risk rousing suspicion, buying a dress?" Jonker asked uneasily.

"No. God-warriors do buy such things. I merely told the woman in the shop it was for my lady-love, and no questions were asked."

"But I'm not your lady-love!" flared Eanna in a tone of horror. Basdon, irked by her sudden ingratitude, was about to tell her how thoroughly right she was when Jonker silenced him with a demanding gesture.

"Whether you are his lady-love or not," the magician said gently to the girl, "that was what he needed to say to the shop woman to satisfy her curiosity."

"Well, I'm not," she replied, somewhat mollified. Basdon watched her flounce away to her tent with annoyed puzzlement.

"What was that about?" he asked, going to the fire and picking up a chunk of roast mutton.

"You were about to deny loving her," said the magician. "That would have wounded her deeply."

"I don't see why," the swordsman growled. "She had just denied loving me."

The magician said slowly, "As an afflicted eleven-year-old, she can't accept herself as a 'lady-love' right now. But if you had denied her, she would remember your words very clearly three or four days hence, when her own feelings might be completely different."

Basdon grunted. "I doubt that. She's the type who'll think her body's too pure to be touched by a lover."

"Maybe so. You know the results of the universal geas with more experience than I. For example, I don't know why it is usual for god-warriors to buy garments for their women. Wouldn't the women prefer to receive gold with which to buy clothing that pleases them?"

"They might prefer that, but it isn't done. Only women who are very degraded, and use sex for their livelihood, accept coins. Respectable girls give themselves in return for presents, if they give themselves at all."

Jonker gazed thoughtfully at the fire while Basdon munched his supper. At last the magician sighed, "The earth has entered a peculiar new age, indeed."

4

In the days that followed they made steady progress along the route of Haslil through regions now inhabited by worshippers. While they made no effort to conceal themselves—a sure way to rouse suspicions—neither did they make themselves too evident. All towns were first scouted by Basdon, then by-passed. The nights were spent in the open, even on those few occasions when a wayside inn was available.

Meanwhile, Eanna lengthened, slimmed, and blossomed into a beauty beyond Basdon's wildest desires. The memory of the unattainable Belissa bothered him no more, because beside him rode a girl whose dewy freshness more than equaled the total of Belissa's charms.

The trouble was that Eanna also more than equaled Belissa in unattainability.

The swordsman rode on in mingled dejection and grim determination, seldom looking at the young woman who was all too inclined to draw back as if his slightest glance were a brutal assault on her chastity.

Jonker sympathized with his plight, but was of no help. The afflictions of the geas were beyond the powers of his magic. He could only urge Basdon to conduct himself in a manner that would not upset the girl and endanger the mission. And he could only suggest that, while passing through some town, the swordsman might take time for dalliance with some willing female.

Earlier in the journey Basdon might have taken the suggestion, but now he was too obsessed with Eanna to wish for any substitute.

"I will take time for nothing," he replied angrily. "We should reach Oliber tomorrow. Then I will see the two of you safely back to the Hif Hills. Thus, in a matter of thirteen days from now, I will escape the girl's presence and thrust her from my mind."

Jonker shook his head sadly. "You fail to reckon on

the days we may spend searching the ruins of Oliber for the talismans. But bear with us, Basdon. Long before you part company with the maiden, your lust will have turned to pity, or perhaps to disgust."

"The pity I feel now, because I can see that she is as unhappy in her affliction as I. But disgust . . ." Basdon shook his head. "Never. Would that it were true."

"It will be, as Laestarp's geas continues its depraved work on the poor child," said Jonker.

Basdon started. "You mean it does not stop? That she will age before our eyes?"

"Not exactly. The geas hastens maturity, which is not the same in all facets as aging. Thus Eanna still has the freshness of a child of six in a body matured to nineteen years. But maturity in time involves processes closely related to aging, and these can kill as readily as aging itself. Also, these processes in an unaged body set up conflicts not ordinarily seen. In most cases, the geas Laestarp imposed on Eanna is fatal in six weeks."

"Just another month, then!" gasped the swordsman in a horrified whisper.

"Yes: Time enough to finish our task and return home, so that her ashes can be scattered by the still kindly breezes of Nenkunal," murmured Jonker.

"You have not told her this?"

"No, and I will not until the disparate forces at work within her make the prospect of an early death a welcome relief."

Early the following morning they by-passed the last inhabited town, with Basdon taking unusual precautions to make it seem he was skirting the evil region of Oliber rather than entering it.

Soon he was leading the magician and girl through a wilderness even more desolate than the Hif Hills. What trees still stood were blackened as if by countless burnings, and the brush was gnarled and stunted.

"How much farther?" he asked Eanna without looking at her.

"I don't know, except that it's close," she said. "Nothing is like it was."

As they advanced such vegetation as there was gradually vanished, as if the soil itself had been poisoned. Rainstorms had taken their toll of the denuded ground. Gullies too steep for climbing frequently blocked their way and had to be skirted.

At last the girl admitted, "I haven't seen anything I knew for a long time. I'm going by the sun. That's all I can do."

"Don't worry," said the magician. "Just do your best, and we'll find it."

They urged their mounts up a rise and onto a rocky plateau where the hardness of the ground had protected it somewhat from erosion.

Before them lay the remains of Oliber-by-Midsea, some thousand yards away. Beyond it, half hidden by a greenish haze, was a murky salt marsh where blue water had once gleamed, as if the sea itself had drawn back, in pious repulsion, from what was now deemed a center of ancient evil.

But the startling sight was not the city or the marsh, but the god-warrior pickets stationed along the outskirts of the ruins. Basdon muttered a curse and loosened his sword in its sheath.

"This I did not anticipate," hissed Jonker, alarmed.

"Who are they?" asked Eanna.

"God-warriors," said Basdon. "They've seen us, I believe. Yes, some of them are mounting."

"Shall we make a run for safety?" asked the magician.

Basdon frowned in thought. "Perhaps Eanna could escape on my horse, but our other mounts are too slow."

"Where would I go? Who would . . . who would . . . ?" protested the girl.

"Never mind," grunted Basdon. "We won't try that, and we won't run. We'll go ahead and see what happens." He jogged his horse into a sedate walk toward a gathering of ten warriors who now barred the way.

"Running would be useless, I suppose," sighed Jonker.

"What will they do to us?" hissed the terrified girl.

"Who knows?" Basdon replied. "Nothing until after they take us. Magician, have your rod ready, but out of sight!"

Basdon was not particularly dismayed by the prospect of battle against totally overwhelming odds. As a fighting man, he had long been reconciled to the likelihood of an early and violent end. And what better time than now, when death would bring the end to bitterness, frustration, and burning eyes?

Nor, he realized, did he have reason to regret the sharing of his fate with Jonker and Eanna. The old magician was an anachronism, a regret-burdened leftover of a happier age, striving absurdly for a re-flowering of The Art in a ridiculously distant future. As for the girl, a quick death would cost her nothing but a single month of increasing pain and misery.

Thus he rode into the presence of the enemy with a feeling of calm and confidence such as he had not known for years. This, it occurred to him, was what he had been seeking for a long time.

"*Hold!*" bellowed the officer of the warriors. "What business have you here, swordsman?"

"The business of the god," Basdon replied brashly, his hand on his sword hilt.

"Ah?" The officer looked past him to give Jonker a fleeting glance and Eanna a lingering stare, under which the girl flinched. The officer grinned. "And who are these?" he demanded.

"Who do they appear to be?" Basdon snapped back.

The officer grimaced with quick anger, then seemed to think better of it. "Very well, you may pass. You will not need a guide, I trust." He gave the ruins behind him a fearful glance as he said the latter.

"We can find our way," Basdon replied almost automatically. In an astonished daze, he jogged his horse forward as the warriors drew apart to make way for him and his companions.

When they had ridden into the edge of the ruins, well out of the hearing of the warrior guards, Jonker murmured in amazed admiration, "Beautifully done, swordsman! I thought you were baiting the officer into the immediate slaughter of us all, but instead . . . here we are! But I confess that I'm totally mystified!"

"So am I," grumbled Basdon, still in a condition of shock at being alive. "I expected no better than you."

Jonker stared at him. "There must be some explanation."

Crossly, Basdon replied, "I don't even know why warriors would be here, much less why they would let us pass."

"I know where we are!" exclaimed Eanna, the fearful encounter with the guards pushed from her mind by the sight of familiar landmarks. "The gold thing we want to get is in that building, deep down!" She was pointing to a hulking structure most of which still stood among the crumbled wreckage of the city.

They directed their mounts to it, and when they were in its shadow Basdon saw why it had not been pulled down with the others. It was constructed of stones too massive to move without extreme difficulty and much labor, and too tough to pound down with ordinary rams.

But when Basdon got off his horse and led the way inside, he saw that it was a hollow shell from the ground up.

"We must uncover a stairway or tunnel leading downward," said Jonker, looking around at the thick rubble as if he had no idea where to begin.

A darker than average pile of stone caught Basdon's eye. He picked his way through the litter to its side, where he bent and picked up a rock.

"Damp," he said to the others who had followed him. "Someone else has tried to uncover something here, very recently." He dropped the rock, drew his sword, and crept around the pile until he reached the edge of a gaping black hole. "Stairs," he said softly to Jonker.

The magician peered into the darkness. "Who could be down there?"

"I know of one way to find out," said the swordsman. He took a step down into the darkness, ducked his head away from the overhanging ledge of loose rock, and continued down the stairs. He could hear the magician and the girl following close behind him.

For a brief moment he mused on the fact that he was acting with the foolhardiness of a man angered because death had passed him by. A man the sting had missed on the first try, now eager to give death another chance.

The darkness underground was not complete, even though the stairs doubled back as they descended three flights. At the bottom Basdon saw why.

"Light down this hallway," he muttered over his shoulder.

"Yes, but neither firelight nor daylight," Jonker whispered.

A muffled, regular thudding sound suddenly started up in the direction of the light.

"I . . . I think that noise is close to where the thing is," Eanna said shakily.

"Then that's where we're going," said Basdon. He strode down the hallway, which was longer than he had judged from the apparent dimness of the light. The thudding was almost thunder loud and the light nearly blinding in the darkness when he reached the door from which the illumination poured and stepped through.

The glistening figure with the heavy sledge whirled away from the wall which he was beating down and glared ominously at the swordsman.

"Sacrilege!" he stormed. "No man enters the god's presence unbidden! Prepare to die, warrior, and for your spirit to burn lingeringly in ..."

The tremendous voice fell silent for an instant as Jonker and Eanna came into the light behind Basdon.

The swordsman stepped aside for them, never taking his eyes from the unbelievable figure before him.

The sledge-wielder was man in form, but to a man as a horse is to a pony. The difference was not so much in size as in molding and strength. Heavy muscles on thick-boned arms and legs seemed almost to glow with power, and the mighty chest gave the feeling that it could suck the room empty of air in one quick breath. The shape of the breechclout, the sledge-wielder's only garment, evidenced a maleness as vast as the musculature.

Now he displayed his formidable white teeth in a broad smile as his eyes gleamed at Eanna.

"So!" he rumbled: "The travelers from Nenkunal have arrived, unwittingly bringing me a well-prepared tidbit!"

Basdon glanced at the staring magician and girl. "He's the god Vishan," he muttered.

"The renegade god-warrior still recognizes his god," remarked Vishan in high amusement, leaning on the handle of his sledge. "It is well, criminal, that you thoughtfully dispatched the spirit of one Laestarp to the keeping of We Who Own All. And well too that those of Us who received him mistook him briefly for one of Ourselves. Their examination of him revealed that evil still remained in my realm, buried in these ruins ... and also that evil lurked in the craven soul of a lard-bellied magician and a bloodshot-eyed deserter."

"Why, he's one of the Great Necromancers!" muttered Jonker in dismay.

"I am one of We Who Own All," Vishan reproved sternly.

"You don't own me," the magician retorted with a show of courage Basdon had not expected.

"Ah, but I will very soon. You and the deserter. Already I own the tidbit." Vishan laughed. "Look at her!"

The swordsman glanced at Eanna and found her gazing raptly at the face of the god. Her expression stunned him, and his eyes felt like twin flames.

"Come stand before me, tidbit," the god commanded.

The girl moved forward like a sleepwalker. Basdon lurched to grab her and pull her back, but was detained by the sudden firm grip of the magician on his wrist.

Rapidly Jonker hissed in his ear: "I *do* lust for vengeance, swordsman! Will you help me get it?"

Basdon swallowed hard and nodded, only half attentive to the magician's words as he watched Eanna approach the carnate god.

"Then we will attack him as we did Laestarp," whispered Jonker. Again Basdon nodded, gripped his sword tightly and moved forward.

Vishan's eyes moved from the girl to the swordsman, and glittered with impatience. "You would interrupt my pleasure, trivial mosquito, for as long as it takes to swat you? Very well! *Die!*"

Basdon stumbled momentarily as a blast of energy

swirled at him and around him. He was not harmed. He lurched forward once more.

Jonker bellowed furiously, "You are embodied, necromancer, which limits your magic to such as I can counter!"

"Presumptuous upstarts!" roared Vishan, now thoroughly enraged. "Very well, renegade, my muscles and hammer against your stringy tendons and childish blade! Come to the first of a thousand miserable deaths I mean to watch you suffer!"

Eanna said in a voice ringing with passion: "I am yours, my god and master!"

Vishan looked aside at her as he raised his sledge against the swordsman. "Yes. I'll enjoy you at my leisure," he said, returning his attention to his enemy.

"Your joy will be my delight," Eanna almost sang, "the pain you inflict my glory, my degradation and destruction by you my pride and uplift, the ruination of my body the salvation of my spirit, the . . ."

She had unfastened her dress and now let it drop to the floor. Basdon gasped, and Vishan himself seemed surprised when she suddenly pressed her bare body against his side.

In a blind rage Basdon lunged. The agile Vishan moved his sledge up quickly and the swordsman's thrust was deflected with a sharp clang of metal on metal. As the god brought his weapon down, he shoved the butt of the handle hard into the pit of Eanna's stomach. She stumbled back to fall to the floor, choking for breath, while the god snapped at her, "Stay out of the way!"

But even as Vishan was knocking the girl aside, Basdon was lunging again, this time to bring blood.

His sword pierced the god's right forearm, and passed between the two bones. Vishan's roar of pain was deafening. He raised the sledge, jerking Basdon, clinging grimly to his stuck sword, completely off his feet. The pain that movement created brought another howl from the god as the blade suddenly slipped free and was flung, along with the swordsman, into the rubble six feet away.

Basdon, stunned and badly bruised, leaped staggeringly to his feet, trying to set himself for the god's assault.

But Vishan was not attacking. He was gazing in tortured wonder at his bleeding arm.

"It's only a wound," Basdon snarled hoarsely. "Come get another."

From across the room Jonker chortled, "How does it feel, necromancer, not to be allowed out of a body in pain? The strength of my art has shrunken, but the power of my rod is still sufficient to keep you trapped in your body! You cannot shift an inch away from its pain, and direct it from outside! So *suffer*, spawn of darkness, *suffer!*"

Vishan's eyes darted frantically between swordsman and magician for an instant, then he made a dash for the latter. Basdon ran after him and slashed at the mighty left arm, which was just launching the sledge in a one-handed swing at the magician. The weapon slipped from the god's numbed fingers to slam clatteringly against the wall twenty feet away.

Vishan was disarmed.

He backed away, making strange guttural sobs, as Basdon advanced on him. The swordsman's lips were drawn tight in the vicious grin of a killer at work.

"Not quick!" Jonker shouted demandingly. "Slay him slowly, swordsman! Much may depend on it!"

Basdon did not know or care what depended on the slowness of Vishan's death, but he liked the idea. He was a small cat with a sharp claw, torturing playfully a giant, fearful mouse. First one leg, then watch and listen while the mouse screeches and tries to hop away. Then slash the metal claw into the other leg. The mouse screams and falls. It looks up at the small cat with glazed eyes, and lays still. Rake the claw shallowly across its belly! Ah! That makes it an active toy again!

"That's enough, Basdon!" Jonker was shouting in his ear. *"That's enough!"*

Slowly the little cat faded and Basdon blinked his scorching eyes and let tension flow from alert nerves. "All right," he mumbled thickly.

He looked around the room and saw Eanna painfully pushing herself up to a sitting position, where Vishan had knocked her. She did not give him a glance as her attention focused on the dying body of the god.

Jonker was saying: "Total physical death won't come for perhaps ten minutes yet, but his spirit would already be gone if I would allow it. Did you know, swordsman, that a soul hardly ever stays with a body to the point of death? It almost always departs seconds or even minutes ahead of that, to escape the trauma." He chuckled. "When Vishan tries to rejoin his colleagues beyond earth, this should leave him such a gibbering idiot of a spirit that he won't be able to explain what happened to him! Why, they might not even recognize him, and think he's merely another poor, battered human soul!"

"No!" screamed Eanna.

She was on her feet suddenly, launching herself at the magician.

"Evil murderers!" she lashed as she tried to tear Jonker's rod from his hands. *"Let him go! Release my god!"*

Jonker twisted, trying to put his body between the rod and the violent girl. *"Eanna! Stop it!"* he yelped. "Pull her away, swordsman!"

Basdon quickly sheathed his sword and grasped the girl's wrists, tightening his grip until she let go of the rod. Then he drew her away, kicking and screaming, from the magician.

"Keep her away from me until this is finished," said Jonker. Basdon pulled her across the room where, after futile efforts to kick and bite him, Eanna stopped struggling and lapsed into soft sobbing. Fearful that he was hurting her, the swordsman eased his grip on her wrists.

Immediately she was a flurry of motion. She jerked free and ran toward the door to the hallway. *"God-warriors!"* she screamed. *"Come quick!"*

"Catch her!" bellowed Jonker.

Basdon dashed after her and caught up with her a short distance down the dark hall. This time he clamped an arm around her waist and held her tightly. She yelled as she squirmed frantically against him.

"Be quiet!" he warned. Her fists were pounding against his bruised chest, and he pulled her close to leave her no room in which to strike.

Then, with her bare body pressed against him, he became indifferent to her weak blows and to her screams.

He carried her down to the floor. Her screams changed in quality but continued as he took her in savage haste.

When it was over, he lay on his back and lifted her limp form onto his, to get her off the rough, cold floor. She lay there in comatose apathy, too exhausted to cry. Basdon, too, was exhausted, and bitter with self-disgust, and with pity for the girl.

Only now, for the first time since he had been the appalled observer to Eanna's reaction to the god Vishan, did the thought occur that her actions were not of her own choosing, but had merely followed the dictates of the universal geas. She could not help but consider herself the property of the gods, of the We Who Own All—property to be kept inviolate from the touch of mere human masculinity.

He hated to think what a lost broken creature his violation had made her. And he wished he had the heart to rise up, seize his sword, and drive it through her heart, thus sparing her a month that his deed of lust could only make a thousand-fold more grievous for her. But he could not.

He was indifferently aware of Jonker coming into the hallway, looking at them for a moment, then returning to the lighted room. Later he heard the thud of stones being moved about, accompanied by the magician's effortful gruntings. But he did not move until the touch of Eanna's body began to stir his desire once more. Then he rose, lifting the girl in his arms, and returned to the room.

The light that had formerly filled it now gleamed through the hole Vishan had been pounding in the wall. Basdon guessed the magician, after enlarging the hole, had taken the light through to search for the buried talismans of The Art.

After a glance at the inert form of Vishan, Basdon carried the girl to the spot where she had dropped her dress. He picked it up and clumsily slipped her into it, then sat cradling her in his arms. Her stained face was peaceful in semi-consciousness; it was a face to remind him forcefully that, in many important respects of mind, this beautiful, demolished woman was in actuality still a child of six years.

He was still sitting there brooding half an hour later when Jonker struggled through the hole in the wall, carrying Vishan's light in one hand and what appeared to be a small, double-handled gold vase in the other.

"Well, I found it," puffed the magician with satisfaction as he brushed himself off. "Now, swordsman, if you can bluff us past the guards with the ease you did before, we will be on our hurried way home."

"What about . . . Eanna?" asked Basdon.

"Um, yes. Well, if she remains as she is now, you could say the god had his way with her, that she will await his future pleasure elsewhere when she recovers." The magician moved closer to touch the girl's forehead and feel her wrist. "However, I fear she will not remain as she is. She's growing alert now, and will certainly betray us to the guards if she has the chance." He shook his head regretfully. "We must leave her here, Basdon."

"I cannot," the swordsman said. "You go, and I will stay."

"Be sensible!" exploded Jonker. "There is nothing

she wants from you, nothing you can do for her! Leave her to the morbid pleasure of mourning herself to death over the body of her slain god! It is urgent to the completion of our highly important quest that you come with me, to help protect the talisman on the return to Nenkunal! You must not let us fail now, swordsman, for no good cause!"

"I have no stomach left for good causes, including your own," snapped Basdon. "I'll stay—and mourn for her while she mourns for that hunk of carrion."

Jonker sighed. "You fought the geas within yourself with valor and determination, swordsman," he said sorrowfully. "But fighting at length wears away strength. Yours is now gone, and the geas controls you as surely as it controls that poor child in your arms."

Basdon realized this was true. He said nothing.

With another sigh Jonker turned away. He walked to where a large block of stone provided a makeshift table, and placed the light on it along with some other odds and ends which he drew from beneath his robe. Basdon watched with dull interest as the magician began working with the stuff.

"You are obliging me to use something very precious— and very consumable—that I found while seeking the talisman a moment ago. I had no idea such an item still existed. Certainly it is the last, and was preserved only by the proximity of the talisman. I would have kept it for an occasion of great need, but . . ." the magician shrugged his shoulders, " . . . perhaps no greater need than that of this moment will arise. For once, I wish I could envision the near future, the years of my own life . . ."

"What are you talking about?" demanded Basdon,

half in worry and half in annoyance, rubbing hard at his eyes which were paining mercilessly.

"This," said Jonker, pulling a small ball of translucent green from his robe and placing it carefully on the rock. "And this!" He tapped a protuberance on the support of the light, which flicked out immediately.

But there was no darkness. Whiteness was everywhere. Not whiteness to see by. In fact, Basdon's surroundings were totally invisible to him. There was just whiteness . . . in front of his eyes, above his eyes, below them . . . in *back* of them . . . everywhere whiteness . . . that kept getting whiter.

The location of the whiteness, he realized, was in his mind. And there, in the midst of all that brilliance, pictures began to race fleetingly past. He recognized none as being events from his life, but he sensed they were all experiences his spirit had known somewhere in the vastness of time:

He was confronting a huge spear-bearing gladiator who (for some unseen reason) it was absolutely vital that he slay. But before he could set himself with sword and shield the enemy had plunged the spear through him. He was dying, but could not let himself die. Defeat was unthinkable. Thus, in his agony, his identity suddenly twisted and shifted to become the spearman and victor.

Ah! he thought in the instant between the vanishing of that scene and the appearance of the next. So *that* is why I foolishly thrust with my sword, as if it were a spear, when I should slash! In his fight with Laestarp's weredogs and again in the battle with Vishan, that habit had nearly gotten him killed. He realized it would not happen again.

The scenes flashed by, too numerous to count, often too hurried to be clearly defined. Then:

Whiter than white, the glowing form of a woman . . . Eanna? . . . Belissa? . . . She was both and neither, a composite of all feminine beauty. But she was not his; rather, he was hers! Her property. Her worshipper, along with dimly sensed legions of others. He lusted for but could not touch her perfection, and his lust was her excuse. The arm of the goddess reached down, and two fingertips, hotter than all the suns, touched and seared his eyes. He fled into blind, pain-filled darkness.

The bitch! he cursed. But . . . but . . . He grunted with the realization. She hadn't been a woman at all! She was a hypnotic construct, a product of outrageously advanced and depraved magic, used to enslave through false beauty!

Shortly thereafter the whiteness faded to gray, then went black. Basdon was aware of the girl stirring in his arms, and of fumbling sounds from Jonker. Then Vishan's light came on.

The swordsman looked down at the girl's face, and saw her eyes were open and looking at him. He smiled at her, wondering why, if she were conscious, she was not pulling away from him.

"Your eyes are blue and white," she said wonderingly. "They used to be red."

He had not noticed before. The burning was gone. That did not seem of any importance. "Your eyes are also blue and white, and beautiful," he replied.

"Do you know you hurt me, out in the hall?" she asked.

"Yes, I know. I'm very sorry. I won't do that to you again, I promise."

"You will, too," she contradicted him. "Or you better. I'll get mad at you if you don't."

She pulled herself up to him and kissed him on the mouth, then giggled.

In delighted wonder, Basdon threw Jonker a questioning look.

"All geases are broken for both of you," said the magician, looking regretfully at a small pile of greenish ash on his makeshift table. "I wonder how many thousands of years will pass before that can be said of any other human beings."

5

Basdon and Eanna would have dallied endlessly along the return route to Nenkunal, but for the pressing anxiety of the magician.

"We may run out of time at any instant," Jonker warned and pleaded. "I fear that They Who Own All have learned by now that Vishan met with disaster in Oliber-by-Midsea. And doubtless they are trying to learn or guess the cause of it. So far we have survived, but only because Vishan's soul was too inturbulated to tell of us. Surely they will guess soon, and raise the countryside against us. Let us hurry!"

So they pushed their mounts hard, through the days and long into the moonlit nights. But the farms and villages of the worshippers remained calm, the people obviously unaware that they no longer had a living god. The Hif Hills loomed in the gray distance ahead of them.

"I'm puzzled by some things, magician," said the swordsman as they jogged along one morning. "Most of all by the geas-breaker you used on Eanna and myself in Oliber."

"That was a device for the production of spiritual energy in its purest form," explained Jonker. "It supercharges any spirit within range of its radiance, and enables the spirit to shatter all the geases that bind it, even those imposed on it a thousand lifetimes ago."

"Very well. My question is this: With that kind of a defense on earth, how did it happen that the necromancers from between the stars enslaved us?"

Jonker lowered his face. After a while he said, "Our world has known no perfect age, swordsman. The age of magic was our most glorious, but it had its failings. As you know, we had our own black-spellers. And even honest magicians were selfish, as all men are. Thus, we restricted very tightly the fabrication and use of the white-energy generators, so that our own geas-making would not be compromised. When the universal necromancers made their assault, we were . . . we were too late in mending our ways."

Basdon nodded. "My other puzzle is this: The souls of each of the three of us will be taken upon our deaths by They Who Own All, will they not?"

"Yes," said the magician.

"Then how will we hide that talisman you are carrying in your saddle-pack?" Basdon demanded. "Can they not probe the truth out of our spirits, and discover the hiding place?"

Jonker grinned. "Not if we do not know the

place ourselves. Are you familiar with the River Heralple?"

"I've heard of it, while in Nenkunal, but I have not seen it."

"It flows down swiftly from the Fogfather Mountains to the Eastern Ocean. But before emptying, the main stream divides into thousands of rivulets that move sluggishly through a vast swampy deltaland. There the River Heralple's burden of mud and silt is dropped. I propose that there, too, will the talisman of favoring destiny be dropped. I've thought long on this matter, swordsman. If the talisman is thrown into the swift portion of the river above the delta, no man nor magician will be able to guess which of those thousands of rivulets will receive it, nor where along their windings it will come to rest and be covered, as the centuries pass, by layers of the earth of Nenkunal. It will be safe from everyone's knowing, including our own."

Basdon could see no flaw in the plan. "Then all we need do is reach that river," he remarked. "For that reason, I hope the storm over the Hif Hills gentles before we reach them."

"Storm?" asked Jonker, peering suddenly ahead. "Yes . . . yes . . . I see. My eyes are less sharp than they once were."

Eanna said, "I see it. Big black clouds, and lightning shooting out."

"It is most unseasonal," Jonker commented with a worried frown.

The clouds, hanging low over the hills ahead, roiled and twisted with a velocity Basdon had never before observed in any storm. And their coloring was a peculiar yellow-gray, rather than white, where sunlight struck their upper edges. Below, they were an impenetrable purple-black.

The farmers the riders passed along the way were viewing the distant turmoil with dumb alarm. If the storm moved down on them, now in early harvest season, its havoc could leave them to starve in the months ahead.

However, the clouds seemed to be holding their position over the hills, neither advancing nor retreating.

That night the travelers camped short of the hills, with gusts of wind flapping their tents and making a fire impossible to maintain. The darkness was filled with noise, loud even at a distance, of the roaring wind and clashing thunder. Several times they felt the earth quiver beneath them.

With the dawn the fury abated somewhat. The horses were mounted and the journey resumed. Soon the Hif Hills were reached, and the riders stared about in shocked dismay.

It was plain to see that the storm had brought no rain. The clouds had been dust and dirt, a pall of which still lingered in the fitful morning gusts. And the hills, desolate before, were now a tumbled ruin. Trees were splintered or uprooted. Hardly a shrub had its roots in soil. In places the wind had scrubbed away everything, down to bedrock. In other places, logs and brush were piled in high, dusty drifts. Here and there, smoke rose from a lightning-set fire.

"That was no natural storm," murmured Jonker.

"I can see that," replied Basdon.

Nothing more was said as they made their halting

way over the broken land. Going was slow and difficult, and kept them too busy watching their horses' steps to brood over the question which, Basdon guessed, had occurred even to Eanna:

If the hills bordering Nenkunal had been tormented thus, *what had happened to Nenkunal itself?*

They learned the answer when they reached the highest crest.

Here the air was clear of dust and they could see ahead for tens of leagues across the valleys of Nenkunal . . . across, but not down into, because all was dust below.

The storm the travelers had seen over the Hif Hills, they now realized fully, was only the blunted edge of destruction. All the wide land of Nenkunal had been shaken, lashed, and scoured by awesome forces. Indeed, the fury was now only partly abated. Cubic leagues of earth were still windborne over what had been green and happy landscapes.

"Sand," muttered Jonker. "I knew it to be Nenkunal's destiny to lie its full length under waterless dunes, but I never dreamt it would come so soon, so suddenly."

"I suppose we know why," said Basdon.

"Yes . . . They Who Own All have struck."

"But why didn't they strike us instead?" asked Eanna her eyes wide with horror.

"Because, being what they are, they assumed wrongly," said the magician. "They guessed that we, like Laestarp, wanted to use the talismans of Oliber that would give us power to dominate—talismans that I found and destroyed as objects of more potential harm than good in the new age. With those talismans

we could have traveled more swiftly, and would have
been here in time to be included in this ruin. And to
make doubly sure that earth-magic would never rise
against them, they destroyed the entire country which
would be the base of operations for such magic."

"Then we're to blame," whispered Eanna.

"Child, everyone and no one is to blame," Jonker
retorted crossly. "The question is, what do we do
now?" asked Basdon.

"Forge ahead, as best we can," the magician said,
with meager hope in his tone. "Try to reach the River
Heralple."

Basdon nodded and started his horse moving down
toward the swirling dust storms. It was futile to assume,
he knew, that the Heralple still flowed, but it would
serve as a meaningful destination.

"And where from there?" he asked over his
shoulder.

"Probably south," hazarded the magician, "into the
tropical wilderness. That, I suppose, is where other
survivors of Nenkunal will try to go."

Late the following day they passed the site of
Haslil's cottage. No trace of the house remained, and
Eanna permitted herself to find relief in tears as they
pushed on toward the lowlands.

"I did not know there was so much sand in the
world," muttered Basdon when they reached the first
valley.

"Perhaps there wasn't until now," replied Jonker.

All next day they journeyed southeastward over the
dry gritty earth, often having to dismount when the
horses floundered in a loosely packed drift. There

was little breeze, or the going would have been more difficult by far.

When they stopped, they shared their supply of sweetroot with the horses, since forage was nonexistent. Fortunately, Jonker's water-purification charm had survived the universal geas, and they could make use of the muddy, rapidly stagnating pools they occasionally discovered.

The next day was different in that the heat was becoming stifling. They stopped frequently to rest and cool their mounts, and were glad when night brought a swift chill to the air.

They were awakened by a rising wind at dawn.

"Shall we try to travel through this?" yelled Basdon, holding his arm in front of his face to shelter his eyes and nose from the painfully cutting grit in the air.

"Our supplies are not plentiful enough for us to wait out the blow," replied Jonker. "We have to move on."

So they walked, leading the horses, throughout the day, cloths over their noses and mouths, and eyes open only enough to glimpse what lay ahead. All day the dust swirled so densely that visibility was limited to a few yards.

"I hope you know which way we're going!" the swordsman yelled once.

"I do, within a reasonable margin of error," answered the magician. Basdon did not want to take more dust into his mouth by asking what a "reasonable margin of error" amounted to.

As the growing darkness of the sandstorm finally spoke the coming of night, they found themselves, rather to their surprise, in the sheltering bend of a low cliff thrown up by one of the earth tremors.

"We had better stop here," said Basdon. "Eanna and the horses can go little further."

"Very well. Get the girl settled in what comfort you can find for her while I unload the mounts," said Jonker.

Basdon led Eanna into the narrowest niche in the bend of the cliff, seated her, and helped her remove the cloth which had been protecting her face. Her bare feet and legs looked near to bleeding from the abrasion of the sand, and he hoped Jonker had some quick healing for them.

"You shouldn't treat me like I'm a baby," she protested. "Go help Jonker. I'm a grown-up woman."

He smiled at her. "So I know." He kissed her and turned to go just as Jonker came waddling up with a look of consternation on his face.

"Basdon! My saddle is gone!" he exclaimed.

"Oh?" Basdon frowned thoughtfully. None of them had ridden that day, but the saddles had been on the horses. "I suppose all this blowing sand worked between the straps and gradually wore them through," he surmised. "Well, you can use my saddle when we can mount again. I can ride bareback."

"But that's not the point!" sputtered the magician. "The *talisman* . . . it was in the saddle-pack!"

Basdon sat down, feeling tired at the very thought of trying to cover the day's back-trail in search of the saddle and its contents. "We'll never find it," he muttered. "We'll never even find our own trail, more than ten yards back from this spot!"

"I admit it appears hopeless," replied Jonker,

sounding stubborn, "but we've got to try. Although the way this sand is blowing, the saddle could well be concealed by now. And we'll have to wait until morning, but then we'll search very carefully..."

"It's *hopeless!*" Basdon bellowed angrily. "We could spend days hunting that thing without finding it! And look at my poor darling's legs! Do what you wish, magician, but I'm getting her out of this deadly land as soon as possible!"

Jonker looked from one to the other, and his heavy old shoulders slumped. "It is hard to accept defeat, after coming so close to success," he muttered sadly. "But you are right, swordsman. I fear the talisman is hopelessly lost."

"But isn't that what you wanted it to be?" asked Eanna.

Jonker blinked and stared at her. "By my long-suffering spirit!" he exclaimed, "*So it is!* The talisman of favoring destiny now lies beneath the earth of Nenkunal! And I, who lost it, haven't the foggiest notion within twenty leagues of where it lies!"

"The sand will keep piling up?" asked Basdon.

"Yes! It's safe!"

"And good riddance!" said Basdon. He moved to Eanna's side and hugged her closely. "In the morning, then, we can turn toward the south, to see what hope and comfort the wilderness has to offer."

Jonker nodded and heaved the sigh of a man suddenly at peace. "Yes... but our real hope lies somewhere under the sand in a saddle-pack... and twenty thousand years in the future."

Forever Enemy

RENSON BROKE WARP a proper five million miles from Nexal. The radiation of the planet's Sol-class sun felt pleasantly warm on his exposed face, chest and limbs, and momentarily opaqued his eyeball shields until he turned his head away from the glare.

The shields cleared immediately, and he had no trouble spotting the gleaming disk of the planet, the capital world of the Lontastan Federation. He went full-inert and promptly streaked toward the planet, feeling a touch of satisfaction with his astrogational skill. His warp-exit coordinates had placed him where his inert momentum would carry him precisely to his destination.

He tongued his toothmike and messaged: "Calling

Nexal Arrivals Control. This is Fait Linler of Stemmons arriving with due prior notification. E.T.A. two hours. Please ack."

The acknowledgment was slow in coming. Renson was beginning to frown uneasily before the response rang in his right ear:

"Linler of Stemmons, this is Nexal Arrivals. Maintain inertia. You will be escorted down."

"Escorted?" Renson demanded, surprised. "I really don't see the necessity of—"

"Maintain inertia!" the voice interrupted. "Nexal Arrivals out!"

"But . . ."

He did not complete his protest. This business of an escort had to mean that, for some reason, the Lontastans were suspicious. Had he given himself away with a false move?

He was—technically speaking—an enemy here, even though he had no intention of causing, or seeking, trouble. However, if trouble waited, his best bet was to warp out while he had the opportunity.

He went semi-inert, preparatory to setting a warp vector, then was stopped by a thought.

Why had Arrivals Control *told* him he would be escorted? Why hadn't the escort simply arrived and surrounded him? Was he being baited into a guilt-revealing action? What should . . .

The hesitation probably saved his life. Zerburst terminals flared suddenly in scorching brilliance on every side, bottling him at a distance of only hundreds of miles in an almost unbroken shell of death. As it was, his skin-field went total reflect to block out the fierce radiation. If he had tried to vector in any direction, one of those terminals would almost certainly have caught him.

A harsh voice barked in his ear: *"Fait Linler! Go inert and STAY inert!"*

Renson obeyed.

Within seconds the escort of Nexali Guardsmen closed in on him. He watched expressionlessly as they spiraled around. They were a tough-looking squad—doubtless barbarian types of the sort usually found performing such duties. With their zerburst guns held in readiness, their black shorts and their overpolished boots, they looked very military and very murderous.

In short, a goon squad—one of the uglier features of the endless Primgranese-Lontastan war. As long as human society had a use for such barbs as these, Renson mused grimly, their genetic strain would remain intact.

"Take off your belt and throw it!" ordered the harsh-voiced Guard officer who had spoken before.

Renson did so, not bothering to protest that his belt contained no weapons. A Guardsman snagged the belt as it drifted away and examined it cautiously.

Then Renson's sight was cut off. The escort had thrown a blindfield around him. He would see nothing during the rest of his journey to Nexal.

Time passed. When they entered the lower atmosphere he knew of it only from the relaxation of his pressor field and from the change of his breathing mode. The sensors of his life-support system, having detected suitable air around him, automatically deactivated the gas-conversion macromolecules in the linings of his throat and nasal passages, and he went on external respiration. What sounds filtered through the blindfield were muffled and uninformative.

When the field lifted Renson saw he was in a small windowless room. He had been left carrying sufficient momentum to slam him backwards into a chair, in which he was immediately confined by a restrainer belt across his stomach.

After a dazed instant he saw the escort was gone. Only one other man was in the room, facing him across a desk.

"I'm Arkay Delton of Anti-Espionage," the man informed him mildly. "Who are you?"

"I'm Fait Linler, from Stemmons," replied Renson. "Look, what's all this about?"

Delton's eyes had lowered to something Renson could not see on the desktop. Now he looked up and repeated, "Who are you?"

Renson blinked. Obviously Delton had an emo-monitor focused on him, and his use of a false name had registered; else Delton would not have repeated the question. Renson had lived with his assumed name, Fait Linler, for five years, and had hoped that, if he were ever emo-monitored, it would register clean. Plainly, it had not.

I AM Fait Linler, he assured himself. *That's my real identity. Grap Renson is no longer real. I accept that as true without reservation.*

But in reply to Delton's question he said, "Nobody you need concern yourself about. I'm not a spy, nor an enemy."

Delton glanced up and said, "Thank you," which probably meant the answer registered clean. "Who are you?"

Annoyed, Renson replied, "Fait Linler."

"Who are you?"

"Fait Linler, of Stemmons."

"Who are you?"

Renson consciously relaxed himself. This interrogation setup—a mild, friendly-faced man repeating a question at him from across a desk—had a strong and intentional resemblance to a psych-release therapy session. Psych-release was a major landmark in the life of every child, opening the way to a sane adulthood.

Thus, the temptation was to regard Delton as a therapist and cooperate fully.

Renson wriggled under the restrainer belt into a more erect position. "Fait Linler," he said.

"Who are you?"

"Look, I told you I'm nobody of concern to you! I'm not a participant in the econo-war at all! In fact, my sole purpose for coming to Nexal is to try to discover why this nonsensical war exists in the first place!"

Delton considered this outburst a moment before saying, "Thank you. Who are you?"

"Fait Linler!"

"Who are you?"

"Fait Linler."

"Who are you?"

The repetition of question and answer went on for half an hour . . . and Renson was beginning to think it could continue forever. Delton would tire, and be replaced by another interrogator, who would tire and be replaced by—

It was futile to go on.

"Who are you?"

Renson sighed. "I've been Fait Linler for five years. Who I was before that isn't important."

Delton smiled. "Thank you. Who were you six years ago?"

"It doesn't matter."

"Who were you six years ago?"

After a pause Renson shrugged. "I was Grap Renson, an engineer with Sol-Veg Systems Corporation in the Commonality of Primgran."

"Thank you, Mr. Renson. What grade engineer?"

"Junior first."

Delton looked impressed. "And you're not here as a spy or a saboteur, or otherwise as an agent of the Commonality or of a Commonality enterprise?"

"No."

"But you are not here as a defector, either?"

"That's correct," Renson said stiffly.

"Thank you." Delton shifted slightly in his seat for the first time. "After your long trip from Stemmons you're probably ready for some bulk food."

Renson nodded.

A tray slid out of the wall to pose a breakfast over his lap. He dug in with good appetite. During warp-flight it was necessary to subsist on food-concentrate pills, with a stomach-balloon countering the empty sensation the pills left. This prevented severe pangs, but the human body had other means of recognizing hunger. And that, Renson realized as he grew more comfortable, was one reason why he had found the idea of a prolonged interrogation so hard to face.

He looked up between mouthfuls. "What alerted your security to me?" he asked.

Delton shrugged and grinned. "Several things. It

seemed likely, when I first read the query on you from Arrivals Control, that you were either a rank amateur at infiltration, or that some Primgranese spy-boss was taking a shot in the dark with an utterly naive approach." He chuckled, "It was foolish of you to expect that a mere five-year record of residence on a low-security planet like Stemmons—where nothing of economic significance is going on—would lead to your unquestioned acceptance as a first-class Lontastan citizen. Notification of arrivals on Nexal are always checked out, and yours was obviously fishy."

Annoyed, Renson snapped, "O.K., so infiltration isn't my line!"

"That's for sure," laughed Delton, studying the captive thoughtfully. "So you came here trying to discover the cause of the econo-war, huh?"

"Yes."

"Which means you don't accept the reasons everybody else does."

"I definitely do not."

"Why?"

"Because I find them absurd! Look, Delton, are all the adults of the Primgran Commonality and the Lontastan Federation sane?"

Delton grinned. "Those of the Federation are. I can't vouch for the citizens on your side."

"Please be serious," Renson snapped. "Humanity *is* sane, to the last adult on the most out-of-the-way frontier world. We've been sane for nearly a thousand years now. Nobody is driven by some neurotic compulsion to accumulate more wealth than he has any imaginable use for, while leaving someone else in economic distress in the process. Only insanity, on the pandemic scale of the

Earth-Only ages, can justify that dog-eat-dog method of wealth distribution.

"Yet, we still go at it tooth and claw, without the tiniest neurosis for an excuse! And the big war between the Commonality and the Federation is just another level of the billions of little wars going on constantly within our ranks. Sol-Veg Systems Corporation versus Philips Interstel, as well as versus Nexxtauri General. And me, while I worked for Sol-Veg, versus several dozen other hard-climbing first-junior engineers. On every level, the organization of both our nations seems to have no other purpose than to provide a battleground!

"Is that what society is for, Delton?" he went on angrily. "Is that the highest purpose we can grasp after all these centuries of sanity?"

Renson ran down suddenly and sat in glum silence, annoyed with himself for expressing his feelings so openly to a man he could hardly expect to understand or appreciate them.

"It could be worse," Delton remarked lightly. "It could be a shooting war, in the old Earth-Only style, instead of economic combat. So you must admit we've gained *something* from our sanity, Renson."

"We've gained precious little!" Renson flared. "There's nothing pretty about industrial espionage and sabotage, or economic oppression of the weak by the strong, or trigger-happy goon squads such as that escort that brought me here! Just because our war involves no wholesale slaughter everyone seems to think it isn't really damaging, or deadly. The obvious truth is that it is deadly indeed to the human spirit! It pits man against man! It makes us enemies when we could—and should—be friends."

Delton smiled. "You and I, for instance?"

"Certainly! Under more favorable circumstances—" Renson's voice trailed off uncertainly.

"Ah, yes, more favorable circumstances," Delton chuckled. "If we were friends instead of enemies, we could enjoy each other's company, discuss our innermost feelings and beliefs, perhaps have an argument as close friends do about some belief on which we didn't agree. Just as *we're doing right now, Renson.*"

"*O.K.,*" Renson nodded, "I'll grant that point. You and I, technically enemies brought face to face, are conversing like friends. But that's precisely what I'm getting at—sane men are friends when face to face, when their proximity crowds out the artificial barriers our social structure normally raises between them. Friendship is natural, enmity is not."

"Friendship wouldn't be natural if both of us were hungry and only one of us had a little food," Delton dissented.

"But there's no shortage of food in our society," Renson retorted, "except for artificial shortages created by the artificialities of the econo-war! We produce a constantly increasing plenty of everything for everybody! That's another reason why the war is inexcusable. We have too much wealth for it to be worth fighting over."

Delton considered that in silence for a moment. Then he said, "Man has always been a player of games, Renson. If you're a student of history, you probably know that one of the key steps in our progress toward sanity was the recognition that life itself is best understood as a game. We need the same things for a good life as we do for a good game—that is, we need freedoms, barriers, and goals. And, of course, a playing field for these things and ourselves.

"But for a really top-notch game, Renson, we need something else—*teams*. The better balanced the teams are, the more absorbing the game.

"That's what the econo-war gives us, Renson, a superb and unifying game, with well-balanced teams. The play gets rough sometimes, especially for the goon squads, infiltrators, and others who choose to play in exposed positions. But there has to be hard play if the game is taken seriously as the basic game of our society.

"So there's nothing artificial or phony about the war, Renson. It isn't something dreamed up and kept going by a handful of government and industrial officials. If you convinced the top brass of the Commonality and the Federation that the war should be ended, and they signed a treaty tomorrow, within a month I bet the war would be starting again! Man *needs* his games, Renson, the same as he needs food, shelter, sex, and life-support. And this econo-war is a great game—otherwise it wouldn't still be going strong after more than three centuries."

Renson said sourly, "I doubt if the economically deprived consider it such a great game."

Delton shrugged, "There have to be losers as well as winners. To quote a bit of ancient wisdom, 'the poor we will always have with us.'" He frowned thoughtfully and asked, "Could that be your trouble, Renson? Are you soured on the econo-war game because you're a loser?"

Renson shook his head. "I was doing very well with Sol-Veg. It was my own decision to quit."

"Are you a married—or formerly married—man with a family somewhere in the Commonality?"

"No . . . I never got around to that. Never found a girl with whom I hit it off just right."

Delton nodded slowly, and Renson wondered why Delton had asked about his marital status. But he said nothing, because he could see no point in continuing the discussion. Evidently Delton felt the same.

"That's all the questions for now, Renson," he said. "Behind you is a door into an apartment where you'll be comfortable while you wait for the disposition of your case."

The restrainer belt dropped from Renson's lap and he stood. He wanted to ask what the Federation officials were likely to do with him, but he knew Delton could not answer that. "Thank you," he said, and left the interrogation room.

During the next two weeks Renson had plenty of solitude in which to consider his situation. And he reached the conclusion that entering Federation territory had been pure folly—a waste of five years.

It was not that his capture was preventing him from gathering data on the cause of the econo-war. The truth was that Nexal, or any other Federation planet, had no data to offer that was not available on any Commonality world. In all essences, the Federation and the Commonality were the same. They were twin societies, operating on the same principles and with the same motives.

And, of course, the Federation's ideas about the war had to duplicate those he had been hearing all his life at home . . . the same glib answers, such as

Delton's life-game analogy, which made a certain amount of sense but failed to explain why man, with all his abilities of creative imagination, had not come up with a far more desirable game for himself than econo-war.

For the first centuries of interstellar travel, a game of conquer-the-universe had been plenty, for instance. And that game was still going on, but it had lost its early excitement. It was too easy, Renson mused. The galaxy offered more room for expansion than man could use for several millennia—and so far man had found no competitor for that room, no alien species to fight.

So he fought himself. That was the explanation for the econo-war, perhaps, but it was no explanation at all. Not for a sane humanity, in Renson's opinion.

He was uncomfortably aware that his opinion was not widely shared. Hardly anybody bothered to question the assumptions that he found so flimsy. In fact, most people with whom he had argued about the war had responded much as Delton had . . . as if they could see and understand some vital point to which he was blind. Was he a prime example of stubborn stupidity, insisting on his rightness and the wrongness of everybody else?

Well, not quite everybody else. After all, there was the Halstayne Independency—a nation far smaller than either the Commonality or the Federation, admittedly—that took no part in the econo-war and seemed to get along quite comfortably nevertheless. The one Halstaynian he had met had shared fully his distaste for and puzzlement over the Primgranese-Lontastan conflict.

His meditations along such lines were interrupted a few times for additional interrogation by his captors, but most of the questioning was perfunctory. Having been away from Sol-Veg for five years, his knowledge of the corporation's activities was thoroughly dated. Also, despite his junior-first ranking, he never had been let in on any of the company's high-security projects. (An indication, he wondered, that the company had considered him a questionable risk?) In any event, he could tell the Lontastans little of value.

Finally he recognized Arkay Delton's voice speaking from the call box. "Renson?"

"Yes?"

"You're to be released, with the understanding that you will not remain within Federation territory. Accepted?"

"Yes," he replied, wondering. *Released? Just like that?* "Is this an exchange of captured personnel?" he asked.

"No, the next scheduled exchange is six months away. And there could be complications if we tried to include you in an exchange. Shall we send out an arrival notification for you?"

Renson grimaced slightly at the insulting truth of Delton's words. The Commonality would not care in the least if he were never released, with his war-critical attitude, and would not be interested in accepting him for a captive Lontastan.

He answered Delton's question: "Notify Bernswa in the Halstayne Independency."

"Sounds like a wise choice for you, Renson," Delton approved. "There you'll be out of the war entirely. Check your life-support and we'll send you on your way."

"Right."

Renson went in the bathroom, stripped, got the life-support meter out of the cabinet, and began testing. He pressed the sensor platelet into the hollow under his ribs on his right side, and saw that the powerpack implant in that location still had a .7 energy capacity, which was quite sufficient. Moving the sensor above his right hip he assured himself that the multifield packet imbedded there was in total working order. A similar check above his left hip verified the functionality of his transport packet.

Then he pressed the platelet against his closed lips, tongued his toothmike, hummed softly, and watched the needle respond. Finally he placed the sensor behind each ear in turn, tapped the soundkey, and heard the clear blips.

This checked out all the major implants. And the macromolecule-sized segments of his life-support, such as those used for gas conversion in the space-respiration system, and the purely mechanical units such as the stomach balloon—these things had to be working right, or he would be feeling sick.

He dressed, stepped out of the bathroom, and blinked when he found three Guardsmen waiting for him. One handed him his belt which he put on automatically.

Then he was blindfielded, escorted out of spying range of Nexal, and sent on his way.

Out of the dozen developed planets in the Halstayne Independency, Renson had picked Bernswa because that was the home world of the only Halstaynian he knew.

The Independency was in a dusty area of the galactic arm, which accounted in part for its autonomy. Warping through dust was not an impossibility, but the prime-field turbulence that resulted was mind-wracking and dangerous. Clear lanes through the dust were eventually found, but their circuitousness kept the Halstayne region from having much appeal for either of the two superpowers. As a result, the Independency was formed and settled in large part by persons who had opted out of the developing Primgranese-Lontastan conflict. It was a pocket of peace, bordered by both of its larger, more contentious neighbors.

Renson made a careful zigzag of warps along one of the clear lanes. Finally through the worst of the dust, he paused in normal space and looked around. The teeming suns of the galaxy were totally obscured. Only fifty-some points of light were scattered sparsely across the blackness—the suns of the Independency—and several of these wore fuzzy halos of dust and gas.

But the sun of Bernswa sparkled un-obscured, and he warped for it. After breaking warp near the planet and clearing his arrival, he messaged Estine Cauval, not knowing what to expect.

It turned out that she was not only at home but in a position—and with the inclination—to be hospitable.

"Sure, come on down, Grap!" she exclaimed eagerly. "I'll switch on my beacon for you!"

"I won't be intruding?"

"Not at all. Oh, I was married for a while after I last saw you, but now everything is casual and simple. Don't forget, Grap, it's been over eight years!"

"Yes. Still a newsgirl?"

"Oh, yes, but not so pushy about it now. I haven't been outside covering the econo-war for years and years!"

"I'll be down in forty minutes," he told her.

Bernswa had several hundred semicities, but Estine did not live in one of these. Her house stood isolated in a richly forested piedmont. This puzzled Renson after a few minutes with her, because he could tell she was still the lover of crowds and swirling activity he had remembered.

"I'm writing a drama," she explained, "and need the isolation of a place like this."

"A drama?"

"Didn't I ever tell you? Dramaturgy has always been my dream. I still do occasional news features but I give most of my working time to my play. I've been at it for over a year."

Renson nodded slowly. Estine was bright, clever, charming . . . but a playwright? That hardly seemed likely. She was too much a reporter, too intrigued by the event to pay much heed to the meanings behind the event. He doubted if she could create a play worth watching.

"Tell me about yourself, Grap," she demanded gaily. "What brings you here?"

He sat down beside her and described his fruitless efforts to learn why the econo-war existed.

"Welcome to the fold!" she exclaimed. "You won't find an answer here, but at least you're among people who share your puzzlement. About the only sensible thing to say about the econo-war is that it's ridiculous!"

"Which begs the question," Renson remarked glumly.

"Yes, but what else is there to say? The society, as well as the individual, of the Independency is *sane*. It *has* to appear nonsensical to us that the rest of humanity finds warfare a normal and *desirable* condition of life. It's all so frantic and foolish."

He grinned. "You seemed to enjoy it when you were a correspondent."

"Oh, sure, as a reporter," Estine said with a toss of her head. "Life in the Commonality has a crazy excitement that was fun to write about, and to watch for a while. It's . . . well . . . have you ever tried writing, Grap?"

"Not the kind of writing you mean—just engineering specs and so on. I've thought if I could solve the mystery of the econo-war, I'd write something about that."

"Yes, but that's not what I mean. I mean poetry, or fiction, or drama. What is called creative writing. Grap, it's next to *impossible* to write creatively, and interestingly, about sane people doing sane things!"

Renson thought this over, and finally nodded. "I can see how it would be," he agreed. "If everybody is sane and reasonable, you don't get much dramatic conflict."

"That's it, exactly," she said. "And that's why I enjoyed covering the econo-war. It's also why modern novelists do historical pieces about Earth-Only days, or else fantasies. I'm not saying sanity is *dull*," she giggled, "only that it makes dull fiction compared to Dickens, or Tolstoy."

"And there is some fiction about the econo-war," Renson put in, wondering why Estine had sounded defensive when she denied that sanity was dull. "Which may be roundabout evidence that the econo-war is as anachronistic as Uriah Heep."

She smiled and grasped his hand. "I sensed that you felt that way when I first met you, Grap. That was one of the things that attracted me to you. And now . . . welcome to our non-fictionalized society."

"Thanks. Hope I'll fit in."

"Oh, you will," she said with assurance.

A few days later he went to talk to Ferd Primlay about a job. Primlay was development director of Halstayne United Life-Support Corporation, largest producer of life-support equipment in the Independency.

"I've not been active in the field for five years," Renson said apologetically after they had talked for a while, "and that may put me a bit out-of-date."

"Not at all!" glowed Primlay. "You may, uh, even find you're ahead of us in some respects. We do tend to lag behind Commonality and Federation companies at times, with them always scrambling for some minor competitive advantage. Although I must say we do all right, considering our size and position."

Renson nodded. It was all a matter, he thought fleetingly, of what one considered "all right" to be. The Halstaynian version of the multifield packet was a cumbersome object, nearly two cubic inches in volume and about sixty years out-of-date by Commonality standards. He had noticed that Estine's packet actually made a visible lump under her skin when she bent a certain way.

"Perhaps I can help you overcome some of those lags," he said. "Also, there's an idea I had on the way here. Why not include an emo-monitor in standard life-support equipment?"

"Hm-m-m. An interesting thought," said Primlay. "I wonder, though, if an emo-monitor wouldn't be getting us too far away from the basic definition of 'life-support'?"

"I think not. The definition has got broader over the centuries. Life-support originally meant providing a livable environment for a man in space, either within a ship, or in protective clothing. In essence, it meant air and temperature control. Provisions for propulsion and communication were called by other names. That distinction was eliminated as it became possible to equip a man for spaceflight without recourse to ships or special clothing. And, after all, motion and communication are as fundamental to life as breathing and maintaining internal pressure, if somewhat less immediately so. An emo-monitor would seem a logical addition to the communication capabilities of life-support."

Primlay nodded gravely. "It would, of course, require extensive research. I can see the advantages. A man wants to understand his woman, a parent wants to understand his child, and so on. Personal relationships would be improved if we could 'read' each other's feelings."

"It could all but eliminate deceit, including self-deceit," said Renson.

"Yes." Primlay squinted in concentration. "Let's keep that idea in mind, Renson, and we'll discuss it further in a few months. You understand such a proposal isn't one to jump at without thorough consideration, and there's something else I'd like to get you onto first."

"Then you're hiring me?"

"Of course! All applicants are hired here. Didn't you know? That's basic to the Halstaynian way of life."

Renson blinked. He remembered reading something to that effect long ago, but he hadn't really believed it, thinking it one of those rules honored more in the breach than the keeping. But, if the Independency was actually free of economic competition, such a rule was probably necessary.

Primlay was watching his expression. "I suppose your former colleagues wouldn't consider that a practical personnel policy," he remarked stiffly.

"They wouldn't," agreed Renson with a slight grin. "But they cling to many things dating from pre-sanity times. What is it you want me to work on?"

Mollified, Primlay said, "Stomach discomfort, especially in older people. Our balloon apparently does not work as well as the Commonality version."

"If the balloon's outer surface is sufficiently random-transportive," Renson said, "there shouldn't be any discomfort."

"Random-transportive," murmured Primlay, not quite making it a question.

"You may have another term for it," said Renson. "The idea is that the balloon shouldn't block pill nourishment away from any portion of the stomach's wall, otherwise a person gets localized pangs. It's mainly a design job, involving the distribution of microtublets in the self-flexing substance of the balloon, with the distribution ordered to provide maximum pressure in areas of maximum resistance."

Primlay nodded. "This is something you're familiar with?"

"Yes."

"Fine! That will be your first assignment. Now, I understand from your friend Estine Cauval that you're quite a vactennis player, Grap."

"Yes, but I'm a bit out of practice now."

"It's my game, too," said Primlay, in a livelier tone than he had used before. "In fact, that's what first roused my interest in life-support systems. A player's game is no better than his equipment, you know. Perhaps we could have a game . . . ?"

"Sure," agreed Renson. "Let me know when you have time."

"No time like the present," laughed Primlay. "Come on!" he leaped eagerly from his seat, strode to the window and dived out. "Let's go!" his fading voice trailed back.

Renson stood motionless for an instant, then grinned and dived after his new employer. Maybe, he guessed, it was part of the rules in the Independency that a man in Primlay's position could play hooky from his job if he liked.

He followed the man up into space and the two of them enjoyed an afternoon of strenuous sport. The Independency, Renson was thinking, was a great place to live.

He spent the next three months changing his mind.

The stomach balloon assignment had not struck him as a major challenge, but more as a preliminary test to assure Primlay that he could deliver. It involved nothing more than was already being done by Commonality and Federation manufacturers, using materials and processes Renson knew well. For that matter, samples of modern stomach balloons from outside were easily available for copying, although at a higher price than many Independency citizens could afford.

He had expected to be through with the project within a month at most. But that length of time found him barely started.

He told Primlay, "I would like to do some shifting about of the personnel on the project. Random-transportive design is a finicky task, in which a minor error by one drafter throws out the work of a whole drafting team. And . . . well . . . some drafters are less talented than others."

"That's very true," nodded Primlay. "However, shifting people about isn't easy. What did you have in mind?"

"Anything that would give me a first-rate drafting team—even a small one. For instance, the less useful drafters could be put on other jobs within the project—"

"Not unless they ask for it without prompting," said Primlay. "The key point there is that these people accepted employment with our company as drafters. As long as they're satisfied with the work they're doing—"

"O.K.," said Renson, "let's take them off the project entirely. Assign them elsewhere in the company."

Primlay smiled. "That wouldn't be exactly fair to our other projects, would it? I assure you, Grap, your project has no more than its share of less useful workers in any category."

"Well, look," Renson snapped, "these people are a drag on our progress! What can be done about it?"

"The best thing to do," laughed Primlay, "is to relax. There's no great rush. Actually, your project is coming along excellently, Grap. Not as fast as such things go in the Commonality, perhaps, but remember there's no war on here. Now, how about vactennis this afternoon?"

After that Renson decided not to bother mentioning his other personnel problem to Primlay: absenteeism. After all, Primlay himself was a heavy offender on that score.

So the project's difficulties boiled down to those overlapping problems—at least a third of the personnel were "losers," people who lacked the ability, or the motivation, to do efficient work. And the entire staff, losers as well as winners, came and went from the lab as they chose. The recommended workday was six hours, but that was treated very loosely as a maximum. There seemed to be no minimum.

Renson tried to acclimate himself to these working conditions. After all, they were absurd only from the viewpoint of a high-competition society, or a society in which the absence of sanity made such a free and easy approach totally unworkable.

And there was no equalitarian nonsense involved in the Independency's way of life, no pretense that everybody had equal intelligence and ability. The system merely insisted that the person of less ability be allowed to make what contribution he could, in whatever way he chose, to the society's progress. That hardly seemed too much to allow.

And aside from all that, the people at the lab, and others he met socially as the weeks passed, were obviously and genuinely *grateful* to Renson for joining them, and working to bring their life-support systems closer to outside standards. It was good to be appreciated, he discovered.

So he hung on, and ignored as best he could the growing sense of frustration he felt with the crawling pace of his project.

"The thing is, it's such a *simple* task," he complained to Estine one evening, "to merely redesign the stomach balloon. I don't know what the lab would do with a really *tough* development problem, like my idea of adding a miniaturized emo-monitor to the standard system. They would probably stretch that one out over several lifetimes! No wonder Primlay's interest in it was so mild."

She grinned at him. "Don't you know we don't have a war on, Grap?"

"Yes, I know that," he chuckled sorely. "I've heard about it from several people, several times. But I still find it a poor excuse for total inefficiency."

"But it's *not* inefficiency, Grap!" she protested. "It's just the sane, comfortable way of doing things. You don't find anyone taking a *negative* attitude toward his work, do you?"

"Not actively negative, but—"

"O.K., then. Everybody on your team is interested in the work. But they're also interested in other matters of importance in their lives as individuals. Society is to serve the individual, Grap, not the other way around. People shouldn't have to behave like selfless machines, you know."

For a minute Renson sat gazing vacantly into the distance. Then he sighed, "I can't help but wonder, though, what kind of future the Independency is making for itself. It's not even trying to keep abreast, economically and technologically, with the Commonality and the Federation, and is falling farther behind every decade."

"We *are* trying to keep abreast," said Estine, "but we insist on doing it within the framework of our own way of life."

Renson chuckled. "So I've noticed. That means nobody works very hard, and no penalty is put on failure to do good work for the society. You *can't* keep abreast as long as your way of life boils down to that."

"Maybe not," she said good-naturedly, "but here's an old saying I just made up: The vegetation on the other side of the fence includes sour grapes as well as greener grass. In other words, we won't discard our way of life for fancier life-support packets."

"It's not just that, I'm afraid," Renson said slowly. "When failure isn't penalized—" He let the thought trail off.

"Go on," she prompted.

"Well, I don't want to belittle the people here, Estine, but it seems to me, from what I've seen in the lab, that the population already includes a large percentage of what we'd call 'losers' in the Commonality. This is a point I hadn't given much thought to until right now, in questioning the econo-war. But the one positive gain that comes out of combat is the culling of the species, the removal of undesirable strains from the gene pool, by killing off low-survival types before they have a chance to breed."

"But the econo-war doesn't even do that," smiled

Estine. "Not enough people get killed in it for that."

"But killing isn't necessary when the persons being culled are sane," he said impatiently. "A loser in the Commonality, or the Federation, knows who he is, and so does everybody else. A loser is far less likely than a winner to find a desirable mate, and he's less likely to reproduce. That keeps the freakish types down to a minimum."

"I don't see that," she objected, "sane or insane, a person's strongest motivation is concerned with himself, the individual. After that, his second strongest drive is to have a family. The needs of his society to keep down the number of freaks runs a poor third."

"Yes, and it is to keep that third from being so poor that the econo-war is being fought!" yelled Renson, jumping to his feet and pacing the floor, more excited than he could recall ever being before. "It all fits together, Estine! The econo-war culls, and it provides unification of motivation for economic and technological advancement! I suppose I had to see your society with my own eyes before I could really understand that. Sometimes I think I'm not very bright."

After a long silence, she asked softly, "What are you going to do?"

"I'm not sure. I'm thinking of going back. I'd like to work on my emo-monitor idea with some company like Sol-Veg, and perhaps write up my ideas about the econo-war, now that they're becoming clear. I had such a hard time understanding it, maybe I would know how to explain it to people who are as dense as I've been." He turned to her suddenly. "Do you think you would like living in the Commonality, Estine?"

"No," she said flatly.

"I'm sorry. You know how I feel about you. Besides, you're too intelligent and capable not to have several children. Stay here if you must, Estine, but I do hope you'll marry again, and have lots of kids next time. Don't let this noncompetitive society cull you, girl!"

"Like the Commonality has almost culled you?" she asked thoughtfully.

Renson looked startled, then angry. "Damned if it didn't!" he said in wonder. "As if idealism was the sign of a loser! Well, I won't stand for that! I'm going home, Estine."

"O.K. It's been fun, Grap." She walked outside with him as he fingered the food pill pouch on his belt to make sure he had an ample supply.

"And for me," he said. "But the war will be fun, too. A good fight always is."

He kissed her, stepped back, and soared off into the black sky.

Heavy Thinker

"MIND INVASION!"

Hage Borat snapped out the alarm as quickly as he could tongue his toothmike. And at almost the same instant, the other nineteen members of Lontastan Exploration Squad 4710Z were shouting the same words.

Their voices rang a ragged chorus in Borat's right ear.

"Does everybody feel that?" he asked. "Sound off if you don't!"

The squad was silent. Then Danta spoke. "I feel it, but I retract the word 'invasion'. Something's looking at my thoughts as I think them, but that's all."

"Same here," several chorused.

"O.K.," responded Borat, "does that hold for everybody? Good. Now, does anybody have a fix on whatever it is? Who can locate it?"

Again silence from the squad. Borat rotated his body slowly in space as his eyes scanned the planetary system in which they had broken out of warp less than fifteen seconds ago. It definitely *was* a system, not a planetless star. He could see two inners plus three more out at gas-giant range.

"Intelligent life, you suppose, after all these centuries?" grunted Orrson.

"It's a weirdy, whatever it is," piped up Baune in her whimsical little-girl voice. "A sure-nuff telepath! I'm not sure I believe in it!"

"It's a telepath all right," Borat said, "and it has quite a range." The squad members had come out of warp with an average separation of over three million miles, as was usual in approaching a previously unvisited star, which spread them over quite an area of interplanetary space. And the telepath was watching them . . . had *started* watching them, judging from their reactions, at practically the same instant.

"What I wonder," Baune was saying, "is, does a telepath have to think? *We* think but don't telepath. Maybe *it* doesn't think, but *does*."

Borat grinned. "Cagoline," he snapped, "report this to headquarters, and keep it terse."

"Right," replied the communications man.

"My guess," said Sherris, "is that anything alive in this system is on the outer of those two visible inners. It could be Earth-type."

Borat had been thinking the same thing. Should

he order part of the squad to approach the planet, or should he . . .

"*Welcome, thinkers!*" came the powerful—but definitely pleasant—roar of thought. "Yes, I'm on the world you have in mind, Captain Borat, and any, or all, of you may come down if you like. Also, forgive the delay in my response to your presence. I had to learn your word-thought-symbols before I could address you."

"Who . . . What . . . Who are you?" asked Borat.

"I have no identity symbol," the telepath replied. "Presumably there must be two intelligent entities in association in order for the name-making process to begin."

"There's just you, in this whole system?"

"Yes, although my world has ample plant and lower animal life. Unfortunately, it never occurred to me to allow an intelligent animal species to develop here. Your existence, humans, is a lesson to me in enlightened self-interest. But without cognating the possibility of such beings as yourselves, how could I cognate their desirability?"

"In what manner do you find us desirable?" Borat asked cautiously.

"As fellow thinkers, as companions, as, perhaps, playmates," came the thought. "No, Baune, this is not a spider-and-the-fly ruse. From your thoughts concerning the chemical composition of your bodies, I do not think I would find you digestible. In actuality, Baune, the man called Orrson finds you far more appetizing than do I."

Baune giggled. "Naughty-minded Orry!" she chided.

But her thoughts—suddenly perceptible to all—were wondering *Why didn't old Tall-and-Tough tell me?*

"I'm omnivorous," Orrson said with discomfited lightness while his thoughts ran: *Old is right! Too old to rate with that delightful little bundle of youth.*

From Baune: *He means I'm too young for him. And he probably thinks I'm too silly, too.*

From Orrson: *No! She's not too young for me. I'm too old for her! Why's she saying things like that with the whole squad listening? I don't mind being kidded by her, but . . .*

From Baune: *Oh, damn, if I only were brazen enough to tell him! But he says I'm not too young, so maybe . . . I'm not saying anything! . . . Or kidding him, either!* "Hey! What's happening to me?"

From Orrson: *Thoughts! Our thoughts are communicating! That creature down on the planet . . . Glowing Baune! Could you possibly mean it?*

From Baune: *Oh, you big mighty monstrous marvelous old supermale . . . WOW!*

From Orrson: *Tremendous! But . . . nine nines are eighty-one, nine elevens are ninety-nine, nine thirteens are . . .*

Suddenly the thoughts of Orrson and Baune were no longer perceptible to the others.

"You humans view mental communication as desirable," the telepath apologized, "but with certain limitations. I believe I have the hang of it now."

Borat's mind was working furiously. Occasional humans had shown vague telepathic abilities, but nothing like this! The creature had inspected the thoughts of Orrson and Baune, decided to put them in close communication, and then, after belatedly discovering that such communion sought privacy, had closed off their thoughts from the rest of the squad!

What other capabilities the creature had—and how it might decide to use them—could not be guessed. Certainly the squad faced dangerous unknowns here.

But also unknown rewards. Functional telepathy! The Lontastan Federation needed something like that very badly in its econo-war with the Primgran Commonality.

And in any event, the being was apparently friendly and well-intentioned. The squad's primary task, he decided, was to learn as much as possible about the creature and its telepathic ability.

He began by asking: "Are Orrson and Baune in permanent communication, or are you acting as a transceiver?"

"A difficult question," commented the telepath. "I am not consciously transceiving for them now, but when I establish a linkage, such as theirs, it continues unless I break it intentionally. Perhaps my awareness of their presence has something to do with it."

"You've linked minds before?" asked Borat.

"Not intelligent minds like yours, but life-flows of various types. That is one method of controlling the ecology of my world."

Borat considered this. "What would happen," he asked, "if Orrson and Baune traveled out of range of your awareness?"

"I have no idea," the creature responded.

"All right, we'll find out. Orrson! Baune!"

"Yes?"

"Warp away from this system in short jumps of

increasing length. Start with light-minutes, and lengthen from there. If your telepathic linkage breaks down, report back, and in any case come back after you've gone out two light-years."

"Right."

"Cagoline," Borat continued, "are you through to Nexal?"

"Sure am! My report's raising a stir in headquarters!"

"O.K. Remain in space, Cagoline, and inform headquarters of developments as they occur. Danta, take charge of Orrson's crew and make a prelim of all planetary objects except the telepath's. My crew will go there. Questions?"

There were none.

"Start, then!" he commanded.

The squad—minus Cagoline, Orrson and Baune— went through a sequence of microwarps to gather into crew clusters. When in formation, Borat's crew warped once more to achieve entry position twenty thousand miles above the telepath's world. At that point the crew went full-inert and plummeted downward.

"Your mobility is delightful to watch, and most educational," observed the telepath. "But I catch thought fragments to the effect that humans were once confined, as am I, to a single planet. Now, however, you identify yourselves with space itself, rather than as creatures of your planets of origin."

"Yes," said Borat. "We could not fly through space until we devised equipment—tiny machines—for propulsion and protection outside our ancestral planet's atmosphere."

"Please continue," requested the telepath. "Your thoughts on a subject become more ordered and complete when you speak of it."

"Very well. For propulsion we need devices for inertial control, which amounts to gravitational control, and a device to insert ourselves into warp vectors which take us out of normal space. For protection we need shielding and pressor fields surrounding us. And a variety of macromolecules have to be imbedded into our body tissues. For example, our nasal and throat passages are lined with molecules that absorb, convert and release gases, to recycle the air from our lungs while we're out of breathable atmosphere. Then we have a power unit, implanted in our bodies along with the other life-support packages, to provide the energy for all these processes."

"I catch the thought," commented the telepath, "that these devices were first used in large vessels rather than in your bodies. Why were ships abandoned?"

"Because of prime-field turbulence. We still use small, unmanned ships for freight transport. Space isn't empty. There's a little gas almost everywhere in the galaxy, and in places the gas is relatively dense. Also, there are scattered clouds of dust particles.

"We . . . or our earlier ships . . . don't collide with this material when we travel in warp at superlight velocities. The warp removes us from normal space-time. But there is a reality underlying every particle of matter, a reality we call prime-field, and we don't get away from that when we go into warp. Our own prime-fields are subjected to turbulence by the fields of every atom of gas or dust that we warp through.

"Now, the more mass an object in warp has, the worse the turbulence. The prime-field of a hydrogen ion, passing through my body in warp, might displace the prime-fields of half a dozen of my atoms, and they in turn might displace to a lesser degree the fields of two dozen more atoms before the shockwave passed through my skin and dispersed. Very quickly, the prime-fields would snap back to their appropriate particles and no damage would be done.

"But if I had the size and mass of a ship, my field would collide with more particle fields, and the resulting turbulences would have more mass to work on. The turbulence would be violent and continuous if my mass were great enough.

"This would do no visible physical damage to me. An atom's prime-field can be disassociated from it without causing the atom to break down.

"But a mind is a prime-field phenomenon, as our first ship-warpers discovered. The turbulence in a large ship could push a man's mind . . . his identity . . . completely out of his body, perhaps to distances of billions of miles. Of course the ego-field as we term it would snap back at the first opportunity, but if that opportunity were delayed for several seconds the man's reality would be permanently impaired. He would, in short, be insane.

"So, we miniaturized the basic components of our spaceships to a point where they could be implanted in our bodies," Borat concluded, "and ceased flying in ships entirely. Also, we wear no more clothes, and carry no more massive equipment on our persons, than we consider necessary."

"Are you not now about to collide with the fields

of this planet's atmospheric gases?" inquired the telepath.

"Yes, but field turbulence is noticeable only at superlight velocity. Our entry into your atmosphere is a purely physical problem and is handled by one of our protective force-screens which shields us from frictional heat and extends, like wings or a parachute, to brake our fall."

The other members of the crew were exclaiming to each other about the appearance of the planet below, and Borat noted that it was, without doubt, the *healthiest* looking world he had ever seen. Not a swath of dead vegetation was visible anywhere on the land mass below, and only a few high-elevation outcrops of raw stone stood bare of plant life.

"Thank you," came the telepath's thought. "I'm pleased that my ecologic control produces results you find attractive."

Borat thought with a touch of awe, *He makes the whole world his garden!* And evidently he did so without hoe and rake, but by thought processes alone—perhaps by "approving" a certain plant, or animal, in a certain place, in the manner of humans noted for their "green thumb," and by disapproving a plant that attempted to sprout, or an animal that attempted to forage, in an unsuitable area.

If this was the power of telepathy, then it was plainly a power the Lontastan Federation had to have!

Borat's crew landed some two hundred yards from the creature, and stood staring.

"We are," observed the telepath, "mutually appalled by one another's size."

"Is all of that you?" demanded Sherris.

"All of this and more," came the response. "Approximately one third of me is underground. My form is roughly spherical."

"Maybe we can name you Monte," Sherris murmured. "That meant mountain in one of our old languages."

"That will be satisfactory," the telepath replied.

The humans walked slowly toward the giant stony-looking ball that soared at least two hundred feet over the rolling grassland. To Borat, the creature . . . Monte . . . resembled nothing else as much as a colossal boulder, lying partially submerged in the soil.

"I had assumed," he said, "that you were basically animal in nature, with locomotive ability."

"I am," replied Monte. "If it became necessary for me to change my location, I could rock myself free of the soil deposited around me, and roll away. When my planet and I were younger, and I much smaller, frequent movements were necessary to escape being crushed, or deeply buried, by diastrophic processes.

"Once," the thought continued, "I overstayed in a spot that became the peak of a mountain, because of the nourishment I found there. When the nourishment was exhausted, the mountainsides were too steep for me to roll down without smashing myself."

"How did you get down?" asked Walver, one of the younger men in the crew.

"First I attempted to forest the slopes with a species of tree sturdy enough to brake my fall, but the climate was unfavorable for the trees. Eventually, I merely waited for erosion to lower the mountain."

"What nourishment was on the mountain?" asked Borat.

"Radioactive minerals. I am, as I told you, essentially animal, but one of my life-processes is similar to the photosynthesis of plant life. Only in my case the process is radiosynthesis. Ordinary light cannot penetrate to the depth of my synthesizing tissues. Thus, I always locate myself over the warmest radioactives I can find."

One of the crew's mineral specialists said to Borat, "There is hot ore under the surface deposits here: I'm getting a strong count."

Borat nodded, still looking at Monte. "You spoke of rolling yourself. How . . . ?"

"I breathe, of course," replied the massive sphere, "thus there is an air cavity inside me. By shifting this cavity I can shift my center of gravity and achieve motion."

"Like a man walking inside a barrel," giggled Baune.

Borat blinked. "Are you two back?" he asked.

"Right," came Orrson's voice. "I think we can put the limit of the telepath's range at seventy-eight light-hours. That's where our linkage faded, and where it began rebuilding on our way back."

Borat frowned. "You lost it completely?"

"Afraid so," said Orrson. "But we have it back now."

"O.K. Come on down."

"Why the bugged expression, Hage?" asked Sherris.

"We need Monte's telepathy," he told her. "But we need it outside his field of awareness. If Orrson and Baune couldn't stay in communion with each other beyond that, I doubt if anyone else could."

"Oh," Sherris nodded. "You thought our people could visit here long enough to become telepathic, and from then on they would have a communication system far beyond anything the Primgranese can produce—except that it won't work."

"Right." Borat turned his gaze to Monte once more. "There is no way to make us permanently telepathic?" he asked.

"Regrettably not," replied the telepath. "Your thoughts concerning 'econo-war' are fascinating, and make me wish I could play on your side. You must find it thoroughly pleasurable."

"It was more fun while we were winning," Borat replied gruffly, "and we were until recent years. Then the Primgranese developed miniaturized emo-monitors—devices that enable one to read the emotional reactions of others—and included them in their standard life-support systems. The resulting gain in understanding gave their teamwork capabilities a tremendous boost, and modified their economic competition among themselves.

"We've been trying to close the emo-monitor gap," he added, "but duplicating what the Primgranese did is a slow, technically difficult task. If we could share your telepathy we would have what the Primgranese have—and more. Otherwise, well, the way the competition has gone recently, the Lontastan Federation will probably be beaten beyond recovery before the end of the century."

The thought depressed all.

"But look!" protested Walver. "All we have to do to use Monte's telepathy is take him home with us!"

Borat grimaced. "Why do you think he remarked

that we were mutually appalled by our relative sizes when we landed and he could make a comparison?"

"Oh, that," mumbled Walver. "He's too massive to warp."

"I would say he's more massive than the biggest starship man ever tried to fly," Borat responded.

"However," put in the telepath, "we have unknowns that might work in our favor. Perhaps I can defend myself against prime-field turbulence, though you cannot. Our minds have their differences. Could not that be one of them?"

"I doubt it," said Borat. "Prime-field turbulence is one of the most basic phenomena of the universe. No kind of matter is immune to it."

"I am willing to put that to a test," Monte insisted.

Borat thought it over. "Well, perhaps—but not until we've exhausted every other possibility."

"Hey!" came Danta's voice from whatever planet in the system she was examining at that moment. "Does he reproduce?"

Grinning, Borat asked, "What about it, Monte? A small offspring of yours—or several of them—could warp wherever they were needed in safety."

"That may be possible," Monte thought dubiously. "I have never tried reproducing because it never occurred to me. The durability of my body has been sufficient to perpetuate me without recourse to a reproductive process. I must give the idea some examination."

The whole crew felt Monte's mental withdrawal into solitary contemplation.

"Gad," breathed Walver, "when we finally found an alien intelligence, it was real alien! And he wants to join our war! Frankly, folks, I don't figure this at all!"

"It makes sense," retorted Borat. "Monte is super-intelligent, and obviously thoroughly sane. Thus he—"

"Why is he thoroughly sane? How do you know that?" demanded the younger man.

"The orderliness of his planet, for one thing," said Borat, "his enthusiasm for another, and his quick understanding of the nature of man, and of a multiple society, to cap it off. You notice he didn't inquire into the reasons for the econo-war. Was anybody doing any concentrated thinking on that subject, by the way?"

Nobody replied.

"Then he recognized our war, as we have only recently done ourselves, as a near-essential game for the progress of human society. He didn't have to have it explained to him."

"But why does he want to play the game with us?" asked Sherris. "Just for the sheer fun of mingling with other intelligences?"

"Partly, I think," Borat replied slowly. "But partly for his survival. He needs radioactives, and his planet is getting older. Diastrophism is slowing down here, and fewer and weaker radioactive ores are emerging on the surface. I think his basic purpose is to work out a mutual aid arrangement with us. He'll help with the econo-war in return for the availability of radioactives."

Monte rejoined them mentally at that instant. "Such a hope had indeed occurred to me," he told them. "However, the production of offspring by me will be of no assistance to you. I find that I can reproduce, but only after a gestation period of fourteen of your

centuries. Also, I recall that the ability to communicate with other life forms did not come to me until
I had attained one-fourth of my present massiveness.
My offspring, with a plentiful supply of radioactives
and other nutritive requirements, might attain that
size in half a billion years."

"Then telepathy is a function of brain-mass?" suggested Sherris.

"Possibly so."

"O.K., reproduction is out," said Borat. "What are
the other possibilities?"

Cagoline spoke up, "Several Council of Commerce members on Nexal are urging a full-scale
research project to investigate Monte's mind. They
say if the telepathic synapse—whatever that is—can
be isolated . . ."

"Tell them telepathy seems to be a function of
brain-mass," Borat replied a trifle crossly. "The trouble
is that research of that kind takes time . . . not as
much as Monte's reproduction, but more time than
we've got. Look how long it's taking our labs to
duplicate the work of the Primgranese on life-support
emo-monitors!"

"You might add," put in Monte, "that my participa-
tion in such a project does not strike me as fun."

"Tell them that, too, Cagoline," said Borat. "Now,
if there are no other suggestions, let's start equipping
Monte for the warp test."

"I don't have a suggestion," said Orrson. He and
Baune had landed a short distance away and now
walked up to join the group beside Monte. The man
was frowning. "But I think we should be sure of what
we're doing—and why. Maybe Baune and I feel a

stronger attachment for Monte than the rest of you, and have a special stake in his well-being. But just the same, it's good sense not to go off half-cocked."

"O.K.," said Borat. "What do you question?"

"Well, as you said yourself, we can't really expect Monte to be able to *nullify* prime-field turbulence. It's too basic. And it's too akin to the stuff thoughts are made of to be cancelled by thought. All we can reasonably expect is that Monte will prove more able than ourselves to *endure* turbulence."

"No mind can endure it long," said Sherris.

"Right," said Orrson. "Just a split-second knockout of your egofield, and you have to get the help of a psych-releaser to clean up the resulting trauma. And, if it lasts two or three seconds, you get a trauma that can't be cleaned up at all—the one form of insanity that doesn't yield. And I'd hate to share the same universe with an insane mentality of Monte's power."

He paused, and the others were silent as the thought sank in. He continued, "If we let Monte make the test, we should keep it extremely brief . . . certainly no more than a second. Now, let's say we find that he *can* endure brief periods of turbulence, followed by periods in which he heals the resulting traumas, with or without human assistance. Over a span of several months or a few years, he could travel into the center of the Federation, to Nexal perhaps, by making several thousand of these minimal warp jumps. It would be risky for him, and probably unpleasant, but chances are he would make it.

"Now, here's my question. Once he was there, what *use* would he serve that would be worth the risk he had taken? And I'm not asking for a glowing generality, but for a highly specific answer. His telepathic range will cover only one planetary system. It can't have the Federation-wide application we need, to serve the same purpose as the Commonality's emo-monitors. So, how do we justify risking his sanity in a test?"

Cagoline's voice sounded in their ears: "Hage, let me take a crack at that one."

"Go right ahead," said Borat.

"O.K., here it is, Orrson," said the communications man. "Nexal's the place . . . the only place . . . we need Monte's services. I'm speaking as a guy who's stuck with a job that keeps him in touch with all too many of those Council of Commerce gabfests back home. The time those brass hats consume arguing! Makes me wonder sometimes if we're as sane as we say we are!"

"Sanity has nothing to do with differences of opinion, only with the manner in which they are settled," Borat put in. "The settling requires the exchange of sufficient information between the disputing parties to provide a basis for agreement. And the most desirable course to follow in dealing with the complexities of the econo-war can't be arrived at without considering a vast multitude of factors."

"And even then the brass comes up with a lot of wrong answers," Cagoline retorted sourly. "But that's what I'm getting at, anyway. With Monte on hand to put all those CofC brains in communion with each other, that information-exchanging routine would go a lot faster and surer. And the same process is needed at lower levels of government, and in corporation boardrooms. Most of our corporations have their main offices on Nexal, and that's where they do their planning and get in their

448 Howard L. Myers

licks against each other. If Monte goes to Nexal, we won't *need* him anywhere else! Not much."

"Could you do what Cagoline has described, Monte?" asked Borat.

"Yes, indeed," came the eager answer. "I am now providing communion channels numbering in the trillions . . . at a sub-rational level, of course . . . among life specimens on this planet. Certainly I could do the same for the mere billions of persons on your capital planet."

"But your beautiful ecology!" mourned Baune. "If you come to Nexal with us, it'll go to pot!"

"That possibility does not disturb me," the telepath replied. "Your econo-war interests me more."

Borat eyed his second-in-command. "Satisfied, Orrson?" he asked.

"I suppose so," Orrson shrugged. "Yes."

"Then let's go to work."

The squad's equipment included several inertial-control packs, warp units, and power modules, brought along for use in the shipment home of discovered items that merited full study. For two days, most of the humans busied themselves around Monte, drilling holes through his tough shell, installing the necessary devices, and working out with him the means by which he could control their operation.

The latter was no serious problem. Monte had ample nerve-ends under his shell, plus sufficient musculature and muscle-control.

When the job was done, Borat said, "On this trial run, Monte, let's keep the warp jump as short as possible. It has to be long enough for you to see what you can do about the turbulence, but not long enough to do you any harm. I would say a one-second jump . . ."

"A tenth of a second should suffice," responded the telepath. "A full second will be better, of course."

"Fine. Be sure to set the warp breakout on automatic, just in case. Go ahead whenever you're ready, and good luck."

Slowly, Monte's mountain-sized bulk lifted free of the grassy surface and drifted upward, semi-inert.

"If no more than this is achieved," the telepath commented happily, "this means of transportation is far superior to rolling."

"Fine. Don't try to warp before you're three planetary diameters up," said Borat.

Monte drifted on upward and out of sight of the members of the squad who were remaining on the ground. They settled down to wait.

An hour later he called, "I'm in position, and *here I go!*"

Then immediately: "That . . . was . . . bad!"

"You couldn't fight it?" asked Borat.

"No. As you said, Hage Borat, prime-field turbulence is exceedingly fundamental. A quarter of a second was all I could tolerate."

"O.K. Come on back."

"Very well, but my return will be slow. I do not care to warp again."

The humans looked at the disappointment in each other's faces. "Well, that's that," Borat said inanely.

Cagoline called, "Hage, the Council of Commerce on Nexal is in a tizzy. I've told them the bad news."

"Do they have any bright ideas?"

"No, people in tizzies seldom get bright ideas," the communications man contributed. "They had their hopes way up. They were counting on gaining something important from our discovery of Monte, or his discovery of us. They still aren't reconciled to taking a licking on this."

"They may as well accept it," growled Borat, "and put some more push behind emo-monitor development." After a moment he added, "Tell them we're staying here to study Monte and mine some radioactives for him . . . and tell them to try to come up with a workable idea."

Monte was four days getting down from interplanetary space, and was appreciative of the concentrated uranium ore that awaited him.

"This is most generous of you," he told the squad, "in view of my inability to assist in the econo-war."

"You tried," shrugged Borat. "After all, *we're* supposed to be the experts on mobility, and it's no fault of yours if we can't find a way to transport you."

"Hey, I just thought of something!" yelped young Waiver. "If we have an insoluble problem here, why don't we stick the Primgranese with it? We simply let word of Monte leak out and they'll tie up thousands of their best spies, saboteurs and sundry infiltrators on him! Monte could spot them as fast as they arrived, and we could capture them."

Borat frowned. "I hate to admit the problem is insoluble, and that our only use for Monte is a largely negative one such as that. At best it would give us only a short-term victory, and at worst, well, the Primgranese might solve the problem." He paused and shrugged. "Although I'm coming to the conclusion that no solution exists. There's no way to get Monte to Nexal."

"Well, frankly, I'm *glad!*' chirped Baune. "Not that I want us to lose the econo-war, but it would be such a *shame* for Monte to go away and let his beautiful ecology fall apart! If those old tycoons and bureaucrats on Nexal want Monte's help so bad, they can come to *him* instead of him going to *them.*"

There was an instant of stunned silence. Then Borat leaped to his feet.

"That's it!" he bellowed jubilantly. *"You've hit it, Baune!"*

"An excellently suitable solution!" came Monte's thought.

The whole squad was suddenly swarming around Baune, everybody trying to hug her at once. "But . . . but—" she tried to protest amid the hubbub, "think what a mess those billions of people will make of Monte's ecology!"

"Not with Monte running things," said Borat happily.

A few months later Monte's world had become the new and bustling capital of the Lontastan Federation.

War in Our Time

THE OTHERS LOOKED up when old Radge Morimet stomped into the chamber of the Primgranese High Board of Trade. He stood, turning his head slowly to look at each of the Board members while the emo-monitor sensor implanted in his chin gave him quick reads of their attitudes.

He read relaxed concentration in them—the kind of attitude that's great, he thought caustically, for a kid trying to work a fairly simple puzzle toy. Here and there he encountered flashes of annoyance, presumably with himself because of his late arrival and the less-than-totally-sane emo-reading they were getting from him.

Morimet was well aware that he was rattling their sensors with the slam-slamming signal-cry of *vengeance*—of a mind busy with schemes of mayhem to inflict on an enemy. He had the prestige of his age and his record of service to protect that chronic attitude. Had he been a lesser figure than he was, he would have been pressured long ago into the care of a psych-releaser to get his vengeance-fixation lifted.

Personally, he considered it a useful attitude to have in the conduct of a war. He wished some of his colleagues on the High Board shared it.

He sat, and his chair positioned him comfortably at his place along the rim of the Board table. "Please go on from where you were," he said.

"We were in the process of reviewing," said Domler, the chairman. Morimet grunted.

Domler said, "To sum up, twenty-three years ago the Lontastan Federation apparently discovered a nonhuman, telepathic intelligence, about which we still have only limited information. The telepath is referred to as 'Monte', which may be suggestive as to its size. The Lontastans shifted their capital from Nexal to what is presumed to be the world on which the creature was discovered, and which has been named Orrbaune. Again, we have an indication in this that the creature Monte is too massive to travel by warp.

"We have not," Domler continued, "been able to obtain direct verification of this information. Our infiltrators have not been able to penetrate to the new capital planet. They are detected by telepathic means as soon as they enter the Orrbaune system.

"We have learned, however, that the telepath is serving the Lontastan capital as a communication system, on a level far surpassing anything previously achieved. This balanced our previous advantage in personal coordination, obtained when we equipped our people with implanted emo-monitors, and enabled the Lontastans to compete with us on even terms.

"Then last year the Lontastans finally perfected an implantable emo-monitor of their own. They now have a decisive advantage over us, and we have in prospect nothing of sufficient magnitude to restore the balance.

"The econo-war, ladies and gentlemen, is in grave jeopardy."

This was not news to any of the members. The emotional atmosphere in the chamber darkened slightly toward depression, however, at Domler's reminder. Morimet's vengeance pattern slam-slammed even harder.

"Comments on my summary?" queried Domler.

Several members eyed Morimet expectantly. He frowned. "Not from me," he growled. "If somebody will come forward with something *new* to discuss, all of us might have comments to make. We've already hashed and rehashed the status of the war to the point of no return. The question is: What are we going to do about it?"

He glared around fiercely.

"Every possibility is being explored," replied Grayme, a touch of tartness in her tone and a flicker of anger flashing at Morimet. "For example, our exploratory teams are now examining an average of thirty-nine stars per standard day on the mere chance that the Monte-type lifeform may have evolved on more than one planet, and we can find a Monte of our own."

Farsit, adjutant of Armed Resort, said slowly, "Also, this Board might seriously consider, in this crisis, the

use of overt force. Assuming Monte is a massive living
creature, we could produce a high-megaton missile
with a prime-field guidance system we are confident
could home on this creature. I'm aware that such
action would violate the traditions of centuries, but
if no other course presents itself—"

"Well, we do have promising preliminary findings
for more conventional approaches," Domler broke in
hurriedly. "It is theoretically possible, for instance, to
jam telepathic communications. Effective hardware is
still decades away, but—"

Morimet was glowering. "I said something *new!*"
he snapped. "We're going down the drain today, not
twenty years from now, or not in whatever century
we happen to stumble across a Monte of our own!
As for bombing that telepath, if it worked at all
it would put the econo-war on an unsustainable
primitive level. Such absurd crudities as that was
what put organized rivalry in such bad odor back
in Earth-Only times. We fight Lontastan commerce,
not Lontastan landscapes and populations! Besides,
they could play the missile game, too, if they were
pushed into it."

"Your desire for a new solution to our problem,"
replied Domler, showing an exasperation-read, "is one
all of us share. Unfortunately, none of us has such a
solution to offer . . . that is, Radge Morimet, unless
you have something in mind."

Morimet stared down at the table. "What we need,
at a minimum, is a counter to the speed with which the
Lontastan Council of Commerce, aided by telepathic
communication, can reach command decisions. Presumably, of course, Monte also improves communication

at lower government levels, and perhaps in corporation offices as well. But it is the CofC that makes the important econo-war decisions for the Federation, just as this High Board does for the Commonality of Primgran. With telepathic communion, their CofC doesn't spend years, or even hours, verbally comparing information and opinions among the members, or quibbling over semantics. They *communicate*, perhaps not instantly, but a hell of a lot faster than we do.

"And we," Morimet paused, sweeping the chamber with a disdain-read, "we have us. With our emo-monitors, we're not as bad as an ancient stockholders' meeting or national congress, in that we can't practice concealment and deceit on each other. But we can consume endless amounts of time, as we're doing right now, while the Lontastans are *moving!*

"In short, good colleagues, our problem is in this chamber. What do we do about it?"

The members stirred uncomfortably.

"We can throw your criticism in your face, Radge," replied Grayme. "What's new about that? We know the limitations that apply to this or any human governing body. As for the absence of concealment and deceit, I wonder if the absence is total here. That yammering vengeance-pattern of yours could conceal a multitude of unrecognizable intents."

Morimet grinned wolfishly. "Maybe it does. For example, my intent in bringing up the shortcomings of this High Board was not to enjoy the sound of my own voice. It was to propose that we do something about us."

"Do what?" asked Domler.

"Grayme just mentioned the 'limitations that apply to this or any human governing body'," Morimet responded. "She was in error. There is one purely human governing body to which the limitations wouldn't apply. I refer, of course, to an individual man or woman."

Everyone tried to reply at once. Morimet's emo-monitor hit him with a confusing flood of anger, disgust, and alarm. Then Farsit made himself heard.

"You object to bombing as a primitivism," he barked, "and then propose one-man rule!"

Morimet did not reply.

Gazing at him coolly, Grayme said, "Let's keep in mind the purposes of our econo-war. Man as an individual requires a demanding challenge at the group-activity level in order to maintain a cohesive, well-culled social structure that is motivated toward progress. Our war provides that, both for ourselves and for the Lontastans.

"A key requirement is group activity at all levels . . . that is, *teamwork*. What would the individual citizen ask himself when he learned the Commonality was being led not by a team . . . by this Board . . . but by an *individual*? Would he not be tempted to conclude that, if one person was better than a group for governing the Commonality, then he could govern himself on the basis of his strictly personal desires and goals without giving priority to the goals of his society?

"Don't forget, Radge, that man is by nature selfish, that self-interest is his strongest drive. That's a necessity for individual survival. Concern for the well-being of the society of which he is a member is also present, but it is less urgent and often must be aroused by the blandishments of others. His morale, as a team member, must be encouraged by reasoned explanation and pep talks.

"Certainly that morale would be dampened," she concluded, "if he saw the highest echelon of his team giving way to what the ancients called a 'personality cult'. It would be an invitation to him to pamper his own personality. Thus, we cannot allow the slightest taint of such a cult to enter this chamber."

Morimet glanced around to see if anyone else wanted to get some licks in before he replied.

Then he said, "Such a taint is already present here. I refer, of course, to myself. Any average citizen with an eccentricity such as mine would have been dragged to a psych-releaser long ago, but I, it seems, am a specially respected person. However, that's a rather quibbling point.

"I don't propose that this Board abdicate, but merely streamline itself. I say that decisions which require speed in the making—mainly those involving strategic and tactical matters—be left entirely to one person."

"Meaning practically every issue of importance that comes before this Board," growled Domler. "You're proposing more than a mere manager."

Morimet continued, "The Board would constantly review the actions of this top man, the one we can call the Executive, but would have no authority to interfere with those actions. The Board's chief authority would be the power to dismiss the Executive when, and if, it found him unsatisfactory. Thus, the Board would remain supreme, essentially, and the Executive would be its tool."

The chamber was silent for a moment after he finished. Farsit fidgeted and said, "The concept of delegation of authority is an old one—"

"I don't claim originality in this," said Morimet. "It *is* an old idea, and a workable one."

"For the sake of discussion," said Farsit, "how would this Executive be selected?"

"From our own membership," replied Morimet. "It would be a simple matter to ask the secretary to review the deliberations of this Board over the past five years and identify the member whose stands have proven correct more often than any other member's. That would be our man, or our woman as the case may be."

Another silence followed.

Suddenly Grayme snapped, "We're getting way off base here! The whole idea is unacceptable in principle! What good can be served by going into its details?"

Morimet looked at her. "I'm inclined to agree, concerning the principle," he said, "but more than a principle is at stake here. The war itself is threatened! That's a matter of urgent practical concern. We have to act!"

"Very well, on a *practical* level," retorted Grayme, "the conduct of the war requires continuity. It has lasted for over four centuries, and may be needed at least that long in the future. But your suggestion would produce a break in continuity at the end of an Executive's life. That's another weakness of the 'personality cult'. When the personality is gone, collapse tends to follow. At best, this would be sporadic, cyclical leadership . . ."

"I grant that," Morimet replied testily. "Maintaining

continuity will be a problem for future Boards. But the immediate need is to maintain the war *in our time*. Without it each citizen would, as you remarked yourself, make a cult out of his own personality. The deadly somnolence we've witnessed in the warless Halstayne Independency would overtake us all. What do you want for your grandchildren, Grayme, a slightly compromised econo-war, as I propose, or no war at all?"

She blinked, registering shock. Farsit spoke up. "Chairman, I ask that the secretary be queried as Morimet suggested, with the understanding that this request won't commit me to his proposal."

Domler nodded and pressed a button to put the computer secretary in the Board table into action. A moment later slips of paper were fed out of slots in front of each member's seat.

Grayme read hers and laughed dryly. "Were you counting on this, Radge?"

Morimet wadded his slip angrily and threw it on the table. "I decline to accept the position," he said flatly.

Domler remarked, "Maybe we *should* drag you to a psych-releaser! This was your proposal, yet when you are chosen by criteria you yourself specified—"

"It's my age, damn it!" Morimet bawled in annoyance that for an instant broke through his vengeance pattern. "When I said maintain the war in our time, I meant more than the next ten or fifteen years! We need a younger person for the Executive!"

Farsit nodded slowly. He glanced at his slip of paper again. "The numerical scores of the rest of us are closely clustered, well below your own, Morimet. I'm in second place, but by too slight a margin to mean much. If your age rules you out, and I agree that it should, then our choice of a candidate is not obvious to me."

"Well, I don't insist that the Executive be one of us," said Morimet. "I'm willing to go along with whatever modifications of my proposal you consider realistic." He hesitated, then added, "In fact, I know of a young man, a recent infiltration casualty, who might make an excellent candidate, although his motivation is rather shot at this moment."

"Who's that?"

"His name is Glan Combrit."

"Oh, yes," nodded Farsit, "Combrit. A brilliant record. He was one of your junior execs when you were an active corporate raider, wasn't he?"

"He was more than that," said Morimet. "He wound up running the whole Exchange end of my operation. Since then he's had a varied and highly successful career, most recently as an industrial espionage agent on several Lontastan planets. And it wasn't a slip on his part that has him out of action now. Even after the Lontastans got wise to him, it's to his credit that he managed to elude their goon squads and get home with a reasonably whole skin. He *knows* the econo-war, and he's a gifted strategist who can play it by the book or come up with creative solutions of his own. He's in recuperation on Earth right now. I visited him there a couple of weeks ago."

"I protest this discussion, Chairman!" Grayme complained loudly. "It is premature! Nothing has been decided!"

"Sustained," said Domler. "The discussion unjustifiably presumes a favorable decision on Morimet's proposal."

Morimet rose from his chair, his vengeance pattern slam-slamming harder than usual. "You have my proposal," he snorted, "and my arguments in its favor. I'm going home, and let you haggle over it as long-windedly as you like. Maybe you can do that better without my emo present to distract you!"

He whirled and stalked from the chamber. Once alone, he permitted himself a small grin.

Outside the building, Morimet glanced up with an old man's caution for obstacles in his path. The sky was blue and empty. He activated his transport implants and soared upward, on semi-inert mode and propelled by repulsor field.

His home, on the other side of the planet, could have been reached most quickly by lifting totally out of the atmosphere, making three right-angle minimal warps, and then descending. But he was in no hurry. He had nothing to do at home but await word of the Board's decision, and he suspected the decision was hours away.

Besides, he was skittish about warping in the vicinity of a planet. There was too much gas, even ten thousand miles above the atmosphere proper, for warping to be totally safe. That was how he had got stuck in his vengeance fixation. Warp did not take a man out of prime-field space, only out of matter-energy-time space. And every particle of gas carried its share of prime-field—and a man's mind was itself a patterned, durable prime-field matrix. A man who warped through a too dense wisp of gas could have his mind knocked right out of his body . . . knocked out at a velocity several times the speed of light.

The trauma of such an experience wasn't mild. The disassociation of mind and body was not bad in itself; in fact, that was a rather useless trick most any sane adult could do at will for amusement. And whether knocked out in warp or wittingly sent wandering, the mind matrix snapped back into place, as if from the end of a taut rubber band, as soon as it was permitted to do so.

The damaging factor about warp knock-out was the sheer speed with which it happened, the sudden recognition by both mind and body of the presence of relative motion of a magnitude both found innately "abnormal". And worse, this superlight motion was *separating* them.

In more respects than one, the experience was more traumatic than death itself. It was, in fact, one of the few types of trauma that a sane adult could not break without the help of a psych-releaser.

Thus it had happened several years ago that Radge Morimet, indulging himself in a moment of vengeful anger after a minor econo-war setback, had warped toward his headquarters planet . . . and had cut it too close. He had come out of warp in the stratosphere—that is, his body had—while his mind matrix had been knocked away by the outermost fringes of the ionosphere. The ionosphere was no mere wisp of gas; its prime-field was *solid*. It had stopped his mind matrix cold.

Reassociation took place in far less than a second, but not before the mind matrix was fixed by shock in the vengeance pattern it was holding at the instant of knock-out.

But, as Morimet had quickly realized, a touch of unsanity had its usefulness, to a man in a position to get away with it. It wasn't pleasant or comfortable, either to himself or to others, but for purposes of fighting a war his particular fixation had advantages over sweet reasonableness. It kept his mind on his job, for one thing. Probably it accounted in large part for his "rightness" score being higher than those of the other Board members.

He took his time going home, riding his repulsor field through the upper stratosphere. It was nearly an hour later before he dropped down on his estate. The local time was about 4:00 A.M., and his house, lawns, gardens and forest were dark and dewy damp.

Still, he lingered outside. There was no one in the house, his wife having "gone visiting" more or less permanently after he acquired his fixation—which was understandable. After all, what kind of companionship could a woman have with a man whose emo-pattern blocked communication?

Morimet blinked on his infrared vision and puttered about in his wife's flower garden until the call came from the Board.

"Morimet?" Domler's voice sounded in his right ear.

"Yes?"

"We've decided in favor of your proposal. It was unanimous except for one abstention."

Morimet grinned. "Grayme?" he asked.

"That's correct," the woman replied for herself.

Domler continued, "We've also studied the profiles of the young man you mentioned, Glan Combrit. He appears to be a suitable candidate, except for the motivation factor you mentioned. Possibly that lack can be remedied by an indoctrination course, which Grayme could conduct . . ."

Morimet straightened up from the flower he had been admiring and walked toward the house. He chortled. "Glan's been around too much to be more than mildly affected by a pep talk. Don't his profiles show that?"

"They suggest it," Domler replied. "However, we've agreed that a mild improvement in his motivation will be sufficient. An Executive who was too hard-driving would tend to aggravate the 'personality cult' problem and—"

"I disagree," Morimet interrupted. "High motivation is essential in that job. Consider my own example. I'm no brighter than many of the Board members, so why did I have the highest rightness score?" Nobody replied, so he hammered his point: "Why have you tolerated my eccentricity? Didn't you do so out of tacit recognition that it was making me exceptionally useful to the Commonality?"

Another silence. Then Grayme snapped angrily, "Radge Morimet, if you are suggesting what I think you are . . . !"

"I'm suggesting that now's the time to do things that just aren't done!" he retorted sharply. "We have a war to keep going, damn it! But if it will make you feel better, Grayme, I'm not suggesting that a fixation

be installed in Glan Combrit without his knowledge
and willing consent."

"To *intentionally* render a man *unsane!*" she
yelped.

"Oh, don't get so appalled," he chided. "You happily supervise the indoctrination programs that direct
the thinking, to a degree, of billions of individuals.
I'm proposing to direct the thinking, to a somewhat
greater degree, of just one man."

Farsit's voice sounded in his ear: "What would be
the content of the fixation?"

"Oh, something to the effect that Combrit desired
most urgently to be on the winning side in the
war."

"The *winning* side?" protested Domler. "But we
don't want to win the war! That would be almost as
bad as losing it!"

"Of course," Morimet agreed. "But the Executive
should be *trying* to win. We can safely trust the
Lontastans and their Monte creature to see that he
doesn't succeed. And bear in mind that this wouldn't
be a hate-the-enemy fixation, such as mine, that
would put Combrit out of emo-communication. It
would simply focus his drives along channels which
are desirable in his job."

After a pause, Domler said lamely, "This will require
some discussion."

"Call me back," said Morimet shortly, flexing his
ear to break the connection. He went into the house
and prepared himself a supper.

Five days later he was sitting on a patio on top of a
forested Asian hill, gazing out over the Sol-brightened

Pacific while sipping a drink and chatting with Glan Combrit.

"I imagine that the decisive point for the Board," he told the younger man, "was that score the secretary came up with. If my stand had been correct so often in the past, they're betting it is this time."

Combrit said slowly, "I accept the position, of course—and the condition attached."

"Good!" approved Morimet, seizing Combrit's hand for a firm shake. "I assured the Board you would. But there's one thing, Glan, I want you to face with your eyes open."

"What's that?"

"You're not going to be a happy man. I'm speaking as one who knows. A fixation is no fun to live with in the best of circumstances. And yours will, of necessity, cause you many frustrations, since it will demand winning. Even if you're effective beyond my wildest dreams, the most we can hope for is to bring the war back to even terms."

Combrit nodded. "O.K. I'll know to expect that. It is something I won't like, but I can live with it. After all, back in the days when this planet we're on was all man had, the entire race was loaded with neuroses beyond count, and they managed to survive it."

"Yeah, but they didn't know anything better," grumped Morimet. "Well, if your life-support is all in order, let's get off our duffs and warp for the capital. The sooner you're on the job, the sooner we'll stop losing this war!"

Combrit stood up. "Right. But don't expect too much. That creature Monte is more than a communications network. If we succeed in putting real pressure on the Lontastans, they might well respond by assigning duties to Monte similar to those you're giving me. And let's face it . . . my brain must compare to Monte's the same way an implant computer compares to that desk job in the Board chamber."

"Well, we'll see," replied Morimet, pleased that Combrit had recognized that key point in the situation without prompting.

Within weeks after assuming the duties of Executive, Combrit began stemming the tide of Lontastan victory. This was most immediately evident in Trade Credit Flow statistics, which had been running in high negative figures for the Primgran Commonality for two decades. Before the end of a standard year, Combrit's fast and effective trade moves had brought the TCF down to within a trillion dollars of parity.

And in one memorable trading day on the Open World of Exchange, the Primgranese General Stock average soared twenty-nine percent—and on low-volume turnover. Obviously, this unprecedented gain was not due to a flood of raid-buying by Lontastan adherents, but to a sudden decline in selling decisions by Primgranese holders. On that same day the more vulnerable Primgranese Frontals ran up a forty percent gain, also on low volume.

The formerly depressed Primgranese stocks were now safely priced and no longer inviting to potential raid-buying.

Then, having brought the econo-war back to even terms, Combrit began swinging it in the Commonality's favor.

He was jubilant, as were all members of the High Board of Trade, except Morimet. The old man took praise for the success of his proposal more grumpily than gracefully. It was evident to him, as well as to some of his associates, that his fixation was getting him down.

"Get rid of it, Radge," Grayme urged him after one of the in-person Board sessions. "Perhaps it served a useful function for a while, but we have Combrit now. Living in unsanity is too far beyond the call of duty. Let go of it!"

Morimet grimaced unhappily. "Not yet," he replied. "Perhaps soon . . . but . . . well, not yet." He turned and hurried away.

Combrit had heard the exchange, and walked up to the woman. "I think he means to hang on until he sees what the Lontastans will try to do to counter our successes," he told her.

"That's needless!" she complained. "You've demonstrated that you can handle any response of the enemy with more effectiveness than Radge possibly could."

"He obviously doesn't see it that way," Combrit replied.

Grayme shrugged. "Who knows how that man sees *anything*? That constant slam-slam-slam shuts him off from everybody."

Combrit nodded. "I'm glad my own fixation involves nothing like that. Fact is, I'm quite comfortable with it. But for him, that trauma must be like a painful wound on an otherwise healthy and alert body . . . not bad enough to dull the alertness and thus deaden the pain for him. It has to be a torture to live with, simply because it stands alone and can't be ignored."

"I'm glad your fixation has worked out so well," Grayme said. "I opposed it, and I'm glad I've been proven wrong."

Then within days the situation changed again.

In a stunningly brilliant series of market maneuvers, Lontastan raiders seized majority control of Midgard Starstream, a pivotal holding corporation on the Primgranese Frontal list that had territorial as well as industrial significance. It had been firmly in Primgranese hands for more than a century and a half.

Combrit's report to the High Board concluded grimly:

"The Lontastan Council of Commerce, presumably with reluctance similar to this Board's in establishing the position of Executive, appears to have responded in kind. I assume from the efficiency of the Midgard Starstream raid that the creature Monte was selected the Lontastan 'Executive'. For sheer mass of brain-power, Monte obviously outclasses any human, or any presently conceivable artificial mental construct.

"Two positive factors should apply, however. First, the Lontastan Federation may employ Monte with restraint, disliking—as would we—relinquishment of a human conflict to nonhuman control. Second, Monte lacks man's heritage of combativeness. This, plus the special preparation I was given for my present duties, should leave us with a definite motivational edge."

Domler messaged Morimet: "Damn it, Radge, a lot of good motivation is going to do us when that Monte monster can outscheme a dozen Combrits. They can murder us!"

Morimet snorted. "Don't bet on it! One positive

factor both you and Combrit seem to be missing is
that we hold the creative initiative."

"*What* creative initiative?"

"They're copying us, we're not copying them. We
establish an Executive, then they imitate our action.
Before that, we came up with emo-monitor implants,
and they followed suit as soon as they could develop the
gadget for themselves. One edge that gives us—among
several—is that it makes the Lontastans tend to hold
back, to guard themselves against whatever unexpected
initiative we may hit them with next."

"All right, I'm not saying the econo-war's lost,"
Domler said, "but I am saying that adoption of your
Executive scheme hasn't gained us a thing, at best,
and for the moment at any rate it's proving costly."

"So it is," Morimet replied agreeably, "but let's wait
and see how it goes for a while."

"Morimet, are you withholding information from
the Board?" the Chairman asked suspiciously.

"Nothing is being withheld," growled Morimet. "As
for certain opinions and expectations I might entertain, based on data known to all of you, those are my
business until I care to express them."

Domler broke off communication brusquely.

The war continued to go discouragingly for the
Primgran Commonality. There were no further coups
of the scope of the Midgard Starstream seizure,
but almost every action wound up favorably for
Lontasta. When the enemy did not achieve a small
victory, at least victory was denied the industrialists
of Primgran.

At last Morimet paid a visit to Combrit's office,

Executive Control. He stood in the middle of the room, staring about critically at the sumcom consoles, the Executive's three immediate assistants, and at Combrit himself. Judging from the man's strained appearance, and by the presence of a cot in a corner of the room, Combrit had been living in his office day and night.

"You're pushing yourself too hard, Glan," he said.

Combrit laughed wryly. "Monte's doing the pushing, Radge, not me! What a brain that creature's got! And evidently he never sleeps. I have to stay on my toes constantly, and . . . and"—he slumped his shoulders—"well . . . we're still losing."

Morimet had observed Combrit's emotions closely while he spoke. Frustration was heavy. Events were running counter to the demand of Combrit's fixation. And there was a definite flicker of admiration when he mentioned Monte.

"O.K.," Morimet replied. "The solution is to *not let* him keep pushing you. You're not glued to this office, Glan! Your assistants know standard economic strategics and tactics and can hold the fort. Get away from these clattering consoles a while, where you can *think.*"

Combrit frowned. "I'd better stick around . . . never know when something urgent will come up."

"But what are communications for!" snapped Morimet. "You can stay in touch wherever you go. Look, Glan, I've lived with a fixation a hell of a lot longer than you have, and I've learned some tricks about dealing with one. And I say get out of here! Warp to Earth for a few days, or even a week. Appease that urge to be on the winning side by hauling a few game fish out of the ocean. Or conquer a couple of mountains by climbing them on foot with all your life-support systems off."

Combrit showed annoyance. "You don't really think such stunts would distract me for a single minute from the hard and plain fact that I'm *not on the winning side,* do you?"

"Well, maybe not. But I have a suggestion to deal with that. Get your fixation deintensified while you're taking your break. A psych-releaser can do that for you. Then it can be reestablished when you return—"

Thoroughly goaded, Combrit flushed and shouted, "I don't *want* it deintensified! I want to *win!*" He whirled away, and quickly calmed down. When he faced Morimet again he was registering surprised concern. "That was quite an outburst, wasn't it?" he chuckled sorely. "Which proves you're right, and I have let this job get me on a thin edge. I'll take a few days off and go to Earth."

"Fine!" Morimet approved. "I think you'll find you'll feel better, and some quiet thinking might produce some useful answers for you as well."

The next day at his home Morimet was informed that the Executive had warped for Earth for a few days of relaxation. "About time," he grunted.

He settled down to wait. The trip from the capital planet to Earth took fifty-three hours—long enough for him to do a lot of floor-pacing if he allowed himself to become impatient, but also long enough for Combrit to think through his position and discover the answer to his problem.

But would Combrit do it? Morimet messaged his

wife. "I might go to a psych-releaser in a day or two," he told her.

"You might? I hope you do, Radge," she replied. "Let me know."

"I will."

He managed to hold off fifty-five hours before attempting to message Combrit. There was no response. He messaged Earth Arrivals Control.

"I'm trying to contact Executive Glan Combrit," he said to the officer in charge. "He must have passed through Arrivals two hours ago. Do you know where he is?"

"Executive Combrit hasn't arrived here, Director Morimet," the officer replied with a touch of alarm. "I'll see what I can learn and call you back."

Morimet grinned. "Thank you."

Then he messaged a psych-releaser and made an appointment.

Four days passed before it was known for a fact that Glan Combrit had defected to the enemy, and was even then in Lontastan territory.

The Board met in emergency session, and Morimet arrived late again. The others noticed, but were too preoccupied to comment upon, the absence of his fixation.

Without preamble, Domler said, "Morimet, this Board isn't trying to shift responsibility for what's happened, but the fact is that you were the key figure in this disaster from the beginning. You proposed establishment of an Executive, you named the man for the job, you suggested and later structured the fixation installed in him."

"And he's feeling *pleased* with himself!" observed Grayme, staring at Morimet. "You didn't plan for this, *too*, did you?"

Morimet nodded. "This was the final act of my scheme," he admitted comfortably. "I'll resign from the Board but I'd like to be sure a new Executive is properly prepared and on the job."

"A *new* one?" muttered Domler. "After what happened to the old one?"

"The next time," said Morimet, "the fixation must be worded differently. The Executive must be locked to the purpose of producing victory for Primgran, specifically, not simply to be on 'the winning side' as Combrit's fixation was phrased."

"Then it was the wording of Combrit's fixation," said Farsit, "wording you selected, that drove him into the enemy camp."

"Yes. He saw no hope for being on the winning side with us," said Morimet, "but with the Lontastans, and most of all with Monte, he expected his fixation could be satisfied."

The other members gazed at him, emoting stunned incomprehension.

Grayme demanded at last in a cold voice, "Morimet, was your vengeance desire directed at us rather than the Lontastan Federation?"

He chuckled. "Of course not! I wanted to injure the enemy, and that's what I've done."

"By giving them our key man?" exploded Domler.

"Right," Morimet nodded, "our key man, and one they will be slow to learn is worse than useless to them, provided what's said in this chamber today isn't allowed to go further."

* * *

He leaned back in his chair and smiled at the others. "How well would a football team play with two quarterbacks calling signals at once?" he asked.

"Oh, I see," said Farsit, puckering his brow. "Or I see what you tried to do. I don't think it'll work that way."

"You don't? Consider these points: First, the Lontastans have grown accustomed to copying our initiatives, to taking our ideas and using them against us. They know that Combrit is *good*, almost as good as their creature Monte, as he demonstrated by holding them to limited victories. Second, they have the same misgivings we would have about looking to a nonhuman for leadership in a purely human fight. They would prefer to limit Monte's role to that of a super-communication system.

"However, they would be as reluctant as you were about rendering a man unsane by installing a fixation in him. Since they had Monte, they could avoid that while not only following our lead but going us one better. They had misgivings about elevating Monte, and they still have them even though Monte has proven himself a winner.

"But now they also have Combrit, already handily fixated for them, with a motivation that will make him loyal to what he considers the winning side. Don't think they won't use him, friends! They will!

"On the other hand, they won't retract all the authority they've given Monte. He's proven too successful for them to do that. They will try to make an Executive team out of the two of them, which is a very promising-sounding idea, you'll agree."

"Damn right, I agree!" growled Domler. "Entirely *too* promising! It'll probably work! Monte's supermentality and Combrit's motivation and fighting heritage—"

"Very promising-sounding," Morimet repeated with self-satisfaction, "and very much in keeping with the concept of maintaining teamwork at all levels." He hesitated and peered expectantly at the others.

Grayme caught on first. "*A committee!*" she exclaimed. "Monte and Combrit will be a *committee!*"

"Right!" approved Morimet. "It only takes two to make a committee, at which point the long gab-sessions begin! Even with one member of the committee a telepath, it will take time to reach a meeting of minds and make a decision. Monte and Combrit will have the same problems directing the conduct of the Lontastan effort that our Board had before we picked an Executive."

"But how long will it last?" asked Farsit. "Won't they catch on?"

"Maybe, but I doubt it. They *prefer* teamwork, for one thing, just as we do, and won't want to catch on. Also, the idea of one man in charge was copied from us, and it is much easier to neglect, or forget, the basic philosophy behind a borrowed idea than one you work out yourself. The Lontastans won't be as dedicated to the single Executive principle as I hope this Board will remain."

"But when Combrit discovers he isn't on the winning side after all—" Grayme began.

"He'll rationalize his way through that problem," said Morimet. "Read the wording of his fixation, Grayme, with careful attention to tenses. He's on the winning side now, and he knows it. What happens from now on can be explained away to his satisfaction."

"Well!" exclaimed Domler. "If all this works out as you expect, Morimet, woe to the Lontastans!"

Morimet smiled and pulled a sheaf of paper from his belt pouch. "That's why I mentioned retiring from the Board. I've got my licks in, and you shouldn't need me any more."

"Radge," asked Grayme softly, "why did you hide behind that vengeance pattern all these years? Did you think we would refuse to go along with you if we knew all the details of your scheme?"

"Partly that. But mostly," Morimet hesitated, his pattern showing a flick of resolved self-distaste. "Mostly, though, it was because I needed a touch of unsanity to go through with it. Combrit was a friend of mine."

He straightened and tossed his papers on the table. "Here are my recommendations concerning the new Executive, and my resignation. My wife's at home rearranging the whole flower garden. I'd better get back there and either stop her if I can, or help her if I can't."

"But look here," broke in Domler, "your scheme is no lasting answer, even if it works for a time. At the best, it can't outlast Combrit!"

Morimet shrugged. "I know, but it gives us war in our time, and that's the best any generation can expect to do. What happens later will be another generation's problem."

He turned and walked jauntily out of the chamber.

Misinformation

❧⟡❧

ROF TOSEN ENTERED the outer office of the
Bureau of Strategic Information and gazed about
with dismay.

There were half a dozen Bureau staffers in the
room, and his emo-monitor picked up high enthusiasm
from each of them. But it was obvious at a glance
that the enthusiasm was not for their work.

Three were huddled in conversation that seemed to
concern, from the snatches Tosen overheard, the doings
of their various children. Two others were seated at
their desks using their communicators. One of these,
a man, was close enough for Tosen to gather that he
was discussing plans for a hunting trip on the planet
Glarsek.

Only one was going through the motions of handling

some paperwork, and her main attention was focused on the conversing group.

Tosen sighed. Just like back home in the offices of his Arbemel Systems Corporation on Haverly, he reflected glumly. Anyone would think the econo-war was over—or had never existed—from the actions of these people. And in the Bureau of Strategic Information, of all places! Regardless of the indifference of Commonality citizenry at large, he had expected somehow to find competitive morale still running strong here.

The woman doing paperwork looked at him. "May I help you?" she asked.

"I'm Rof Tosen," he said. "I have an appointment with Stol Jonmun."

"The Bureau chief won't be in this week," she replied. "Dave Mergly will see you instead. This way, please."

She rose, ignoring the flash of annoyance from Tosen, and led the way up a jumpshaft and along a corridor. Dave Mergly was the one man in the Bureau Tosen had hoped to avoid. He was Stol Jonmun's top assistant in charge of saying "no." But if Jonmun was out gold-bricking like everyone else . . . well, it would have to be Mergly.

The woman guided him into Mergly's office and departed. The two men studied each other for a moment. Dave Mergly was middle-aged, several years Tosen's senior, and was one of those men who remained slender with minimal exercise. He could burn up energy simply sitting at a desk. A high-tension type, Tosen reflected—and clearly that way as a matter of genetics, because psych-releasers made doubly sure, when treating government officials, that every possible source of unsanity was fully lifted.

Tosen's emo-monitor read the bureaucrat's attitude as one of detached curiosity, which gradually shifted into reserved approval, as they studied each other.

Mergly's thin lips bent in a slight smile. "Still competing, Tosen?" he asked.

"Trying to. You, too, I would judge."

"Yes. Not many of us around anymore. Welcome into the shrinking minority. Have a seat."

Tosen lowered into a chair, asking, "You holding the fort alone, here in the Bureau?"

"Not quite. How about your company . . . Arbemel Systems, isn't it?"

Tosen nodded. "I've got two good men. Mike Stebetz in Management and Clarn Rogers in Research. Makes two out of a payroll of sixty-seven hundred."

"Three, counting yourself," observed Mergly. "A little better than average, I would say." He studied Tosen for a moment, then asked, "How do you explain the situation, Rof?"

With a shrug Tosen replied, "I don't have any original thoughts on the subject. The obvious answer is that the public at large considers the econo-war to be over, so they're no longer participating in it. The Lontastan Federation, with its telepath Monte, has an overpowering advantage over us. So the average citizen considers it all over but the official surrender and seizure."

Mergly frowned. "The Commonality has been in tight squeezes before, and managed to squirm out, and morale didn't go to pot while we were doing it. Remember old Radge Morimet?"

"No, he predated me by ten years. But, of course, I'm familiar with what he accomplished—and what he didn't accomplish. His motto was 'war in our time,' and let the next generation worry about war in its time. Well, we're the next generation, and the compromises he made to keep the econo-war going have made our position even more difficult. He managed to squirm, but in doing so he left no squirming room for us.

"I think the public realizes that," Tosen continued thoughtfully. "The time is past when we can find a short-term answer by compromising the philosophical foundation of the econo-war. Morimet didn't leave us any compromises to make. Except for a handful of diehards, which includes the two of us, nobody sees any possibility of bringing the war back to life."

"And the public doesn't seem to care," grunted Mergly.

"Oh, the people care, all right," Tosen disagreed. "I have talked to a lot of the people in my company about it. They regret the ending of the war, but without panic or grief. That's the sane way to face a loss, no matter how tremendous it is. We're inclined to misjudge their reaction—and this is something to think about—because this is the first major social crisis humanity has faced since we attained racial sanity, nearly a thousand years ago. We listen for screams of anguish and look for people wringing their hands, or lashing out angrily at everybody and everything, or sinking into the apathy of defeat. But such responses from the Earth-Only days are no longer in character."

Mergly nodded slowly. "A good point. The people write off their loss and fall back on what they have left—their purely personal interests, their love for their families, and what not. Meanwhile, our social structure collapses about us."

"Yes," Tosen agreed. "That's what the econo-war was for, essentially . . . to stimulate the individual's motivation as a functioning member of a racial social structure."

"Then why," demanded Mergly, "are we few die-hards still hanging on?"

"Maybe because we're more informed than most on how damaging a social collapse could be. At the best, we would have a stasis civilization. At worst, we could slide back into unsanity. Unless . . . and this is a trillion-to-one shot . . . some sublime genius of a philosopher discovered some presently unsuspected Higher Purpose for humanity to pursue."

Mergly gave a dry chuckle. "Another explanation for us diehard types," he said, "could be that we still see, or imagine, some thin hope to cling to."

"Yes," nodded Tosen, "there's that."

"Which gets us around to the real reason for your visit, doesn't it?"

Tosen hesitated. "I'd rather not have my scheme termed a 'thin hope' before you've even heard it," he said with a grin.

Mergly nodded, and his emo reading was a cold nothing. He was, Tosen guessed, all set to listen analytically—and thoroughly critically—to the proposal. "Go ahead," he said.

"What I have in mind," Tosen began, "would get us away from damaging compromises, and hit at the basic imbalance in the econo-war. That is, at the fact that the Lontastan Federation has Monte, and the

Commonality of Primgran doesn't. Essentially, Monte was the first compromise. The Lontastans should never have allowed a nonhuman to participate in what was a purely human conflict. Do you agree with that?"

"Yes."

"Unless, of course, Monte isn't a nonhuman life form at all," Tosen added, eying the Information man closely.

Mergly blinked. "Oh? You think there's room for doubt about that?"

"That's what I'm here to find out. Let's consider what we think we know about Monte, and why we think we know it.

"First, he's a huge globe in form, perhaps a hundred meters in diameter, with a stonelike shell of sufficient thickness and strength to support that tremendous weight on a planet of approximately Earth-gravity. Second, he's a one-member species that does not produce offspring, and presumably had his genesis in the earliest stages of the life-formation processes on his planet, perhaps a billion years ago. Third, a Lontastan exploration team entered his star's planetary system and discovered him, and he volunteered his services in the econo-war very soon thereafter.

"Now, we aren't dealing with impossibilities in any of those three areas—that is, Monte's present form, his history, or his discovery by man. But I suggest each of the three holds substantial improbabilities, and when all of them are combined the likelihood of truth is statistically slight.

"For example, such giant size and mass would create problems of inadequate muscular strength for mobility, of finding sufficient nourishment, and of dissipating body heat. A Monte creature ought to be immobile, and stewing in its own weak juices.

"And yet, this creature reportedly has survived and grown through most of the geologic ages of his planet. Earthquakes, floods, volcanic eruptions, ice incrustations . . . he got through them all.

"And then this creature, after a billion years of total intellectual solitude, becomes a 'joiner' as soon as he encounters humanity!"

Tosen paused, then added, "I don't say all this is impossible. Merely improbable."

Frowning, Mergly countered, "Perhaps; perhaps not. Every difficulty you cite can be explained. The matter of nourishment, for instance, seems to be handled in large part by a process similar to photosynthesis, called radiosynthesis. Radioactive ores would have been plentiful and rich in Monte's youth—and incidentally there may have been many small Montes back then, making the survival of one far more probable. The nourishment problem would have built up with the passage of time, I agree. And according to some reports I've seen, that could explain Monte's eagerness for human associates. People can mine and refine radioactives for him to bed down in.

"I won't bother to cover all your 'improbables'," Mergly concluded with a shrug. "Presumably you've studied the matter sufficiently to know the explanations yourself. My question is why do you even bother to bring the subject up?"

"Because despite the explanations, the improbables are still just that," retorted Tosen. "And if there is any reason to believe the account of Monte we have is based on misinformation, we might be well-advised to assume a more believable account of what he is, and how he got that way."

Mergly's eyebrows raised and he flickered annoyance. "Misinformation?" he said.

"That's what I want you to tell me," said Tosen quickly. "What are the sources of our data concerning Monte? How close has one of our own agents ever got to him? Have we ever captured and questioned a Lontastan who had *direct* knowledge of Monte's physical nature?"

There was a moment of silence. "You're suggesting the Lontastans have sold us a comet tail," Mergly said slowly.

"Could be. I want to know if any of our data on Monte is unimpeachable enough to prove me wrong."

"Well . . . as you know, Lontastan security around Orrbaune is extremely tight," said Mergly. "As soon as one of our agents breaks warp anywhere in the planetary system he's detected telepathically. And he can't stay long . . . everybody's jumpy about intruders these days, partly because of the crisis condition of the econo-war, and partly because Radge Morimet brought unsane motivation into play. The Lontastan Guardsmen blast away at an agent immediately, on the chance that he might be some kind of nut with a superweapon in his pocket.

"As for picking up direct data on Monte from a captured Lontastan, I'd have to check on that, but I believe all information from such sources is third-hand at best. For the moment, I'll go along with your notion that the Monte story has been falsified. The question remains, what good would this falsification

do the Lontastans? And what can we gain by penetrating it?"

"Easy," smiled Tosen. "If Monte's not a living being,
the most probable alternative is that he's a machine
built by the Lontastans. If we are led to *think* the
Monte machine is a being, we won't try to build one
of our own. After all, anything the Lontastans can
build, so can we. But a telepathic life form isn't one
of those things . . . biotechnics just isn't up to it. Thus,
the Lontastans develop a telepathic device, make us
believe it's a natural life form, and keep a monopoly
on their gadget."

"But why on such an out-of-the-way planet as
Orrbaune?" protested Mergly. "Would they actually go
to the trouble of shifting their capital way out there,
if Monte were indeed a machine that could be built
presumably anywhere?"

"Sure, for verisimilitude!" exclaimed Tosen. "And
for security reasons, too. Keep in mind that, back
before they had Monte, we had the upper hand in the
war. They hadn't broken our monopoly on implanted
emo-monitors then, and our undercover agents and
saboteurs were having a field day on their central
worlds. When they hit on the telepathy gimmick, they
had to spirit their development team off somewhere,
to such an undeveloped world as Orrbaune, to keep
the project secret from us.

"But if they had started building Monte machines
on all their major planets, we would have caught
on quickly. So they built just the one . . . and on
a planet where a startling life form might possibly
have been discovered, and started spreading their
tall story."

Mergly nodded slowly, and Tosen felt a calm elation.

"Of course," Mergly said, not quite willing to be convinced, "what you have here is a purely supposi- tional structure."

"Yes, but one that, if I'm right, could straighten out the entire econo-war mess and get everybody back in competition. But I agree it would help if we had more dependable data to go on."

"Such as what?"

"Such as an agent might get during a very close— though necessarily quite brief—approach to Orrbaune. For a moment our man would be in the thick of the telepathic communications network that Monte provides the personnel on the planet, not merely within range of telepathic detection. He might get a surprise reaction from Monte, especially if it is a living creature. And he might pick up thoughts from the local humans who have first-hand knowledge of the telepath."

Mergly was radiating impatience. "Who's dealing with extreme improbabilities now?" he snorted. "But never mind that for a moment, since I can see from your emo that you think you know how such a close approach could be made. If you're asking me to assign a Bureau agent to that mission, the answer is NO. For the very good reason that we no longer have an agent fit for that type of job."

"No agent?" murmured Tosen.

"They've all turned noncompetitive," grunted Mergly. "Which makes sense from their viewpoint. Agents are among the few people who actually risk their lives in the conduct of the econo-war. That takes strong motivation, which present conditions don't provide."

"But if it was explained to one that this mission might revitalize the econo-war . . ." Tosen began.

"He would laugh at you," Mergly responded. "Have you tried to explain your scheme to a non-competitor?"

"Well, yes. To my wife."

"What did she think of it?"

"She laughed," Tosen admitted lamely.

Mergly's smile was sour. "So there you are. You have a suppositional structure, which you need more data to substantiate sufficiently to impress someone who has turned noncompetitive. But to get that data, you have to impress a noncompetitive agent with your suppositions. Quite a dilemma."

After a silence, Tosen said, "There's one answer to it: I can make the jaunt to Orrbaune myself if you'll agree."

"That's a deadly game for an amateur," replied Mergly.

"I know," said Tosen.

Four light-days away from Orrbaune's sun Tosen came out of warp, well outside telepathic detection range.

For an instant he felt a purely subjective chill, so distant from a sun's warmth and clad only in the shorts, sleeveless shirt and low boots normally worn by space travelers. However, the tiny implanted devices of his life-support system were keeping him warm while they protected him from the vacuum, and from the high-energy particles of interstellar space. And embedded in the tissues of his throat and nasal passages were gas-converting macromolecules to permit normal breathing.

He torqued his repulsor field to start himself spinning slowly, blinked tightly to turn on his ampli-sight, and peered about for the equipment pod which had been set to follow three seconds behind him through warp. This was an uncertainty-filled point in his mission—finding his equipment—because warping over a two-hundred-light-year jump was not totally precise. His pod might emerge on top of him or fifty thousand miles away. And it could not make any blatant announcement of its location so near the Lontastan capital system . . . it had a powerful red blinker for Tosen to look for, and that was all.

Without the equipment in the pod, he might as well warp for home immediately. He had to have it, and it could not have made the trip through warp with him. A man-sized mass was about the maximum that could move at warp velocities without stirring up mind-wrecking turbulence in prime-field.

So Tosen spun slowly in space, straining for a glimpse of the red blinker.

He almost missed it. It was a dim flicker in his peripheral vision that vanished when he tried to look directly at it. But he had its direction spotted. He activated his propulsor field and zoomed toward it on semi-inert mode.

Within fifty yards of the pod he went full-inert and drifted in slowly. The pod was a slender torpedo of dull red, and the color went black when he reached and killed the blinker. After activating the automatic setup system, he drifted a few feet away while he

watched the pod unfold, extend a framework of slender lattices, and fan out a thin pie-slice of silver into
a six-meter telescope mirror. When the components
clamped together and motion stopped, he drifted to
the eyepiece and swung the instrument to point in
the direction of Orrbaune.

Basically it was an ancient device that would have
been readily recognized for what it was back in Earth-
Only times—an astronomical reflector telescope. It was
rendered more effective by an ampli-sight attachment
and tight-line tracking, but its mirror optics differed
little from those used by men to peer into space
even before man himself could leave old Earth's
atmosphere.

Tosen grinned at the sheer size of the instrument.
Who would imagine a spy using such a big, cumbersome gadget?

And that was the whole point. Nobody had imagined it, and that was why it had never been tried.
People were used to thinking of space equipment in
pill-sized packages . . . devices small enough to place
in the various available nooks and crannies of the
human body without making noticeable bulges. Like
ampli-sight, for example, for which a specialized field
phenomenon was produced by speck-like transmitters
located within the eyeballs.

Being sane, Tosen mused as he busied himself with
the telescope, only gave individuals access to such abilities as they inherently possessed. It was no guarantee
of great wisdom, or of creative imagination. He felt
himself fortunate to possess the latter of these.

He spent fifteen hours working with the telescope
and its computer attachment, getting the data he

needed. When his series of observations was complete, he knew his position and motion relative to Orrbaune with more exactitude than any earlier Commonality agent. He figured on a maximum margin of error of ten miles.

Satisfied at last, he activated the breakdown system and watched the telescope collapse back into the compact pod configuration. When the process was complete, he switched on the systems of the pod's record-and-home automatic sequence.

Then he drifted away from the pod, carefully set up his approach vector, and warped toward Orrbaune.

He exited into norm space almost sitting on the planet. His altitude was only two hundred miles, and his inert momentum in relation to the surface was near zero.

But he had no time to congratulate himself on this success. He was too busy observing with every implant-augmented sense he could bring to bear. He had a lot to try to learn in the two seconds he had allowed himself.

At that, he nearly overstayed. The Lontastans were skittish indeed about unheralded visitors—and especially one appearing almost on top of their heads. Tosen realized as he automatically went into warp and zipped away that he had felt the first few milliseconds of a zerburst flare that had blossomed within a few hundred meters of where he had been. He could feel the burn all across his back, and could detect his medicircuits going to work on the damage.

What had he learned?

He wasn't sure, but he hadn't expected to be at

this stage. The important information, he hoped, was that which had been gathered by his special sensing devices and transmitted to the pod, to be recorded and transported home.

But at any rate, his memory of those two seconds held nothing to indicate Monte was not a device.

There *had* been telepathic contact. It had come so swiftly after his exit from warp that he had noticed no time lag.

But the . . . the *feel* of that contact was, at first, impersonal, without even mild emotion. Would a living telepath have such a feel? Tosen had never experienced telepathy before, but he doubted it.

Then, a split-second later, that impersonal feel was lost in a welter of obviously human thought-patterns as alerted Guardsmen came storming into the telepathic linkage with the expected reactions of alarm and anger, and harsh demands that the intruder identify himself instantly.

All in all, Tosen considered his mission to Orrbaune a complete success.

He left a confused flurry of exchanges behind him.

Who was that? demanded Frikason of the Lontastan High Board.

Monte replied: *His identity was not revealed as his attention was so totally on receiving data that he transmitted very little. However, he was from the Commonality, and his purpose came through clearly.*

Oh? What was it?

To obtain information to verify his belief that I'm a machine, not a living being. Monte's thought was obviously amused. *If I were a machine, it would be possible for the Commonality to build my counterpart. That was his intention.*

Frikason along with several others present shared Monte's amusement.

Then from Frikason: *In a way it's too bad he's so completely off the track.*

True, agreed Monte. *The deterioration of the econowar game is regrettable, and my equivalent on the Primgranese team would be the ideal way to restore the balance. But extensive studies by myself in collaboration with a number of your scientists has produced the unavoidable conclusion: a telepathic device, or machine, lies totally beyond all present skills and knowledge, and may, in fact, be an impossibility. Whereas certain of the reasoning capabilities of the mind can be duplicated by computing devices, telepathy lends itself to no such mechanical production. It is too purely a life-function for that.*

After a moment of relative telepathic silence, a thought came from Garsanne of the High Board: *Surely even the Primgranese should have figured that out. Why did this spy think otherwise? Did he have an unsane motivator?*

No, replied Monte. *My impression was that he bases his belief on a logical—if thoroughly wishful—interpretation of such data concerning myself as the Commonality has obtained.*

Wishful indeed, remarked Frikason. *By the way, did he warp out safely?*

Yes, barely. He escaped with the equivalent of a bad case of sunburn.

Sadder but wiser, huh?

No, not wiser, Monte informed them. *As you know, there is practically nothing of what may be called personality in any one of my billions of telepathic attention units. Each is simply a circuit. The spy would not be able to distinguish the attention unit that detected his presence and revealed him to the nearest Guardsmen as the product of a living mind. As for the Guardsmen with whom he was in mental contact, able though they are for their assignments they are genetic barbarians of meager intellectual curiosity. Their knowledge of me is only of the hearsay type the spy discountenances.*

So he's going home, still thinking you're a machine he can duplicate. observed Garsanne. *Look, Tedaboyd, you'd better dispatch a couple of agents to learn his identity and see what he comes up with, just in case.*

The Lontastan Intelligence chief's thought was annoyed: *What couple of agents? I told the High Board months ago that I haven't got a decent agent left! They've all become slack-outs! And I can't say I blame them. Why should they stick their necks out for a war that is already won?*

Yes, I'm afraid we non-slack-outs are a vanishingly small minority, agreed Frikason. *Never mind trying to track down that spy. He can't possibly succeed, as Monte's told us. Let's get back to the task at hand of devising the least disastrous means of bringing the econo-war to an official close.*

Monte observed: *The Commonality of Primgran, though defeated, still has one strength we lack.*

Oh? What's that? Frikason asked.

One highly-motivated agent, still on the job.

* * *

Tosen soon found himself needing all his high motivation.

"Why," demanded Mergly, glowering across Tosen's desk, "didn't you tell me you didn't have even the backing of your own research man?"

Tosen glanced sideways at Clarn Rogers, who was emoting offended surprise, then replied, "Because I didn't know." He grinned wryly and added, "I didn't bother to check with him."

"Why not?"

"Because I suspected what his answer would be."

Mergly growled, "So you got me to go to bat for you before the Council to get you an R-and-D contract, with my neck way out—not that I give a damn about my neck, but wasting what competitive push we've got left is another matter!"

"I don't think it's a waste," Tosen returned. "I think Rogers is wrong."

"But, Rof," Rogers complained, "a telepathic machine just doesn't make sense. Every piece of substantial research on the subject indicates that telepathy is a function of the ego-field, or the spirit, or soul, or whatever you want to call it. Definitely, telepathy is *not* a function of the physiological nervous system. Or at any rate, not basically. A proper nervous system, such as that of the creature Monte, doubtless is essential machinery to facilitate an ego-field's telepathic abilities—otherwise all humans would have it. But you certainly can't produce telepathy with a mere machine!"

"Psionic devices have been around for several centuries," Tosen remarked softly.

"Certainly," Rogers said, showing impatience, "but they function as accessories of the users' nervous systems, as relatively simple additional nerve-ends, so to speak. Very useful as controls for our life-support implants and what not."

"But it's the ego-field that makes a psionic device work, isn't it?" said Tosen.

Rogers wriggled. "Well, of course. But as a *small* added part of the nervous system under the ego-field's control! What you're proposing wouldn't be small. It would be several orders of magnitude more complex than the human brain itself, according to my understanding of what Monte is. You couldn't merely focus your attention on such a thing and make it work. You don't have that much . . . that much *attention!* Certainly not that much to spare."

Mergly asked Rogers, "Then what would you expect to be the result of the project if we carried it out?"

Rogers shrugged. "We would have a very large, very expensive, and very inactive conglomerate of close-connected macromolecules."

"As large as Monte is reported to be?" demanded Mergly.

"No. We can crowd more functional capacity into artificially produced macromolecules than you find in living tissue, and use more concentrated energy sources. The construct would be less massive than Monte's living brain, but approximately as complex. I would estimate the diameter at two meters."

Tosen smiled inwardly at Rogers's insistence on thinking of Monte as a living creature, despite the flat, mechanical emo-quality of the telepathic contact made with him on his spying jaunt—that quality having been duly recorded and scrupulously analyzed since his return.

Now he kept silent as Mergly and Rogers continued the discussion. He was for the moment in the bad graces of both men for getting them involved in a project they considered half-baked at best. But they were both good constructive competitors who would, if they could, find a way to salvage something useful from the mess his "irresponsibility" had created.

In the meantime, his research man and the government's Information man were a team from which he was excluded. So the less he had to say, the better.

"Assuming that Monte is a natural life form," Mergly said, "with a brain as massive as that assumption would suggest, wouldn't our artificial construct be superior to him, provided it worked at all?"

"Interconnections would be much shorter," Rogers nodded, "which would permit faster responses. But, of course, it wouldn't work at all. It would be a sumptuous mock-up of a superior central nervous system, capable of producing billions of responses of the quality Rof picked up from Monte. But it would be an *uninhabited* mock-up. It would be dead."

After a pause, Mergly said, "Yes, but would it stay that way?"

"What do you mean?"

Mergly shifted in his seat and frowned. "There's much we don't know about the disembodied ego-field, even though that's a state we've all gone through. The experience just doesn't carry over to the normal embodied state; perhaps there are too few similarities to use as guides. My own impressions of disembodiment are completely vague. I'm wondering . . . would our artificial construct be attractive to a disembodied ego-field? Could it be *made* attractive?"

Rogers blinked. "That's a possibility, I suppose. We don't know what attracts an ego-field into a newly-created life form, such as a human baby, although there's no shortage of conflicting theories. There are, certainly, the physical pleasures, such as sex. Perhaps a structure that facilitated telepathic communication would have its attractions."

"O.K., and if that didn't do the trick," Mergly persisted, "couldn't pleasure-producing circuits, or physical structures, be added on?"

"Well, yes, in an artificial way. But let me put it like this: Would you want to live in a body composed completely of prosthetics?"

Mergly frowned. "No."

"Well, that's what we would be offering any interested ego-field. Strictly ersatz, second-rate physical pleasures. I think telepathy would be the real—perhaps the only—attraction we could offer."

Mergly considered this in silence, displaying a varying emo-pattern as he did so. Then suddenly his pattern went clean and he rose from his seat. Obviously, he had decided.

"O.K., Clarn," he said to Rogers. "Get on with the project. Build that structure, and we'll see if anyone moves in. We're taking a shot in the dark, but," he shrugged, "these are rather frantic times." His eyes moved to Tosen and he added, "Frantic enough to justify frantic schemes I'm sure."

Tosen was radiating triumph, and the contrite tone of his "Thank you, Dave" fooled nobody.

*   *   *

He stayed on the side lines of Project Bauble as the research and development work moved ahead. He assisted Rogers mostly by seeking out people in the company who hadn't gone completely non-competitive, giving them exciting sales pitches about "something big and revolutionary" going on in the lab, and sending on to Rogers the recruits who responded with genuine interest.

Within a month, there was a notable difference in atmosphere at Arbemel Systems Corporation. It wasn't back to the status of Hot Econo-war times, but had shifted in that direction. Even Tosen's secretaries were showing alert interest in their work, whereas before the project started their attention had been dispersed over such areas as the care and feeding of each other's children, beauty regimens, and in a few cases astrology. Now they were trying to outdo each other once more in demonstrating their efficiency.

Tosen was pleased. Whatever the outcome of the project, he had restored for a while, and within the limited confines of his company, the old spirit that had brought humanity so far and so fast.

But he knew the spirit would die quickly if the Bauble did not come alive.

Mergly was spending at least as much time on Haverly, at the Arbemel lab, as he was on the capital planet. Project Bauble was, after all, about the only real action going, so far as econo-war effort was concerned. Mergly wanted to keep an eye on it . . . and make sure there were no Lontastans doing the same.

"I've taken the liberty," he told Tosen after the

project had been underway for several months, "of having the Arbemel floating stock purchased quietly for a Commonality trust."

Tosen nodded. "A good move," he said. "Since the bottom dropped out of the market three years ago, I've been uncomfortably aware of the possibility of being descended upon by a team of referees from Exchange World, with the news that Lontastans had bought a majority interest in the company for peanuts and had voted to liquidate."

"That wouldn't have been likely," said Mergly. "Why would they want this company, even for peanuts, the way things were? But now, because of the project, which they might find out about, we can't have a majority of the stock loosely held."

"How much did you buy for the trust?" Tosen asked.

"Forty-one percent."

"With my fourteen, that makes us safe." Tosen fiddled with the antique ballpoint pen he kept on his desk. "Been in the lab lately?" he asked.

"I just came from there."

"How are Rogers and his people doing?"

"They're coming along." Mergly paused, then added, "The Bauble will be complete next week, he says. This has been an expensive undertaking, Rof. The Council wouldn't have stood still for it if they had known what a gamble it is, or if other projects had been competing for R-and-D funds."

Tosen made a face. "O.K., you can consider me chastised. But despite all informed opinion to the contrary, I still believe the evidence favors Monte being an artificial, Lontastan-built structure, concerning which everyone but a few top Lontastans has been fed a load of misinformation."

"Maybe so," Mergly answered coolly. "We can hope so. If *they* haven't sold us misinformation, then you certainly have."

The Bauble had a pearl-like luster, and Tosen decided as soon as he walked in the lab and saw it that it was well though deceptively named. A big bauble in appearance, but no bauble at all in price.

Rogers and Mergly were both there, gazing expressionlessly at the two-meter globe of glittery gray.

"That's it, huh?" Tosen said to announce his presence. "When are you going to turn it on?"

Rogers gave him a blank look. "It's turned on. It was built with its energy sources activated. It stays turned on."

"Well?"

Rogers said, "It's not doing anything. No life in it."

"O.K. So we wait for an interested ego-field to come along and discover it," said Tosen.

"We've already waited three hours," Mergly complained. "What's more, we've paraded every pregnant woman on the company payroll through here . . . two hundred and seven of them."

"What for?"

"Oh, one of the ego-field traditions that seems solider than most," shrugged Mergly. "Disembodied ego-fields are supposed to hang around pregnant women, waiting for the moment one of them can inhabit her child."

Tosen nodded. He had never thought highly of that idea. Ego-fields like a swarm of starving beggars, all of them after a tidbit only one could have! It carried the concept of competition to an unpleasantly ugly extreme.

"You may as well have a seat and a drink and be comfortable, if you're going to join the watch," said Rogers.

Tosen did so. The three of them sat with little conversation for over an hour.

At last Mergly said, "We ought to take this in shifts."

Rogers agreed. "This could keep up for days."

"I started last," said Tosen, "so I'll take the first shift if you like. Until midnight, say?"

"O.K."

The others left and Tosen got himself a fresh drink.

How long, he wondered, would it be reasonable to wait? With knowledge of ego-field characteristics so uncertain, a definite answer to the question was impossible. But his hunch was that, if an ego-field were ever going to inhabit the Bauble, it would have done so before now. From all accounts, ego-fields were numerous. And they moved around constantly. One should have discovered the Bauble before now. Probably one had—and had either considered it an undesirable habitation, or had not even regarded it as a *possible* habitation.

And unencumbered by a body and brain, an ego-field could presumably act with the swiftness of thought. Perhaps a hundredth of a second was all the time required for an ego-field to recognize a body's desirability and move in.

In which case the Bauble should have been inhabited within less than a full second after its completion. But that had not happened, not even in the first minute—nor the first hour—nor the first six hours.

Tosen sighed. So far as orders of magnitude were concerned, he realized uncomfortably, six hours resembled a century more closely than it did a hundredth of a second. So, if the Bauble were ever going to be occupied, chances were that it would have been so by now.

Another uncomfortable thought struck him for the first time, seriously undermining all his reasoning on the nature of Monte.

The Lontastans had, over the centuries, been less noted for innovation than the Primgranese. Usually, the Lontastans were content to copy, or improve upon, basic advances first made in the Commonality.

Would the Lontastans have gone to the extreme expense of a Project Bauble without foreknowledge that it would work?

It would have been most uncharacteristic of them, for sure. And Mergly could never have got Council support for *this* Project, except by arguing that this was something the Lontastans had already shown was possible.

Tosen chuckled, because in the final analysis none of that mattered in the least. The econo-war was lost, thanks to an obviously alive Monte on the Lontastan team. So what resources and effort had been spent on Project Bauble was merely decreasing the wealth that would be available for Lontastan claimancy, when the Lontastans got around to demanding settlement of the war.

So, as far as he was concerned, the project had been a good final try, even if a rather frantic and poorly thought-out one . . . at the enemy's eventual expense.

Tosen leaned back in his seat and relaxed, gazing at the Bauble.

A very handsome piece of workmanship, he mused, whether it did anything but look pretty or not. Actually it could be more accurately described as something grown rather than something built, being produced by chemical processes that had their genesis back in Earth-Only times when crystals were grown for solid-state electronic components. While the Bauble could theoretically be subdivided into millions of individual macromolecules, it was in fact one super-macromolecule, since the linkages between its theoretical units were themselves molecular in nature.

It would have been one hell of a gadget—if it had worked.

Why did the ego-fields turn up their ectoplasmic noses at it? he wondered with sudden irritation.

Maybe he could find out.

He put down his drink, let himself go limp, and left his body. This was something any psych-released adult could do easily enough, but was a rather useless trick except when the body was dying, at which time the ego-field usually went exterior to escape the death trauma.

Now Tosen drifted a few feet behind and above his head, still controlling his body from a distance and looking at the Bauble with normal sight and at the same time perceiving it with vague field senses. He drifted forward very slowly and entered the Bauble.

It was . . . like and unlike a body. Or more exactly, like and unlike a mind. It was difficult to pin down the flaw of the place as an abode. A poor analogy would be the interior of an empty house, with no furnishings, no fixtures, no doors. Just walls that were, strangely, both stark and indistinct at once.

He realized that he was exterior rather than fully disembodied, and that this might alter his view considerably from that of a totally detached ego-field. But his impression was strong that the Bauble was so totally lacking in *hominess* that no ego-field could possibly find it livable.

He pulled out of it and returned to his body. The mental exercise had, unaccountably, left him slightly exhausted and very hungry.

He walked over to an autospenser, dialed himself a tray of supper, and returned to his chair to eat. When he finished, he lay back and napped for a couple of hours.

Mergly came in promptly at midnight. "Nothing yet?" he asked.

"No, and I'm afraid not ever," said Tosen. He quickly explained why the time they had already waited should have been more than adequate for the Bauble to take on life, and why the Lontastans would not have tried to develop an artificial telepath.

"As a final check," he wound up, "I exteriorized and entered the thing to get the feel of the place. I wouldn't care to live there."

Mergly nodded slowly. "What was your feeling inside the . . ." he began, then hesitated. "Never mind describing it. I'll take a look for myself."

He sat down and relaxed. Tosen waited quietly

for close to ten minutes before Mergly stirred and looked up.

"Well, what did you think of it?" Tosen asked.

"A vast empty place with hard echoes. That's about as close as I can describe it," Mergly replied thoughtfully. "Even with you along for company the emptiness felt overwhelming."

"I didn't go along," objected Tosen. "I stayed right here in my own comfortable noggin."

Mergly frowned. "Oh? Perhaps you didn't, at that. What I sensed, I believe, was that you had been there before me. Maybe some of you rubbed off inside."

Tosen laughed. "Could be. I felt half exhausted when I came out."

"So do I." Mergly yawned, and stared at the Bauble from beneath drooping eyelids.

"I'm going home," said Tosen, heading for the door. "Tell Rogers I'll contact him around midday to see if he thinks it worthwhile for me to stand another watch."

"O.K.," replied Mergly. "I'll suggest that he take a feel inside the Bauble, too. He might have some ideas on how to make it more homey."

Walking down the hallway Tosen replied, "O.K., no harm in asking him. But I feel the Bauble's flaws are too basic to be remedied easily or cheaply." He paused outside the lab to gaze upward into the clear, starry night. Then he activated his transport implants and soared up and westward toward his home. "At the least," he added, "we would have to start again from scratch and build a completely different kind of Bauble. What would the Council say to that?"

Mergly emoted such a violent shudder that Tosen chuckled.

"I'm glad you can feel amused," complained Mergly with a flash of anger. "Unfortunately, I can't share that don't-give-a-damn attitude you've taken on. It smacks of non-competitiveness to me."

Tosen flinched. "Sorry," he said. "I got us into this thing, and I'd have no business turning deserter now."

"I didn't say you were a deserter," Mergly denied.

"No, but you felt it . . . or thought it." Suddenly Tosen gasped and whirled his body, searching the upper atmosphere for sight of Mergly. "*Say, where the hell are you, anyway?*"

"Why . . . right here in the lab, in my body."

Tosen watched through Mergly's eyes as the Information man looked away from the Bauble to search the room for the man he had been talking to. "Where are *you?*" Mergly demanded, then added, "Oh . . . I . . . see."

The damned thing works! Tosen exulted.

But just for us? from Mergly, whose mind was tumbling confusedly.

Sure! The Bauble's not a living telepath like Monte. It's merely a gadget! It doesn't reach out. We have to reach in. Give it our individual punched cards, so to speak. And so far, only you and I have reached in! You felt I had been there before you, remember. That was because it had my pattern. It has yours, too. I'm going to flip on this antique toothmike of mine and call Rogers, while you warp for the capital to give the Council the news!

Very well, but . . . but this is difficult to take in, Rof. Not thirty minutes ago you had me convinced the Bauble couldn't possibly work, that the whole project was based solely on your wishful thinking and misinformation . . .

Tosen thought a big happy smile. *Dave, we'd all still be living in Earth caves if we hadn't wished for things we couldn't possibly have. And as for misinformation . . .*

Yes? Mergly prompted.

Well, when misinformation says the impossible can be done instead of the other way around, then it just might turn out to be the truest information you ever heard!

Little Game

❧❧❧

1

THE AWOL GUARDSMEN had taken over an E-type wildworld called Jopat, the Primgranese contingent holding the northern hemisphere and those from the Lontastan Federation the southern. The tropics between served as their battleground.

And a battle was in progress as Gweanvin Oster approached the planet. She could see nothing of it, even with her amplisight blinked on, from where she hesitated fifty thousand miles out. The barbs had evidently agreed to limit their combat zone to the ground and atmosphere—perhaps because space-fights were too deadly even for them.

What Gweanvin could not see, however, she could

hear quite distinctly over the comm implant in her left ear. Cryptic commands and responses were snapping like verbal firecrackers among the Primgranese forces, along with savage yells of glee and occasional grunts of dismay. She had no trouble recognizing the deep bark of Spart Dargow, general of the Primgranese barbs, as he bellowed his orders.

Using her psionic comm tuner, Gweanvin scanned the band and found the frequency being used by the Lontastan forces. All she could get was a meaningless garble, since her unscrambler could not handle the Lontastan code. She listened only a moment before tuning back to General Dargow.

" . . . *Red-seven, red-seven, horseback dawn, horse-back dawn! . . . Jato. Blue-forty, jato, damn it! . . . Red-ten, red-ten, washout, washout!*"

As a frontliner herself, Gweanvin had worked with Guardsmen enough to be familiar with their command language. But she could make only limited sense out of what she was hearing. Dargow was using a couple of terms she had never heard before, such as "horseback dawn." And she wasn't sure such familiar commands as "jato" meant the same thing here on Jopat as back home.

Here, after all, the language was being used in a situation that had never existed before—a pitched battle between massed forces of Guardsmen. In the econo-war, Guardsmen guarded. They defended their worlds, whether in the Primgranese Commonality or the Lontastan Federation, against entry by such enemy frontliners as spies, saboteurs and subvert-ers. Occasionally a squad would vector out a few light-years to the assistance of a returning and hotly pursued frontliner, and a brief running battle would ensue. But never anything so insane as this combat on a wildworld.

Gweanvin grimaced in disgust. What boneheads these genetic barbarians were! Very useful in keeping the econo-war honest, very competitive, very high-survival—but boneheads!

She went full inert and let her momentum carry her slowly downward, her velocity perhaps ten thousand miles per hour relative to the planet. Except for being hungry after five days in space, she had no reason to hurry. Could be that it might be best to let the battle end before she tried to land. She had now located the scene of conflict as the late-afternoon zone, and she guessed hostilities would end by the time night fell if not before.

A Lontastan voice, speaking uncoded, suddenly boomed at her: *"Hey, you at forty-seven thousand altitude! Identify yourself!"*

Gweanvin's zerburst pistol was in her right hand instantly and her detector implants out full. She had trouble spotting her challengers, with the mass of the planet behind them and they only a few thousand miles up. There appeared to be about twenty of them, hanging south of the battle area, probably as rear guards and observers.

She tongued her toothmike and replied: "I'm Gweanvin Oster of the Commonality. Don't let me interrupt your stupid game. I'll wait here till it's over."

"Like hell you will!" boomed the response. *"You got no business up there! You're south of the equator! Haul it north, doxie, or we'll blow you north!"*

"Just try it, foghead!" she snarled back, and went on

with a suggestion that the Lontastan go amuse himself
in a manner both vulgar and physically impossible.

The twenty vague specks vanished abruptly. Gweanvin held her position a precise two-fifths of a second,
then warped away on a minivector of some five thousand miles eastward. At that, she moved a trifle too
soon to sucker the entire squad. Only six zerburst
lances were fired, to terminate into flares of supersolar
energy around the spot she had vacated. Gweanvin
fired two quick shots of her own at the sourcepoints
of two lances and vectored away quickly without waiting to see the results.

"*Gweanvin Oster, what the hell are you doing?*"
General Dargow's voice was blasting at her. He sounded
angry and concerned. "*Vector north, girl!*"

"Stay out of this, General Bonehead," she snapped,
making another miniwarp when she found herself
without a clear target.

"*You're breaking our rules!*" he protested furiously.

Her new breakout point put her close enough to
one Lontastan for her to drill him cleanly through
the belly. Her lance flared late, however, a hundred
miles on the other side of him. Still, he would be
one sick barb for a couple of weeks. "So what?" she
snorted as she fired.

"*So we'll come help the Lonnies blast you, if you
keep fooling around!*" yelled Dargow. "*You'll still be
gas when the universe coalesces!*"

Her new minivector carried Gweanvin straight down,
as close as she could warp toward the atmosphere
without traumatizing herself. Here she had a few

seconds respite from detection. "Send men you don't want!" she retorted warningly. As soon as she had the Lontastans above her well located, she miniwarped into their midst. This time she stayed long enough to get off three shots before making another quick drop out of normspace. She had an advantage in that she could shoot at any target she detected, whereas the Lontastans needed an extra split-second to make sure an unwarping figure was not one of their comrades.

She grinned. Playing a lone hand had its good points.

Dargow's voice was still yelling in her ear, threatening to send Primgranese fighters out to help the Lonnies blast her. But she made no response. Dargow was smart enough to know that mixing a squad of Grannies with the Lonnies would only add to the confusion already working for her, so his threat could be considered idle. She concentrated on her deadly game.

A few seconds later she noted that Dargow's yells were no longer directed at her but at some Lontastan commander. *"Pull your men back!"* he was urging. *"Ignore her. She's just an interloper from back home, not working with me!"*

The general's new tack suddenly worked. The space around Gweanvin emptied as the Lonnie squad warped away.

She blinked and looked around. Far below, three bodies were tumbling planetward. Two other squadmen, evidently wounded and with damaged transport implants, were going down in controlled inert mode. That made a Lonnie casualty list of six, she figured, because she was sure she had flared one into vapor.

Below, the barb battle had ended, too, evidently broken off short because of the distraction she had created. She could hear a bedlam of pull-back commands over her comm as she vectored northward and began descending toward Primgranese territory.

"*Gweanvin Oster, what the hell are you up to?*" Dargow snarled.

"Coming in for a landing," she replied nonchalantly. "Give me a location."

"*You know what I mean!*" he stormed.

"Yes, I know. I also know I'm not playing your damn-fool game so I don't have to abide by its silly rules. I wasn't bothering the Lonnies, until they came up and started shooting. Are you going to give me a location?"

"No! I'm telling you to warp for home right now."

"Nuts to that. I've been in space five days and I'm starving. Welcome or not, I'm coming down to eat."

"Okay, damn it! Somebody will meet you at forty-one north, four forty-five realtime solar. But tomorrow you head for home, girl."

"That's tomorrow's problem," she replied.

2

As she hit the fringe of Jopat's atmosphere her shieldscreen stiffened automatically, protecting her body from air friction. At the same time the screen bulged out to act as braking wings. A few minutes later her breathing went exterior. After five days with nothing to do, her nose sniffed the fresh smell of Jopat's air with appreciation.

She holstered her gun as she approached the location the general had given her. There she detected only one barb waiting for her, hovering at five thousand feet. She swooped to a halt six feet in front of him and saw that it was Nathel Gromon.

He grinned at her. "Well, well, Skinny Hips." He chuckled. "Come all this way because you can't live without me. Right?"

"Meatheads aren't my type," she retorted.

He chuckled some more. "And you're not old Spart Dargow's type, chicken. He's mad enough to skin you."

"This conversation reminds me of how hungry I am, for some reason," she said.

"Okay. Follow me down."

The barb dropped groundward, leveled off sharply just above the treetops and headed westward. Gweanvin trailed him closely.

"One thing puzzles me about you, Nathel," she said.

"What's that?"

"Most of you idiots came to Jopat because the econo-war back home was fizzling, and out here you and the Lonnies could have a little war of your own. That made a primitive kind of sense under the circumstances. There was nothing for genetic barbarians to do at home, and nobody seemed to know how to get the econo-war heated up again. I even dropped out myself for a couple of years . . ."

"I remember."

"But you stuck out the doldrums at home, Nathel.

You didn't leave until three months ago. That was after our Bauble telepathic communicators had been developed to put the Commonality back on even terms with the Lontastans and their telepath, Monte. The econo-war was coming to life again. Guardsmen were needed—especially for planets where Baubles were being installed. There was the prospect of plenty of action for you. And that was precisely when you pulled out. Why?"

Nathel Gromon grimaced. "You said the dirty word. Bauble."

"What does the Bauble have to do with it?"

"It opened my eyes," he grunted. "It showed me how other people really think of us barbs."

"How do they think?"

"Oh . . . that we're stupid."

"Hell, did you need telepathy to find that out?" She snorted. "I've called you stupid a hundred times! Did you think I was kidding?"

Gromon frowned uncomfortably. "It's not the same thing. You and me mentacommed once, if you recall, after they got the Bauble on Prima Gran."

Gweanvin nodded. "How could I forget?"

"Well, the way you thought about me was okay. You think kind of hard and snotty about everybody, did you know that? But all them pencil-pushers . . . it's like I'm some kind of animal, the way they look at it."

"Aw-w-w," Gweanvin cooed mockingly. "Did the mean old pencil-pushers hurt Nathel's tender little feelings?"

"Go to hell," the big man grunted. "It's just that who needs it! The econo-war is a pencil-pusher's war. It fits them, not us. Hell, they outnumber us a million to one. It has to be their kind of fight. So I say, let them have it their way, and we'll stay on Jopat and have ours our way."

Gweanvin shrugged. "Prima Gran sent twenty doctrinists out here a few weeks ago. They were supposed to try to reason with you lunkheads. If they couldn't talk you out of such fallacious attitudes as that, far be it from me to even try." After a moment, she added, "All those doctrinists suddenly went out-comm. What happened to them?"

Gromon grinned. "Oh, we listened to them, till they started repeating themselves. That got too boring, so we field-stripped them and grounded them on a semi-tropic island. They're safe enough. The insects here don't like the taste of humans much, and we parleyed with the Lonnies to keep the fighting away from that island."

Gweanvin was not especially fond of doctrinists but she failed to share Gromon's amusement. Field-stripping a man was as ugly a crime as horse-thievery had been on an earlier frontier, and for the same reason. A man lived and moved by the life-support devices implanted in his body: power packets, shieldscreen generators, inertia nullifiers, propulsors, communicators and so on. To field-strip him—to cut out those devices that could be removed by simple operations—was the dirtiest of dirty tricks. In the econo-war not even captured frontliners were subjected to such treatment.

But Gweanvin saw no point to making an issue of the transgression. She could guess that the barbs had made it to put everybody on notice that on Jopat the game was played by barb rules, and outsiders had better not try to interfere.

"Getting back to the way pencil-pushers think of barbs," she said, "that's something the doctrinists, being pencil-pushers themselves, could hardly explain to you. They take that attitude toward all frontliners—toward me the same as toward you idiots. And it boils down to the fact that they just don't dig killing or being killed. They can't play, or even appreciate, a game played on that level."

"They're narrow," growled Gromon. "Killing is just bodies. If I get killed, all I got to do is find me a new one. And that ain't hard, because babies are being born every second."

"Right," Gweanvin agreed. "You know, all through history the most atheistic societies, the ones that didn't believe in the survival of the ego-field, were the most squeamish about killing."

"But that don't hold any more," objected the barb. "People don't have ignorance as an excuse now."

"No, but they have other reasons. Killing is destructive, wasteful—and the whole point of the econo-war is to have hard competition that is essentially constructive. It can't be all one way, true. But the vast majority of participants, the pencil-pushers, have to view conflict as a motivator for non-destructive activities."

Gromon grunted noncommittally.

"Also," Gweanvin went on, "killing and being killed are both traumatic. They were basic to the anatomy of unsanity. Pysch-releasing removed that problem quite a few centuries ago, of course, but the old association with unsanity gives killing an ugliness that's still remembered."

"Well, I can see all that," Gromon conceded, "but you ain't talking me into going back, girl. I like it here."

520 *Howard L. Myers*

"Hell," Gweanvin grunted, "if twenty glib doctrinists couldn't talk some sense through your thick skulls, I'm not going to try. Propagandizing's not my line."

Gromon turned his head toward her briefly to study her emo-pattern. "Old Dargow figures Prima Gran sent you out here to bring us home," he said. "Do you say different?"

"No. That's what I'm here for."

"Well, how can you do it, if you don't talk us into it?" he demanded. "You can't force us to go back."

"I'll be damned if I know, Nathel," she replied, flashing annoyed frustration. "I'm flying blind on this stupid mission, and that's the disgusting truth."

Gromon considered this information with surprise for several seconds before chuckling. "I guess we really got the high brass running in circles back at Prima Gran HQ," he said smugly.

"Maybe so," murmured Gweanvin.

She had puzzled over the question for hours during her flight to Jopat, and it still made no sense to her. This mission wasn't spying. It wasn't sabotage. And if it was subversion, it was not the kind she was accustomed to. So, being none of those three, the mission simply wasn't in her line of work.

And in the past, even when engaged in work that was her line, Gweanvin had always gone out with detailed and specific orders—with a plan to put into operation. But this time all she had been told by the Special Assignments Bureau was to go to Jopat and bring the Primgranese Guardsmen home.

Gromon had been watching her emo as she glummed over her problem, and was radiating glee. "This is going to hand everybody here a hell of a big laugh," he chortled. "I can't wait to see old Dargow's face when I tell him! But slow down. We're on top of my camp."

Gweanvin followed him as he eased down among the tall trees to come to ground in a widely dispersed and rustic-looking campsite. A well-endowed young woman with dark hair was watching them from beside a stone fireplace, on which a crude earthware pot of stew simmered. It sent out odors fit to drive Gweanvin mad.

"Gweanvin, meet Valla," Gromon muttered, a touch of embarrassment showing. Gweanvin knew Gromon's wife, a barb named Samis, who had refused to come to Jopat with her husband. Guardsmen seldom had difficulty getting women, however, barb or otherwise. Gweanvin was not surprised to find a young beauty presiding over Gromon's cookfire.

Valla's emo-pattern showed dislike and misgiving for a moment as she studied Gweanvin's slim, almost boyish figure. Then, evidently deciding that such a wispy though pretty girl was no real competition, she smiled. Half-regretfully, Gweanvin decided not to disabuse her on that score. On a wilderness world like Jopat it would be foolish to get on bad terms with a talented cook, while available men were more than plentiful.

"That stew smells wonderful, Valla," she cooed.

Before Gweanvin had more than started eating, numerous barbs began dropping by that part of the camp. Some were old friends of hers desiring to renew acquaintanceship; most were strangers eager for a close look at the doll-faced little dish of dynamite whose skirmish with a whole squad of Lonnies had tizzied the top brass of both sides. Gromon, meanwhile, drifted away, presumably to report to General Dargow.

Gweanvin enjoyed the evening—being the center of attention was always fun. At least ten of the younger AWOL Guardsmen, either unattached to women or lightly attached, courted her unsuccessfully. Not that she didn't regard sex as fun. It was just that she would not want the barbs to think of her as a camp-follower and, with her thus classified to their satisfaction, dismiss her from their curiosity. To accomplish anything at all toward the completion of her mission, she felt, she would need to keep the barbs attentive—and if possible, mystified.

The cookfire was finally permitted to die down and the last of the visitors departed. Gromon had returned, but Valla had already discreetly lured him away to safety, evidently suspecting from the male attention Gweanvin was getting that she had underestimated the Prima Gran girl as potential competition.

Gweanvin chuckled to herself. Women were bigger idiots than barbs sometimes. That chick Valla, trying to own Nathel Gromon, who was certain to drift back to his wife sooner or later. If he didn't get vaporized first, of course.

She yawned, went semi-inert, and kicked herself up into a secluded treetop. There she hooked a beltsnap around a limb as a tether, and relaxed. After a moment she activated her tightbeam comm, tongued her toothmike, and said softly:

"GO to HQ SA-Forty. Smitwak?"

"*I'm here, Gweanvin,*" came the response from distant Prima Gran. "*Report.*"

"I'm on Jopat, in contact with our barbs," she said. "Nothing new here since the last time you heard from the doctrinists. They're alive, by the way—field-stripped and isolated."

There was a pause on the other end. Gweanvin giggled as she imagined the angry thoughts that must be passing through the Prima Gran Bauble.

Smitwak spoke again. *"Get us the precise location of the doctrinists,"* he snapped. *"We've got enough loyal barbs to send out a heavily armed rescue party . . ."*

"Cool down, Smitty," she replied. "I can dicker the barbs into letting you rescue them without a fight. These knuckleheads wanted to show how ornery they could be if anybody tried to interfere with them. They've made their point, and I think that now they'll let the doctrinists go."

"Okay, work on that. Meanwhile, the rescue team will be on its way. Now, any progress with your mission?"

"What the hell do you think?" she snarled. "I don't even know how to begin. Don't you have further instructions?"

"No. Continue under your original orders, Gweanvin."

"Those damned orders don't tell me a thing!"

"Sorry. You're on the scene, Gweanvin. In a position to evaluate the situation more thoroughly than HQ can and devise a practical plan to pursue. Give yourself time to think it through . . . not too much time, however. The need for those experienced Guardsmen is getting urgent here."

"Take my time, but hurry, huh?" she grunted

disdainfully. "Thanks a lot. I'll set your words to music and sing myself to sleep with them. Out."

"Stay in touch, Gweanvin. Love and out."

A light rain had started falling. For a few minutes Gweanvin listened to the drops bounce off her invisible shieldscreen. Then she went to sleep.

3

The general wanted to see her the next morning.

He was waiting outside when Gromon brought her to Battle Headquarters, the only solid building Gweanvin was to see on Jopat. Constructed of meltstone, it had feet-thick walls and roof that were obviously flareproof.

Gromon and a few other staff officers stood around grinning as Spart Dargow glared disapproval at the slim shorts-and-haltered figure. Gweanvin glared back with cool disdain. Dargow was a seven-footer, several inches taller than the barb average, a middle-aged man of perhaps sixty-five whose hair and beard were grayshot.

"You look the same as when I last saw you, and that was a good seven years back," he growled. "When are you going to become a woman?"

She made a gesture of indifference. She was well aware of the striking contrast between herself and the normal woman of twenty-seven E-years. But she had never found the contrast disturbing. "Who knows?" she said. "Maybe never, like some boneheads I know whose brains never develop."

His reaction to the verbal jab was minimal. "I recall somebody describing you," he said, "as fifty-five pounds of brass and fifty-five pounds of viper venom. I see that hasn't changed, either."

"Right. I still weigh one hundred and ten," she replied.

Dargow's frown deepened, and his emo slowly shifted from disapproval to curiosity. Gweanvin knew what he was trying to do—understand her well enough to categorize her, and thus discover how to deal with her.

"I keep thinking," he finally muttered, "that you must be the victim of an incompetent psych-release, but that doesn't hold up. And I never heard of a physical deficiency the docs can't handle. Just what the hell is it with you, girl?"

Ask a polite question and get a polite answer, thought Gweanvin. "The physiologists tell me I'm a mutant, with a characteristic of late physical maturity."

"Oh . . . any more like you around?"

"I don't know of any yet."

"And I guess you won't ever," he grumbled. "That's a damn-fool mutation if I ever heard of one. Late maturity gives you too many chances to get killed before you breed. Especially if you go around frontlining like a wild morimet or something! Now, we genetic barbarians breed early—"

"And often," Gweanvin inserted.

"We're high-survival," he went on, "but unless you get your skinny rump home, and settle down behind a nice safe pencil till you're ready to have kids, your genetic line is going to be awful short."

Gweanvin shrugged. "Crap," she sniffed.

"Good sense," the general retorted angrily.

"Where's the good sense of trying to perpetuate a strain so low-survival that it needs that kind of protecting?" she countered. "If I don't have enough survival abilities to do the things I want to do, and still stay alive to have babies some day, to hell with my genetic line."

Dargow snorted. "You think you got those survival abilities?"

"I think I'll be around to spit in your vapor, general."

"Lots of luck!" he snapped. "Now, what's this about you trying to talk us into returning to the Commonality?"

"I'm not. The doctrinists used every conceivable argument to try to get some reason through your thick skulls, and they failed. So I'm not trying to talk anybody into anything."

"You are here to get us to go back, though."

"Right."

"And you don't know how you'll go about it?"

"Right again."

Dargow grunted an obscenity. "Maybe I ought to find that funny, but I don't like it a damned bit."

Gweanvin's eyes widened. This was a favorable development she had not anticipated. Plainly, Dargow could not counter her play if he did not know her game. And he could not force her to tell it, because she did not know it herself.

"I've changed my mind about making you leave Jopat this morning," he said after a pause. "The more convinced the pencil-pushers become that we're here to stay, despite any tricks they try to pull, the better for everybody. If I made you leave, they'd think you had us worried, unsure of ourselves. So stick around as long as you like—but try to stay out from underfoot."

"Thanks, general," she replied. "Since I'm at loose ends right now, as far as my mission is concerned, I may as well participate in this little game you and the Lonnie barbs are playing. I'm not much on teamwork, since I usually operate alone, but—"

"You want to fight the Lonnies?" gasped the general.

"Why not?" she demanded. "They're the enemies of Prima Gran, aren't they? They would kill me if they could. Besides, I don't relish spending my time gossiping with your camp followers. And if I'm in the fight, maybe I can cut the number of you boneheads who get killed before I figure out how to make you come home. How about it?"

"You're on! Gromon, Green-Ten has lost a couple of snipers lately. Take this recruit over to Green Camp and tell Dak Surants she's his new man."

Two days later Gweanvin was approaching her first battle station, on or nearly on Jopat's equator. The jungle was slightly less dense than a typical rain-forest because Jopat had fifteen percent less than typical E-world moisture. And as she flitted through the tree trunks and hanging vines on semi-inert, Gweanvin passed through several flare-burned clearings in various stages of regrowth, evidence that there had been plenty of shooting in the area although it was not a favorite battle zone.

A mile and a half short of her assigned spot, she dropped to the ground, went inert, and reported in.

"Rocket to Axe."

"Axe here, Rocket," responded Dak Surants' voice.

"Rocket in place," she reported. *"Oke and out."*

She had wondered if Surants would challenge her "in place" claim when she was obviously short of her assigned position. He had not, but probably he would raise hell about it later.

But Gweanvin had worked under cover entirely too much to start taking damn-fool risks in the manner of the careless and rather lazy barbs. She had no intention of doing a semi-inert flit all the way to her post. Functioning transport implants, with their high power-drain, were too easily detected. She meant to walk the rest of the way with power packs at minimal output.

And walk it she did, in less than thirty minutes, using no life-support other than a tight shieldscreen to ward off the brambles she shoved through and to provide necessary air-conditioning against the heat. On enemy detectors she would be little more noticeable than a large native animal stomping through the undergrowth.

When she reached her assigned spot she climbed into the highest, sturdiest tree she could locate—still moving under muscle-power alone—and found a concealed perch. Then she settled down to wait for action.

She drew her zerburst pistol and studied its settings thoughtfully. The gun was basically a laser projector, the characteristics of its lance and flare governed principally by the intensity of the beam. At lowest intensity it produced a lance which never flared—merely a bolt of monochromatic light. That bolt would punch through the hardest shieldscreen as if it were not there and drill deeply into whatever flesh, stone or metal it struck.

But above a certain intensity threshold, so high that the light-energy took on aspects of mass, relativistic effects came into play. The front end of the lance propagated at normal light-velocity for the medium through which it was traveling. Because its concentration was such as to make it behave like mass, however, it underwent spacetime contraction, this effect increasing in magnitude from the front end of the lance to the rear. The net result was that the rear portions of the lance propagated progressively faster than the speed of light. That caused the lance to telescope in upon itself until, at flarepoint, its length came so close to zero, and its raving energy so closely confined, as to constitute a time-space "singularity"—an unsustainable state. So it flared, releasing nearly all the energy of the entire lance at one point and in one tiny fraction of a nanosecond.

The higher the intensity of laser beam fired, the more quickly it would flare. Maximum practical flare range was about two million miles—a very weak flare—and minimum was a mile and a quarter. At that short range the gunner ran a real risk of getting a bad case of sunburn from his own flare.

All in all, the zerburst pistol was an excellent weapon for Guardsmen, operating in space but in the near vicinity of their planet. But for ground-fighting or aerial combat? "Lousy," Gweanvin muttered to herself.

She realized she could not argue with her weapon, even though she could think of three other types of handguns she had used in the past that would be preferable in her present situation. The point was that the zerburst gun was the weapon of the Guardsmen. It was their baby. And of course they would not consider using anything else in their private little war on Jopat.

She turned the beam down to low, non-flaring intensity, with maximum-duration lance. She could change it back quickly if she spotted Lonnies stupid enough to be bunched so that a flare could catch several. Otherwise, she would rely on the accuracy of her aim to drill—maybe slash—any singletons she spotted.

Jopat's sun climbed higher in the sky. And higher. It was overhead. It crept lower. And lower.

A helluva lousy way to play a game, fumed Gweanvin. It dawned on her that there might not be any action at all in her sector that day. Or the following day.

But she had agreed to play by the barbs' rules. That meant she did not desert her post, no matter how little action came her way.

It was midafternoon before she heard Dak Surants snap: *"Motor through Target, ho the fox!"*

That meant someone had spotted enemy elements approaching the line on which she was posted. Probably forward scouts on anti-sniper patrol, she guessed. Such deployment was a standard opening move, according to what she had been told.

She killed her shieldscreen and gasped when the sullen heat of the jungle, no longer held at bay, hit her like a blow. But detectable power usage was now down to the barely perceptible trickle required for sense amplification and emo-monitoring. Until she used her gun, an enemy would have to look at her to know she was there.

Minutes later she detected a Lonnie advancing on a line that would take him through the trees a thousand yards to her left.

The incautious speed of his advance indicated that he was not really expecting opposition here. Gweanvin guessed that, as she had hoped, Lonnie observers had pinpointed her at the spot a mile and a half north where she had made her last comm transmission and switched off her transport implants. The passing Lonnie seemed to be making for that spot.

She let him go by.

Less than a minute later three more Lonnies came into detection, well spread out, following the lead man. None would pass within feet of her, so as to actually be visible through the curtains of foliage. But all would pass within reasonable range for detection-aiming.

They arrived abreast of her. She blazed away with the zerburst gun, first to the left, where two of the barbs were passing, then to the right, her lances of light *stoom-stoom*ing through the air and vegetation in tight patterns that riddled the vague detection images of the enemy barbs.

Without pause, she flicked into semi-inert mode just long enough to streak down from her perch. Before touching ground she had returned her comm to the frequency Lonnie patrols were using. She caught the garbled but identical reports made by two of the downed men. From the third came only silence. Conclusion: two wounded, one dead.

She was running northward. Her perch would no longer be tenable, of course. For several seconds, vapor trails marking the passage of her zerburst lances would hang whitely in the air, pointing telltale fingers back to their source point for any aerial observer to see—and as soon as the nearest wounded Lonnie could move himself to a safe distance, that tree would be the target for a Lonnie flare.

And that lead Lonnie—the one supposed to have drawn her fire—was up ahead somewhere. She didn't like the idea of leaving him to her north while she was looking for action from the south. He just might try to sneak back on her . . .

He did. Almost, but not quite, as cautious as she, he was coming through the concealing ground growth toward her, his transport implants off. But his shield-screen was on, while Gweanvin was suffering unprotected the stings, scratches and heat of her jungle run.

She halted when she detected him, aimed her gun, and stood puffing while she waited for him to emerge into visual contact. When he did . . .

"Hi!" she chirped. He had an instant in which to view her grin before she lanced him through the brain.

Immediately she activated her shieldscreen, and with only seconds to spare before the expected flare erupted back at her vigil tree. The airblast bounced her around for a moment.

"Axe to Rocket, report," Surants' voice demanded.

She was up and flitting hurriedly toward the spot of the flare, taking advantage of the detection-jamming miasma of ionization from induced radioactivity that would hang over the spot for several seconds.

She tongued her toothmike. "Two Lonnies killed, two wounded. Out."

"*You're drawing the crowd. Out.*" replied
Surants.

Which meant that the ruckus she had stirred up was
going to make her the focus of the coming battle. That
was often the way the barb battles developed—each side
pouring forces into the scene of the hottest action.

The Lonnies would be eager to blast the Granny
sniper who had so quickly disposed of an entire anti-
sniper patrol.

She dived into the small crater now marking the
site of the tree in which she had perched, and went
full inert. The backwind had littered the ground
with smoldering embers so she had to keep up her
shieldscreen. Tumbling to the deepest, most sheltered
position the hole offered, she halted in a crouch,
peering up through the drifting smoke with zerburst
gun held ready. She had switched it to flare intensity,
range tentatively set at a mile and a half.

Ten seconds, fifteen seconds . . . Lances appeared,
three of them simultaneously, foreshortened because
they were aimed close to her position. Gweanvin
upped her gun's range to three miles and fired back
at the source of one lance before glare and flying
debris and hard gusts of superheated air made aiming impossible. Her crater was now the center of a
pattern of four craters—then of six, then of eight, as
two of the aerial gunners fired again and again.

Rocks and dust, tree trunks and splinters—chunks
of debris of all shapes and sizes—were raining down
on her. Impatiently she maintained her crouch, protected by the shieldscreen, and waited for the worst
of the deluge to end so she could jump over to one
of the newer and therefore safer holes.

But when the stuff stopped falling, she was completely buried in it . . . a good fifteen feet deep! Her hole was now a mound slammed together by the pattern of surrounding blasts, and she was under it. She cursed.

Not that she couldn't get out. That would be easy enough. But in so doing she would use so much power as to draw the fire of every Lonnie within range. She was effectively immobilized.

And outside the battle was getting hot. She could detect it fuzzily through the junk piled on top of her.

"Axe to Rocket!" came the concerned voice of Surants.

"Oh, shut up," she said crossly, then hit him with a string of utterly blue vulgarities, making clear her total disdain for this simple-minded and primitively pointless little war game.

"Glad you're in one piece, Rocket." he responded lamely.

"Go take a barbed-wire enema, you anachronism. Out!" She settled down to wait out the battle, mindful that the wait might end any instant if a stray flare caught her mound, but not fretting about the possibility.

4

It was three hours after sunset before all was quiet above. From comm talk she had listened in on, Gweanvin gathered the Grannies were claiming an overwhelming victory, which was not surprising. Thanks to the rules under which they fought, the Lonnies and Grannies were usually so evenly matched in combat that any unanticipated success or failure could set a trend that would hold throughout a battle. And Gweanvin's victory at the very outset, from which she had emerged vitriolically alive though discomfited, was more than enough to carry the day.

She was mildly pleased by this. As she had told General Dargow, a main reason she wanted to get into the war was to keep as many Primgranese Guardsmen as possible alive to return to duty in the Commonality. If that entailed killing Lonnies before they could kill her Grannies, so be it.

The annoying thing was that she still had not the slightest idea how to get those vac-skull Guardsmen to stop this stupidity and go home. Why bother keeping them alive just to waste themselves playing bang-bang-you're-dead?

She spent most of her hours of burial trying to think of a plan. She had been told to get a first-hand acquaintance with the Jopat situation, and formulate a scheme based on that direct knowledge. So she tried to formulate. The result was a big empty zero.

The damned barbs were where they wanted to be, doing what they wanted to do. And they knew what their duties in the Commonality were like—that their little game here was a war much more to their taste than the econo-war.

And though she called them stupid, she knew they were not weak-minded. They knew what they liked—that was for sure. And nobody was going to trick them into thinking they would like something else better when experience told them otherwise.

So . . . what should she do? What *could* she do?

Not a damned thing.

She sighed finally and returned her attention to her surroundings. All was still above. The battle was over and the barbs had retired.

Slowly she expanded her shieldscreen, employing it as an earthmover. The debris yielded stubbornly with creaks and scrapings as she poured power into the screen. The surface of the mound bulged up. Rocks and tree trunks rolled and toppled down its sides, and the bulge pushed up still higher. Finally an opening appeared at the top and Gweanvin, semi-inert, squirted herself through it, the hole collapsing back as she lifted above the dark treetops and streaked northward.

When she reached the Green-Ten camp she dropped quietly to the ground, hoping the barbs had left her some supper. More than food was waiting for her. Her arrival triggered a celebration, in the loud, tumultuous barb style, that lasted into the morning hours. She was hugged, kissed, fondled and fed until she nearly turned on her shieldscreen in self-defense.

General Dargow came shortly before midnight to bestow the Best in Battle award for the day on her. After that brief interruption, the party resumed. And Gweanvin had to admit it was fun.

But a similar shindig, following the next battle three night later, was too much of a repetition to be quite so enjoyable. The barbs of Green-Ten were even more delirious than before. They were carried away by the glory of their cute little snip of a sniper taking two Best in Battle awards in a row!

The battle itself had not developed quite the same as the first. The Lonnies had sent no anti-sniper patrols forward in the Green-Ten sector, and when fighting had begun to develop elsewhere Gweanvin and the others along the line had been allowed to advance in search of the enemy. She found them, to their regret.

The third time she saw action, the Lonnies hit the Green-Ten sector with a sudden massive assault; no preliminaries. Gweanvin had halfway anticipated that tactic, and with Surants' prior approval had never perched at all. She kept walking and crawling south throughout the long midday waiting period without benefit of life-support. When the Lonnies struck, she was far enough behind their front elements to bob up unexpectedly in their midst, where she had a lone-hand advantage similar to, though not as great as, that in her space encounter on the day of her arrival. She created confusion and havoc while vaporizing one Lonnie and lancing at least five more before she caught a lance through the right shoulder and had to stage a zig-zag-zogging retreat northward.

Another Best in Battle award, and another celebration.

She was transferred to command of a twelve-man assault squad in Purple-Eighteen. Training a whole week for that new assignment, she missed two battles.

Back in action with her shoulder totally healed, she demanded no less from her squadmen than she did from herself. They did not come through brilliantly in her opinion, and she let them know it. But they drew the crowd in four successive engagements, with resulting Granny victories.

Then General Dargow called a staff meeting and ordered Gweanvin to be present. The assembled officers sat in a natural amphitheater near Battle Headquarters, studying the half-chagrined emo-pattern of the general as he stood up to face them.

"I've had comm with General Brastig of the Lonnies," he announced. "He wants a parley, to consider rules revisions. I'm inclined to agree with him."

"What the hell for, chief?" someone in the crowd called out. "Because the game's got one-sided, that's what for!"

This brought silence. Gweanvin could read the concern of the barbs around her. Maybe the econo-war was not their game, but the basic philosophy of it—that competition is an end in itself and must never be allowed to decay by becoming uneven—was something they understood. It was great to win battles, but winning a war was as unthinkable as losing one.

"We got good rules!" a rumbling voice objected. "Them Lonnies oughta get theirselves a Gweanvin of their own, if they want the sides evened up."

Gweanvin blinked. Damn! Was this business of changing the rules all on account of her?

After a moment of thought, she realized it was. It had not occurred to her before that in a bloody fight with close to a million barbs engaged on each side, her own escapades, award-winning though they were, could make that much difference.

Dargow was answering the rumbler: "I guess they would like to. But the Federation hasn't sent a Gweanvin out to try to bring them home—if the Fed's got Gweanvin's equal, which I doubt. Now, what I want us to do is figure out some rules changes that will give the Lonnies a better break without hampering ourselves too much. That way we can go to the parley with—"

"Hold it, general!" yelled Gweanvin, leaping to her feet.

He stared questioningly at her. "Leave your silly rules alone," she told him. "I've said all along that this is a little game you yaps are playing, and I see now I wasn't kidding! It's too damned little for me to fit in. You can count me out—because I'm going home!"

Bellows of protest roared from the officers. Gweanvin stood unswayed, her chin jutting with determination. And despite the yells, she could read a growing agreement in the crowd, and also in Dargow, that her departure would be the best answer—better than tampering with the rules. Soon the protests died away.

"What about your mission?" asked the general.

She spat an obscenity. "I'll tell the desk-riders back home where to shove their mission."

"Damn it, Gweanvin," Nathel Gromon spoke up. "I hate to see you get pushed out of the game."

"Don't bawl about it," she told him. "This is a boring war you're having, and I've been playing just to kill time while I tried to formulate a plan. I've had a bellyful, thank you." She turned slowly to glance over the sobered faces. "So long, meatheads." She grinned at them. "Good shooting!"

She went semi-inert and streaked up through the trees. For a moment she thought of going by her squad's camp to tell her men goodbye in person, but she decided to hell with it. She soared on up through the atmosphere and into the vacuum of space, her breathing going on internal mode.

Once in clear vacuum, she set a vector for Prima Gran and went into warp. Only then did she contact headquarters.

"GO to HQ SA-Forty."

"Yes, Gweanvin. Smitwak here."

"Chalk up one flop to the cute little broad," she gritted. "It was a stinking mission to start with, and I'd like to get on mentacomm just once with the wise guys who dreamed it up!"

"You can't, Gweanvin. They're off the Bauble network. Security, you know."

Gweanvin grunted. Smitwak often took a remark literally when caught unawares. "Never mind," she sighed. "Just tell them I'm coming in, mission unaccomplished."

"Okay. Win some, lose some. That's life, Gweanvin."

"Thanks for the platitudes," she snarled. "I'll quote you in my memoirs. Out."

"Don't kick yourself all the way home," Smitwak said. *"Frankly, you kept working on this one longer than I expected you to. You have great perseverance. Out."*

Smitwak's solicitude was unnecessary. Gweanvin had no intention of blaming herself for the failure of the mission. When the directors of the Special Assignments Bureau misfigured as badly as they had on this one, the fault did not lie with the operative in the field. The directors had flubbed, and she looked forward to telling them so.

But now, with five days of warpflight ahead of her, she relaxed. Soon she was in the space traveler's semi-doze—a hibernative state that could eat up the light-years with minimal awareness of time's passage. Every ten hours she would rouse long enough to swallow a food-concentrate pill and check on the progress of her journey. Then she would slide back into dormancy.

"HQ SA-Forty to GO."

The call snapped her alert when she was three days out from Jopat.

"Okay, Smitty, I'm awake. What is it?"

"Bard Lustempo will tell you. Here he is."

Lustempo was one of the Bureau's directors. Gweanvin's lip curled. If that guy tried to give her a song and dance—or send her back to Jopat . . .

"Miss Oster," came Lustempo's voice. *"I wanted the pleasure of giving you the good news personally. Your mission was a success. The Guardsmen are returning. Dargow reported their departure from Jopat twelve minutes ago. Congratulations are in order. Miss Oster."*

"But . . . but . . ." Gweanvin sputtered. "The mission flopped!"

"By no means," the director assured her jovially. *"It went essentially as we expected."*

"But I never even figured out a plan," she protested. "If those lumpybrains are coming home, it's because they finally got as bored with their little game as I got in three weeks—not because of any plot of mine!"

"Precisely, Miss Oster. And why do you suppose they got bored?"

"You asked that question for the pleasure of answering it yourself," she told him evenly, "so go ahead."

Lustempo chuckled. *"I will. Our Guardsmen fought*

*one battle following your departure and discovered the
excitement you brought to their game was gone. Also,
there was some business about changing the rules to
accommodate your presence. That helped bring home
the point to them—a point they could not be TOLD
convincingly, but had to be shown. I refer, of course,
to the limited scope and interest of their game . . . in
short, to its littleness."*

"It was too little for me," she said.

"Correct. And despite the shortcomings of the
econo-war from the viewpoint of the genetic barbarians, Miss Oster, you convinced them by your actions
rather than by words that any competition in which
you participated had to hold more excitement than a
competition that excluded you. In short, Miss Oster,
they want to be in your war."

"Oh . . . then I wasn't expected to come up with
a scheme at all," she replied thoughtfully. "That was
just your way of getting me to hang around Jopat
and—and play their game for a while."

"Yes. Some situations, Miss Oster, are not really
soluble by plot alone. This is a lesson that should
be well learned by those who seek to direct the
activities of others. No scheme we—or you—might
have formulated could have overcome the stubborn
determination of the Guardsmen and brought them
home willingly. That situation had to be resolved by
allowing the persons involved to pursue their natural
inclinations. Our formulation was thus one of selection
of a person or persons to inject into the situation to
bring about the desired resolution. Thus we saw to it
you became involved in the Guardsmen's game—and
allowed events to take their course."

"Nice of you."

"*While you are not an overly modest person, Miss Oster,*" the director continued, "*I wonder if you realize the powerfully catalytic effect you tend to have in all matters in which you . . .*"

Gweanvin yawned. That was the way of desk-riders like Lustempo—jabber-jabber-jabber! Well, maybe they needed to talk a lot as a substitute for action. Old Lustempo's praise of her, which was still droning on in her ear, was really patting himself and his Bureau colleagues on the back for being so clever in sending her to Jopat.

Well . . . It had been pretty bright of them, at that.

She yawned again, keyed herself to rouse and say "thank you" when Lustempo finally unwound, and dozed off.

The Frontliners

1

"RAYEAL PROMTON, I presume."

The voice was an assured feminine purr behind Gweanvin Oster. She twisted her head to look up at the smiling woman, then rose from her chair at the work console.

"Yes, I'm Rayeal Promton," Gweanvin said, "and you must be Marvis Jans, girl security agent."

The woman nodded. "How did you identity me so quickly?" she asked.

"Because I was expecting you. What's being done here on Narva, and more specifically here in Gordeen

Consolidated Systems Lab, calls for the presence of the Federation's sharpest security agent. That's you. And you wouldn't come here and not take a look at your genetic sister. Of course, now that I've had a close look at you, I see that your nose is like mine . . . based on permanent bone instead of cartilage."

"And just what is being done in this building, Rayeal?" Marvis Jans asked softly.

Gweanvin laughed. "Is this a friendly visit or a security interview? Okay, so I've guessed a lot more about this project than my job requires me to know. Does that surprise you?"

"No." Marvis smiled. "A mind like yours is wasted on circuit growth technology, Rayeal. You should be a frontliner like myself. It's far more challenging work."

"I don't know," murmured Gweanvin. "I've thought about it, but sabotage, spying, counter-spying and other such derring-do strikes me as awfully masculine."

"Humpf! I like that!"

Gweanvin giggled. "No aspersions on your femininity intended, Miss Jans. Maybe I'd be more willing to swash about with a zerburst pistol on my hip if my hips were as curvy as yours." She paused, giving the older woman's figure an admiring once-over. "Gosh, how gorgeous you are! I hope I'm that well-stacked when I grow up."

"Thank you, dear." Marvis let her pleasure show. "You are twenty-seven standard years old, aren't you?"

"Yes. And you're about thirty-four."

"Right. If you develop at the same rate I did you'll start budding very soon, Rayeal."

"I've already started," Gweanvin grinned, "and not a minute too soon to suit me. I'm tired of looking like a boy."

"I wish you *were* a boy," Marvis remarked wryly.

"I'll bet you do," snickered Gweanvin. Then she asked more seriously, "Any clue of where one might be?"

"A male of our species? No, not a clue."

Gweanvin considered the undertones of that brusque reply. "That bugs you, doesn't it?" she asked.

"When your urges become as strong as mine . . ." She shrugged and turned away. "Isn't there any coffee in this joint?"

"Sure. Over here."

Gweanvin led the way to the spenser and drew steaming mugs for Marvis and herself. She motioned her visitor into a chair and seated herself nearby.

"Why not talk about it?" she asked. "Your search for a male is no secret from me."

"Aha! Spying on a Federation security agent, hah?"

"Oh, don't be such a warrior!" snorted Gweanvin. "Of course I've been spying on you, and you've probably known it all the time. Or certain friends of mine have, but don't fret. They're security people, too, and haven't told me any deep Federation secrets. They've merely kept me informed on your male-hunt."

Marvis sipped her coffee. "I was kidding you, dear. Of course I know what you've been up to. I haven't tried to keep my hunt all that secret anyway—because there may be a male somewhere as eager to find me as I am to find him. I wanted a bit of publicity."

"But nobody turned up?"

"Oh, a lot of guys turned up, but not one of us. Some looked like good bets but cases of delayed maturity are not unheard of among ordinary homo sapiens; that's all any of them turned out to be." She studied Gweanvin's face questioningly. "Just how much did your friends tell you about my search?"

"Well, they told how you finagled a permit to go into the Federation's central personnel files and run a computer check for individuals with genetic charts that match your own. My name was the only one thrown out—and you already knew about me, didn't you?"

Marvis nodded. "Go on."

"All right. Next you enlisted Monte's help. It assisted by working out a scheme to get one of our agents into the Commonality's personnel files to see what they had to offer."

"Monte's a *he*, not an *it*," put in Marvis. "The feel is definitely that of a masculine mind, as anyone who has ever been on Orrbaune knows."

"Which I haven't," said Gweanvin, "but we'll soon know the feel of Monte's mind here on Narva, won't we? If the project's a success, that is. Right?"

Marvis gave her a cool smile. "If you expect a security agent to join you in loose talk about a secret project, dearie, think again. Get back to the subject."

"Well, that's about all I know, except that you had no luck with the Commonality files. All that search produced was another female . . . somebody about my age named Gweanvin Oster."

Marvis nodded slowly. When she said nothing, Gweanvin added, "I'd like to know more about that Oster wench."

Marvis smirked. "Don't ask me, Rayeal, dear. Check

with those spies of yours. If they can't tell you anything, tough."

"Not that tough," Gweanvin replied equably. "If
you find out Miss Oster has located a male—and
that's the only thing about her I'm really interested
in—I'll know soon enough. When you vanish into the
Commonality."

Marvis gave a little chuckle. "You think I'd be so
unpatriotic as to defect for a man?"

"Yep. And so would I."

"Well . . . you could be right about that," murmured
Marvis. "Actually, Rayeal, I don't mind telling you
about Gweanvin Oster, but there's precious little to
tell. She's a Commonality frontliner. We're unable to
obtain data about her appearance, present activities,
or whereabouts."

"Then . . . she may have found a male!" breathed
Gweanvin, all wide-eyed ingenuousness.

"Unlikely. Our information is fairly solid on one
point—that she's on assignment, not off in the
bushes."

"Oh."

For a while Marvis gazed at Gweanvin without
speaking. "You needn't peer at me like that," Gweanvin
protested. "I'm not Gweanvin Oster, and I've got a
long pedigree to prove it."

"I almost wish you were," grumbled Marvis.

"Why? Would you and the whole security bureau-
cracy enjoy looking like champion idiots?"

"I'm referring to the odds," Marvis said.

"Which odds?"

"Those against three mutant females being born

without a single matching male." She frowned. "Don't tell me that hasn't occurred to you, too."

Actually, it had not, because Gweanvin knew there were only two females, not three. She realized she had made a slip with that "Which odds?" question . . . a rather subtle slip, but one that could nevertheless blow her cover sky-high . . . and just when her assignment was reaching the pay-off point. Had she shown dismay? No. Like Marvis, she had the ability to maintain a perfect poker-face at will.

"Surely you understand the laws of probability better than that!" she exclaimed. "Or does security work dull the reasoning powers?"

Marvis replied flatly: "I know the odds are eight to one against flipping a coin for three heads in a row. If there were no factors working against the conception of a male . . . if the odds were fifty-fifty in any given birth, then at least one of us three should be male."

Gweanvin laughed. "Have you actually done any coin-flipping recently?" she asked.

"Of course not! Why should I?"

"Try it sometime. It should make you happier about those 'odds'. I tried it myself not long ago, and flipped a sequence of five tails, one head, another tail, three heads, two tails, two heads, a tail, and so on. What were the odds against my starting out with a sequence of five tails like that?"

"Well . . . thirty-two to one. But a run like that is unusual."

"Sure, but it happens! I made over a hundred tosses without getting another string of five. But I had three fours, and five runs of three.

"The point is, Marvis, that probability works out

to what we call 'the law of averages' only when we're dealing with a statistically significant number of events . . . the more the better. A gambler can actually have a lucky streak, you know. But he doesn't leave the game a winner unless he gets out at the right time. If he keeps playing long enough, the law of averages catches up with him. Don't depend on what you've read about probability, Marvis," she concluded with a grin. "Get a coin and start flipping it. The results should prove therapeutic."

Marvis thought about it for a moment. "You're right about mathematical probability, Rayeal," she said at last, "but the circumstances leave the possibility open that something is repressing conceptions of males of our species."

Gweanvin shrugged. "A possibility, sure. In which event, we're not the next evolutionary step for man, just three more old maids in the making. And if so, so what? I see no signs that man's about to cave in for lack of a new breed, anyway. But I don't really think that, Marvis. I think we're being balked out of motherhood, temporarily, by a streak of bad luck."

"I hope you're right. I . . ." Marvis paused in the listening attitude that told Gweanvin someone was speaking to her via her communications-implant. "Right away, Thydan," she responded to the call, then looked up at Gweanvin. "I must run along, dear. Some people I'm supposed to join for lunch."

"Oh. I'm sorry. We've got so much to talk about," said Gweanvin, rising.

"I'll have some time later," Marvis assured her, walking toward the door. "I'll get in touch."

Gweanvin followed her. "One thing I simply must

ask you now. You've been mature, sexually, for some years, Marvis. Are you *sure* we can't procreate with an ordinary homo sap male?"

Marvis paused on the balcony jutting into the building's west wing scramble area and turned. "I'm positive, dear. And that's not theoretical." She gave a slight smile. "Maybe I did not bother with coin-flipping, but *that* I checked out with experiment. Many experiments, in fact. We're a new and different species, Rayeal. We can't cross-breed with the old."

"I was afraid of that," nodded Gweanvin, soberly.

"Sorry. See you later, dear."

Marvis stepped off the platform and plummeted downward on semi-inert transport mode. Probably on her way to the tightly restricted basement test-chambers, Gweanvin guessed. She knew the project was due to reach its climax very soon, probably that very afternoon. The arrival of Marvis Jans made that almost certain . . .

Across the scramble area from her balcony was the balcony and open door to Don Plackmon's office, with his desk so situated that he could sit looking out. When she glanced that way she found Don watching her. She waved, and he waved back. Don was supposed to be a circuitry growth technician . . . and he wasn't too bad at it . . . but she suspected he also had a security function. On a project like this one of every two people were probably involved in counterespionage.

And how many were spy-saboteurs?

None but her, she guessed. An operation such as this was too thoroughly guarded. First, it took the ability to lie to an emo-monitor without detection, which was something not one human in a thousand could do. Also it took a personal history that could be checked out by some of the most suspicious eyes in the Federation without revealing a flaw. That kind of cover took time, effort and money to build. Actually, it took a long-established family, one which had devoted itself for generations to the job of resembling loyal citizens of the Lontastan Federation, for Gweanvin Oster to be "born into"—with a minimal and painstaking doctoring of public records—as Rayeal Promton.

And getting inside this kind of project required one more thing: a reason for being there. To work on something that would of necessity involve circuitry growth one became an expert circuit-grower. The more expert the better. And with her mental equipment, Gweanvin had not had too much trouble becoming tops in the field, so far as the Federation was concerned. The Primgranese Commonality had the real leadership there, and Gweanvin had the benefit of being coached for her assignment by some of those leaders.

She knew more of circuitry growth than she was using on this project—and she was using more than her Lontastan colleagues knew.

Thus, she might actually wind up a net contributor to the Lontastan project if she were caught, or her assignment goofed in any way.

She returned to her work console. It lighted as she sat down, revealing the bitbox diagram she had been studying when Marvis Jans interrupted her. In a sense, this was make-work she was doing—the examination of alternate possibilities for the Lontastan version of a Bauble. Just in case the Bauble her section had completed, and that was now resting well-guarded in one of the basement test chambers, failed to work.

She knew it would work . . . and do other things the Lontastans would find far less desirable. This territory had been explored by Commonality scientists over a decade earlier, after the success of the first Bauble telepathic-communication systems led to a great deal of experimentation into the potentials of various Bauble-type constructs.

Was anything happening in the test chamber yet?

While continuing to gaze studiously at the console screen, she exteriorized from her body and—as an ego-field—dropped to the basement room. There she touched the Bauble gently, not really entering it, but establishing enough contact with it to use some of the special features its circuitry contained, features the Lontastans knew nothing about.

She found the Bauble was unchanged. It was in contact only with the pedestal on which it sat, like a beachball-size pearl. Nor was any field, ego or electronic, impinging on it. Judging from the silence of the room, no human was in the test chamber where it waited.

So Marvis Jans and the others who were to be on hand for the test probably actually were at lunch. Nothing would happen for at least an hour. And speaking of lunch . . . she had better start the afternoon with a full stomach herself. Her cover might be blown if her plans slipped just a little, in which event days might pass before her next solid meal.

2

She walked out on her balcony, semi-inerted and soared across the scrambleway to Don Plackmon's office. He watched her approach, and stood up and stepped around his desk when she came in. He gave her a squeeze and a kiss to which she responded with casual pleasure. Don was nice—and handsome as well.

She pushed herself back from him after a moment and said, "I know I'm early for your invitation to lunch, Don, but I'm starving. Let's go now."

"Sure, Rayeal," he agreed, nuzzling her. "You always give me an appetite."

"For what?"

He chuckled. "I'll settle for food right now. Look. Old Marchell wants to join us, and much as I'd prefer to be alone with you, it's not good form to say no to the boss. I'd better give him a call."

"Okay," she nodded.

Plackmon tongued his toothmike and commed briefly with Boll Marchell while Gweanvin considered the point that Marchell was not with the lunching group of bigwigs, which probably meant he would not be present at the upcoming test. Security wraps must be on very tight indeed to exclude one (and perhaps both) of the two major production chiefs, she mused.

Plackmon reported, "Boll says for us to go on and he'll join us in a few minutes."

"Good. Let's go."

They left the office and soared up through the scramble area to the dining garden level, which they entered and found a table for three where Marchell would see them when he arrived. "I'm going to try something on the ancient Egyptian menu today," said Plackmon.

"Go ahead. I'm in a steak and potatoes mood myself."

He laughed. "You weren't kidding about being starved."

They punched their orders, and Plackmon said, "Was that dish who came to see you who I think it was?"

"How you ever get any work done with all your girl-watching, I'll never know," Gweanvin replied tartly. "Yep, that was my fellow mutant, Marvis Jans."

"You're much prettier than she is," he murmured, leaning close. "She doesn't have your full lips."

"Yeah, but she's got a lot of full other places I don't—as you might just possibly have noticed."

Plackmon laughed. "Give yourself time, Rayeal. You're beginning to bud very nicely." Their lunches arrived and they busied themselves with eating for a moment before he said, "I find it very hard to think of you as a mutant, you know. You don't look all that unusual. Neither does she. It's hard to imagine your genes being so different from mine."

"Genetic tension," she replied around a mouthful of extremely rare steak.

"Tension?"

She nodded. "That's part of evolutionary theory which post-dates Darwin by several centuries, after geneticists began to find out how such things really work. You're the same species as *Homo Neanderthalensis,* who was chipping flint on Earth thirty thousand years ago. He was homo sapiens the same as you, but if you saw him you probably wouldn't be sure he was even human—and he would be just as dubious about you. But still you could mate and produce offspring. And knowing you, you probably would."

"Only in a pinch, my dear," he chuckled.

"The difference between you and Neanderthal Man can be summed up as genetic tension," she continued her explanation. "The species changes, adapts to new environmental demands and to somatic responses to our conscious ideas of what man should be. Changes in the genetic structure go with these adaptations, but they aren't the kind of basic changes that mark a difference of species . . . only the difference between individuals or races *within* a species.

"But they do place something of a strain on the original pattern. This strain, genetic tension, gradually builds toward a point where no further departure from the original is possible without breaking the species pattern itself. Humanity reached that stage in late Earth-Only times, it seems. People have been pretty much the same ever since.

"But in the meanwhile, we've changed our environment drastically. We have our life-support implants that enable us to live on almost any half-way habitable planet—or go streaking through interstellar space stark naked, for that matter. We've found the psych-release techniques with which to clean up ourselves, as ego-fields, and eliminate insanity. We've developed the econo-war as our major social institution, simply to make existence more of a competitive challenge than it would be otherwise. All of which adds up to the fact that homo sapiens needs to change into something as different from present man as present man is from the Cro-Magnon. But he can't, because his genetic tension is already as tight as it can get.

"So," she finished, "here we are, Marvis Jans and myself—and Gweanvin Oster in the Commonality. We have some structural differences that set us apart from homo sapiens, such as nasal bridges of solid bone. Also we mature more slowly and probably live longer. But the really important difference is that genetically we're a new species, with zero genetic tension. Our offspring can adapt like mad for a long time to come. *They're* the ones who'll really be different."

Plackmon nodded slowly, and started to speak but at that moment Boll Marchell joined them. "Hope I'm interrupting something intimate," he remarked, favoring Gweanvin with his best dirty-old-man leer.

"Rayeal was just explaining why my love for her is tragic," Plackmon replied. "Sit down, Boll."

Marchell sat, punched his selection on the menu. "Gene-crossed lovers, hah?"

Gweanvin said, "I think Don's real throb is for a big-busted visitor I had this morning. His eyes bulged out into the scrambleway when he saw her."

"Marvis Jans?" asked Marchell.

"Yes. Have you met her?"

"Just briefly."

"What do you think of her?"

"Well, if you and she are does I'd hate to tangle with the buck!" Marchell chuckled. "She's quite a doll, but hardnosed in more ways than one."

"One step farther from the primordial flat-faced apeman," said Gweanvin. "Do you really find her formidable?"

"Damned right I do. And you, too. That's why I'd hate to tangle with a male of your species."

Gweanvin thought about it, puzzled momentarily. "Oh, you mean because men are more competitive, more combative than women," she hazarded.

He nodded. "Yours would make a terrific econo-warrior—if he bothered with the econo-war at all."

Gweanvin considered the point with interest. She hadn't thought of the missing male from that standpoint before. What Marchell had said about the male role was certainly true for humanity and numerous other species.

"What else is the male's job?" she asked.

"Finding and courting a mate, of course," said Marchell.

"Well, ours is certainly goofing on that," she replied.

"Or biding his time perhaps. I get the impression Marvis Jans is trying to do both his job and her own as well. The typical female role is merely to make known her presence and readiness, by whatever means of communication is appropriate for the species. Miss Jans has done that. Now she's searching, and that's usually the male's prerogative."

Gweanvin chuckled. "Then it's enough for Marvis or me to announce, 'Here I am. Come get me.' And then wait for Mr. Super-Econo-Warrior to show up."

"Probably. And just keep yourselves amused in the meantime, you with the project and such as poor Don here, Marvis with her frontlining and every homo sap who lays eyes on her."

"Speaking of which, I have a hunch big things are about to happen on the project, now that Marvis has come to make sure our labs aren't spy-infested. Pay-off time may be here, gents."

Plackmon grinned. "You still think our project is Monte-related?"

"What else?" she shrugged. "We are on Narva, a

nothing-planet except for being Orrbaune's nearest habitable neighbor—a mere six light-years away from where Monte is, of necessity, permanently located. And our section has been building a . . ."

"If you're going to give us one of your speculative commentaries on the nature of the project," Plackmon broke in, mashing a button on the table's control box, "let's keep it between the three of us." A baffle-screen snapped on surrounding the table, effectively curtaining the occupants and their words from others in the dining garden.

Marchell laughed. "We don't need security agents with Don around," he said.

"Yeah, I wonder sometimes if his interest in me is as ulterior as he pretends that it is," said Gweanvin.

"I'm merely a conscientious little econo-warrior," Plackmon contended stoutly. "As you were about to say . . ."

"Well, our section has been building what we hope is a reasonable facsimile of the Primgranese Commonality's telepathic transceiver, the Bauble. We don't know—or I don't—what the other section's been doing. But my guess is that they're working on a communications link to tie Monte on Orrbaune in with the Bauble here on Narva.

"Now, essentially, a Bauble is just a dead device," Gweanvin continued, with the eagerness of a bright child showing off its talent, "whereas Monte is a living being, not only capable of receiving and sending telepathic messages, but of originating thoughts of his own. This makes him far superior, and more useful, than a Bauble could ever be. But one shortcoming of both Monte and a Bauble is limited range. One can cover a single planetary system, and that's all.

"What we really need to get ahead of the Primgranese is a Federation-wide telepathic comm system, something that can spread throughout our portion of the galaxy. Maybe it would be possible to link Baubles alone into that kind of network, but the Primgranese must be trying that, with no success that I know of.

"Anyway, we have Monte, and would want him in our network. And if we have some linkage system to tie him in with a Bauble at interstellar distance, the logical place to locate the first test Bauble would be right here on Narva. Otherwise, this under-populated ball of dirt would be about the *last* place in the Federation to rate a Bauble."

She paused, looking at Boll Marchell, then asked, "Well, what do you think?"

Marchell grinned. "I think it would take one hell of a comm system to link Monte with the Bauble when they are six light-years apart."

"Yes," she nodded, "that's what fascinates me. All our section has done is try to duplicate Primgranese work. But Hobard Dawnor's section . . . gosh, I'd give my eye teeth to know what they've got!"

"You never had any eye teeth," said Plackmon.

"Figure of speech," she replied absently. "Of course the actual spanning-signal could be an exceedingly broad-band version of standard subwarp communications. What intrigues me is the nature of the interface between Monte and the transmitter on Orrbaune, and between the receiver and the Bauble here on Narva. In other words, how is telepathy translated into transmittable signals, and how are those signals then converted back into telepathy? That's the real breakthrough involved in this project."

"And you can't figure it out?" asked Marchell.

"No. In fact, I bet Monte himself had to figure it out. Who else would know enough about telepathy?" She studied him closely. "You know if I'm right or not, Boll," she accused, although she knew he did not, "but you won't tell me."

He chuckled. "That's econo-war for you, Rayeal. Never let your right hand know what your left is doing."

"Suppose you are right, Rayeal," said Plackmon, wearing a serious frown, "don't you think such a project has some disturbing implications?"

"I don't see why it should," she lied. "I would think it might bother my new friend Marvis Jans, though. If Monte's telepathic ability is extended over the whole Federation, that'll put all our internal security agents out of work, her included."

"That's what I'm getting at," said Plackmon. "Every Federation citizen's mind will be subject to scrutiny. As matters now stand, those of us who prefer to keep some mental privacy have the option of staying away from Orrbaune. If your speculating is accurate, we're going to lose that option."

"That doesn't sound much like the conscientious little econo-warrior," Gweanvin kidded. "Actually, though, I'm a little hesitant about giving up mental privacy, too. But if everybody else does . . . and the people on Orrbaune don't seem bothered by it. They say Monte is a perfect gentleman and very discreet. He doesn't spread around the thoughts that need to remain private. And since he's not human, it doesn't matter much if he knows a person's thoughts. He doesn't take advantage. And if you're worried about some kind of thought control, he steers totally clear of that."

"Now, but will he always?" Plackmon argued.

Gweanvin shrugged. "What's 'always'?"

Marchell put in, "The Primgranese gave up emotional privacy long ago. They use emo-monitor implants, and it doesn't seem to bother them. It merely improves communication."

"We would have had emo-monitor implants of our own by now," said Gweanvin, "except that if this project is a success we won't need them—so they're dragging their feet on getting them into production."

"You sound so sure of everything you say," laughed Plackmon. "Is that because you're a woman, or is it a characteristic of the new breed?"

"It's because we're having an argument," she replied. "If I'm right about the purpose of the project I don't want my triumph weakened by a lot of 'perhapses' and 'maybes'. And if I'm wrong you guys won't be polite enough to remember any 'maybes' anyway.

3

The lunchtime conversation was a mild disappointment to Gweanvin. She had hoped to learn something from Marchell about plans for the test, but obviously he knew no more and had guessed far less than she had.

After the normal amount of dawdling about after lunch, she returned to her work console and pretended to be absorbed by her task while she exteriorized once more and returned to the test chambers and the Bauble.

She found it still untouched but now there were sounds in the test chamber. Equipment was being brought in, she judged.

"This has to be turned slightly to the left," she heard someone say.

"That enough?" said another voice.

"Yes. Good. Now roll it closer. It has to be in contact with the Bauble."

"Okay . . . how's that?"

Gweanvin felt the contact. Something was touching the Bauble over about thirty per cent of one side of its surface. Aha! This was it! The interface system that she had to probe. She shifted all her attention to that part of the Bauble surface, but found nothing but touch-pressure. The interface was inactive.

"Hadn't we better switch it on and check for good contact?"

"No. We turn nothing on until the test begins. Don't worry about the contact. It's good, all right."

Footsteps moved away from the Bauble and the test chamber was silent once more.

Gweanvin used the delay for one last review of her contingency plans.

The Gordeen Consolidated building was not designed for the convenience of spy-saboteurs. Its outside walls were thick, tough, windowless. To leave in the normal manner meant going out on her balcony, semi-inerting, flying up through the scramble area to the roof exit seventy-one floors above, where one of the gates would check her identity and let her through.

Minimum exit time: ten seconds . . . *if* she ran into no traffic jams, and *if* the gates had not been alerted to detain her.

Still, that would be the best way out if she had time to use it. If not . . .

She opened a drawer of the console desk, considered its clutter of contents, took a light-pen out of it. She used the pen to streak a pair of trial vectors across the diagram on the console screen, and gazed studiously at the result.

The drawer's contents were such as most anyone might accumulate over a period of a few years on a job. Some items, such as the light-pen, definitely belonged there. Others, such as a zercrown and a couple of sheets of slightly worn warprag, did not belong but were readily explainable, in case anyone asked. The warprags, for example, she had swiped from one of the shops—which no one would mind—with the intention of taking them home to see how they would work as abrasives on gold sculpture, which she made in her spare time.

Also, most of the jumble of stuff in the drawer was as harmless and useless as it looked; anyone would have to take a very close look indeed to know that some of it was not.

Unfortunately, she mused, suspicion would have been aroused had she added a charged implant power-unit to the accumulation—and if things got really tight, she would doubtless need plenty of power in a hurry. She had an answer to that, of course, but it would have been better if . . .

There was a murmur of voices and footsteps down in the test chamber.

"If everyone will find seats," spoke an authoritative voice. "Thank you. Now, how are we on security, Marvis?"

"We're snug, Thydan," the voice of Marvis Jans replied. "The Gordeen people have done a good job of keeping this project tightly wrapped."

There was a murmur of appreciation, in which Gweanvin could make out Falor Dample's rumbled, "Thank you, Miss Jans."

"This room could not possibly be bugged, then?" demanded a voice she did not recognize.

"Not unless the Primgranese have developed an entirely novel technique," replied Marvis Jans with a touch of disdain, "which is most unlikely. And if they had, the likelihood of their both knowing of this project and getting an agent inside approaches zero."

"Okay, Marvis," chuckled the man she had called Thydan. "I have one specific question: what about Rayeal Promton?"

"All clear there, and I might say Rayeal is drawing more security attention than she merits simply because she happens to match a particular Commonality operator in age and basic genetics. Admittedly, the question, 'Could Rayeal Promton be Gweanvin Oster?' is a tempting one to consider . . . and it has been—but just because it is such an obvious one the Primgranese command would not have sent in the Oster woman on an assignment where . . ."

"They could have counted on us discounting our suspicions," put in Thydan, "for that very reason."

"Well . . . the important thing is that right now, she is forty-one floors above us working in her office and under observation from across the scrambleway."

"I'd like to be sure she'll stay there," grumbled the man who had asked about bugs.

"That can be arranged—if you think it's necessary," said Marvis.

"Good. Arrange it."

Thydan said, "One point that bothers me about Miss Promton is that she has speculated accurately on the nature of this project and has discussed her speculations rather freely."

"She's a very bright girl," Marvis broke in. "If I were in her position, I would probably have drawn the same conclusions. And she has been discreet in her indiscretion—only with people such as her boss, and agents such as Don Plackmon and myself. Obviously she's playing give-the-security-boys-a-hard-time. We're used to stirring up a little resentment."

"If I may put in a word," rumbled Falor Dample. "Miss Promton's contribution to the project has not been a small one. Without her, that Bauble we're looking at might still be only on the drawing-board. That doesn't strike me as something to expect from an enemy agent."

"In any event," said Marvis, sounding impatient, "if the test which we might get around to after a while is a success, Monte can tell us very quickly if Rayeal Promton or anyone else on Narva is a Primgranese infiltrator."

"Good point," replied Dample. "Why don't we get on with it?"

"Very well," agreed Thydan. "Marvis, you'll alert Plackmon to keep Miss Promton confined?"

"Taken care of."

"Good. Mr. Dample, as chairman of Gordeen

Consolidated, I believe the honor of pushing the button is yours."

And that, very suddenly, was *it*. The loss of her preferred escape route could not concern Gweanvin now. No tenseness over that or anything else. The task at hand required totally relaxed attention.

She entered fully into the Bauble for the first time. It felt different from Primgranese Baubles, partly because this one carried no idents of previous ego-field entrants, and partly because it was different on the physiochemical level. She felt an instant of relief at finding no idents there. If somebody around the lab had broken the rule forbidding entry in the Bauble she would now be open to telepathic contact with that person, and he could have blown the whistle on her.

Immediately she turned her attention to the portion of the surface touching the interface. Glowing bright traceries filled her mind. *Beautiful!* But this was no time for esthetic appreciation. What were the shapes of those traceries? What made them? How did they function?

And what did they remind her of? Some natural structure . . . She allowed herself no awareness of seconds passing. Taking time to observe that this was taking too long would have made it take even longer.

When Thydan spoke, his voice came dimly to her, and its content made no impression: "Readings indicate optimum operation. Now I'll comm Orrbaune to turn on their end."

Were the traceries like the optical-synapse interface? The summation of thousands of retinal cell messages into a coherent visual scene? . . . No . . . Something else . . .

Auditory! The complex interconnections of cilia nerves, involving feedbacks and resonances and a dozen other phenomena that enabled a listener to distinguish subtle variations in pitch and quality of sound. That was it! . . . In part, and not exactly.

Gweanvin kept at it until the whole picture clarified. She knew the nature of the interface and could guess from that the parameters of the comm system behind it. She could break contact right now, sabotage the Bauble and head for home at the earliest opportunity. It would be easy enough to get a vacation after the test proved a "failure", and back in the Commonality she could write out detailed instructions on how to build a Bauble-to-Bauble comm system . . .

And that system wouldn't work. That realization came almost intuitively from her grasp of the characteristics of the interface. It wouldn't work.

Which wasn't the same as saying it *couldn't* work. It could. An ancient automobile with a defective starter could work, but wouldn't—until someone gave it a push to start it. The same was true of this system. There was near-complete randomness of orientation of the tiny, fine-texture fields of the interface traceries. This would prove extremely resistant to any flow through the system, too resistant for a flow to move.

But given the right kind of push, the fine-texture fields would align and resistance would vanish.

What kind of push, though? And by what . . . or whom?

Gweanvin could not even guess at the answer to the first of these questions. But the answer to the second was obvious.

She could not pull out of the Bauble yet, she realized. A vital question was still unanswered. She had to stay . . . perhaps until it was too late to pull out at all . . .

She stayed. But at the same time she started her body through a previously planned program of activities that could be carried out with minimal mental supervision. Her hands twisted off the top of the light-pen and her fingers deftly plucked out the instrument's control assembly and minipower unit. Next, the zercrown was brought out of the drawer, slid over the point of the light-pen, and taped in place.

"Orrbaune's switching on immediately," Thydan reported. Gweanvin kept her attention spread over the interface glow, watching for any change.

Now her fingers were wiring the device with strands of superconduct equipped with ready-weld tips. The two loose ends were then attached to insulated probe-needles.

The interface was beginning to alter in an area near its center. Something was happening there. Gweanvin moved in tightly on this area. Yes, it really was something like a push coming from the other side . . .

Her hands had left the finished device on the console and had picked up the two sheets of warprag. Her body had stood up and was walking toward the door.

. . . and in a way the push resembled a magnetic field. It was swinging the fine-texture fields into consistent orientation. But how was it doing this, specifically?

Her fingers separated the two sheets of warprag, and her hands slapped the exposed active surfaces

into position, overlapping the edge of the door and
the door frame. Absently, like a well-rehearsed piano
player with a wandering mind, she watched her hands
press firmly against the sheets, imbedding their grip.
Only a powerful smashing could force the door from
the balcony side while those warprags remained in
place.

. . . Ah! She was getting it! Monte was coming
through! And for the instant he was too occupied
opening up the interface to notice what lay beyond.
Gweanvin *watched* him work. She saw how it was
done . . .

Her body had returned to the console. Her hands
picked up the probe-needle contacts of her device
and plunged them through the flesh under her ribs
on her right side, seeking and finding the terminals
of her main power pack imbedded there.

. . . *Anger!* A flash of anger now and she would
have the job finished. But emotions, while controllable,
work more slowly than clean thought. The split-second
required to work up a burst of rage was too long.
Monte spotted her. *Damn!* Her rage flooded out in
a quick spurt and was gone. And so, of course, was
contact with Monte . . .

"*Security break!*" Thydan was yelling. "*It's Gweanvin
Oster! I caught a thought from Monte! The Bauble's
dark!*"

Gweanvin grinned as she pointed her device at the
wall of her office opposite the door and activated it. A
thin, superhot laser-beam flashed from the zercrown,
cutting a curving slash in the wall as the device kicked
in her hand. For an instant her shieldscreen turned

on automatically to protect her from the intense back-flare. She had pulled out of the ruined Bauble, but was keeping a light contact with its sound-sensitive surface segments which, not being destructible by emotional overload, were still functioning.

"I'm going after her," came a grim bark from Marvis, as Gweanvin re-aimed and made another curving cut through the wall. The curves came together at two points, and a two-foot-wide slice of metal-mass teetered for an instant and fell outward.

Gweanvin had semi-inerted and slipped through the opening long before the chunk of wall reached the ground. She streaked upward from Narva as fast as atmospheric resistance against her shield screen would permit.

"Alert the Guard!" came Thydan's voice. "She's out of the building and getting away!"

"What happened to the Bauble?" came the rumble of Falor Dample.

"How should I know?" Thydan returned bitterly. "Among those major contributions of hers you were just praising was a twist she didn't bother to tell you about! I'm trying to get a report relayed from Monte. Maybe he knows what happened."

Gweanvin allowed herself six seconds of unswerving upward flight before taking evasive action. She figured on that much leeway before the Guardsmen could mount an effective response to the alert at upper-atmospheric levels. Out in open space, which she was fast approaching, they could react quicker, but so could she. She kept her laser device ready for use. It was clumsily small as a hand weapon and wasteful of energy, so low in resistance as to act as a virtual short-circuit across her power implant. It was no match for a zerburst pistol, though it worked on the same principle. She hoped she could get away without using it again.

"Monte says she knows how to work the interface!" came Thydan's alarmed voice. "And she may be listening to us! Let's get out of this room!"

4

Gweanvin pulled away from the Bauble completely. It wasn't a good idea to enter warpflight with the ego-field lagging behind the body, anyway.

She tongued her toothmike to her "father's" frequency. "Hey, Pops!"

"Hello, Rayeal," the reply murmured in her left ear.

"Cover's blown, Pops. Out."

"Thanks, Gweanny. Out."

That warning would give her "family" members a chance to scram before Lontastan counterespionage teams closed in on them. But she was the one the heat was really on. That report relayed from Monte to Thydan would make it plain that she had information she must not be allowed to carry to the Primgranese Commonality. The Guards had probably been ordered to shoot on sight . . .

One of them did. Just as she was passing the forty-mile altitude level the flare from his zerburst pistol sparked less than three miles to her left. She caught a quick glimpse of the ionized trail of the beam leading to the flare. It hadn't missed her by more than fifty feet and wouldn't have missed at all if she hadn't made an evasive zag less than a second earlier.

She risked a mini-warp—dangerous in the atmospheric fringe—and came out of it seventy miles higher, with body and ego-field still together. Her detector immediately revealed half a dozen Guardsmen within range. She had warped into the middle of a platoon! She quickly warped again, and came out to see a spectacular display of flares blossom around the spot she had just vacated.

Nobody was close enough this time to get a good shot at her, but her detector showed the sky was now full of Guardsmen, above, below, and on all sides. This was a time to scoot, she decided, not to stand and fight. She would have to risk going into warp and staying there.

She did so . . . and got away with it. No body/ego-field dissociation that came when one warped through a too-dense wisp of gas or dust, wisps that were always drifting unpredictably about the near vicinity of stars.

Now the sun of Narva was shrinking to a pin-point and she was safely through the gauntlet of Guardsmen—thanks to the fact that the alarm had not gone out until she had escaped from the Gordeen building and was on her way. Two seconds later and she would not have made it.

She would be pursued, of course, and Guardsmen from other Lontastan worlds would be swarming out to try to intercept her. But interstellar space was vast, and she possessed less mass than any of the Guardsmen—neobarbs were all big men—and therefore had a higher sustainable warp velocity. She'd be hard to either catch or head off.

Nevertheless, she knew she could not make it to the Commonality without help. The necessity of cutting her way out of the Gordeen building had made that impossible. Those two blasts from her makeshift laser knife, brief though they were, had drained an awesome amount of power from her pack. Those packs weren't designed to be stingy; often a person in an emergency needed plenty of juice in a hurry, and a pack would supply current at the rate needed . . . while it had current to supply.

But on a short-circuit discharge, and especially through superconduct wiring, an implant pack could be drained completely in ten seconds or less. Gweanvin's pack had not been fully charged to begin with, and had been on short-circuit for a good three seconds. It was, she guessed, at something less than half capacity now.

And the Commonality was a long way off. Narva was located at the far side of the Lontastan Federation, and that put her home ground some twenty thousand light-years away, with nothing but unfriendly territory in between. Perhaps she had power for two-thirds of that distance.

There was, however, no point in heading in the other direction, into the unsettled region of the galaxy behind the Lontastan worlds: That region had been explored for quite some distance. There were planets on which she could play a female Robinson Crusoe for the rest of her life, but that was all.

There was just one destination within reach that made any sense—the Halstaynian Independency.

The Independency lay roughly between but somewhat to one side of both the Federation and the Commonality, and bulged on the Federation side in the general direction of Orrbaune. It was not a participant in the econo-war, having been settled by people who viewed competitiveness with distaste, as a childish and demeaning habit man should have given up long ago.

Gweanvin shared the majority view of Halstaynians—that they were somewhat less than half alive and getting more so every year. But when somebody from the Commonality or Federation went into the Independency, which was not often, the Halstaynians were friendly enough—if in an absurdly condescending manner. And from there she certainly shouldn't have any trouble getting her pack recharged and returning to the Commonality.

The important point was that she had the power to reach the Independency.

After a moment of consideration, she threw away her laser device. It was her only excuse for a weapon, but it was also mass, and if she made it out of Lontastan territory, she would do so by running, not by fighting.

Next she considered her clothing, but her flimsy blouse and shorts really had too little mass to make discarding them worthwhile. The same was true of her sandals. As for her belt and pouch, they had mass but could not be parted with. She had to have something in which to keep her food pills, if nothing else. However, she went through the pouch and threw away everything in it she could possibly do without.

After that she broke out of warp momentarily, got

herself coordinated on a star beyond which was an entry through the gas cloud banked on this side of the Independency, and returned to warpflight on the new course.

Then there was nothing to do but relax into dormancy from pill-time to pill-time, for the several standard days the journey would take. And despite the all-out search the Lontastans were making, this routine went undisturbed.

The gas clouds that lay between the Halstayne Independency and Earth accounted for the Independency's existence. As humanity began spreading out among the stars, forming the colonial societies that eventually became the Primgranese Commonality and the Lontastan Federation, the explorers moved along the edges of the clouds without attempting to penetrate. Much later, when gas-free passageways through the clouds were found and charted, neither the Commonality nor the Federation saw much potential in the hard-to-reach handful of habitable worlds the clouds concealed.

These worlds went more or less by default to the individuals and small groups who, for various reasons, wanted no part in the econo-war. Gweanvin had never felt much affinity for any such drop-out philosophy; in fact, she had never visited the Independency before. But it was part of her job to know her way about the inhabited portion of the galaxy. She had learned the charts of the passageways through the clouds, and the locations and descriptions of the habitable worlds within.

Also, she knew enough of the down-hill history of

the Independency to have some idea of what to expect on those worlds. No more than a century ago, when fair numbers of people were still moving into the Independency, it was a fairly successful society. But of late the movement had been in the other direction. The more capable Halstaynians were realizing that a society that forbade the competitive spirit was, in essence, a denial of the basic nature of man ... of life in general, for that matter. And being unrealistic, that kind of society had to either change or fall.

The Halstaynians who could see this flaw for what it was usually found their personal solutions to it by immigrating to the Federation or Commonality, rather than staying home and pushing revolutionary reform against an opposition composed principally of a formidable mass of public inertia. As a result, the Independency as a whole had rusticated. It no longer even tried to keep up technologically with the econo-warring societies. What technology it had once had was falling into disuse. The population was dwindling.

All of which was all right with Gweanvin. If that was the way the Halstaynians wanted it, she mused, that was the way they could have it. All she asked was a simple recharge of her power pack—and surely that much technology was still left.

She was more than halfway through the series of short, zigzagging warps required to follow the charted passage through the cloud when she felt a warning twinge in her side. The power pack was advising her it was ninety per cent drained. She grunted. But at least she knew now precisely how much power she had left, and how stingy in its use she would have to be.

No corner-cutting was advisable going through the passage, however. When she came into view of the Halstaynian suns she calculated she had enough power left for one sizeable or two short jumps.

Okay, which planet was it to be? Bernswa was reportedly the most advanced Halstaynian world but unless she had greatly underestimated her remaining power it was out of reach. And Felis, with a so-so reputation, was barely within range. The only world that could be called close was Arbora, which was so far gone that the Halstaynians had blithely designated it a wilderness preserve nearly fifty years ago.

Gweanvin ate a food pill while she pondered the matter. This was a crucial decision. If she made the wrong choice, she could wind up stranded in space . . . and the Halstaynians might not have a functioning space-rescue service these days. Or, if she went to Arbora, she could be stranded there, too, if there were no functioning power supplies.

She needed more information before deciding. She tuned her comm receiver to the open-broadcast channels and drifted in space for several hours while she listened attentively for a few useful facts. There was little to hear except music, most of it ancient, interspersed with trivial gab. But there were a couple of mentions of persons on Arbora, which assured her that world wasn't totally deserted.

In any event, she decided it almost had to be Arbora, because of the possibility that she was overestimating her remaining power. That could be the only world actually within reach.

She was making the painstaking calculations needed for a precise warp when a bogie flicked into existence, a small glowing spot on the detection field surrounding her head. Whoever it was couldn't have been more than a thousand miles away, she saw, suggesting that it was someone who had followed her through the cloud.

A Lontastan agent on her tail? Very likely, indeed.

Gweanvin had gone full inert while listening to her comm, to save a trickle of power. Thus, she would not be as visible to the bogie as the bogie was to her. In fact, she might easily be mistaken for a chunk of space debris, so long as she remained inert.

She played possum and watched. A couple of minutes passed, and the bogie flicked out, the person having warped off. But others might be following, so she continued to watch.

Nobody else appeared, which was a bit puzzling. Was that bogie a single Lontastan agent, playing a lone hand on a hunch? Well, if so, Gweanvin herself had a hunch who the agent would be.

She had left clues enough behind to give somebody as sharp as Marvis Jans a clear hint of what might have happened. Marvis would know that she hadn't blasted her way out of the Gordeen building with a zerburst pistol, for the obvious reason that as a security measure hardly any such weapons were allowed inside the building. Marvis would have accounted for those weapons quickly. Then she would have checked (if she hadn't already) to be sure the building's energy outlets were fused against short-circuit overdraws, also as a security measure.

And Marvis would therefore conclude that the likelihood was very good that she had used her power pack implant, for lack of any other sufficient source, to blast through the wall. A little more checking would reveal how long it had been since Gweanvin had gotten a recharge. Marvis could then guess she would have to head for the Independency as the only non-enemy territory within reach.

But it would be a guess, not a sure thing. And it would be like Marvis—or like herself if their positions were reversed—to play the guess on her own.

Would Marvis investigate Arbora first?

Perhaps. The agent's movements were not predictable. She could see no percentage in delaying planetfall any longer. The sooner she was on the surface of a world, the sooner she could make herself impossible to find.

She warped for Arbora . . . and missed. Only by some two hundred thousand miles, but that was enough to require a mini-warp approach jump. This brought her within five hundred miles of the surface. There she went full inert and let Arbora's gravity bring her down, knowing she would be less noticeable that way than in a semi-inert approach, and also would use less energy.

When she hit air her shield screen reacted automatically, protecting her from friction and heat, and spreading into a wing conformation to slow her fall and allow her to steer. Not that it seemed to matter where she landed . . . all was field and forest below, with no indications of where the people might be.

She angled toward a small grassy valley as she neared the surface, waiting until she was down to one hundred feet before trying to go semi-inert to soften the landing. Nothing happened when she did. She came down with a jarring thump, slowed only by ground-effect compression of the air between her shield and the surface at the last instant.

She rolled over and sat up in the long grass. Her shield was off, and her respiration had gone on normal exterior mode.

Once more she tried to semi-inert, without result. Which could mean only that her power pack was totally drained. Just to be sure, she tried the shield screen again, and it did not respond.

She was definitely on Arbora until she found a recharger, and she would do her searching for it on leg-power alone.

But more urgent was the subject of food. The instant her breathing had gone external, bringing her the varied aromas of field and forest, she had become ravenous. She had been on the food-concentrate pills and stomach balloon for an uncomfortably long flight, and needed something solid.

She stood up and walked through the tall weeds to the small brook that gurgled through the valley, her eyes searching for anything edible. Arbora had, she recalled, a seeded Earth ecology—which obviously had turned out better than most other Halstaynian experiments. She recognized a number of briars and bushes that produced edible fruit in season, but the coolness of the air and the yellowish hues of the not-distant eaves of the forest told her this was not the season. It was autumn in this region of Arbora.

At the brook she knelt and drank, and splashed her face with the clear sweet water. Standing, she considered following the brook downstream, but the thick growth of brambles and weeds would make difficult walking. Instead, she headed uphill toward the nearest trees.

There her luck improved. Some of the trees were hickories, the ground beneath them liberally sprinkled with small nuts. She spent two hours smashing their tough hulls between two stones and picking out and eating their tiny but rich kernels.

Then she moved on to a rocky bald on top of the hill. It was late afternoon by now and she scanned the horizon in all directions, searching for a wisp of smoke or any other sign of human presence.

"Hey!" she yelled at the top of her voice. *"Anybody home?"*

The startled birds in her vicinity obligingly ceased their chirping while she listened for a reply. Nothing.

She turned around and yelled again with the same lack of results.

So . . . start walking—or try to build a fire and some kind of shelter for the night. The low position of the sun made her choose the latter.

Try to build a fire . . . ?

The quickest way was to strike a spark between rock and metal into easily-lit tinder, but she had thrown away everything metallic when she cleaned out her pouch. She tried hitting rock on rock instead, but the stone thereabouts was wrong for the job. It crumbled instead of sparking.

So . . . she would rub two sticks together, making a groove in one with the end of the other.

She tried that for a vigorous forty minutes and was surprised when the groove finally began smoking. She dumped the spark into a handful of cedar bark fiber she had gathered and fanned it into flame. A few minutes later she had a roaring fire going.

For a while she sat beside her fire, resting her arms and rubbing the fatigue out of them as twilight deepened. Then she rose and began searching the nearby trees for pine and cedar boughs to break off for bedding. That would be better than a mound of dry leaves, which were certain to be insect-infested.

5

"Huy! Was that you yelling a while back?" a man's voice called out of the gloom.

Gweanvin turned, trying to see him. "Yeah . . . I didn't hear you answer."

"I was stalking a deer at the time. Couldn't make noise," the man explained. His form moved closer to the fire, and she saw he was carrying something large over a shoulder which he heaved to the ground a moment later. "I finally got within bowshot and brought her down. Then I started looking for you, and saw your fire."

He turned to look at her, and she could see his face dimly in the flickering light. He was clean-shaven, which she had not expected from a buckskin-clad man of the wilderness, and appeared to be in his thirties.

"Looks like you've strayed a long way from home, young lady," he said. "You from Bernswa?"

"Farther away than that. The Commonality," she

replied. "My power pack's exhausted. I had to land here to get a recharge."

"A recharge on Arbora?" he laughed. "Well . . . probably you can, at that. There ought to be a few rechargers scattered about. I don't know for sure, though."

"You don't know?" demanded Gweanvin. "Where do *you* go for a recharge?"

He chuckled. "The only thing I recharge is my stomach. And I'm about ready to do that right now, if you'll let that fire die down to a bed of coals fit to cook over. You hungry?"

"I'm starving."

"More than plenty for both of us." He slid the large backpack off his shoulders and busied himself with knife and deer carcass.

"Then you don't have a life-support system?" she asked.

"Just Arbora. No implants. I guess that sounds primitive to you, doesn't it?"

"It sounds restrictive," she said diplomatically, not wanting to offend the source of her supper. "Doesn't anyone on Arbora use implants?"

"A few do. That's why I say you might be able to get a recharge. There's a settlement called High Pines about five days hiking west of here, and about eight days to the southeast is Lopat. You could almost call Lopat a town, I suppose."

"What's in between?"

He shrugged and motioned vaguely at the surrounding woods. "Just this. Good hunting country. And not many hunters. I don't average running into somebody three times a year out here."

Gweanvin considered this information. At last she said, "Then I'd better start walking for High Pines in the morning, if you'll tell me the way."

"Sure." he agreed. "Or maybe you should head for Lopat. It's a longer trip, but . . . well, I can't say for sure which place is more likely to have a recharger, but I'd guess Lopat is."

There was a silence. Gweanvin was waiting for the man to offer some assistance in her search, perhaps hiking to Lopat while she went to High Pines. But he made no offer. Perhaps the primitive life deadened the chivalrous inclinations . . . or perhaps he needed to know her better to exert himself in her behalf . . .

"My name is Gweanvin. Gweanny. Gweanvin Oster."

"Glad to meet you, Gweanny. I'm Holm Ocanon."

"There are a lot of Ocanons in the Commonality," she said.

"That's nice," he said. Which was a conversation-stopper if ever she had heard one.

When supper was ready they sat by the fire eating the broiled meat strips, roasted roots too fibrous to be potatoes but with a pleasant nutty flavor, and some kind of raw greenery Holm had had in his pack. Also he had brewed a bitter tea that was invigorating, and might have actually been tasty with a little sugar.

"I have a blanket you can wrap yourself in," he said. "As near naked as you are, you'll sleep mighty cold without it."

"Thanks. It seems strange to need a blanket on a comfortable E-type planet, when ordinarily I'm perfectly comfortable just like this in interstellar space. It's easy to take life-support for granted."

"I imagine so," he mused. "It's easy to take living conditions of whatever kind for granted. And some conditions are less dependable, less stable, than others."

"Yours seem stable enough, but awfully strenuous," she said. "Wouldn't life in or near one of the settlements be easier?"

"Yes, and wouldn't life in the Commonality be easier without the econo-war?" he returned.

"Too much easier—as we found out a few decades ago when the war got too one-sided and almost ended."

"Yes, that was after the Lontastans found the non-human telepath they call Monte, and brought him in on their side," Holm said. "We heard about that. Then your side developed the Bauble to even the sides up again."

"I hardly expected to find an econo-war fan here in the Arbora wilderness," she said, smiling.

"People are interested in other people's games . . . to watch if not to play," he said musingly.

"That's true," Gweanvin replied. "For instance, I'm interested in your game, and why you choose to play it. I would think the game of family-raising near one of the settlements would have more appeal for an Arboran, and be plenty challenging."

He nodded slowly. "I'd be playing that game if I could."

"Why can't you? A shortage of women on Arbora?"

"No. I could get the women all right. I can't get the children."

"You look like a thoroughly functional male to me," said Gweanvin, still hoping to recruit Holm's aid with a bit of flattery.

He laughed. "I feel like one, especially with you sitting next to me. But just the same, I'm out of whack, somehow. I don't reproduce."

"Oh . . . That's a problem I know a bit about."

"Probably you don't. It's not simple sterility. We still have medical treatment here, to take care of problems like that. No . . . I seem to be too different . . ."

Gweanvin started. "D-different? In what way?"

"Well, if there was enough light for you to see my nose, you might notice a bony look, because—"

She slipped close to him. "Let me feel it," she breathed.

"Why . . . sure! Go ahead," he laughed.

Her fingers found his nose in the dark, and explored its ridge. Solid bone was underneath the skin! Just like her own nose! And Marvis Jans'!

"Oh, golly! Wow! Oh, golly!"

He laughed again. "My nose doesn't usually get such a flattering reaction. What's so thrilling about it?"

"Your turn to feel my nose!" she giggled. As he did so she kept giggling. "This beats everything! We search the files of the Commonality and the Federation, cybernetically examine the genetic profiles of billions of people. Then I land on Arbora of all places, and who walks up to my fire first thing! Oh, Holm, this is a miracle! I've found you!"

Holm sat without moving or speaking for a long moment, apparently stunned. Then he grunted, "Damned if you haven't!" and took her in his arms.

*   *   *

When Gweanvin woke the next morning Holm was gone, but his pack was still there. She found some live embers in the ashes of the fire, and succeeded in blowing some twigs into flame. Then she went down to the brook for an icy bath and was back at the fire warming herself when Holm returned. He was carrying a rough-woven bag that Gweanvin hoped contained breakfast.

"Hi," she chirped. "Been hunting?"

"Yes," he grinned, kissing her tightly. "More than hunting, really. I left you shortly after midnight. Did I wake you?"

"No." She had felt him leaving, but had not come fully awake.

"I wanted to check on a cabin that's a couple of hours walk from here," he explained. "I suppose it's been deserted for a century but it's in good condition. We can use it unless you want to be closer to a settlement."

He took utensils from his pack, some large brown eggs from the sack he was carrying, began working on breakfast.

"Holm, I can't stay," Gweanvin said softly.

He hesitated. "What's wrong?"

"An obligation. My job in the econo-war. I'm a spy-saboteur for the Commonality. I have to go home to report on a matter that could be crucial to keep the war in balance. Somehow I have to get my power pack recharged, and do that. Then I can resign and come back."

Holm put the teapot on the fire and began cutting fat into a frying pan. "How long will that take? A couple of months?"

"More like three years, I'm afraid. You see, the critical part of my report involves a technique that I've seen employed, and that I can do myself but can't describe verbally. I'll have to show others how it's done, and some special equipment will have to be built before I can do the demonstration. That's what will take time."

After a moment, Holm nodded. "Okay, Gweanny, I won't give you any argument—except that I don't want you giving birth to a child of mine in the Commonality."

"Don't worry," she giggled. "I'll wait till I get back for that."

"And you can't do anything until you're equipped to travel on foot through the forest," he added. "You need a bow and training in how to use it to bring down game. You need warm clothing. We should stay here at the cabin for at least three days getting you prepared. Then you go to High Pines while I go to Lopat. That's the fastest way we can find out if there's a recharger at either settlement. We'll meet back here. Okay?"

"Fine. But there's one thing you should know, Holm. I'm sure I was pursued into the Independency by at least one Lontastan agent."

He nodded. "Right. I'll keep my mouth shut about you—but there's probably nothing to worry about. The people here won't cooperate with the Lontastans, of course. And Arbora would be the last planet your pursuers would expect you to land on. Even then, there are thousands of villages on Arbora, in all of which they would have to make inquiries. I'd say they don't stand a chance of finding you until after you're recharged."

"That's good to know," she said gratefully. But what pleased her most was his assumption that there were several agents on her tail—not just one female with a big bust and bony nose. Above everything, she could not allow Marvis Jans and Holm Ocanon to find out about each other. Thank goodness, the likelihood of that was slight with Holm out of communication this way, playing his game of self-sufficiency in the wilderness.

But even Marvis Jans' presence in the Independency was in itself more of a risk than she was willing to accept. She resolved that when she resumed her homeward journey she would make sure Marvis pursued her right out of the Independency.

The three days at the cabin passed swiftly and busily. She had much to learn before undertaking a two-week trek alone . . . how to handle the bow Holm made for her, how to find edible vegetables in field and forest, how to quickly build a shelter that would keep out most of the rain. She was a good student, however, and often asked questions that gave Holm pause. Perhaps, she mused, there was no such thing as a completely expert woodsman. Holm, who had lived in the wild most of his adult life, seemingly had missed many points.

He was often away from the cabin for stretches of ten or more hours, ranging far among the scattered derelict habitations in search of bits of equipment she would need. His finds included a good knife, a chunk of sound velveen fabric from which she made herself warm trousers and jacket, a few pots and pans, and a flint and steel for firemaking.

Then one clear morning they began their separate journeys, she heading west and he southeast. She had a roughly sketched map Holm had made for a guide, showing the major landmarks on the way to High Pines with a line indicating the best route to follow.

Even with that help, it was a tough trip. Gweanvin guessed it had been years since Holm had actually traveled this particular course, because she kept coming up against impassable thickets and bogs that must have formed since then.

What he had described as a five-day hike turned out to be seven. But at last she came to the settlement of High Pines—some two dozen houses in a loose cluster under the trees with a scattering of cultivated fields nearby.

There she was welcomed with hospitality, a couple of good meals, and a cozy bed for the night. But no recharger.

Did they know if there was a recharger in Lopat, or anywhere else nearby?

No . . . they weren't sure. Only seven of the villagers had life-support implants, and didn't use them much. The last person there to get a recharge had gone to the planet Bernswa for it—and that was seventeen years back.

The picture wasn't encouraging as she began the long hike back to the cabin. The chance of Holm finding a recharger in Lopat seemed slight indeed from what she had learned.

Well, if that meant she was stuck here indefinitely, then the econo-war would just have to get along without her. Perhaps getting the new breed started would have more long-term significance anyway.

And she *could* get home at some indefinite time in the future. A couple of oldsters in High Pines had told her that when one of them died she would be welcome to salvage his partially-charged power implant from his corpse.

Both of them were discouragingly spry and healthy. She wondered how much use her report would be to the Commonality, if it didn't arrive until twenty years from now.

Holm was waiting for her when she reached the cabin. "Poor Gweanny," he murmured, taking her in his arms and kissing her.

"You look exhausted."

"I can believe it. Did you . . . have any luck?"

"Yes, I brought a recharger back with me," he replied, surprisingly. "It's inside."

"Wow! That's a relief! From what I was told in High Pines, I wondered if there was one this side of Bernswa."

"At least one," he smiled, giving her a squeeze, "and you've got it."

"Golly! I don't know how to thank you, Holm!"

He grinned. "Maybe I'll think of some way."

"I get the impression you're not as beat as I am," she laughed.

"I shouldn't be. I got back three days ago. Been taking it easy ever since."

"How did you manage that?"

"I was given a lift by a fellow in Lopat, the man who loaned me the recharger. He wanted to know where I was taking it, anyway, so he flew out here with me riding on his back."

She thought about it for a moment. "Doesn't that compromise the location of our little love-nest?"

"Not really. I know that guy. He won't talk to any Lontastan agents about us."

"Had any agents been in Lopat?"

"I don't think so. Of course I didn't ask, but someone would have been likely to mention such unusual visitors."

Gweanvin nodded, and asked no further questions. Holm hadn't been as discreet as she would have preferred, but then he wasn't a frontliner, experienced at disclosing not one datum more than he wished to disclose. Considering his backwater background, so far away from the econo-war, he had done very well indeed.

They entered the cabin and he brought the recharger out of a closet. It was a large clumsy device, in a plastic block. It weighed at least twenty pounds, typical of the comparatively unpolished technology of the Independency of a century ago.

But it worked. It generated energy. Gweanvin punched its probe-needles through her skin to the contacts of her power pack—rather gingerly because the needles were painfully dull—and thirty minutes later she had her recharge.

"When are you leaving?" Holm asked.

"Soon . . . tomorrow morning. I really must, Holm."

"Okay. I'll hate to see you go—but you know that."

"Returning will be more pleasure for me than leaving," she said. "And Holm, I don't want you to see me go. It would be best if you were far away from the cabin before I go on power."

"Oh . . . in case the Lontastans spot you leaving and follow your backtrail?"

"Yes. My light weight makes it possible for me to outwarp any agent I ever met, so the chances of my being caught are slight. But there's nothing to stop the agents from coming here and questioning you."

He laughed. "A lot I'd tell them!"

"You could wind up telling them more than you intended," she said grimly. "You know no more of their tricky games than I knew of woodsmanship—and if they find out I'm coming back . . . well, you can kiss our plans for a long and happy mating season goodbye."

After a moment, he said slowly, "I'll leave around midnight, Gweanny, just as I did the first night. When you go, I'll be more than twenty miles away."

He was gone the next morning. Gweanvin prepared a large breakfast and ate it slowly. She was in no hurry to lift off, since each moment of delay now would put Holm farther away. Of course it was not really likely that she would be backtracked, but she did not want to take even a slight risk of bringing Holm and Marvis together.

She was not, she realized, being completely reasonable on that score. But neither would Marvis be, if their roles were reversed. Had she and Marvis been devoted sisters, perhaps they would willingly share the only available male of their species. But they were not. The expediencies of the econo-war could not be left out of the picture. She and Marvis were competitors, and frontline competitors at that, which meant they were among the relatively small group of econo-warriors who might, on occasion, carry the conflict to the point of shooting at each other.

Sharing the available male would be reasonable. It would be the surest way to give their new species a toehold on continued existence. But circumstances did not really allow her to be reasonable . . .

. . . Not even if she wanted to, which she didn't. She grinned. It was such fun to outdo Marvis of the big bust!

Not that Holm was . . . well, was her *ideal*. Gosh, he was close to sixty Standard Years, old enough to be her father! Even though, by the homo sap norm, he only looked thirty. Of course he doted on her; he made that all too obvious. Letting her have her way about everything, instead of forcefully taking charge. For instance, letting her leave for three years, or maybe even longer, without the least ruckus, although he plainly hated the idea.

Oh, well. It was too much to expect the one available male would be someone she could fall madly in love with. At least she found him attractive enough for all practical purposes. And he *would* make a terrific father, here on Arbora. She had sized his woodsmanship up wrong earlier, because he had trouble teaching it to her. But that was because he hadn't ever bothered to verbalize a lot of what he knew before.

The things that man could do . . . the success he had had scrounging equipment for her trek to High Pines . . . and that bow he had made for her, as good or better than any wooden bow that could be bought in a Primgran sporting goods shop . . . and these lovely breakfast eggs she was eating. Despite his instructions, she hadn't yet been able to find a wild chicken nest, but when Holm went egg-gathering he always came back with a sack of beauties.

And if he was lacking somewhat in youthfulness and forcefulness, he was nevertheless plenty masculine. And with him sex could have a purpose beyond play. She suspected that difference alone would hereafter make dalliance with homo sap males too trivial to bother with.

What was that quote she had noticed in that ancient treatise on the experimental crossing of donkeys and horses to produce mules? Oh, yes:

" . . . it is a curious fact that once a male donkey has served a female donkey, it is often reluctant to transfer its attentions to a female horse."

A "curious" fact, indeed. Seemingly even donkeys have an intuitive preference for producing a viable strain of offspring . . .

6

She rose from the table and prepared to leave. That consisted mainly of removing the warm velveen clothing which would no longer be needed when she went on power. She walked through the cabin and paused, looking at the bow Holm had made her. It was a handsome piece of work, and she was tempted to take it and a few arrows along as mementos.

Well, why not? If Marvis Jans were still around, she wanted to lead her away, didn't she? The extra mass of the bow ought to slow her just enough to keep Marvis from growing quickly discouraged. She

slung it across her shoulder and tied the quiver of
six arrows to her belt.

Gweanvin stepped outside, took a final glance
around, then semi-inerted and activated her propulsion
field. Rapidly she soared up into the clear morning
sky, lifting directly away from the planet, enjoying the
physical comfort of having all her life-support systems
going again and the freedom of motion which could
come no other way.

Her detectors showed a spot of activity off to the
southeast . . . the settlement of Lopat, she guessed.
Nothing showed at High Pines; none of the few pos-
sessors of life-support systems there were using them
at the moment.

There were no signs of pursuit yet. She had not
expected anything this quickly. Marvis might well have
stationed herself near Arbora by this time, working
on the assumption that if Gweanvin were still in the
Independency at all, it was because she was on a planet
where a recharge was hard to find. In short, on Arbora.
But Marvis wouldn't be on the ground. She would be in
space, ready to pounce on Gweanvin when she emerged
from the atmosphere.

Gweanvin hoped she would be waiting for her.
That would save the trouble of buzzing every planet
in the Independency looking for her.

Soon she had cleared the atmosphere, and immediately went into warp toward an opening in the gas
clouds that led into the Commonality. Within two minutes she was sure Marvis had not picked her up.

She frowned in thought. Was it really worthwhile
to search the Independency for Marvis, when the
Lontastan agent might even have given up the chase

by now and returned home? Or, if not that, might be waiting in ambush at one of the warpshift points in the cloud crevice ahead?

It was not, she decided. If Marvis wasn't hanging around Arbora itself, what chance was there that she would encounter someone who would say, "Hey, I know a guy with a nose just like yours"? Almost no chance at all.

So the only real risk was that Marvis was near Arbora, but Gweanvin's quick departure had caught her napping. Or perhaps the planet had been between them and had blocked out detection.

Well, that possibility could be checked out quickly.

Gweanvin reversed warp and went back to the Arbora system, overshooting the planet some thirty thousand miles. She had departed from the early-morning side, and now she hung over the early-evening side, studying her detector-screen.

Nobody was on power anywhere in nearby space. The only flickers came from the planet itself, and not many of those. Only one of those flickers was dop-plering, indicating a person moving upward through the atmosphere. Marvis Jans? Hardly likely.

Gweanvin hesitated. Was there anything else to do before heading home? Well . . . not really. There came a time when the best thing to do was leave well enough alone and—

The dopplering spot on her screen flicked off, and Marvis Jans emerged from miniwarp less than fifty yards away. Before Gweanvin had time to react, the Lontastan fired her zerburst pistol.

An intense pain lanced through Gweanvin's left hip.

be more in the situation for which it was intended. Marvis could set the weapon's intensity to flare at a certain range, then bide her time until she maneuvered herself to precisely that distance from Gweanvin.

Perhaps, thought Gweanvin, if I can circle behind that gas giant I can lose her long enough to—

But again she dropped out of miniwarp too quickly. The condition of her transport packet wasn't improving. She caught a flashing glimpse of a large object off to her left and with no hesitation warped to put it between herself and her pursuer.

This time she had allowed properly for her malfunctioning implant. Her warp exit was less than half a mile above the surface of the object, one of the gas giant's airless minor moons. Immediately she went full inert, killing all power consumption except for pressor field and detector. An instant later the detector screen showed the spot that was Marvis flash quickly on and off several hundred miles up as the Lontastan agent jumped around searching for her. Gweanvin, under the gravitational attraction of the moonlet, drifted slowly to the ground.

"Very bright of you, Gweanny, dear," came the voice of Marvis. "Taking cover could add whole minutes to your life-expectancy."

Which was accurate enough, Gweanvin supposed, as she touched ground feet first with an experienced knee-jiggle to prevent bouncing. All Marvis had to do was close in on the surface to a range where Gweanvin would be detectable, despite low-power usage, and circle on semi-inert until she spotted her target.

Gweanvin looked around for shelter, but saw no good hiding-place, no hole to crawl into. A rill-cliff, its top in sunlight and its base in deep shadow, was the best cover she could find. A few long leaps brought her into the shadow where she stood, back to the cliff, watching her detection screen.

A hell of a way to be caught, weaponless and with a loused-up transport implant, she told herself bitterly.

Weaponless?

She swung her bow off her shoulder and gave the string a testing tug. Surprisingly, the wood responded normally, as if it had been treated in the manner of professionally made bows against deterioration in vacuum. She wondered fleetingly how Holm had come to anti-space the wood, but this was a bit of luck too good to question.

She fitted an arrow to the bow and held the weapon ready, making sure that more arrows were poking handily out of the quiver for quick drawing.

A ludicrous situation . . . pitting a bow against a zerburst pistol. She snickered grimly at the thought. Why, Marvis could fire, miniwarp, and fire again while a single arrow was crawling its way toward her original position!

But if she could score a hit, the arrow would penetrate the agent's defensive screen. Though an arrow was light in weight, it still packed a lot of mass in relation to the size of its penetrating tip. More than a bullet did, or many other far more sophisticated projectiles that defensive screens were designed to stop. Its relatively low speed in effect would "fool" the screens into treating it as a minor threat, since the screen could not see all that inert mass behind it.

However, the only possible advantage she could

expect from an on-target arrow was one of surprise, in that Marvis would not expect her to have any weapon at all . . .

And there was Marvis! She came into view and into detection at the same time, flying slowly over the top of the cliff and not far to Gweanvin's left.

Gweanvin raised the bow, drawing back the string, and released. Without waiting to see the results, and while Marvis spotted her and aimed her zerburst pistol, Gweanvin miniwarped right up from the surface to a point fifty feet above her enemy. There she went on inert propulsion and drove straight down at Marvis. There was a slight jar when her shield screen banged into that of the semi-inert Lontastan, and a bruising jar when her impetus slammed both of them down on the rocky moonlet, with Marvis on the bottom. A shield screen had to flex under such punishment.

7

Gweanvin sat up groggily on the spot she had bounced to, ten feet from where Marvis was stretched out. Where was the pistol? Oh, there it was, beyond Marvis. She leaped across the woman and grabbed it just as Marvis began to stir.

Gweanvin tucked the pistol in her belt and watched the Lontastan warily. How knocked out was she? Badly hurt or playing possum?

Although she had no intention of aiding her traumatized enemy, Gweanvin exteriorized and moved into the woman to check on her injuries. That was something an ego-field could do far better than physical hands, because the care of bodies was a prime ego-field skill, and . . .

Stunned, Gweanvin withdrew and stood staring at the older woman.

Marvis was not badly mangled. A couple of broken ribs, a little internal bleeding, and an arrow through the left shoulder. Nothing her life-support maintenance system could not mend in a few hours, once that arrow was out of the way. After a moment, Gweanvin stepped forward and gently pulled the arrow free.

Oh, yes. Marvis would be fine. And so would her baby.

Pregnant!

By about two weeks, as near as Gweanvin could guess.

Oh, my, what a fine country bumpkin Holm Ocanon had turned out to be!

"Marvis," she said.

The woman roused slightly. "Uh-huh."

"You'll be okay in a little while. I removed the arrow. I'd better run along now."

Marvis managed to open her eyes and stare questioningly up at her. "Where are you going?"

"To the Commonality, naturally. I have a report to make, in case you've forgotten."

"Uh. See you again?"

"Not if I can help it. So long."

Gweanvin lifted off. She decided not to bother retrieving the bow she had left back by the rill-cliff. But before warping out of the Arbora system, she paused in thought. Despite what the pregnancy of

Marvis told her, the point remained that she had promised to return in about three years ...

She tongued her toothmike to nonspecific frequency and called, "Holm Ocanon?"

Silence.

"Speak up, Holm," she snapped. "I've caught on."

"Hi, Gweanny," his voice sounded in her left ear. "I'm sorry."

"I'll just bet you are!" she scolded, narrowing down to his comm frequency. "Quite a set-up you arranged for yourself. Not that I really blame you of course. Males of our species probably have polygamous instincts, just like homo sap, I suppose. Too bad for you your scheme didn't work. Wow, how you had it made!"

"Uh ... how's Marvis?"

"Oh, don't fret! She's out cold at the moment, but she'll come limping back in a few hours."

"Does she know as much as you do?"

"Not from anything I said. But you won't gain anything from your masquerade now, Holm, so why not be honest with her?"

"Maybe I should," he replied glumly. "How did you catch on?"

"From her being pregnant. How stupid I was, admiring your woodsmanship! Wild chicken nests, indeed! What farmer did you buy those eggs from, Holm? Did you pick up that bow at a sporting-goods shop in Lopat, or did you have to hop on semi-inert to a bigger town to find it? Maybe a town halfway around the planet from where I was stuck, but close to the nest you shared with Marvis? Did you have to go all the way to Bernswa to pick up that recharger? Damn! No *wonder* that map you drew had me mired in bogs and scratched in briar thickets! The least you could have done was to survey it at a lower altitude!"

"Gweanny, I set things up like this because I'd given it years of thought, along with a lot of patient waiting for the right opportunity. Try to understand, won't you?" he urged. "We're a new species, too new to know what we really are, or even have a name for ourselves. We and our children should develop as much as possible on our own, not as members of the econo-war society of humanity. We should find our own paths and goals, Gweanny, as we can on a world like Arbora. Don't you see the reasonableness of that?"

"I decided earlier today not to be reasonable," she replied. "In any event, I don't see the reasonableness of starting our species off with personal relationships based on deception. Damn it, Holm, I wouldn't treat anybody but a Lontastan in the tricky, scheming way you've handled Marvis and me! I wouldn't . . ."

She paused as another light dawned on her. "But of course, you'd be good at things like that, as a *former frontliner!* Were you Primgran or Lontastan?"

"Primgran," he grunted.

"I'll be interested in looking up your personnel file, when I get home," she mused. "I want to see how you doctored your genetic chart to conceal yourself. And how you managed to keep tabs on Marvis and me, without us ever dreaming you existed! Very cleverly, I'm sure. You had to be bright indeed to anticipate by several hours that she and I might come to Arbora, so you could be on hand to welcome us separately.

Well, so long, Holm. Fess up to Marvis, and have plenty of kids."

"You'll be back, Gweanny," he told her.

"Don't count on it."

"It pleases you now to be unreasonable, but in the long run you won't be unrealistic." He chuckled. "And the reality is that I'm the only available male."

"Don't count on that, either. You concealed yourself. Maybe another is somewhere around, doing the same. Not likely, maybe, but even so I'd prefer to spend my whole life waiting for him rather than be your second-stringer."

"I don't understand you," he complained.

"My unreasonableness. If you understood that, you would have anticipated my unreasonable decision to decoy Marvis away from Arbora when I left. If I hadn't tried that, I wouldn't have gotten wise to you."

"Well," he said confidently, "jealousy on your part was hardly expected. And, of course, feeling that way, you'll surely return."

"Meaning I love you?" she sneered. "Hah! If I did, do you think I'd fret over competition from Marvis? I'd just blow a hole through her! I was trying to prevent a competition I didn't care about enough to win! Love you? Hell, Holm, I don't even *like* you!"

With that she warped for home. She had meant what she said, but, golly, how she was going to need a male when she reached Marvis' age!

Hours later, and far from Arbora, a voice piped in her left ear: "Nice going, Gweanvin Oster."

"Huh? Who's that?"

No response.

Who could it have been? It had sounded like the voice of a boy, perhaps twelve years old. But what would a kid be doing way out here, and how could he have known of her?

She guessed the answers, of course, long before she knew them for sure nearly a decade later. By then the boyish voice had deepened and matured.

Gweanvin never returned to Arbora. Her children did.

Questor

❦

MORGAN'S POSITION in the fighting formation of the Lontastan raid brigade was well back, but on what would be the Earthward flank. Certainly he was not out of harm's way, but neither was he particularly in it. It was important that, when the Primgranese defenders studied the records of the coming skirmish, Morgan should not look special in any way.

His left ear hissed softly as the ultralight carrier came on, and he heard the voice of the brigade's navigator: *"Delay in warp exit, three point four two seven seconds. Reset cut-outs for delay in warp exit of three point four two seven seconds. . . . Exit now due in eighty-five seconds. Prediction: Combat will commence four point five seconds after exit."*

Morgan reset the timing of his warp cut-out and

twisted his head for a moment to gaze toward the navigator's position. He couldn't see him, of course. The distance between the two men was something over twenty-three hundred miles, and also normal vision was of scant use at superlight velocities.

But he looked anyway as he thought half sympathetically of the navigator, as burdened with equipment as an ancient was with clothing. Morgan glanced down at his own well-muscled body, bare and exposed to space except for his black minishorts, his weapons belt, and his low boots.

For an instant he entertained himself with his daydream of encountering a famed ancient, mysteriously transported forward in time about a thousand years from the Early Interstellar Age, back when men still traveled in ships. How astonished that worthy would be to see almost naked men zipping routinely about the galaxy! And how puzzled by the microchemical mysteries of a modern life-support system!

The thought made him aware of his breathing, and of the pounding of his heart which was speeding up in anticipation of the coming battle in spite of his efforts to think of other things. He inhaled deeply and slowly, conscious of the oxygen and nitrogen coming out of combination with the chemicals lining certain nasal passages to fill his lungs. Then he exhaled, and other doped surfaces, mostly in the lower throat, quickly absorbed the gases and almost as quickly broke down the carbon dioxide. After three breaths, he would be using the same oxygen over again.

Meanwhile, he had not neglected to draw both of his zerburst guns and wave them about a bit to loosen his arm muscles. His comrades of the brigade, randomly spaced with an average separation of fifteen hundred yards, were doing the same thing. Most of these men would fight the Primgranese Commonality defenders of Earth for fourteen long, furious seconds . . . and probably live to tell about it.

Morgan expected to be out of the fight within six seconds.

The brigade made warp exit less than a million miles out from Earth, and automatically went semi-inert. A quick glance at the ancestral planet assured Morgan that the navigator hadn't blundered; the brigade's trajectory was carrying it Earthward in a slanting, curving power dive that would peri at maybe two thousand miles from the surface.

And the defenders were coming in a swarm! Satellite bases were ejecting Primgranese Commonality guardsmen like slugs from antique machine guns, precisely aimed to intercept and parallel the course of the raiders of the Lontastan Federation.

The battle was quickly joined. Zerburst terminals flowered in deadly beauty in both formations as the first shots were exchanged. Pale purple lances of light . . . the beams along which zerburst energy poured from gun to terminal point . . . criss-crossed the narrowing gap between the formations.

Morgan got off a few shots in rapid succession, less conscious of his aim than his position relative to the rapidly swelling Earth. Also, he needed a terminal for cover—one not close enough to terminate *him*, but one sufficiently near that, with luck on the side of the Primgranese gunner, some vital area of his life-support could conceivably be knocked out.

He felt the glare on his back of the terminal he needed two seconds before the time to make his move. That time came.

Instantly he went full inert and tumbled Earthward from the raider formation, a pinwheel of flailing arms and legs that quickly spread-eagled as if his pressor system were giving way and exposing him to the effects of space vacuum. In fact, the pressors did weaken sufficiently to assure the spread-eagling did not look faked.

That far, all was according to plan. But then came the unexpected . . . the statistically possible but improbable accident.

He was holed by a zerburst lance. It could have been fired by friend or foe, and could not have been aimed at him. It terminated too many hundreds of miles away for him to pick out its flare among all the others. He felt the intense burning pain as it drilled a neat quarter-inch hole in his side, and looked down to see blood spraying out of him.

His life-support went to work on the injury immediately. Localized pressor intensity stopped the blood loss, and internal reagents threw up sturdy walls of pseudo-tissues to contain organ ruptures for the hour that would be needed for normal healing.

But that lance of energy had punctured more than human flesh. From the way the injury felt, Morgan suspected it had also holed a major life-support packet carried in that part of his body.

Which could prove disastrous.

When he hit the upper fringes of the atmosphere he discovered what the damage was. His re-entry field came on full, taking up the heat of impact with the air and braking his fall. But he did not go semi-inert for even an instant! The inertial unit had been smashed.

It could have been worse, he told himself. With his re-entry field fully extended for maximum atmospheric retardation he could slow for a reasonably soft landing. But he was going to take a battering from G-forces on the way down.

At least his life-support wouldn't let him black out, and would give brain damage priority attention. He had to remain alert to pick out a landing site where he might expect some privacy for a while, since he was going to be in bad shape.

His target area was in the northern Rockies, on the dawn line and just breaking out of Earth's unmodified winter season. That area was, perhaps, the key spot in the galaxy, so far as the future of humanity was concerned, but if the Primgranese suspected nothing there shouldn't be a human within eighty miles at this time of year.

At an altitude of ten miles his ionization trail began to dim as he slowed, and soon vanished. Unless there was a very close tracking antenna, the Primgranese would not be able to pinpoint the remainder of his descent. He tilted himself to slant his fall slightly north of vertical as soon as he picked out the place he wanted to ground.

It was at the south end of a high valley, on a slope where snow lingered in—he hoped—a heavy drift. He wanted the snow not for softness but for concealment, because his body was overwhelming him with painful distress signals. He was quite sure that, once he was on the ground, he would not be able to move about, seeking cover, for quite some time.

He killed his re-entry field a split-second before hitting, to avoid making a broad dent in the snow. There was an icy crust on top, which shattered easily with his impact, and his body came to a halt several feet below the surface. Gratefully, he blacked out.

His revival came slowly, like a drowsy awakening. For a minute he remained motionless, monitoring his body sensations and considering his position. He had been out for a little more than two hours—a dangerously long time if the Primgranese were making a serious effort to find him. Since he was still buried under the snow and not in captivity, it seemed a reasonable assumption that the Primgranese had disregarded him, thinking he was merely one more dead or dying Lontastan whose inert trajectory had happened to intercept Earth. Or at most, they had made a cursory search from the air, and given up when they found no clear trace of him, perhaps assuming that his re-entry system had failed and he had burned like a meteor in the final stage of his fall.

For the moment, then, he was probably safe.

He pushed against the weight of snow that had caved on top of him, to come to his hands and knees. Then he began wriggling and crawling, pushing his way downhill through the drift.

Finally his head contacted harder stuff, and he butted through the icy crust and into the morning sunlight. As he looked around he felt his breathing mode change, his life-support having automatically sampled the air and found it suitable—with minor nasal warming—for human respiration. Now he could smell as well as see the snow and, not many yards away, the stunted trees and early growth of grass of this high and rugged valley. Off to his left somewhere he could hear the roar of water.

He pulled himself free of the snowdrift and ate two rations from his food pouch. It was an easy, well-prepared-for task of a few seconds to modify the appearance of his boots, weapons belt, and shorts to pass for an ordinary Primgran citizen. Then he turned his attention to the scars left by the zerburst lance.

Mentally he constructed an image of the area through which the lance of energy had passed, and ran a straight line from scar to scar. The line passed through the center of the inertial control complex of the life-support packet, but touched nothing else of importance.

However, the damage done was important enough. Without inertial control, his entire transport system was of little practical use. His repulsors wouldn't raise him a millimeter off the ground against full inertia; nor, if he should manage somehow to get into space, could he go into warp.

If he hoped to get home, he would have to stun or kill a Primgranese, and take the inertial-control complex from the enemy's body.

But that could be dealt with when the opportunity arose, or when it became necessary. What he had to do now was get out of this valley and start his quest.

He walked toward the sound of water and soon came to the rushing, swollen stream, with the intention of following its course down through the southwest end of the valley. The going was difficult, at times through a solid jumble of boulders, and after a mile Morgan found his route blocked completely. The valley narrowed to a steep-walled canyon. He could neither follow the stream nor climb the wall.

For a moment he eyed the water speculatively, but it was a rolling rapid, and even with the protection of his skin-field he could be battered into a lifeless pulp if he tried swimming down it.

It was annoying indeed to be impeded this way by such petty trivialities as a minor river and a rock wall! But without inertial-control, which would let him leap over such obstacles without a thought . . . well, he would have to find another way out.

He turned back upstream, found a place where he could cross the water by leaping from boulder to boulder, and began exploring along the western slope of the valley, which was free of snow and appeared less steep than the eastern side. At several promising looking spots he tried to climb, but always he was stopped by a blank stretch of rock where he could find no further holds for hands or feet.

Finally he halted, sat down on a boulder, and tried to develop a solution to his problem. In the distant past, he knew, men had climbed mountains often—perhaps because they could not fly. Mountains far higher than the walls of this valley, and steeper too. But they had used equipment of some sort, judging by pictures he had seen: ropes, and spikes which could be driven into stone.

He glanced down at the items attached to his weapons belt, but raiders traveled light. He had nothing that could be improvised into a rope or spike. Of course, if he had kept his zerburst guns he could blast his way out—and take a chance on attracting the Primgranese to the energy release—but he had let his primary weapons go flying when he pretended to be wounded. His remaining gun was a stunner, effective enough on a human enemy at close range, but no hewer of stone.

His eyes swept the valley, in search of anything that might prove useful.

A stone clattered loudly behind him.

He refused to let himself go tense. He turned, more with the appearance of alert curiosity than startled fright.

But it wasn't an enemy, nor even a man. It was merely a mountain goat, standing high on the rim of the valley and looking down at him. Such creatures were thought to be numerous in these mountains, he recalled. In fact, the Primgranese had set aside most of the Rockies as a wildlife preserve for such animals as this one.

Morgan started to look away just as the goat moved. It began descending toward him with an ease and agility he found hard to believe, its hooves locating firm footings where he would have sworn his fingertips would have found nothing but blank stone. As the animal came closer to the floor of the valley, he ceased to marvel at its movements and began to puzzle at its purpose. He frowned. Wild animals had territorial instincts. Did this one consider him an invader to be attacked? He did not wish to inflict pain and injury on the animal, but he drew his stunner to use if he had to.

The shaggy beast stopped ten feet away and regarded the man curiously. Morgan watched and waited.

"Looks like you got in a hole, mister," said the goat in rough but perfectly understandable Universal. "What's your name?"

The man blinked. A talking goat was no great cause for surprise. Men had experimented with genetic modification of several animal species. It was puzzling, however, to find an intelligent goat living in the wild. Also, this animal's skull was no bigger than that of an unmodified goat.

"I'm Morgan," he replied.

"And I'm called Ezzy," said the goat.

"Where do you carry your brain, Ezzy?" Morgan asked.

"Under the shoulder hump," said Ezzy. "A goat's skull ain't the place for a brain. Takes too many licks. But like I was saying, Morgan, looks like you got yourself in a hole."

"You mean this valley? Yes, I'm having a little trouble getting out. Is there a path?"

"Afraid not," said Ezzy.

"Well, where can I climb out?"

"If you can't do it at them places I watched you try, you can't do it nowhere," said Ezzy. Morgan was sure the goat was grinning at him.

"I hope I'm not violating your territory," he said rather stiffly.

"Matter of fact, you are," said the goat. "but that's okay, I saw you don't want to stay. I guess this place don't look much like home to you, does it? What Lontastan planet you from, anyhow?"

Morgan's grip on the stunner tightened. "What makes you think I'm a Lontastan?" he demanded.

"Cause you landed way up here, and cause you

ain't calling for help. I guess some of your stuff ain't working, or you could get out, but some of it is, or you'd be freezing. So you could get help if you wanted to call the Primgranese."

This goat had a brain all right, Morgan thought tensely. But ... although it could *guess* he was Lontastan, it could not be certain. Maybe it was trying to verify its suspicions by tricking him into admitting his identity, after which it would curry favor with its Primgranese masters by reporting his presence.

Morgan grinned. "With all respect for your territorial preferences, what would a Lontastan be doing in such a nowhere place as this?"

The goat waggled its head. "Humans hang around a lot of nowhere places. Like where there ain't even air."

There was a long pause.

At last Morgan said, "Your reasoning about my identity could be right, Ezzy. But it's also possible that I hesitate to call for help because my predicament is a silly one to be in, and I would be embarrassed to let my friends know a mere mountainside bested me."

The goat appeared to consider this possibility before saying, "That don't tell why you lit here to start with."

"Sheer accident," said Morgan. "I misjudged the terrain."

"Well, it ain't much business of mine, nohow," said Ezzy. "I guess you want me to help you get out."

"I would appreciate it if you'll tell me the way."

"There *ain't* no way. Like I said, where you was climbing is as good places as any, and you couldn't make it." The goat looked him over—rather belittlingly, Morgan thought. "Guess I'll have to tug you out."

"Tug me?"

"Yep. You take ahold of my hind quarters and jest hang on tight."

Morgan visualized what Ezzy was suggesting, then glanced up the steep slope. Maybe the goat could do it, but did the goat really mean to help him? Morgan realized that, once the climb was started he would be utterly dependent on Ezzy's good intentions. A sudden backlash from those sharp rear hooves and Morgan would be dislodged from goat and ground alike. He would tumble back to the valley floor. And his life-support system had not been intended to solve this kind of problem in this manner. It would afford him little protection during such a tumble.

"No, thanks, Ezzy. I don't care to risk it."

"Up to you," the goat said airily. "I don't mind having you for company, so long's you don't eat no grass." Ezzy turned away from him and began munching the spring greenery.

Morgan kept a cautious eye on the goat as it wandered slowly away, but its sole interest appeared to be in filling its belly. And his own interest should be in getting out of the valley, he reminded himself. And there was no reason to take the goat's word that he couldn't get out without help. After all, a rough, tumbled valley like this . . . *surely* there was some way!

He resumed his search along the western slope, moving slowly up the valley floor, attempting to ascend at every promising break in the wall. It was arduous and tiring work, which left him exhausted within a few fruitless hours.

He stopped, drank from the stream, ate a ration, and sat down to rest a while.

"Hey, Morgan!"

He turned to face the approaching goat. "What is it, Ezzy?"

"I been thinking, Morgan. You don't trust me, do you?"

"Not much," the man admitted.

"Can't blame you for that. This here's a Primgranese Commonality world, and you'd be foolish to trust anybody on it. Particular if they didn't level with you."

"Didn't you level with me?" asked Morgan, half amused.

"I reckon not. Thing is, Morgan, I know who you are, and what brings you to these parts. There was Primgranese all over these hills, eight years ago just about, for the same reason. I know, cause I helped 'em what I could, showing where the old diggings and things are, stuff like that, and hearing them talk about what they was after. So I got that reason I didn't tell you about to know you come from the Lontastan Federation."

Morgan had grown tense. "That search eight years ago. How did it turn out?" he demanded.

"They didn't have no luck. Guess there weren't nothing to find. Least, that's what they finally figured. Morgan, you give yourself away with that question, and the way you ask it. Why don't you quit butting the ground?"

"You assume I'm hunting for what the other search failed to find?" asked the man.

"That's all I can figure," said the goat.

"And what was that?"

"Sometimes they called it the Grail," Ezzy replied.

Morgan paused, then nodded. Why not talk about it? The goat obviously had helpful information and—if the goat became a threat in any way—it could be killed.

"The Grail is as good a name as any, I suppose," he said. "Or it can be called cornucopia, or Aladdin's Lamp—or perhaps Pandora's Box. Its precise appearance and function is uncertain. The only certain information is that it has vast power, and has been around a long time."

The goat chortled. "That's what them Primgranese was after, all right. That's just like they talked about it. They was sure it was around here in the mountains somewheres. Said it had to be. I never could tell jest how they figured that."

"Historical investigation," said Morgan. "Evidently they saw the same pattern our own historians discovered—the similarity of legendary evidence that couldn't be satisfactorily accounted for in terms of human imagination alone. The Primgranese historians seem to have been a few years ahead of ours."

"Well, it didn't do them no good," said Ezzy. "Maybe it ain't for me to say, being just a goat, but I wonder about them historians sometimes. You sure they ain't chewing on cobweb?"

Morgan shook his head. "Historical investigation is an exact science, limited only by the completeness and accuracy of available information. And information weakness can be taken into ample consideration in making a historical evaluation. In this instance, the probability that the so-called 'Grail' object is now located within fifty miles of this spot is . . ." He hesitated, reluctant to disclose the 95.3 per cent figure to a creature of the Primgranese, " . . . is very high," he finished.

"That's what the Primgranese thought," said Ezzy. "They talked about something called fortune-shifts, way I recollect, that showed how the thing was carried about in ancient times. They figured it was in a place called France for a while, but was brung over the ocean by the first Yankans."

"Between 1720 and 1750, probably," agreed Morgan.

"And they figure it's got to be right around here," the goat continued, "cause this is where the Yankans hung on in their diggings in whichever year that was."

"In 2106," said Morgan. "The key fact there, of course, was that the Yankans were in an impossible position but managed to win that war just the same. Their victory is the strongest single piece of evidence in favor of the 'Grail' object's reality."

Ezzy chortled again. "It sure beats me. All the fancy molecules and things you humans got, to fly you in space, or so you can walk on places like Jupiter. Looks to me like if you wanted a Grail thing, you ought to jest figure out and build yourself one. Anything all them thousands of years old I reckon is easy for you to build, cause you learned so much."

Morgan frowned at this speech. Ezzy's vocabulary seemed limited, and his sentence structures clumsy, which left the man with occasional doubts of the goat's meaning.

"As I said before," he explained slowly, "we don't know what it does, much less how it works. Thus, we don't know how to start building one. We only know it appears to assure the survival and success of whatever society has it in possession."

"So the Lontastan Federation wants it," said the goat.

"Of course. And not just for our own benefit. You see, Ezzy, the econo-war with the Primgranese Commonality has lasted for centuries, but almost always the fighting has adhered strictly to a set of unwritten rules which keeps the damage to both sides down to an acceptable level. Some people call it a game, but it is a *serious* game. Lately, our side has developed a permanent superiority. And the Primgranese are slowly but definitely losing the war.

"At some stage, and perhaps soon," the man continued, "the Primgranese will become desperate enough to throw out the rule book. We will have total war, and that could spell the end of interstellar civilization. *Unless* the 'Grail' object, in our hands, can prevent it. In fact, it's possible that the Primgranese, knowing that we possessed the object, would be deterred from total war. So, for everybody's good, the Lontastans must have it."

The goat was chewing a wad of grass, and swallowed it before speaking. "Got my own angle on that, Morgan. Don't want the war moving in on me."

"But if the Primgranese go all-out," said the man, "we may have to attack Earth."

"Yeah. That's what I figure. Especially if you think that Grail's around here somewheres. That's how come I offered to help you up the rocks, Morgan. If you can find the thing and tote it off the Earth, or satisfy yourself and the Lontastans that it ain't here to start with, I figure on being a lot safer."

Morgan considered this at length. "Don't you feel any loyalty to the Primgranese?" he asked.

"Well, maybe a little. But it ain't my fight."

The man nodded thoughtfully. "I wonder," he mused, "how a prehistoric Greek would have felt, watching the war of the Gods and the Titans. Or a Norseman the battle of his Gods and the Frost Giants. You're in a similar situation, Ezzy."

"Then I reckon the way they felt was, they didn't want no stray lightning bolts hitting them," said the goat.

Morgan made his decision and stood up. "All right, Ezzy. Get me out of this valley, and I'll do what I can to keep lightning bolts out of the Rockies."

But Morgan did not escape the valley that day. Even hanging onto the haunches of the sure-footed Ezzy did not make the ascent easy. He was constantly in the goat's way, and Ezzy had to climb with unaccustomed caution, making no jumps and being careful not to put a rear hoof on the man's foot or in his groin.

Morgan spent the night on a fairly comfortable ledge about halfway up. When they reached the spot he threw himself on the ground and said, "I don't know how you made it, Ezzy."

"Weren't easy," the goat replied. "Some places I had to use my fingers. Don't never do that very much."

"Fingers?" said the man.

"Yeah." The goat lifted a foreleg, and Morgan watched the hoof snap into two heavy, horn-backed fingers and a similar opposing thumb. Ezzy flexed the digits a few times, then closed them into a fist once more and put the hoof down. "I reckon you humans figure if they give us big brains, they got to give us hands, too. Like they have to go together. I ain't real sure of that, myself. Don't hardly ever use it." The goat paused, then finished, "I'm going back down where the water and grass is. Be back about sunrise."

With a couple of leaps Ezzy was out of sight. Morgan sighed with misgiving. He had to trust the goat to return. But finally he slept.

And Ezzy was back with the sun, and the climb was resumed.

They reached the crest shortly before midday.

"I reckon you can make it without me from here," the goat said.

The man studied the terrain for a moment and nodded. "Yes. Many thanks, Ezzy."

"Weren't nothing," said the goat. "Where you figure to head?"

"I have to find a way into the old caverns."

Ezzy said, "Well, I showed the Primgranese how to get in, so I reckon I could do the same for you. Got a map?"

Morgan nodded, drew a sheet from his belt pouch and unfolded it. The goat studied it and then put a finger on a spot. "Right there. It's a tight crevice with a hole in the side. Nothing close to mistake it for. Best way to get there from here is like this . . ." The horn-backed finger described a route across the map as the man watched closely.

"Good," he said, "and thanks again."

"Well, but don't figure on finding nothing," warned the goat. "I don't reckon there's something there to find. The Primgranese is already looked."

"That's my problem, Ezzy. Don't worry about it. Goodbye."

The goat stood on the crest watching the Lontastan questor depart in search of the Grail.

Lontastans and Primgranese . . . they were pretty much the same. All shared Earth as their ancestral home . . . a home they had grown up and left. Even the Primgran citizens who resided on the planet weren't Earthmen. Not really. Like all other humans, they were . . .

The goat paused in his thought.

. . . They were Spacemen. Or Starmen. Or Galaxymen.

Were they like the ancient Gods and Titans and Frost Giants mentioned by Morgan? Ezzy had not heard of those mythological races before; no Primgran had ever happened to mention them to a goat. But it could be, he meditated, that long ago other creatures had matured and left the Earth, to fight battles in the sky. And primitive man waited in awed fear for the chance blow that would doom him . . .

Now, however, man was in the sky and goats were on the ground. In times still distant, would goats be stupid and forgetful, and follow the same pattern?

Ezzy lifted a foreleg, studied the hand man had given his kind, and made an annoyed sound in his throat.

But the distant future would have to take care of

itself. Ezzy had his duty to perform in the present, to perhaps assure the survival of his kind.

There was no question of where the Grail object really belonged. Not with the Primgranese, and not with the Lontastans. They had passed beyond the Earth. And Whoever or Whatever had endowed this planet with the object had meant it for Earth's creatures, not for conquerors of the universe. Else, why was the object still here after all the ages?

Also, there was no question of who really needed the object's protection. *Earthlings* needed it.

Ezzy turned to survey the valley from which he had assisted Morgan, and felt a mild pride in a job diplomatically done. He had been worried for a while, because the man had chosen this particular spot to land. But that was mere happenstance. Morgan had suspected nothing, and had been very glad indeed to leave the valley empty-handed, to do his questing elsewhere.

Once more Ezzy turned to look in the direction the man had taken and caught sight of him passing over a ridge about a mile away, following the route Ezzy had suggested.

Then the goat trod northward along the crest, continuing his watchful guarding of the Valley of the Grail.